Praise f

'Pure comfort – warmt'   '

'Cosy and uplifting – a real treat.'
Debbie Johnson

'Family, friendships, farming and fabulous food'
Heidi Swain

'Warm, romantic, emotional . . . gave me ALL of the feels. A
truly lovely read'
Carmel Harrington

'A delightful, life-affirming story. I wanted to retreat to
a cottage by the sea after the first chapter!'
Ali McNamara

'Such a wonderful book, heart-wrenching and uplifting and
joyful!'
Cressida McLaughlin

'Cakes, castles and oodles of charm: this book is huge fun and
pure escapism'
Cathy Bramley

Family, friends, food, a glass of bubbly and, of course, a good book make me smile. I believe in following your dreams, and my love of writing led me here to HarperCollins Publishers. Stunning Northumberland is my home – golden sandy beaches, castles and gorgeous countryside that have inspired my novels.

Also by Caroline Roberts

The Second Chance Supper Club

Christmas at the Second Chance Supper Club

CAROLINE ROBERTS

ONE PLACE. MANY STORIES

HQ
An imprint of HarperCollins*Publishers* Ltd
1 London Bridge Street
London SE1 9GF

www.harpercollins.co.uk

HarperCollins*Publishers*
Macken House, 39/40 Mayor Street Upper,
Dublin 1 D01 C9W8
This edition 2025

1

First published in Great Britain by HQ,
an imprint of HarperCollins*Publishers* Ltd 2025

ISBN: 9780008769734

Printed and bound in the UK using 100% Renewable
Electricity by CPI Group (UK) Ltd

MIX
Paper | Supporting
responsible forestry
FSC
www.fsc.org   FSC™ C007454

For more information visit: www.harpercollins.co.uk/green

For Mum and Dad x

Chapter 1

That kiss …

Wow. They'd only stepped apart a few seconds ago. Bloody hell, her knees were like jelly, her fingers trembling.

So, how did that compare? Her giddy teenage self asked the middle-ager she now was.

Hmm … tender, sensual, sincere, sexy (hell, yes!) … it was certainly reaching parts that hadn't been reached for a very long time. It was unexpected and beautiful, bold and brave. It was all new, and yet felt like home. Like the past and future had melded together.

A smile crept over her still-tingling lips.

Despite all the baggage (and quite honestly, the pair of them could go on a world cruise with that lot) they both carried from mature lives full of love and loss, parenthood, grief, and betrayal, that moment of being held in Will's arms again was *exquisite*.

Hah, even with the sneaky gang of supper club friends gathered outside, witnessing the momentous scene through Will's window. The whoops and hollers from the village street giving the onlookers away, after a heap of white lies and excuses as to why they *all*, at the last minute, couldn't make the supper tonight. Cath couldn't help but grin. Oh yes, the posse were making their noisy way up the path right now, about to explode through the door in a bubble of supportive chat, giggles and delight.

But there was a secret, as well as this kiss, that lay between Cath and Will. The supper clubbers who were about to crash in on them had no idea that this *wasn't* in fact their first kiss. You'd have to rewind over thirty years for those answers. But for now, with the emotions of this second-chance love flooding through Cath, it didn't feel like the right time to be revealing the truth of their youthful romance to the others. Jeez, they were still trying to come to terms with it themselves. This moment, whilst beautiful, was also more than a little complicated … being wrapped in a gossamer web of tangled history.

'Hell-ooo!' Dan, in his late forties, with cropped grey hair and steely-blue eyes, was first through the front door. Cath could hear the amused smile in his voice.

'Congratulations, guys,' his partner Andreas added, his chestnut-dark hair and tanned face appearing around the kitchen doorframe with a beaming smile – his Greek-Cypriot heritage evident in his skin tone, even in an English autumn.

Next was Nikki, late thirties, grinning away, her dark-blonde hair pulled back into a bouncy ponytail. 'And about bloody time too! Should have happened weeks ago.'

'We were standing around like weirdos,' Lily, Nikki's seven-teen-year-old niece, chipped in. 'Had a few odd looks from passers-by. It was getting well chilly out there.'

'Hmm, hasn't anyone told you it's rude to hang about on street corners spying on people?' Cath kept up the pretence of being affronted, adding to the humour of the situation.

The group merely scoffed and giggled.

Will, *gorgeous Will*, was grinning away.

'Well then, lovelies, is there any food left?' asked Andreas cheekily. 'I'm famished. With all the goings-on, we never had chance to have our own supper.'

'Hah, I only made our two starters, and Will's bake is now packed away in the fridge what with you lot dropping like flies. But hey, there's plenty of pudding, thanks to Lily's pavlova,' Cath explained.

Will had, in theory, been hosting a supper evening for the six of them. Being a hesitant cook, it was to be the first foodie event in a long time to be held at his home in their rural Northumberland village of Tilldale.

'Passionfruit, was it?' Dan gave a wink.

They were in bloody cahoots the whole way through, weren't they?! Cath shook her head and then joined in the laughter.

'Tea, coffee, fizz, anyone?' Will offered, slipping into the role of 'mein host'.

'Oh, some fizz would be fabulous. We need to celebrate.' Nikki was buzzing, delighted that her scheming had finally worked out.

'Aw, it's so cute seeing you two all coupled up.' Youthful Lily's reaction started sweetly, then she added, 'Even if you are kind of old.'

'Hey, less of the old.' Will pulled a mock grimace, as Cath raised her eyebrows, but neither of them could be grumpy really. Being in their early fifties, they must indeed seem ancient to a teenager; they were her parents' age after all. But age never stopped anyone from falling in love.

Nikki then suddenly burst into song, with a blast of 'It's in His Kiss!'

Cath laughed as she gave her friend a jovial dig in the ribs.

'Right, let's get this party started. Will, where do you keep your wine glasses?' Nikki leapt into action.

Glasses were found and charged with bubbling Prosecco, and the kitchen was filled with merriment, an emotion it surely hadn't seen in some time, Cath mused, feeling a tug inside. Will was a widower, and Cath knew well that despite the developments of the day, he was still trying to deal with his grief. He'd lost his wife only two years ago.

'Aw, best of luck, guys. You make a lush couple,' Lily added.

'Thanks … though I still can't believe you lot engineered this evening.' Will was struggling to take it all in.

Nikki arched her eyebrows. 'Well, someone had to get the two of you together.'

'Indeed. Well then, to new beginnings!' Dan lifted his champagne flute.

And to second chances! thought Cath, raising her glass, remembering in a sudden wave of nostalgia that they'd never made it past their first magical week together as teenagers.

'It's early days yet,' Will reminded them all, as his eyes flicked to a framed photograph of his late wife, Jane, whilst his hand rested gently on Cath's shoulder.

It felt like the two worlds were colliding, with Will and Cath very much in an emotional spin. But it also felt good. Cath looked around this room filled with her newfound and already special friends – she'd only arrived in the village six months ago – hoping upon hope that life would stay as sweet as the sugary-toffee pavlova that Lily had made for them all.

A feeling of hope and joy surged within her, but with it came a reality check. Cath was all too aware that there may yet be trouble ahead. After her recent experience of splitting up with her husband, following his bruising betrayal, she was no fool. That was the main reason behind her move to Tilldale. Romantic relationships were never easy. Was she really ready to jump back into the fire again?

This friendship group was so precious to her. They'd helped pick her up when she was lonely, adrift, and trying to establish a new life for herself. A knot of unease tightened in her chest. Would a romance in its mix just serve to stir things up in the long run? Might it, in fact, make a right Eton mess of things?

They'd piled into Will's neat lounge with its slate-grey linen sofas, chatting away and catching up on village life: the amiable antics in the stores owned and run by Dan and Andreas, Lily's latest cakes and bakes (this creative young woman was a pastry chef in the making, and studying determinedly in her final year at high school), and Nikki's hectic family life – a juggling act with three young boys and a not-so-domestic bear of a husband to look after, whilst toiling in the fast lane of her cleaning business.

Time slipped away with much fizz, laughter and camaraderie. Will occasionally giving Cath a tender glance across the room; both trying to fathom where they now were with their blossoming relationship. Cath smiling back warmly, with a touch of shyness. This shift between them was pretty momentous after all … and so was that delicious kiss.

It was soon almost midnight, and time to head home.

The emotionally charged evening, though exciting and beautiful, had left Cath feeling drained. It was wonderful how their caring group had schemed to give her and Will some together time, and boy, had it worked, but just at the crucial point post-kiss, when they might finally have had chance to talk about how they were really feeling, their friends had come bowling noisily in. Their interruption was lovely, of course, but darned untimely. It was like Cath and Will's relationship was primed ready to unfurl, and then *bumph*, it was swiftly nipped in the bud. Nestled on the sofa next to Nikki – it had seemed all wrong to carry on being lovey-dovey with Will once the posse had invaded – Cath now found herself battling to stay awake. Her eyelids flickering open and shut like a dodgy blind.

'Oh, I'm shattered,' admitted Nikki, giving a yawn beside her. It was evidently catching. 'Far too much excitement for one day. Time for the off. I'm back at work at seven-thirty tomorrow. Got to be up and ready, keeping the offices and homes of my clients fresh as a daisy.'

'Yep, the road is calling us, too.' Dan gave a stretch. 'Need to be up bright and early as always. Newspaper delivery, bread van, the works.'

'Oh yes, and there'll be breakfast bakes to make,' added Andreas. 'Croissants and baklava tomorrow, if you fancy a little treat, anyone.'

The lads ran the Tilldale Stores. A quaint stone-built shop at the very heart of the village, in every sense. They lived in a cosy little flat above it, along with their characterful West Highland terrier, Shirley, named after the sassy Shirley Ballas from their much-loved *Strictly Come Dancing*. 'Our little lady will be waiting for us, too.'

'Oh, how is she?' asked Cath, who walked the dog now and again for them.

'She's fine … still trying to chase those rabbits and squirrels, the little monkey,' said Dan.

'Hah, we're keeping her on the lead! She's been having far too much fun lately …' Andreas added.

Cath nodded, remembering all too well Shirley's escapee antics across the riverside meadows that summer, whilst in her charge. They'd managed to put that drama behind them, thankfully.

'Yeah, I'd better be making my way back, too.' Cath glanced towards Will as she spoke. 'It's been a really lovely evening. Thank you.' Her words felt loaded with meaning, but in front of the group she was unable to voice anything more. She was still trying to sort it out in her head, in all honesty.

'Well, it's been a bit of a night …' added Will with a wry note to his voice. 'It's lovely to see you all.' He stood, ready to see everyone out.

Coats and shoes were gathered, as they were herded towards the front door.

'Thank you so much,' said Nikki, as she leaned towards Will for a quick peck on the cheek. 'And well done, you two, you finally got the memo at last.' She gave a cheeky grin.

Will merely smiled, as Cath felt the warmth of a blush creep across her cheeks.

'Well, after all the ducking and diving with the matchmaking,'

Will added, 'you lot weren't really here for long in the end. You didn't even get to taste my food. So, I'll have to host again some other time and put my newfound cooking skills to the test.'

'Now that sounds a great idea,' responded Andreas.

Next, it was Cath's turn to make her farewells. Oh blimey, what did they do here? She and Will edged closer, somewhat awkwardly. The original moment of passion having passed. Did they kiss on the lips … the cheek, like friends? Have a hug?

'Ahm …' Will flailed his arms out to his sides, evidently feeling self-conscious too.

'Umm …' Cath leaned forwards and decided to kiss his cheek as they would have done at the end of every other supper club evening. She wasn't sure she was ready for anything more in the way of public displays of affection tonight. 'Ah, thank you.'

'You're most welcome.' His words sounded polite, but rather formal and perhaps a little distant.

What was he thinking? Cath couldn't help but wonder. Was he regretting their kiss already, or left wanting more and wondering how Cath was now playing it so cool?

In some ways, she'd have loved to stay on a while longer, just the two of them, and ask the myriad questions lurking in her mind, but perhaps it would be too much, too soon. This way, at least, she'd get a chance, back at home, for a little time to process everything.

The hand she placed on Will's shoulder tingled. Mini electric shocks still triggering between them. 'We'll chat soon, yeah?' A hint, a hope, that there was more to come for them both.

'Yeah, of course.'

'Right, you two lovebirds. Break it up. If you want a chaperone, Cath, then it's time for home. Unless, of course …' Andreas raised an eyebrow suggestively.

Oooh my! She hadn't even thought of staying over or anything like that. 'Yep, I'm on my way.' Cath's pitch was high, wanting to make that very clear, indeed. A kiss was a kiss, but anything more … well, that was a whole other dimension. If she'd been blushing before, she was now in full hot flush mode.

'Night then.' Will's voice was soft.

He moved in for a hug, his gorgeous woody-amber aftershave scent filling the space between them, as she felt herself drawn in, and then, oh so close against him. Andreas's words firing warning signals in her head. Yet her body was booking itself in for the night already.

'Ni-ight.' Her head might well have been full of shooting stars at that point. She took a slow breath, and then stepped back to regroup with the parting posse.

'Bye', 'See you soon' and several 'Thank yous' rang through the hallway.

Dan opened the front door, and out they drifted into the cool night air, a soft autumnal breeze stirring.

Darkness was suddenly all around, bar the glow from a street lamp further along the pavement. Inside Cath, however, the brightest of lights was still glowing.

Their clonking shoes and chatter echoed down the empty late-evening street. Cars were parked up for the night. The group made their way past two-hundred-year-old honey-stone cottages, all with their own stories to tell, and on by a new-build house, designed in keeping with the old, slotting other lives into the village. And, tucked behind that, there was Lily's family's barn conversion.

They took a short diversion to see her home.

'Thanks, guys. See you all soon.' Lily gave a cheery wave, as she stepped over her threshold.

'Night, petal.'

'Bye.'

Nikki's turn next, and they soon reached her house, back on the main street. The lights were all out, bar the porch.

'Well, that's me. Let's hope they're all asleep. Night all.' Her voice softened to a whisper as she unlocked the door. They watched her creep in stealthily, trying her best (tricky, after several glasses of Prosecco) not to disturb her three boys and hopefully snoring husband.

'Night,' Cath found herself whispering back. 'See you soon.' She also sent a silent thank you for the efforts made by her friend to get her and Will together.

They reached the village stores, built from the local creamy-grey stone, its sills and door painted a smart navy. In the window was a display of kindling wood, firelighters, matches, a stack of books and a bottle of red wine, against a backdrop of autumn leaves and a well-placed twig or two. They had even got the fairy lights out, which gave a twinkling welcome.

'That looks so pretty, very autumnal,' Cath commented.

'Thank you, lovely. That's Andreas's remit. He adores doing all the creative stuff. Setting the scene.'

The lads would naturally peel off here, back to their flat above the shop, but they insisted on seeing Cath safely home to her cottage.

'Crikey, it's a sleepy little village. I'll be fine,' assured Cath.

'Nope, absolutely not,' affirmed Dan. 'We'll see you back.'

'Haven't you seen all those murder mysteries?' added Andreas with a mischievous twinkle in his eye. 'This is exactly where it all happens … quiet little villages. Think Miss Marple and all that.'

'And *The Thursday Murder Club*,' chipped in Dan.

'Stop it, you two! You daft things.' Cath found herself giggling.

'Whatever … we're seeing you home, and that's that.' Andreas had the final word.

Cath found herself walked to her cottage door, and gave her chaperones a warm hug before stepping inside. 'Thanks, guys. For everything.' She found herself feeling emotional all over again. Tonight had been crazy, but special, and they'd both been so supportive since she had moved in to Cheviot Cottage and first set a slightly wobbly foot in the village.

'You're very welcome,' said Andreas.

'And hey, it's been lovely to see you and Will both smiling so much this evening,' added Dan.

Cath was still feeling that glow. 'Yes, it really was a wonderful night.'

'It was fab-u-lous, darling,' said Andreas.

Hah, she could tell they were feeling very pleased with their part in the supper club matchmaking. But only time would tell if their matchmaking efforts would turn into something that might last.

Cath watched the couple go, seeing Andreas slip an arm gently around Dan. They looked so at ease with each other. Comfortable. Stood hovering on her step, feeling happy about Will, and the chance for a new relationship, but also damned scared. She wasn't sixteen anymore; when they'd first met and life had seemed simple. A world of experience had shown her that life and love could go wrong. Falling for someone made you vulnerable all over again. Bloody hell, she'd only just patched up her battered and bruised heart. Starting a new romantic relationship, what on earth was she thinking?

Oh, what a night!

Cath lingered at her moss-green-painted cottage door looking out into the dark. The lads' footsteps now distant, and the village quiet, sleepy. The last of the pink summer roses that climbed the door arch wafted fragrantly beside her. A scent that reminded her of her childhood. She and her sister, Susie, plucking and drying rose petals (much to their gardener dad's disgruntlement) for 'potpourri' for their shared bedroom; sometimes it even doubled up as wedding confetti for their Barbie and Ken dolls. All those childish dreams of romance. And later, the real-life happily-ever-afters that would in time come crashing down.

She stepped into the hallway of her home, still feeling in a whirl. There was no way she'd be able to get to sleep just yet – there had been far too much fizz (in her glass and her brain) and excitement for one evening. So, she headed for her cosy kitchen, where she made herself a cup of camomile tea. The simple task of putting the kettle on, finding her favourite blue spotty mug and popping a teabag in a tonic in itself. As she stood stirring the fragrant infusion a few minutes later, she gave a small happy-but-anxious sigh. Whoa, there was just so much to take in.

It was a shame she and Will hadn't had more time to chat between themselves before the gang arrived. Time to confirm how they both felt, about the now … and the past, and the future. What *had* that kiss meant? Was it just a moment of passion released, or the start of something more? Crikey, she hadn't even had chance to ask when they might next get to see each other.

She took a sip of the scented tea, and gazed out into the midnight sky of her back garden, where the stars glinted a million miles away. Cath remembered that precious time, a few weeks back, stargazing with Will. That evening had felt like the start of a shift between the two of them. And tonight, a landmark kiss. She lingered on that moment for a few lovely seconds.

Her thoughts then shifted to her grown-up son, Adam, who was still finding and, to be honest, floundering on his own path in life down in Leeds. Leeds, where her own life was once entrenched. The family home now sold. Her ex-husband Trevor still there in their old city, living in a new flat, with his new girlfriend. Were they all loved up, or arguing by now? Did she even want to know? All of those lives and so many more, all going on under the same sky.

Why were love and relationships so damn tricky? You'd think you'd have it all sussed by fifty-two years of age, but no, you still felt like a daft teenager. The uncertainties, the *do I jump right in or hold back?* as strong as ever. She hugged her mug. Should she message Will? Thank him for a lovely night? Sleep on it? The memory of the kiss was still aglow inside.

Later, in her white-walled cottage bedroom, lying under a crisp white-cotton duvet, Cath reflected further. Thinking about how her supper club friends had engineered their soiree for two. She and Will, at last, being a little more honest about their feelings, or at least revealing what they'd been holding back in that spontaneous and unexpected kiss. This, coming hot on the heels of the recent revelation that Will had in fact been her first love 'Matty' – real name, William Matthewson – all those years ago. Oh yes, the attraction had been building between them these last few months, but with past pain on both sides, they had been trying their best to shield their battered hearts.

But how would this work out, for her and Will? Here in a place where everyone knew everyone's business? Would a fledgling romance put at risk a lovely friendship *and* friendship group? And she was all too aware of her own recent hurts and betrayal. This village was meant to be her escape, her haven. Did she really want to stir things up with romantic ties, and all the confusion that might bring? And Will, oh yes, she knew that he was still grieving. Two years on, after more than two decades of love, was nothing, after all.

But she held on to that moment of their beautiful, surprise kiss this evening. It had lit a flame within her once more. The connection still there after all the years. But they weren't teenagers anymore, were they, and life wasn't always that simple.

It was all well and good having a lovely, romantic moment, but where on earth did they go from here?

Chapter 2

After finally drifting off into a surprisingly settled sleep with no dreams to disturb her – perhaps last night had been dreamy enough – Cath woke to bright-golden shafts of early-October sun peeping through her sash window. She had coffee and hot buttered toast with a generous dollop of local strawberry jam, and then was inspired to get out into her garden for a tidy-up. It was a fresh and lovely morning, the kind of a day to crack on with life … And, keeping busy and physically active would definitely help keep all those confusing thoughts at bay.

Gardening hadn't really been her thing back in Leeds. Trevor had cut the grass, and yes, she had a few pots on the patio and did the odd spot of weeding, but her job as a deputy head and maths teacher at the local secondary school kept her more than occupied. Since moving in to Cheviot Cottage, and inheriting Reggie's – the elderly gentleman who'd lived there before her – overgrown but once-treasured garden, she'd enjoyed tidying it, and planting some herbs and vegetables. Sowing parsley, thyme, onions, leeks and carrots (great for her home cooking) in the raised beds.

It had been rather wonderful watching all that had come into bloom, or sprouted up magically from the soil, during the spring and summer months. The colours in the perennial borders changing in a gentle shift, her garden having a life and rhythm of its own. A favourite discovery being the cobalt-blue clustered bells of the tall delphiniums, which came up from a low burst of green leaves, and just got higher and higher.

Being early autumn, the borders had now lost their flowers, bar the roses, stubbornly clinging on to their blooms, and some tall soft-pink anemones that swayed in the breeze in their corner near the back patio, but the fire-hued autumn colours and the bronze of the beech hedge took over beautifully.

Cath tackled some weeds, and did some 'guesstimated' pruning with her recently purchased secateurs. A robin hopped nearby watching her work, moving in every now and then to catch a grub or worm from the freshly turned earth. Next, after loosening the soil and then pulling out one or two by their frothy frond tops to check the size, Cath dug up a row of carrots from the raised bed, which looked to be ready. Hmm, a warming carrot and ginger spiced soup might be the way to go with those. One thing she loved far more than gardening, even as a small child watching and helping her mother in the kitchen, was cooking.

Glancing up, with her bunch of mud-dusted carrots to hand, she spotted her revamped garden shed – another of Reggie's relics. She was proud of the renovations she'd made to it this spring. She'd repaired some of the wooden side strips, re-felted the roof, and replaced a broken glass pane in the double doors, finally painting it a weatherproofed (time would tell on that!) sage-green. Inside, the wooden walls were now a fresh white and she'd touched up the original shelves. She'd placed her old kitchen table in there along with a mismatched, but pretty, selection of wooden dining chairs. A cosy six seats in all, perfect for the supper group. The hard work had paid off, as it had proved to be a gorgeous venue for her summer suppers.

Hmm, perhaps, before the weather got too cold, they could have one last fling there? An autumn supper club get-together?

Oh, that'd be a lovely social event to look forward to, *and* it'd be a way of meeting up with Will again soon. That might well test the waters between them. But, perhaps initially should she bite the bullet and call or message him? She'd been putting it off, as she really hadn't known quite what to say. After all, last night … that kiss … had been pretty remarkable. The thought of it still flamed in her mind.

But yes, she'd definitely arrange an evening here at the cottage, and weather permitting, give the supper shed an autumnal make-over. She felt excited at the prospect, as they'd had some great social gatherings this summer, each one building the foundations of their friendship.

After tidying her tools and heading in to the cottage, Cath popped the kettle on for a much-needed cuppa. But instead of messaging the group about this get-together, she suddenly felt compelled to contact Will separately. She felt ready. She intended to keep it simple and thank him for a lovely evening. And then, from his response, she might get an idea about how he was feeling post-kiss too. Eek.

Bloody hell, why was she feeling all giddy as she typed?

Thanks for a really lovely evening. x

Keep it simple. That would do.

She pressed send and waited nervously. What to do now? She clicked on the kettle again, then stared at the phone, willing a response to drop in. Had it even been read yet? She checked for the double blue ticks. Her anxiety notching up. Nope.

See. All this angst. Why was she doing this to herself? Hadn't she learned anything? Okay, time to divert her mind. She started chopping the carrots for the soup.

And then, ping. *Oh* … She reached for her phone.

It was a great night. I enjoyed it too xx

The swift response and the words warmed Cath's heart, plus his *two* kisses. She 'hearted' the comment, and smiled to herself.

Later, her mug of tea now a mere stain in the cup, and the soup simmering gently, in came another message, as though Will had been thinking on it:

Do you fancy going out for a walk later today? Say 3pm? x

That sounded gorgeous. A walk with Will. The chance to chat. But it also felt like the first domino in a line towards dating, perhaps even coupledom. Should she leap in? Was she ready to start again on what she had learned was a heart-wrenching road of romance? She gave herself a few moments, gazing out of the sash window across her garden, fixing on the rise and fall of the country hills. Her stomach a swirl. Time to pause for thought.

Oh, damn it! She'd been doing far too much thinking lately. She couldn't resist a smile as she typed:

Yes, that'd be lovely, thanks xx

Will didn't seem to be wasting any time, and how wonderful was that? A walk in the sunshine with the chance to chat – and perhaps catch up on all those things they never got the opportunity to voice last night. It was low key and lovely, and sounded the perfect combination to Cath.

So why was she feeling so damn nervous?

Cath spotted Will pulling up outside her cottage in his blue hatchback. Her heartbeat quickened, and before opening the door, she made herself pause to take a breath. It was just a walk after all, she reminded herself. It was mild for early October, so she'd popped on a gilet over her navy-and-white Breton top, paired casually with jeans. She had plumped for walking boots, being unsure as to where they might be going. Knowing how sporty Will was, it might well end up being a bit of a hike.

Greeting him with a cheery 'Hi' and a brief kiss on the cheek, which felt the safe option, but also seemed a little weird after their passionate moment last night, she slid into the passenger seat. Despite taking that slow breath, her heart was going ten to the dozen and even the safe-zone peck gave her a zing of electricity. He looked and smelt gorgeous, dammit: slightly tousled dark hair, the salt-and-pepper dash to the sides, those meltingly hazel-brown eyes, and his woody-amber cologne. Had Trevor ever looked or smelled this good? She didn't think so.

'Hey, this is a nice idea, going for a walk. Thanks.' She smiled.

'Yeah, it's such a lovely day, seemed a shame to waste it.'

'Definitely. And you've been at the cycling shop today?' She'd learned that Will had opened his cycle repair shop, after taking early retirement from his long-term career as a fireman a few years ago.

'Yeah, early finish this aft. Been mostly regular servicing jobs, so lots of cleaning, re-oiling, new brake pads, inner tubes, and pumping up tyres. Sounds a bit boring, but it's really quite satisfying. It's good to think everyone's that wee bit safer cycling about afterwards.'

'Yeah, I can see that. Whatever you do, it's always a good feeling to do it the best you can.' Casual chit-chat seemed to be the safest option for her and Will for now, though their recent kiss still lingered tantalisingly in Cath's mind. They'd been getting to know each other as a slow burn over these past few months, and more so as part of the social supper group. Cath was finding this new development of going for a 'date-style' walk tricky to negotiate.

'And you? How's your day been?' Will asked.

'Good, I've been doing a spot of gardening,' Cath continued. 'Mostly tidying up, this time of year. It's been such a gorgeous day – I wanted to be out in it.'

'Exactly, hence my idea for a walk ... before those nights start pulling in again.'

'Yep, winter will soon be on its way.' Autumn was already here. She wondered what the colder months would be like in her new village home. What would winter bring for her, for them? Would her rural idyll be the same when the ice and snows came in? An image of the two of them cosying up by her log burner popped into her head. Oh, she suddenly felt all warm and fuzzy.

'And the colours at this time of the year are stunning.' Will's words broke into her thoughts.

Off they drove out of Tilldale village and away through winding country lanes. Nature putting on its show. The hawthorn hedgerows were dappled with red berries, the leaves on the trees turning to fading greens, brushed with copper and gold. October in all its glory. Autumnal treasures.

They came to a halt, a mere fifteen minutes away, at a woodland car park set on a hillside, which gave a gorgeous viewpoint across the valley. Gently rolling farmland surrounded them. The last of the circular golden-straw bales waiting to be collected after the late harvest. And farther along the valley, fields of green with cattle and sheep calmly grazing. Despite it being near to the village, it wasn't a spot she had discovered as yet.

'Well, here we are.'

'It's lovely. So scenic. And look, you can see the whole valley.' She smiled at Will. Northumberland was still delighting her with its many treasures. As she opened the car door, she heard the hoot of a cock pheasant, and the distant hum of a tractor at work. So different from the city sounds she'd grown up with and got used to over all those suburban years.

The track from the car park led them into a canopy of trees, surrounding them with a blaze of colour: golds and browns, russet reds of the wild cherry, the burnt bronze of the beech, and the bold berry clusters and fern-like leaves of the rowan. Birdsong filled the air with a mass of twittering, accompanied by a dashing display of darting wings and tails – blue tits, coal tits and finches.

Initially, she and Will seemed cautious of each other, strolling about a metre apart with the first of the falling leaves crunching crisply underfoot. A shaft of sunlight came through the overhead branches, warming their way. There was something enchanting about woodland at any time, but Cath felt this was its most glorious season – the striking melting-hot colours of autumn, a final joyous fling as summer faded.

Oh, could this be their chance for a final fling? She and Will? Perhaps even something more meaningful to tide them through the autumn of their lives? Life was short. Would it be so bad to let these feelings unfurl?

'It's beautiful,' she commented with a smile, turning towards a thoughtful-looking Will as they strolled.

'Yeah, I love it. I often come out this way on my bike.' Will was super-fit. He found cycling an escape, and a means to help keep his mind off recent heart-wrenching events.

'Must be great. The views are amazing.' She could appreciate the sentiment and the scenery, even though cycling wasn't really her thing. She much preferred staying on her own two feet.

There were no other cars parked when they'd arrived, so for now, it was just the two of them, the birds, and the gentle whisper of the breeze through the leaves.

Will paused, turning to look at her, his lips lifting into a warm smile, and as they walked side by side, he reached his arm into the space between them. Aw, he was still keen to be close. For a second, she wasn't quite sure if she was relieved or scared. She took a steadying breath as she slipped her hand into his, interlacing fingers, as they strolled together. The gesture *so* much more than friends. She felt all warm and tingly. Last night's kiss wasn't some kind of fluke or faux pas.

She sneaked a sideways glance at his handsome face, his conker-coloured hair, likely in need of a cut, but it kind of suited him slightly ruffled. His skin, like hers, was ageing of course, light wrinkles on his brow and the etched lines of both laughter and sorrow by his eyes – a sign of a life well lived, the marks of experience, and grief. She took in the curve of his lips, which she had now relearned.

He caught her staring. 'Everything okay?'

'Ah, yes … all fine, good thanks. This is nice … walking …' She was lost for words, remembering his sensual kiss from last night. Would there be a repeat performance? Cath very much hoped so. But things felt far more hesitant and polite between them today, even if they were holding hands. It was a fine balance, getting this right. After everything he'd been through, and he'd already admitted he wanted to take things slowly; she had to respect that.

'Yeah, it is.' His voice was steady, calm. He quirked an eyebrow.

A penny for your thoughts, as her nanna used to say, came to mind. They walked on, fingers still laced tinglingly together, taking the track that made a circular trail through the forest. Bracken and brambles tumbled and tangled each side of the path, along with twisting tendrils of honeysuckle – the blooms now spent. Cath saw sycamores with their swirling keys, ancient oaks with little acorn hats, and the fluttering leaves of the rusty beech, and then higher again, the tall, thin trunks of the towering firs. Layers of nature doing its thing.

'Hey, how's your son getting on?' Will asked, his tone full of kindness. They had talked recently about Adam's recent mental health issues.

'Ah, he's doing okay, definitely on the up. Thanks for asking.' Adam had had a real down patch just a few weeks prior. He'd come back from travelling around Southeast Asia after university, to the lingering mess of his parents' failed marriage, and the Leeds-based family home they'd shared for most of his child-hood sold. On top of that, the job market for fresh graduates was proving to be a dog-eat-dog world. And zoology, though he'd loved his degree, wasn't the easiest to link with job hunting whilst living in a city. It was no wonder he was having problems and had lost his way. It was still a big worry for Cath. 'I went down to visit him last week. To see how he was coping ...' she continued. 'It's so hard to tell over a phone. Anyone can put on a cheery tone and cover things up. He seemed in good form. And his flat looked much cleaner than when I was last there, thank God. I purposely didn't give him much notice before I popped in.'

It was almost a three-hour drive each way for a 'pop-in', but that was fine. Cath had wanted to see that he was all right in person. Whilst she knew he needed his independence and to find his own way, she wanted to show that she was there for him, to be his support come what may. You didn't stop worrying about your kids, whether they were two, twelve or twenty-two, perhaps even fifty-two if her parents had still been alive. 'And he's promised me he's off the drink for now, thank heavens. That wasn't helping things at all.'

Will gently nodded, giving her the space to talk.

'Trev's been keeping an eye on him, too. My ex has actually stepped up. They're in the same city, so he's been seeing him regularly and keeping me posted, which has been good.'

'Well, that must be reassuring.'

Their joint love of their son was at least making them work together for his wellbeing. Perhaps Trev's guilt at being the catalyst of the whole sorry split was finally kicking in. Although this past year or two had been bloody tough, with the bruising crush of Trevor's affair to deal with, Cath was trying her best not to be bitter. In the last couple of months, in fact, it felt like things between the pair of them were finally moving on.

'And I'm so glad Adam's picked up. That must be a real relief. It's such a worry when your kids aren't happy.' Will had two grown-up daughters, Maddie, a nurse, and Sophie, a student.

'So, how about your girls?'

21

'Ahm, they're great.' He paused, as though pondering how much to reveal. 'Ah, Maddie's just heard she's getting a promotion in the hospital, moving up to a Band 6; that's a junior sister role. She's delighted, and I'm so proud of her. We've all had so much to deal with of late.' He gave a sigh.

'Wow, sounds like she's done really well.'

'Yeah.' He gave a proud dad smile. 'And Sophie's now just started her third year at uni. Doing a law degree, so it's pretty full-on for her. She has the right attitude, realises she needs to study hard and put the work in.'

'Hah, it wasn't 'til the last few months of his final year that Adam got that memo.' Cath had to smile. 'He made it through, and did well in the end, though. Zoology. He's been crazy about animals since he was a little lad. I'd discover all sorts in his room … shoeboxes with mice in, crickets jumping about, worm farms, spider collections.'

'That sounds fun.'

'Not when you find half of them hopping around in his bed.'

Will gave a chuckle. 'Parenthood, hey. They're good girls, my two. I miss them being around …' He paused, seeming thoughtful. 'The house seems very quiet now.' His voice dipped.

She gave his hand, which was still laced with hers, a squeeze.

They stopped walking and took a few moments, looking towards the canopy of trees and through to an azure sky. Feeling the warmth of the sun's rays on their cheeks, hearing birdsong, and knowing that life was still going on. In spite of everything – the hurt, the loss – the world was still turning.

It was so nice, just *being* together. That silent strand of communication. It reinforced Cath's feeling that there really was something there between them. A bond.

They ambled on, the conversation tailing off for a while, and that was fine. Cath felt comfortable in his company, here. They came to a break in the tall firs, which opened to a vista of the Cheviot hills on the skyline. They paused to take in the scene.

Cath was aware of Will's closeness – shoulders brushing, hips touching – as they stood side by side.

The kiss from last night, and how things might have changed for them, from friends to something much more, suddenly felt like the elephant in the room … well, the woods.

'Ahm, I enjoyed last night.' Cath felt like she needed to put it out there.

'Hey, those supper club meddlers …' He was smiling. 'What are they like?'

'I still can't believe how they schemed it all.'

The two of them shook their heads, smiling at their group's antics.

'Ah, about last night …' Will suddenly sounded serious. He faced her, and as he did, his hand loosened around hers.

Cath felt a shift. Like a cloud had appeared, casting a shadow over them.

Will continued, 'This is lovely … coming for a walk, having your company. And I really do like you, Cath, but I'm finding all this so hard.'

Cath stayed quiet, letting him try and find the words he needed, whilst a flutter of panic filled her. Was it all about to end before anything had had time to start?

'It's going to take time, I think, is what I'm trying to say.' His dark eyes looked caring, if showing signs of confusion.

She held his gaze. He looked fragile, wary. 'It's okay, Will. You've been through such a tough time. I can't begin to under-stand that level of grief. But I do know how it feels to hurt, to feel vulnerable. I've been in a pretty dark place too, lately. Honestly, there's no rush.' Yet even as she said the words, she couldn't help but feel a dip of disappointment.

One day at a time – that's all they needed to think about. And yes, though she'd felt giddy and part of her could have rushed on in with this relationship, another part knew that slow steps forward had to be the best way for both of them.

He looked at her with affection. 'Thanks. Hey ...' He opened his arms, in an offer of embrace. And it felt so natural to step forward into that hug.

Wrapped in his strong, warm arms, she found the tenderness of the moment soothing. Cath's breathing slowed to match Will's own steady beat. *There was no rush* ... There was already this bond between them that went way, way back to their youth. As well as the simple joy of now, and the hopes of things yet to come.

She let her head nestle against Will's shoulder, heard the twitter of the birds around them, felt the warmth of the October sun that filtered through the gaps in the firs, with their pine-fresh scent. She also breathed in the scent of Will, as she pressed her cheek against his chest, all fresh and citrus-woody. It wasn't a kiss, this moment, this time, but it felt like so much more.

It was a hug that was healing. Like their beaten-up hearts were trying to mend.

Chapter 3

She was falling, falling, falling … like the autumn leaves.

She shouldn't be feeling like this.

At fifty-two years of age, Cath thought she should be past all the schoolgirl excitement of the tentative start to a relationship. Certainly after everything she'd been through, every brutal lesson in love learned with Trevor. So why couldn't she better control her feelings now than the sixteen-year-old she once was, when she'd first fallen for Will – her Matty?

She was buzzing and yet oddly anxious once she got back to her cottage. So much had happened in these past few days, and she felt she wanted to share that with someone … someone she trusted.

With a cup of tea near to hand, and an hour to spare before her evening tuition session, sat in her cosy armchair in the living room, she called her sister. 'Hey, Susie, hi. How are you?'

Cath felt a tremble through her fingertips that held the mobile as it hit her how quickly her life had changed from 'we' to 'I'. Was it already time to move back to 'we'? Would Will become part of her equation? Or was it all too fast, too risky?

'Oh, fine thanks. You? How's village life?'

'Ah, good … yeah, all fine.' The image of Will burned brightly in her mind.

'Hmm? And?'

'Yep, everything's good.' *Too good*, an excited voice reminded her. Her body still felt like it was tingling a little. The kiss, that hug today, had left her with aftershocks.

'Come on, sis. Your voice is all giddy. Something's up – I can tell. Spill the beans. What's been happening?'

There was a telling pause, as Cath chewed a hangnail momentarily. Where to start? Susie was sure to be discreet, but Cath was still digesting it all herself. She wasn't sure how to put it into words. Good Lord, she felt like a daft teenager again … A teenager, hmm, that's where it had all begun. Was this fate? Second time lucky? And yes, Susie had been there with her the first time around, too.

'Oh, it's not that hunky guy in the pub, is it?' Susie hazarded a guess. She'd visited a couple of months ago, and Will had come over briefly to say 'hello'.

Hah, how did she *do* that? Hit the nail on the head every damned time. Was Cath that blooming obvious? It must be down to all those years of sharing a bedroom when they were kids … then on through the riots of youthful hormones, on to adulthood, parenthood and beyond.

'Maybe …' Cath felt suddenly coy. Was it too soon to be sharing any details? It might yet fizzle to nothing, and she also felt a little protective towards Will.

'The good-looking one – touch of Marti Pellow about him,' Susie continued.

'Umm …'

'It *is*. You lucky girl. I bloody knew something was up. Tell all …' Susie then started humming 'Love Is All Around' with a short blast about feeling it in her fingers.

Cath snorted with laughter. She certainly *had* been feeling it in her fingers and her toes, and probably a few other more sensitive places, as well. 'Okay, you've got me on that one.' But the thing was, Susie still had no idea that she, *they*, in fact already knew this 'Marti Pellow' chap from years ago. 'Okay, so we may have kissed ... last night. And went for a walk in the woods today, that's all. Nothing major.' White lie alert – that kiss had felt pretty seismic, and had caused a tsunami of emotions ever since.

'This *is* major, Cath. You haven't kissed anyone other than Trevor since 1992. Well, not unless you've been secretly playing the away game, too, and never told me?' she added cheekily.

'Of course, I bloody well haven't! I stood firmly by my wedding vows, unlike some. Anyway, all this is lovely and early days, but I'm also scared that it's all a bit much ... and too soon.' There, it was out. Coughed up like a confessional furball. She couldn't bottle her confusing feelings any longer.

'Well, I think it's great you've met someone. But you don't have to sign up to a whole new relationship – just have some fun. What's the problem? He's hunky. He's free, I imagine. And he seemed like a nice enough guy when I saw him in the village that time. Hey, it's high time to get back in that saddle, girl.'

'Oh jeez, that's just it.' Perhaps Susie had hit the nail of her anxieties on the head again. What if it did develop into anything more? What if their relationship was about to become *sexual*. 'Christ, I'm terrified of that,' she confessed. 'It's just been me and Trevor all these years. I'm middle-aged now for goodness' sake, with a saggy mummy tummy.' She began to feel a thrum of panic at the mere thought of taking her clothes off in front of Will, excitement and horror hitting her in equal measure.

'Hey, he's bound to be nervous too. And yeah, he was fit-looking, but he wasn't exactly Tom Cruise. He'll not be expecting a model.'

'He'll not be getting one.' Cath had to chuckle.

'Anyway, cuddly is good.'

'Hmm.' Cath wasn't convinced, but hey, they were jumping the gun here. It might not even get that far between them. Oh, and then that hit her like a little gut-punch too. There she was getting nervous about something happening, and now even more worried that something might not. She was a bag of bloody anxieties.

'Look, if you get to that point, just have a large glass of wine, and then go with the flow. That's my advice, for what it's worth. I still use that ploy with Mark now.'

The pair of them got the giggles.

Susie had been married to her second husband Mark for eighteen years, having been left at only twenty-nine with two young girls to bring up single-handedly, and what a brilliant job she'd done of that. Mark was the extra layer of support and love they hadn't realised they all needed, and he'd taken Beth and Hannah on as if they were his own.

Cath took a sip of tea, then became more thoughtful. 'On a more serious note, Suz, yes, he is *really* nice and we're getting on well, but I know he's struggling with bereavement, so it may not all be plain sailing. His wife died from cancer a couple of years ago. She wasn't even my age,' Cath shared.

'Oh my God, that's awful. The poor chap.'

'I know. So, I don't think he'll want to jump in all guns blazing romantically. He does seem lovely though. He's been coming along to those supper club dos we've had in the village.'

'Ah, well, that's a good way to get to know each other.'

'Yeah, it has been.' And that reminded her: she needed to organise another supper evening to look forward to soon. 'And Suz,' she then continued, 'oddly enough, you already know him.'

'I do?' Her tone was quizzical.

'Strangely, we go a long way back. Remember our Northumberland holidays with Mum and Dad? Does the name Matty ring any bells?'

'Shit ... you're kidding me. No, Cath, it can't be.'

'Uh-huh.'

'Matty, the lad you went all goofy over. You made that mix

28

tape … with "Angel Eyes" on repeat. Oh, Christ, that really was "Wet Wet Wet", hah. And then you mooned about him for weeks after you got back.'

Cath remembered it all, too. That and so much more. Was it true that first love never dies?

Chapter 4

'Oh my, something smells amazing in here.'

Andreas popped his head around the doorframe from the kitchen area behind the shop. 'That'll be me and my bakes,' he answered, giving a cheeky smile. 'I have honey cake, Greek style, made with our best local Chain Bridge Honey, and it's fresh out of the oven.' He appeared in full, wearing his favourite Greek statue apron, the one that always made Cath grin. It was an image, old-masters style, of a naked man in marble. You were guaranteed service with a smile and a touch of fun in this fabulous rural shop.

'I'll just have to let it cool a little. But I can always pop some around to you in a short while.'

'That would be great.'

'So, what's on the shopping list today?' Dan stepped forward at the counter.

'Hah, that's it. I always get diverted as soon as I walk in. I never intend to buy cake. It's dangerous, this shop.'

'Naughty but nice. Designed to entice.' Andreas chuckled to himself.

'Okay, so what I actually came in for was some milk and bread, a pack of butter and some granulated and demerara sugar. I'm planning on making a crumble.'

'Ah yes, it's certainly a crumble time of year. And we can help with all of that.'

Cath had a haul of sun-ripened juicy blackberries in her freezer, which she'd picked from the nearby hedgerows back in September. And the apples were now ripe on Reggie's Bramley cooking apple tree. She'd tested one this morning with a twist of her hand, and off it had popped. An apple and blackberry crumble would make the perfect pudding for her next supper event.

'Oh, and I wanted to set a date for the next supper club, thought I'd moot it with you two, first.'

'Oh, so what's the plan then, lovely?'

Since Cath had arrived in the village, they'd had some fantastic themed events, each taking turns to host, and putting their personal twist on things. The bar was set at a relaxed high.

'Are we back in action at Will's?' Dan asked. 'We still need to test out his cooking skills! He got away with it, the last time.'

'Well, seeing as you all bunked off that day, it's hardly his fault.' Cath sounded miffed, but she couldn't help but smile. So far, she'd loved the results of their meddling, truth be told, even if it had sent her into a bit of a spin. And the two of them had chatted again last night, just easy conversation, saying how nice the walk had been. Slow, steady steps.

'I'd like to host again, so let's give the old summerhouse a last blast for the autumn.'

'Oh, marvellous.'

'I just need to find a date that works for everyone. I was thinking maybe next Saturday?' Cath suggested.

'Oh, we have a cinema trip planned. The latest Joker movie is released then. Lady Gaga's in it, looks rather fab. Shall we go for the Friday evening instead?' said Andreas.

'Great, I'll put a message out to the group,' said Cath, feeling a frisson of anticipation.

'And might young Will be helping you in the kitchen?' Dan quirked an eyebrow.

31

Cath felt herself blush. 'Possibly … he might be.' He had in fact already offered his sous-chef services, when they'd chatted about doing another group event on the phone last night.

'Hah, I knew it.'

'Well, it'd be a shame to waste those cooking lessons we gave him,' added Andreas. 'He needs to build on his skills.'

'I don't know about cooking lessons, Dan. The last supper club was more like "Lessons in Love".' The partners bantered on.

'Yeah, he'll need to build on those skills, too.'

The pair of them grinned broadly.

'Hah, you two are incorrigible. Shush now, or I might just withdraw that invitation.' Cath was, however, giggling along with them.

The bell above the door jingled, announcing the arrival of another customer, and the cheeky chat ceased. Being true gents, the lads didn't intend to spread any gossip about Cath and Will from their shop. An elderly lady walked in, wrapped up in a smart black woollen coat teamed with a fuchsia pink scarf, with an old-fashioned tartan shopping trolley in tow.

'Morning, Agnes. How are you, my lovely? Is Frank's cough any better this week?' Dan asked kindly. After eight years running the local stores, they knew everybody in the village and its environs.

'Oh, so-so. Thanks for asking. I've been trying to get him over to the doctor's for a check, but he won't have any of it. Actually, I'll get him some more of those lozenger thingies. The honey and lemon ones – they seemed to help a bit. And I'm here for my *Daily Mail* and some semi-skimmed milk.'

'Of course, lovely.' Dan came out to the tall glass-fronted fridge to fetch the milk for her, her paper already saved behind the counter with the regular orders.

Cath said a cheery 'Hello', and then finished gathering her provisions, and settled up with Andreas, whilst Agnes browsed for some fresh fruit and vegetables.

'Oh, and I'll bring your cake order over in a little while, Cath,' called out Andreas as she headed for the door. 'Home delivery. No extra charge. It's all part of the service.'

'Ah, thank you.'

'He's hoping for a coffee, mind you,' chipped in Dan. 'I'll know what's going on if it takes you twenty minutes, when it should be five, Andreas. There's bound to be a rush on too just as you disappear. It always happens that way.'

'Well, don't forget to take your pinny off as you leave the stores,' said Cath, 'or you might shock the neighbours.'

'Hah, perhaps. But they might get a laugh.' He chortled.

'Well, don't mind me, I rather like it.' Agnes's voice, then face, lifted wryly from behind the fruit stand. Her eyes were smiling.

They all chuckled.

Community and friendship were key at the Tilldale Village Stores, along with a generous sprinkling of flamboyant fun.

Chapter 5

It was foodie Friday. The day soon coming around, and with it the next supper club. Hurrah!

Cath had been praying the balmy Indian summer weather would last, allowing them to enjoy her revamped garden shed for one more social gathering this year. Her plan was to decorate it with a pumpkin-style harvest-festival theme, and with Halloween on the horizon, she had found a big orange pumpkin and some fabulous speckled green-and-yellow squash in the garden centre yesterday. She was going to display them along with a purple swede and a bunch of her fresh carrots strung together by their feathery fronds.

She'd also gone back to the woods where she'd taken that gorgeous stroll with Will, and collected some fallen autumn leaves in an array of beautiful burnished colours, and some pine cones.

The man himself had offered to come around in the early afternoon to 'help her cook'. She pondered whether the *real* reason was that Will wanted to try and pick up a few more tricks of the trade to improve his limited cooking skills, and hey, that was fine by her. But hopefully, he was looking forward to seeing her too, and the chance to spend some time together before the rest of the gang arrived. Either way, the thought of having him all to herself for a while made her happy. He could be her sous-chef anytime.

After trawling through her cookery books last night, sat curled up on her sofa by the log burner, she'd decided on a slow-cooked casserole as the main dish. A heartwarming ensemble of beef and autumn root vegetables in a rich ale gravy. She'd already made the trip to the butcher's in Kirkton to get the stewing beef. And she'd stuck with her dessert plan. Her black-berry picking in the country lanes meant she had a ready supply of the dark, juicy fruit, along with tart ripe apples from her bountiful tree in the garden, perfect to make a crowd-pleasing crumble for pudding.

It was almost two p.m. when the doorbell went. Her pulse rate lifted with a stirring of anticipation. She wiped her hands on her apron, fluffed her hair a little, and swiftly applied some peachy lip balm from her handbag. She then strolled to the door, catching sight of herself en route in the hallway mirror: dark wavy hair, recently recoloured to keep the greys at bay, her mascara still in place, a touch of rosy blusher and the fresh gloss on her lips. She'd do.

She opened the door, with her heart thrumming. 'Hi.' She gave a nervous smile.

'Hey.' Will was standing there in dark jeans, and a black top under a shirt-jacket in a cosy-looking red and black tartan, bearing a sexy smile and oh, those hazel-green eyes.

Taking him in, she felt all warm and fuzzy. How did he do that to her just by standing there?

'This is great. I'm looking forward to our cooking session and …' he raised a quirky smile '… with what limited skills I have, I am at your service. Feel free to boss me around.'

'Oh, I will do.' She laughed, her mind whizzing off to some pretty steamy places that definitely weren't the kitchen.

Hah, so maybe he *was* here for the cooking class, but hopefully for something a little more personal too. Their recent woodland walk had been lovely, but things had quietened off between them these past few days, and despite their occasional messages and a friendly chat over the phone, it still felt somehow measured. He'd been working, of course. And well, life took over; she knew that. Perhaps they had both also needed a bit of time and space at this point.

Not wanting to pressure him – his situation as a recent widower being a complex one she knew she couldn't fully understand – Cath'd held back from over-contacting him. But she couldn't help but wonder where they stood in this blossoming relationship. She'd agreed to slow things down, after all. Rushing in to a full-blown relationship might well just burst their balloon and call time upon the whole thing.

'Ah, it'll be fun.' Cath pulled herself back to the task in hand. This afternoon was going to be a busy one. 'Cooking's not so bad if you keep it simple and use good quality ingredients.'

'Well, I tend to stick to the basics at home: steak, salads and pizza. I can roast a chicken, too. Outside of that, well, I have to confess I'm pretty hopeless really.'

'No worries, I'll ease you in gently. Come on through, and let's have a coffee first.'

'Okay, great.'

'So how are you?' she asked, trying her best to sound relaxed but, in reality, feeling like a coiled spring. What was the matter with her? He was here to help her get set up for the supper club, she reminded herself.

'Yeah, good thanks.'

'I went back ... to the woods,' she broached, perhaps hoping to remind him of their walk and trying to regain a little of that previous closeness.

'Ah, right.'

'Yeah, I picked some greenery and some colourful leaves for tonight's table.'

'Sounds interesting.' Despite the words, his voice held a note of indifference.

'It was nice in the woods, our walk ...' she persevered, feeling even more nervous mentioning that.

'Yeah, it's very scenic there.' His response seemed non-committal, non-personal.

She felt a bit hurt, put out. Had he not felt that same sense of togetherness? Had she built that hug under the trees into something more than it was ever meant to be? *Oh*, well that put her whizzy emotions in their place.

'Ahm, yes, it is.'

Cath then found herself filling the gaps with polite conversation as she sourced milk and mugs, and popped the kettle on. It was such a domestic, homely situation, both of them there in the kitchen, which somehow made it all the more awkward. She stifled a sigh.

Cooking together, acting like a couple, what had she been thinking?

Five minutes later, over mugs of rich coffee with frothy milk, Will looked up, his brow creased thoughtfully. It was so hard to read him.

'Hey, thanks for offering to help teach me how to cook today.' His tone had softened.

'Oh, that's no problem.' She had been looking forward to doing that, too. 'I tend to take my cooking skills for granted, to be honest. Even when I was younger it seemed to come naturally; perhaps it was all the time I spent watching my mum in the kitchen. And I was only interested in licking the bowl back then.' She smiled. 'And then, cooking for my own family, trying out new recipes here and there, well, it was a pleasure, most of the time.' She paused, her chatter stalled by a sudden flush of memories. An image of the three of them, her family, sat around the dinner table. The past always nearer than you imagined.

'And, hey,' she continued, pushing herself back on track, 'having friends around for a social evening like tonight, well, that's even better. Our happy little band here, chatting away and enjoying the fruits of my labours. It doesn't seem like work at all.'

'Well, I haven't had much incentive to do a lot cooking-wise, what with the girls away,' Will confessed. 'It hardly seems worth it just for me. But I've been thinking …' he hesitated, the sorrow there in his eyes once more '… if perhaps I could cook a bit better, and maybe more often, then the girls might want to come home more. Look, I know it's the stereotype of uni students coming back for home-cooked food and getting their laundry done, and I can certainly put on a wash, but I'd love to be able to do more for them, to be able to look after them in that way. It seems like another thing the girls have lost. With everything that's happened, it's like we're still struggling along rather than anywhere near enjoying ourselves.'

'Oh, Will, I'm sure they enjoy seeing you, whether or not you can cook. And hey, it's bound to feel difficult for you all,' Cath tried to reassure him, her heart full of sympathy. 'But I'll certainly give you a few tips today. You'll soon be feeling much more confident in the kitchen.'

'Thank you.'

They sipped their coffees, briefly lost in their own thoughts.

'Well then, there's no time like the present. Shall we?' Cath stood up, taking their now empty cups to the sink.

With that, she placed the veggies for the casserole out on the kitchen side, and Will helped to peel, then cut up the carrots and cube some parsnips, whilst she deftly sliced a large onion showing him the easiest way. Working side by side at the kitchen work surface felt kind of right.

The butcher at Kirkton had already cubed the stewing steak for her, which she dusted with flour, salt and pepper. She opened a large bottle of local brown ale, and then made up a jug of hot beef stock. They were ready to begin cooking.

'Okay, here we go. Time for the "cheffy" stuff.' Cath gave a broad smile.

As the oil began to warm in the pan, Cath watched as Will fried the onions to a golden brown, after a few minutes adding the other vegetables. Setting this aside, she got him to add a splash more oil, and then turned up the heat. Under her guidance, Will tipped in the floury steak cubes, searing them to a toasty brown, then slowly poured over the fragrant ale and rich beef stock. He happily stood and stirred, watching it all come together, whilst Cath sprinkled in a good pinch of seasoning, and a dollop of pungent mustard and a teaspoon of horseradish sauce for good measure.

'That smells delicious already.' Will grinned, raising his head above the steam. It was lovely to see how the act of cooking had lifted his mood.

'It may well do, but it now needs around three hours to become meltingly tender. So, we need to just pop it in the oven on medium, and let the slow-cooking do its magic.'

'I'll take your word for it.' Will was beaming.

Oven gloves on, and in it went. Cath felt calmer now, realising that she'd relaxed as they had cooked together. The process of chopping and stirring taking over from all those anxious thoughts about where they went from here.

'Well, that was pretty straightforward,' said Will. 'I think even *I* might manage to have a go at making that sometime.'

'Great. And whilst that's cooking away, we've got some decorating to do.'

'Jeez, you haven't got me lined up for some DIY as well as cooking?' Will grimaced, evidently imagining they were about to paint walls or something.

'Hah, nope, just a bit of autumnal styling in the shed – our supper club venue for this evening. Walk this way ...' Cath gestured for him to follow her out into the garden.

Cath picked up the tray that she'd already loaded with cutlery, vintage cut-glass wine glasses (a gift from her parents many moons ago), green-and-orange-checked paper napkins (a lucky find in the minimarket), and a couple of green-glass tealight holders. She asked Will if he'd carry the big storm lantern up for her.

Earlier, she'd placed her pumpkin selection by the summerhouse door, and the red-and-gold leaves and pine cones were strewn rustically along the wooden table, with some starlike dried-hogweed heads looking pretty in two posy jars.

'Wow, this looks amazing here, Cath.'

'Aw thanks, but this is only the start of it. Okay, so can you pop the lantern there by the pumpkin patch?'

'Right-io.'

The pair of them set to work, and in no time at all, the shed was transformed. The tealights were ready to light, either side of a small orange pumpkin, which she'd reclaimed for the centre table and draped some glossy-green ivy strands around. Each place setting had an antique cut-glass tumbler, sparkling-clean cutlery, and a folded napkin with a shiny brown conker (another lucky find on her stroll in the woods) placed upon a named brown-card luggage label. She'd handwritten them last night in black ink.

The storm lantern and the remaining larger pumpkins and swede were welcoming sentries by the open doors.

'Looks great. I love it,' Will commented, scanning around the shed. 'How do you even think of all this? You make it look so damned easy. If it was my place, you'd be getting a placemat and a knife and fork put out, and that's if you were lucky.'

'Ah, I enjoy doing it. It's kind of fun.'

'Hah, well, you're obviously *way* more artistic than me.' He grinned. 'I might have come up with a can of beer and a conker, at best.'

She chuckled. 'Well, that would have worked fine, too. Don't overthink with theming. Just have fun with it. Anyhow, that's the small stuff. The food's the important thing. And on that note, we'd best get back down to the kitchen. I'll give the stew a stir, and then our crostini await.'

'Our what?'

'It's the starter, well, nibbles. They're dead easy, I promise you.' She froze as she let slip the word 'dead'. Oh no. Would Will pick up on that? Might it make him feel sad? Wreck their happy afternoon? Oops. She couldn't help but feel hypersensitive around him.

'Ah well, thank heavens for that. I need easy,' he responded.

Phew, she seemed to have got away with her unintentional faux pas.

'And now, it's what—' Cath glanced at her wristwatch, as they reached the bottom of the garden steps. 'Blimey, almost five o'clock. I think the yard arm might be getting near? Fancy a cheeky glass of vino for the cooks?' She might well need one to settle her nerves. Whilst enjoying the cooking and dining-area decoration, it seemed very much that they were on their best behaviour this afternoon, keeping a polite physical distance.

Will seemed more relaxed, however, as he quipped back at her. 'It'd be rude not to. Don't want to be upsetting the hostess.'

They were drawn back to the kitchen by delicious aromas of beefy gravy. Cath took out and stirred the casserole, which looked mouth-wateringly rich, the meaty aromas even more pungent and alluring up close. After popping the dish back into the oven, she poured them each a small glass of Malbec.

'Cheers.'

'Cheers, and thank you. I've learned a lot already. Hey, I might even dabble with a theme whenever it's my turn to host, or when the girls next come home.'

'Ah, they'd like that, I'm sure.'

Cath started the crostini by slicing thin circles from a ready-to-bake baguette, and popping them on a baking tray. 'Now *this* is the easiest starter in the world. Watch and learn.'

'I'm on it. Circles, thin, bake.' His lips curved into a cute smile. '*Cooking with Cath* is going well. You ought to do a TV programme for beginners like me. It'd go down a storm, I reckon.'

'Hah, just imagine. *The Cheviot Cottage Cooking Show.* Sounds rather fun. My teaching might take on a whole new twist. Move over maths, and in with the food.' It was a crazy dream, but fun to chat about. And hey, who knew what life might hold for her in time? This was her second-chance moment after all. She did so enjoy cooking and chatting.

Cath took a sip of the fruity red wine. The bread discs were baking to a nice golden crisp in the oven. Once cooled, they'd just need some toppings. Cath was going to show Will how to chop and mix a traditional tomato, garlic, oil and basil bruschetta topping, and a blue cheese alternative. Perfect to nibble on, along with a glass of wine as their guests arrived. A great alternative to a formal starter, as they could chat and graze in a wonderfully relaxed way.

They had a five-minute reprieve whilst the discs baked and cooled, and pondered a suitable music selection for this evening. Will was keen on playing his Chilled Acoustic and Fifties Classics mixes on his Spotify, and Cath, wanting a relaxed atmosphere plus loving the Fifties tracks too, was more than happy with that. He said he'd fetch his mini speaker to use in the hut, when he'd call back home later to get changed. They enjoyed a sip or two of their wine, and then Cath got Will to help her prep the crostini toppings.

He was deliciously close at this point. How did a man cooking in her kitchen, concentrating as he chopped basil, manage to look so darn-well dishy? The pungent leafy aromas, as well as his aftershave, filled the small space between them. Hmm, perhaps it was because Trev rarely ventured there, other than to make a cup of coffee or load the dishwasher – only when asked to, mind. The kitchen had always been her domain, but hey, she was more than happy to share it in this instance.

Cath was aware of the time slipping away. There was still

plenty to do; it was already almost five p.m., and their guests were due to arrive at seven.

'Right then, we can't relax too much: next up's the crumble,' she announced.

'Oh, I thought we were finished, what with it being wine o'clock?'

'Not qu-ite. No resting on your laurels here.'

'Jeez, you're some taskmaster.' He was smiling as he spoke, his soulful eyes glinting.

'Come on then, we have pudding to make.'

'Yes, sergeant major.' He stood to attention. 'I'm starting to feel like I'm in Gordon Ramsay's kitchen, here.'

'Oh no, I'd need to be swearing far more, with a few choice Foxtrot Oscars aimed at you.' She laughed, as she began to weigh out some butter, then cube it up, next sifting flour into a large mixing bowl. 'Here's where the fun begins,' she said, as she dipped her freshly washed hands into the mix, ready to rub the fat into the flour.

'Oh, I quite fancy the look of this bit …' Will gave his hands a rinse at the sink, and then moved in closer, standing behind her initially to take a look at what she was doing.

'You do it like this.' She rubbed and pushed the mix through her fingertips. 'It needs to look like breadcrumbs by the time you've finished.'

She became very aware of his face close to hers, just over her right shoulder. Ooh, his breath was now soft by her ear. It reminded her of that scene at the potter's wheel in the film *Ghost*. Oh crikey, she could feel a hot flush coming on. Bugger it! She'd bet Demi Moore wasn't all hot and sweaty at that point … well, perhaps a lot later in the evening, but not at the bloody start.

'Like *this*?' He reached around her, and then dipped his hands into the mixing bowl beside hers. As he did so his body was, ooh, pressed gently against hers from behind as they stood at the kitchen counter. Things were definitely hotting up. She was no longer in a relaxed cooking lesson state, oh no.

'Uh-hmmm.' She'd suddenly lost all power to speak.

'Actually, I could quite get into cooking, I think,' he uttered cheekily, his breath warm beside her.

She couldn't see his face, but she knew absolutely that he'd have a naughty twinkle in his eye.

'Hmmm,' she murmured again, as she kept rubbing the mix, even as his hands took hers in his, all sticky and gooey.

Before she knew it, he'd flipped her around towards him, and swiped a blob of the mixture down over her nose.

'Hey.' She pretended to be affronted, and gave him two swipes of buttery raw crumble across his cheeks, laughing as she did so.

'It's a crumble war!' He grabbed a chunk, and with a dab gave her a doughy moustache.

'Enough! There'll be no mixture left.'

'Shame, I was thinking about licking that one off.'

And a glimpse of the old, carefree Matty from years ago struck her. 'What? Really?' Hmm, that might not be so bad …

They collapsed into a fit of giggles. It was lovely just to laugh and muck about. She couldn't remember the last time she'd laughed like that. Suddenly, they went quiet as they paused to stare at each other for a momentous second. His eyes drew her in, and Will moved to gently kiss her gooey nose, and then he tasted the buttery mix, drawing his tongue in a glide along the top of her lip.

The air between them felt charged. What had happened to taking things slow? She shifted to meet him full-on with her lips … and oh, her hips. *It'd be a damned shame to waste the moment*, she mused. The uncooked crumble was not the best of flavours to be honest, but the kiss beneath it was warm and tender, and very sensual indeed.

BRRING. With that the doorbell went.

Dammit.

They pinged apart like they'd been stung.

'Oh … I'd better go see …'

'Yeah … suppose you had …'

As she stepped away and turned to head for the door, she spotted Will's eyes trailing after her longingly. *Oh my.*

Cath brushed herself down in the hallway, checking for crumb mixture on her clothes. Oh, might there still be mix on her nose? She swiped the end of it with the back of her hand, and then licked her lips, which still tasted of Will.

She opened the front door, feeling flushed indeed, to find Nikki there on the step. 'Oh, hi.' Cath tried her best to sound normal.

'Hello, lovely. You okay?'

'Ah … yep … fine.' The colour was rushing to her cheeks, up her neck. Will was there in her kitchen. Of course, that in itself wasn't too bad but the kiss they'd just shared felt like it was *so* obvious.

'I've just finished work. Thought I'd bring the fizz around for tonight. Thought it might be nice to get it chilled and ready in your fridge.' She held aloft two bottles of Prosecco. 'It's been a hectic week. Figured we deserve this.'

'Aw, that's kind of you.' Cath was still trying to land back down on earth.

Nikki was hovering on the step. 'Well, can I come in?'

'Ah, yep, yeah. 'Course.'

'You sure you're okay?' Nikki frowned.

'Absolutely.' Cath opened the door wide, to let Nikki past.

Her friend swept in ahead of Cath, reaching the kitchen first; she must have been angling for a brew, or maybe something stronger. Perhaps she was hoping to find out all the latest goss. Well, she wouldn't have to look far …

'Oh, well, look who's here. Hi, Will. You're a tad early for supper.' Nikki's voice had a cheeky lilt.

'Hi, Nikki.' He looked up with a quirky expression. 'And, believe it or not, I was actually helping to make it.'

Bless him, while she'd answered the door, he'd taken the remaining crumble mix, and was spooning it over the sliced apples and blackberries in the dish that Cath had prepared beforehand. He looked a dab hand. Actually, oops, there was still the sugar to add, she realised. Oh well, she'd sprinkle plenty over the top, and give it a quick fork-through for good measure.

'One I made earlier.' He deadpanned as he gave Cath a surreptitious wink.

There was a trace of dough across his cheek, which made her grin.

'Ooh, well, look who's come over all Mary Berry then,' Nikki teased. 'I thought cooking wasn't your thing, Will?'

'Exactly … I'm having lessons.'

At that, Nikki merely raised an eyebrow with a smirk. 'Well, I hope I wasn't interrupting anything.'

They both answered 'No' far too quickly.

Nikki's eyebrows went up a notch.

'We were just doing some prep for this evening,' Cath added. All the while thinking, *what the* hell *were we just prepping for?* And getting a weird fuzzy feeling inside as her imagination let loose.

'I *see* …' Their friend had definitely sussed something was going on between them. 'And you're on the wine already? Like your style, guys.'

'Chef's prerogative,' Cath quipped back.

Nikki joined them, taking a seat at the small kitchen table, as Cath fetched a further glass for her.

'Well, I've had a right couple of days of it.' Nikki sighed. 'Can't wait to chill out a bit here this evening …'

Cath guessed Nikki had popped around early to offload a little.

'I cook, I clean, as well as work all day, and I know Kev works too, but honestly trying to get anyone to lift a hand to help at home, well, that'd be a bloomin' miracle. Just last night, I'd done a deep clean at the Kirkton Café as well as my usual four house cleans. And bless him, one of my regulars, old Henry, was in a bit of a state, needed a hand with putting some washing on. He must have had a bit of an accident with the bedsheets, I reckon, so of course I helped him. Well, by the time I got in, with my grubby work clothes on, I was straight up to the shower and there's Hamish asking, "How long 'til tea?" Well, I gave him one of my looks, handed him the potato peeler and Angus a tea towel, with young Scott still holed up in his room. Well, you'd think I'd asked them to clean the bloody loo with their own toothbrushes. Shock horror – an eleven-year-old asked to wipe up, and a teenager to peel a potato.'

Cath and Will chortled whilst giving supportive smiles. They were used to Nikki's rants on the joys of having a house full of boys.

She took a large glug of wine. 'Ah, I love them to bits really, but sometimes … honestly. It's like you have to prise them away from their phones and the Xbox to do anything useful. Kev's as bad, too. "*Had a hard day, love,*" he grumbles as he sits in his chair watching the football. Well, what the hell does he think I've been doing?' Nikki shook her head, looking as though she might growl. 'Argh, there's far too much testosterone going round. How did I land with a house full of boys?'

'Well, we were all girls in our house bar me. That took some handling at times too.' Will softly chuckled, then a sadness dulled his eyes. The grief always there, lurking just below the surface. My, how he must long for those tricky moments with his houseful of girls to be back.

'Ah, we shouldn't moan, should we? It's just family life in all its glory. The good, the bad, and the stroppy,' Nikki conceded, empathising with Will's loss.

Cath took a slow breath, feeling for this gorgeous, grieving man. How had he felt kissing her, just before? Was she the first person he'd kissed since Jane? Was it strange? A relief? Filled with guilt? An escape from the gloom?

'Well, I'd better get back up the road. Get myself changed into something a little smarter for this evening.' Will suddenly stood up. 'I'll leave you ladies to it.'

'Oh, and remember we're up in the shed,' said Cath, picking up on the matter of clothing, and letting them off the emotional hook for now at least. 'So a warm fleece or jumper might come in handy.'

'Oh, are we?' Nikki chipped in. 'Back in the summerhouse, hey. I loved it up there. Glad you mentioned that. I'll let Lily know. Might put on my jumper dress and boots then, and I'll bring a cosy scarf.'

'Yep, final fling for the autumn … then I'll shut down the shed until the longer days reappear with the warmer weather, next spring.'

'Sounds a plan.'

'Well, thanks for the cooking lesson, Cath.' Will was popping on his jacket, ready to leave.

'My pleasure.'

They shared a knowing smile, and despite his evident grief, he had clearly enjoyed the chance to flirt, the chance to forget just for a little while. Of course, they were still working on this being 'more than friends', one step at a time. But that had seemed a pretty big step today.

'See you later, Nikki,' Will added, politely.

'You too. Bye, hon.'

Cath followed him to the door, where she gave him a small hug. 'See you later.' She wiped a small smudge of dough from his cheek.

'Looking forward to trying the crumble,' he added, giving her a cheeky wink as he stepped out of the door.

'Me too.'

She'd never be able to look at a crumble in the same way again.

As Cath returned to the kitchen, Nikki was on the case. 'Ooh, well, you two don't seem to be wasting any time. *Cosy* cooking lessons, is it? Not just the oven getting hot?'

Hah, well if she'd arrived five minutes earlier, Nikki may well have seen exactly what had been going on for herself. Spicy cooking lessons was more like it.

'Hmm, perhaps ...' Cath wasn't ready to give much away. Whilst she and Will had enjoyed some flirty fun just now, it was all too early, too vulnerable, too unknown, to be shared as gossip.

'So, it's going well, then?' After the supper club set-up to get them alone together, Nikki was keen to find out more.

'Pretty good, but honestly there's not much to tell ...' Cath felt her cheeks flare with the white lie.

'Ooh, but you're hoping there will be, yeah?' Nikki was grinning like a Cheshire cat.

'Maybe ...' Cath smiled cautiously. 'Look Niks, I really do like Will, and he seems to like me, I *think*. But it's very soon for us both. I can see how hard it is for him; he's still so obviously missing his wife, and no wonder – losing his life partner like that.' She paused. 'And well, I've not exactly had the best of experiences myself, have I? What with my dickhead ex-husband. Maybe it's just too soon.'

Right people, wrong time, yet again. Was history about to repeat itself? That thought made her stomach sink.

Did she confess the truth of their youthful romance to Nikki? But surely, it was only fair that she and Will decided on when, or if, to share that together. For now, her lips stayed sealed.

'It's got to be worth taking the plunge, though? Nothing ventured, nothing gained,' said Nikki. 'And let's be honest, he's such a dish.'

'Maybe you're right,' Cath continued, 'part of me would like to get to know Will more. But you know what, in all honesty, another part of me is terrified. What if we start developing real feelings for each other? And then it all goes tits up again? I don't think I'm ready to put myself through all that again. I came here to Tilldale, to my lovely little cottage, to get away from all that messy relationship stuff. And the village, it's so small; there'd be

no avoiding each other. I can't move, uproot myself again …'
She puffed out a sigh.

But somewhere deep in her heart, she knew it was already too late. She was already falling, *had* bloody well fallen for him all over again. Should she take a step back, hand herself a safety net right now? Before it all went too far? Before going back to being friends was no longer possible?

'Aw, I can understand that fear, hon. But you know what, life's too short. Isn't getting hurt a risk we all take in relationships? It's got to be better than being bloody lonely, surely? Or living to regret that you never gave it a chance?' Nikki looked up at her and then gave a grin. 'Or having to look at that damned athletic body, wishing you'd given it a try. If I wasn't married to Kev, I wouldn't be wasting time dithering, I can tell you.'

Cath shook her head as she laughed. It had been lovely, Will helping her in the kitchen earlier, and that crumble-fuelled kiss, which was way better than crumble itself, and she loved crumble, *but* where did they go from here? Seeing how things went with their get-together tonight might just help her decide.

Chapter 6

After tidying the kitchen, and a whirl of washing up, Cath did a quick hoover in the lounge, in case they ended up back inside should the shed prove too chilly later. A new roll of loo paper was placed in the downstairs toilet, and her tealight candles refreshed in the lounge and kitchen with cinnamon-and-orange-scented ones, to add some spiced autumnal notes.

She then headed upstairs to get changed, and put on a little make-up, brushing away a fleck or two of crumble mix from her hair with a smile and a heady sigh. What to wear? Pretty top, or warm jumper and jeans – practical for the shed – or a dress, tights and boots combo? Options, options ... Gorgeous Will was flashing like a Belisha beacon in her mind after that steamy crumble session. She knew she wanted to look her best whilst still casual enough to cook, plus also no doubt dashing to and from the shed. She plumped for a dress, choosing a button-through ditsy-floral-printed navy-and-red cord number. On a quick check in the mirror, she undid one more button at the neckline to reveal a little more decolletage. Well, that was the nearest to living dangerously she felt she could manage just now.

All too soon, the doorbell was ringing once again, this time heralding the arrival of the evening supper clubbers. She dashed back down the stairs.

First to grace her threshold were Andreas and Dan.

'Well, hello, my lovely. And aren't you looking absolutely adorable tonight. Oh, that dress!' Andreas gave a broad grin and made her give him a twirl.

The time spent on her outfit had paid off then; the dress teamed with thick tights and her charity shop long brown-leather boots. She'd also spent more than five minutes on her make-up, miracle of miracles, with a sweep of eyeliner and a swish of black mascara to accentuate her green-grey eyes, and some daring-for-her red lipstick. It was time to come out of the kitchen! Well, not quite, she actually *loved* the kitchen. She just needed to feel a bit more glamorous whilst she was there. Actually, thinking about it, she was rocking the Nigella vibe somewhat.

'Oh, yes, *love* the dress!' added Dan. 'Stunning.'

These boys definitely knew how to make you feel good, bless them.

Dan handed over a bottle of posh French fizz, and Andreas a Rioja. 'One to set us off, and one to go with the meal. A little bird told us beef was on the menu.'

'No secrets around here, are there?' Cath smiled. 'Does the village have the entire menu by now?' Village life was a revelation. It was lovely in so many ways, with the community very much welcoming her these past six months, but blimey, you couldn't lose yourself like you could in a big city. Everyone seemed to want to be updated on your business, and though she felt the lads were generally discreet, having friends at the heart of it all in the village shop, could at times be the equivalent to a broadsheet update.

'We saw Will,' Andreas explained. 'He was in the shop looking for a nice wine to pair with the meal, asking our advice.'

'Ah, okay.' Well, that was sweet of him.

She wondered how it would feel seeing him walking back in

so soon after their 'crumble' kiss. The doorbell buzzed again, and oh, her answer might soon be apparent.

But it was Nikki with her niece, Lily, bearing floral gifts and a rectangular tin of something homemade, hopefully. It was wonderful to see, and sample, the baked creations Lily had made.

'For you. Thanks for having us.' The young woman handed over the tantalising tin.

'Lily's made petits fours for after dinner,' shared Nikki. 'Or, of course, you can save them and keep them as a treat for yourself another day. Not that we'd talk about you behind your back or anything, if you actually did that.'

Oh delicious, Cath couldn't wait to peek in. 'Hah, sharing's caring. I wouldn't dare deprive you all.' Cath gave a wink. 'Thank you, and the flowers are gorgeous, girls.' They were a bunch of autumnal blooms, with bold orange roses and peaches-and-cream carnations. 'Come on through, and I'll get these popped into a vase.'

They made their way to the kitchen, where the others were waiting, greeting Lily and Nikki warmly.

'Mmm,' commented Nikki, 'something smells absolutely delicious in here. And before you pipe up, Andreas, I'm talking about the food, not you,' she added with a grin.

'Now stop spoiling my fun.' Andreas gave a wink.

'Not that anyone could accuse Andreas of ever trying to steal the limelight,' chuckled Dan.

'Cheeky.'

'Well then, I've got some Prosecco chilled in the fridge. So, Dan or Andreas, perhaps you could do the honours with that,' Cath suggested, 'whilst I quickly sort these lovely flowers. There are some flute glasses ready for the fizz, there on the side.'

'It'd be my pleasure,' said Dan.

As the cork popped jubilantly, the final guest arrived, announced by another ding of the cottage doorbell. 'I'll get it,' called Lily, who happened to be standing nearest the hallway.

Cath, though busy at that point, felt slightly disappointed that she wouldn't get to see Will in herself. Just to have a second or two with him alone, before it was all go with the group. Mind you, her stomach had started doing that washing machine thing, remembering their recent antics in this very kitchen, so perhaps it was for the best.

'Hi, everyone.' The man himself appeared, looking fresh and stylish, dressed in black jeans and a pale-blue chambray shirt under a thick navy jumper. He was holding a black padded coat across his arm. 'I'm prepared for the outdoors.' He gave a dashing smile.

'Well, we'll have a drink here first, and then we'll head on up.' Cath gave a nervous smile back, trying to still the fluttering that was going on inside. She was going to have to get a grip on herself. He did look absolutely gorgeous, mind.

They gave a 'Cheers', raising their glasses, with a 'Here's to a good night' from Dan, and 'Thanks for having me' from Lily.

'Well then, let's head up to our supper club shed while we still have some daylight,' Cath announced, as they reached the bottom of their welcome drinks. 'I thought we'd try a last summerhouse blast before the autumn comes in good and proper. I'm not sure how the cosy blankets I've put out will cope, if it gets any chillier. We can always move back in here if it is too much.'

'I'll be fine. I've got my thermals on underneath,' quipped Andreas.

'We've brought our fleeces,' said Lily.

'And I'm just your average hardy cyclist – used to all weathers,' Will added with a grin.

Hmm, there was nothing *average* about him at all, mused Cath.

'Okay then, let's recharge the glasses, and we'll head on up. And I'll grab another bottle, for good measure. The lanterns are already lit, so even though it's a bit dark out, we'll be fine.'

Lily illuminated the way for them up the steps with her phone torch. As well as the lanterns, Cath had earlier carved out the largest pumpkin with a spooky-toothed face, placing a tealight to give a glowing warmth from within. It greeted the guests from outside the shed, along with its vegetable friends.

'Ah, this is beautiful, Cath,' said Nikki.

'Love it. It's so cool,' added Lily, taking in the storm lantern and pumpkin display, and snapping a few photos on her phone.

'Oh, and inside is fabulous, too.' Andreas's face lit up with delight as he stepped in.

'You're a marvel. The autumnal theme is perfect.' Dan grinned.

Will looked proudly on, without commenting that he had in fact given a helping hand; the creative flair was all Cath's, after all.

'Oh yes, it's "pumpkin fest" for us at the shop too just now, what with Halloween fast approaching,' said Dan. 'We can hardly keep up with the sweetie supplies for trick-or-treating. But hey, all too soon, it'll be November. That's when things really start hotting up in the stores. We've ordered in most of our Christmas stock already.'

'Yep, best be prepared. Christmas will be here before we know it!' Andreas added animatedly. 'We're already thinking about Christmas cards, wrapping paper, local gifts, arts and crafts. Then, there's deciding which festive bakes I'll be making. And of course, we need to plan the store's festive window display for this year. Gotta get the theme just right.' He was off in a world of festive planning.

'Honestly, you'd think he was designing the Fenwick's Christmas window, the way he goes on.' Dan was smiling affectionately.

'All right, Mr Killjoy. It's all in the detail, I'm telling you.'

'Well, we've been in the shop for eight years; we should know what we're doing for the festive season, by now.'

'No, Mr Boring. We don't have to do the same thing, year on year. I find the run-up to Christmas rather exciting, that's all. You can't help but get wrapped up in a bit of Christmas spirit, can you, my lovelies? The lead-up, the lights, the gift buying

– everything. It's just such a magical time.' He paused, and then gave a slow sigh. 'Ah, but it's going to be so much trickier this year …' His eyes had misted.

Dan reached for his hand, knowing what was coming.

Andreas drew a breath, then explained, 'It'll be the first Christmas without Mama.'

'Oh, Andreas. That'll be very difficult. She'd still want you to enjoy it though.' Cath understood how hard losing a parent could be. Her mother and father had both passed away a few years ago, and within a year of each other.

The group had grown very fond of Andreas's mother, Maria, Cath having visited her a couple of times at her nursing home in the nearby town, in the weeks before her passing.

'Ah, she used to love Christmas,' Andreas reminisced with a happy-sad smile on his lips. 'The big family gatherings down in London. She'd clean the house from top to bottom, and be baking like some crazy woman through December: *melomakarona* and *kourabiedes* biscuits, feta spinach pastries, and so much more. You had to be prepared and have something ready to offer anyone popping by, as well as all the goodies for the main feasts.'

'Oh, heaven forbid a Greek-Cypriot mama not having a full pantry for the festive season,' added Dan with a wink.

'Oh yes, and Christmas Day, everybody was off to Mass first thing in the morning, followed by a feast of roast chicken,' continued his partner.

'It was great fun, if noisy and bloody chaotic,' Dan confirmed with a grin, having been welcomed to the family and invited to many a seasonal celebration in his early years with Andreas.

'And then New Year, St Basil's Day – that's a huge celebration in the festive calendar,' Andreas continued. 'That's when we'd finally be able to open all our main presents. Can you imagine, as a kid, your mates getting theirs on Christmas Day, and you had another whole week to wait? Another feast that day, naturally, too. Oh yes, even living in London, it was a real Greek-Cypriot-style Christmas.'

'Sounds wonderful,' said Cath, enjoying their reminiscing.

'Then, when she moved up here, to be nearer us,' Andreas continued nostalgically, his voice becoming a little thick, 'living on her own – as Papa had passed away a few years before – it was a much quieter event. But she still used to love coming to us for her turkey dinner with all the trimmings. Ate like a horse, enjoyed a sherry or two, and then complained loudly about indigestion through all the best parts of the Christmas movies.'

Dan chuckled, remembering too. 'And when it was time to ferry her back to her little bungalow,' he added, 'she'd end up taking home a goodie bag, with a plated second dinner all ready to warm up for the next day, along with gammon for sandwiches, boxes of chocolates, Andreas's baklava, traditional cookies, and a feast of treats.'

'Hah, it was enough to keep her going for a week, bless her.' Andreas smiled warmly.

'Oh, it sounds great, and very much like you looked after her really well,' observed Nikki. 'You can take some comfort from that, for sure.'

'Aw, and she used to love getting spoilt on Christmas Day, even when she was at the home. They'd give her the full turkey dinner along with the other residents there.' Andreas was on a roll.

Cath's mind flicked to the elderly gathered together there in the care home. The ones she'd briefly met when she'd called by to visit Maria. Some larger than life, others retiring to a quiet corner content with a little calm.

'But even then,' Andreas added, 'Mama was determined not to miss out on coming to ours. So, a couple of days before Christmas we'd pick her up, and bring her over to Tilldale for a day trip. An alternative festive feast, full of all the Greek-style things she loved.' Andreas's eyes were twinkling, the food and the memories very much wrapped up in love.

'Such lovely memories, chaps.' Will had a glisten in his eye, too.

'This year won't be the same though, will it?' Andreas was softly shaking his head.

'Of course, it won't be the same, but you can still celebrate Maria and her life,' Lily suggested gently, with a wiseness beyond her years. 'Perhaps you can think of something special she liked, or used to do around this time of year.'

That seemed to cheer Andreas up. 'Oh yes! Dan, we can have a *Commandaria* wine toast in her honour before we eat. She used to love that drink. And I'll have to make some *melomakarona* in her memory – cinnamon and orange cookies, with delicious honey syrup and crushed walnuts. That was her absolute favourite at this time of year.'

'Oh, they sound lush. I'll have to get the recipe for those!' Lily beamed.

The group had grown to know and love the feisty, characterful Greek-Cypriot mama, who'd spent her last days happily, if a little frustrated that life was passing her by far too quickly, with all those amazing adventures coming to an end, in the nearby Kirkton care home.

'Ah, that sounds lovely. Here's to your gorgeous mama.' Cath lifted her flute of fizz.

'To Maria,' added Nikki.

'Maria,' Lily echoed, raising her glass.

'To those we have loved and lost …' Will added, poignantly.

'Cheers, everyone,' said Dan.

Andreas wiped a stray tear with the back of his hand. 'Now then, enough of me going on and getting all sentimental. What are you lot up to for Christmas?' he asked the group.

'Well, we're doing "The Usual",' Nikki began. 'The family at ours, so that's both sets of parents, a day of Christmas chaos, far too much food, and Granda falling asleep and snoring in the chair, while I try to rally the boys *and* Kev – who'll also be about to nod off – to help with the mountainous pile of washing up.

All followed by a very large Baileys for me, some choccy treats, and a Christmas movie. Manic, as ever … but I do love it.'

'Sounds like fun.' Cath could picture the family gathering in all its chaotic glory.

'So, how about everyone else? What's on the festive agenda?' Nikki asked.

Lily, who was hoping to be heading out on Christmas Eve with her mates, said her mission after that was to keep awake through Christmas Day. 'And I'm looking forward to making the yule log,' she added. 'I've found a cool new recipe to try using dark chocolate and rum. I've already got the boozy brandy Christmas cake underway.'

'Anyone else notice there's a bit of a theme going on here?' Nikki raised her eyebrows.

'Like how to get away with as much alcohol as you can in the name of baking?' said Will. He had two girls of his own, just a little older than Lily, after all.

'Yep, you've got me.' Lily merely smiled.

'Absolutely, I like your style, girl,' said Andreas.

'Yeah, we pop over to Auntie Nik's for drinks mid-morning Christmas Day,' Lily explained. 'That's a family tradition, but then we tend to do our own thing. Mum and Dad like things a bit quieter. *Yawn.*' Nikki and Lily's dad were brother and sister.

'Hah, it's a madhouse at ours,' said Nikki. 'No wonder they look to escape before the lunch!'

'Mind you, I might actually be working over the festive season this year,' Lily added, with a secretive smile. 'Haven't given the parents the lowdown on that possibility, yet.'

'Oh, this is news. How come?' Her aunt was curious.

'We-ll.' The young woman pulled an excited-anxious face. They all knew of her hopes to work in catering, and her dreams of becoming a top pastry chef or artisan baker. 'I'm actually waiting to hear if I've got a part-time job with Saveur. You know, the new restaurant in Alnwick? I'm already lined up for some work experience with them this term, which is so cool. And I've now heard they're looking for help over their pre-Christmas season. So, I've messaged, and got my name down.'

'Wow, that's great, Lily!' Nikki was beaming.

'I'm still really keen to go to catering college after finishing my A levels,' she explained further, 'and this'd be brilliant for my experience and CV. They're trying to get a Michelin star there and everything. The food is meant to be a-mazing.'

'Sounds like a great opportunity.' Cath was delighted for her. Lily was talented and ambitious. They'd all enjoyed the fruits of her culinary labours recently at her fantastic Puddings and Patisserie Night. 'They'd be lucky to have you, Lily.'

'Oh yes, I hope you get lucky for the extra shifts, Lils, and that work experience sounds great,' Dan said.

'Yeah, I'll have a few lunch sessions there on my work experience week. Mainly washing up and stuff I think, and a bit of sous-chef prep. But if I land this job for the run-up to Christmas, then I might get to be more hands-on. They might even let me progress to plating up the desserts.' She gave a hopeful grin.

It was lovely to see the young woman so animated. She'd been quite shy when she'd first joined their supper group only a few months back, understandably as they were all a few decades older. But they loved having her.

'Well, that's fantastic, Lily. Fingers crossed for you,' said Andreas.

'You go, girl,' reaffirmed Dan. 'And what's on for you then this Christmas time, Cath?'

'Oh, I'm not quite sure yet,' said Cath. It was lovely listening to all the jolly Christmas activities planned, but it had also left her feeling strangely unsettled. 'I'm waiting to hear if Adam's planning to be with me or his dad … or perhaps, jetting off somewhere else entirely.'

She really hoped he'd want to join her here in the village, but Adam was now an adult with a life and friends of his own. Last year, they'd spent a 'last' Christmas together in the wreckage of the Leeds 'family' home, with the 'For Sale' sign up outside, and her ex-husband Trevor off in his love nest. They'd struggled through. It hadn't been the best day by any means.

So yes, this year would be very different for her too, and of course, it was the first in her new Northumberland cottage home. Whilst that was exciting, she was still learning to adjust to life without her long-term partner, and the ghosts were bound to be there from all those family traditions from years past. A part of her was looking forward to any upcoming village festivities, but another part already felt slightly anxious that she might find it a lonely time, particularly the big day. What if Adam didn't come up for Christmas? Her new friends would naturally have their own plans for Christmas Day, and that was how it should be. Enjoying that special family and couple time together. But for her, well, it might prove to be a tricky day. She wasn't sure what it was she was feeling about it. It wasn't envy as such, as she was genuinely pleased for them all … it was just all so new and unexpected, this being on her own. She had a lot to sit with emotionally. But hey, no point worrying about that now; she needed to think positively. She wanted to make the most of this evening.

'Crikey, I haven't even thought of Christmas yet,' confessed Will.

Cath saw Will's face drop. It sounded like he didn't even want to think about it. He had his daughters, of course, but no doubt Christmas was a really tough time for them all. It was so very hard to have lost a loved one, and Christmas brought that absence home more than any other time of the year. She wanted to give Will a hug, but held back. His grief was intense and so personal that it might seem too much, especially with the group there. Instead, she laid a supportive hand over his. He looked up at her, and tried a smile but it broke down into a look of barely disguised anguish.

Bloody hell, Christmas could be a tough time for sure, a time when loss was felt even more fiercely. There must be many lonely souls out there, finding the festivities difficult, or perhaps wishing they could join in and not be alone.

With that thought, the germ of an idea began to stir in Cath's mind. And as she headed down to the kitchen to plate up the crostini starters, its roots were already growing.

Chapter 7

To the crunch of crostini nibbles and with the glow of the summerhouse tealights, Cath looked around her supper club gang: five very different souls so warm and friendly around her. Friendship lifted you like a buoy, and these guys had been there like a life raft when she'd been tossed up on the shores of Tilldale village all battered and bruised.

She was still wondering how the festive season might pan out here. Her first taste of a tinsel-dusted Tilldale. 'So, what kind of things happen in the village on the run-up to Christmas then?'

Unusually her gang were rather quiet.

Nikki started with an 'umm' and Dan an 'ah ...'

'Well, is there a village tree, decorations? Any carol singing?' Cath quizzed. Her mind had already created a festoon of sparkling lights along the main street. And a huge fir tree adorned with baubles and coloured bulbs on the grassy triangle of the village green. She'd seen enough romantic movies in her time to sink a boat with Christmas scenes of snow and sentiment. That's what English village life was all about, surely.

'Craft fair for gifts? Christmas coffee morning?' she continued.

'Umm, no, not been a Christmas coffee morning in our time here,' admitted Dan with a shake of his head.

'Bruh, no craft fair either, though that's such a sweet idea,' said Lily.

'Nothing like that goes on really. And we don't have a village Christmas tree. Not a public one, anyhow,' admitted Will.

'You don't?' Cath was surprised.

'Nope, never have,' said Nikki.

'I did try to warn you the other day.' Andreas pulled a grimace. 'We always put on a good show at the shop, but I seem to be the only sparkling soul who lives for Christmas here.'

'Well, are there *any* decorations? Like village ones, I mean? I know the shop window will be looking festive and lovely, but I thought that'd just be the start of it.' Cath was curious and a little taken aback. Leeds centre was covered in sparkly lights. It had always given her a lift seeing the festive displays. Had she moved into the quietest place for Christmas, ever? There were sleepy villages, of course, but this sounded positively dormant.

'Oh, the pub, yeah, they put some decs out,' added Nikki.

'Good Lord, yes, the gaudy plastic Santa and his sleigh.' Dan grimaced. 'Along with the half-bald furry reindeers who look like they've come from the 1970s.'

'They actually have.' Will laughed. 'I remember seeing them when I was a kid.'

'Well, at least there's something jolly here. Thank goodness for that.' She'd been picturing the village in darkness in December, with no sparkly lights at all. Her cottage and the shop being the only ones lit up like twinkly beacons.

'It's just, people seem to do their own thing around here at Christmas time. We do get in the festive spirit. But there's not a particular village event,' Nikki explained further.

'It's a bit boring, is what she's trying to say,' added Lily.

'Well, our house is never that!'

'Yeah, everyone seems to decorate their own home, and do their own thing really,' agreed Dan.

Well, that insight into village life left Cath feeling even flatter than before. She hoped to goodness Adam was going to be wending his way back to her for the festivities.

Over warming bowls of beef stew and gravy, served with chunks of crusty homemade bread, the conversation moved on. Unfortunately, rather too close for comfort for Cath and Will.

'Anyway, how's life going for you two lovebirds?' Dan asked teasingly. 'Did we set the romantic ball rolling at the last supper club, or not?'

Nikki gave a knowing smile, having already quizzed Cath earlier. She was happy to let the lads lead this one.

Cath felt herself blush, and though she knew it was merely Dan's friendly banter, she couldn't help but fidget in her seat. She felt protective of these recent meet-ups between her and Will. And though it all felt new and vulnerable, there was also the fact that the 'romantic ball' had been set rolling thirty-six years ago. 'Ah, we're doing fine …' she started.

Were the two of them ready to share that snippet of information yet? She was still trying to get her head around it herself. But these were their close friends, and after all they wouldn't have taken these first tentative steps without them. Cath felt they had their best interests at heart.

'Well,' Will began, as though he'd been mulling this over too, 'there's a little more to our story than you may have realised …' He gave Cath a look, as if checking he had her approval to continue. She responded with an affirming nod, along with a shy smile.

Well then, here goes, she thought. The truth will out.

Will held Cath's gaze warmly with his toffee-hazel eyes as he began, 'The thing is Cath and I have met before—'

'Oh, he's not harking back to that car park prang again, is he?' Nikki heckled with affection.

Cath and Will's first meeting had literally been a clash of bumpers in the local supermarket's car park earlier in the year. Will hadn't been best pleased at the time.

'Nope. We go back way longer than that,' Cath interjected, feeling a tad nervous that their secret was about to be revealed.

All ears were now pricked in the supper shed.

Will resumed, 'Cath or Cathy, as I knew her back then, and I were actually childhood sweethearts back in the late Eighties.'

All eyes had now widened.

Cath was nodding, unable to stop the smile that was spreading over her lips. 'And this is my Matty. We fell for each other when I was staying here on a caravan holiday at Belford with my mum, dad and sister. I was sixteen.'

'Wow,' from Lily. 'That's a-mazing.'

'But Matty? How's that?' Dan's forehead was scrunched, trying to work it out.

'It was a holiday romance. And I was the lad from Belford. Back in the day, known to my mates as Matty ... William Matthewson,' Will explained.

'But we hadn't realised, not until a few weeks ago, that is,' Cath took up.

'Ah, that's such a coincidence! You coming here, meeting again.' Andreas was pondering it all.

'The years had rolled on,' Will added, 'and of course, we didn't recognise each other when we met again, not at first, but there was something there. And then, when Cath's sister turned up the other week, and with talk of holidays in Belford, it all began to add up.'

'Hah, I thought there was something between you. But wow, that's incredible.' Matchmaker Nikki, who'd thought she knew it all, was stunned by this new revelation.

'That's cool. And so romantic – it's like something from a movie,' said Lily.

'Bloody hell, guys. We thought there was a spark—' Dan shared a look of surprise with Andreas '—but we'd *never* have guessed that.'

'First loves, hey.' Nikki grinned, now the news was sinking in.

'Well, that was all very much a long time ago.' Will was keen to put things back into perspective. 'And we've both been through a hell of a lot since, so it's early days yet. No one's rushing into anything here.'

And although he and Cath had already discussed this, agreeing to take things slowly, Will's tone sounded cool and somewhat dismissive, in contrast to that playful crumble kiss in the kitchen earlier, leaving Cath feeling confused and a little disappointed.

The evening air was cooling, along, apparently, with Will's desire for anything more meaningful for their fledgling relationship. Cath hugged her fleece blanket tighter around her.

Was she wanting more from this, a deeper relationship? Already her heart was saying one thing, while her head was agreeing with Will about taking things slowly.

She gave herself a mental shake. Was some daft part of her still clinging on for a 'happily ever after'? A new rush of romance? After Trevor, she should bloody well know better.

Chapter 8

Last night's goodbye between Cath and Will had ended up being a muted affair. The promise of the day, starting with that flirty fun in the kitchen with Mr Let's Get Ready to Crumble, dissolved into him being Mr Cautious once more. A careful hug, a kiss on the cheek, and she was left with an unresolved longing. A stark contrast to the loud and jolly farewells from the Fab Four – Dan, Andreas, Nikki and Lily.

With a spell of early autumn sunshine upon them, and needing a distraction to keep those confusing thoughts of Will at bay – *would he call her, or should she call him, or was it back to being 'friends'?* – Cath made the most of the fine weather by doing a spot of weeding in the cottage garden. Digging and turning the rich, brown earth beneath the established shrubs, she pulled out dandelions with their long, skinny parsnip-style roots, and strands of stray grass. Then, she began trimming the border edges. In old jeans and a long-sleeved black T, her hair pulled up in a high ponytail, she felt quite at home here tending her patch of Northumberland earth, garden fork to hand.

Her resident robin, Robbie – as she'd decided to name him – was back hopping around beside her, ready to take advantage of the newly revealed worms and insects. Her summer busy lizzie pots were beginning to fade, so she made a mental note to go and buy some tulip bulbs, which would be lovely to herald the spring in several months' time.

She could hear the bleating of the sheep from the fields in the valley beyond the garden, and the odd car trundling its way through the village. All this toil was working up a thirst, and beginning to nag at the base of her back if she were honest; a cup of tea was calling. Perhaps, after all that hard work, a little treat wouldn't go amiss either. And she knew exactly the place to find one.

Still in her gardening clothes, but with scrubbed hands, and a freshen-up of her peachy-pink lipstick, she set off for the stores. Well, you never knew who you might bump into in the village … especially on his bicycle. Dammit, Will was never far from her thoughts these days.

Cath spotted her elderly neighbours, Mary and John, and stopped to say a quick hello, asking how they were keeping. They told her they were fine, and off to do a spot of shopping over in Kirkton to get a few bits in, as they were looking forward to their daughter coming to visit tomorrow. It would be lovely to have a bit of company, they said. And oh, that seed of an idea from last night came to Cath's mind again. It stayed with her all the way to the shop.

Dan, sporting a blue-and-white floral short-sleeved shirt, greeted her with his usual warmth from behind the counter. 'Hello, lovely, and thanks so much for a fabulous evening.'

'Ah, you're very welcome.'

'And how are you today? No niggly hangover, I hope, unlike our Andreas here. Went in a little heavy on the red wine, I do believe.'

'No, thankfully, I'm good.' She'd gone steady on the booze on purpose, wanting to keep her wits about her as hostess, and also around Will. 'What a gorgeous morning, I've been making the most of it, out in the garden.'

'Oh, sat with a good book and a cup of coffee, I hope.'

'Hah, no, with a border fork and a pair of secateurs, actually.'

'The work's never done, is it.' He smiled.

'Keeps me out of mischief, I suppose,' she added.

And talking of mischief, Andreas appeared in the shop then. 'Morning, petal.'

'Hi, Andreas, and how are you?' she asked with a smile, giving Dan a knowing look.

'I'm fine … ah, if a little jaded. I think I enjoyed myself a bit too well last night.' He did in fact look rather pale.

Cath was stood browsing the cakes and pastries, wondering which delight to select to go with her morning coffee.

The shop's jingly bell announced a new arrival, and with that, dear old Kenneth arrived, looking for a couple of tins of soup, some bread, milk and butter, and of course his cup of complimentary tea and a chat with the lads and whoever else might pop in.

Watching Dan and Kenneth chat, Cath's germ of an idea from last night began to sprout. A Christmas event, something to perk up this village over the festive season and get people together. Along with Mary and John, Kenneth was exactly the kind of person who Cath felt might need a little extra light in their lives. It was time to spread some festive joy. A sprinkling of festive fairy dust was needed over Tilldale. Cath just had to work out how best to do that.

Sitting in her garden, mulling the Christmas event idea over a coffee with a slice of Dan's delicious chocolate-orange cake, Cath's thoughts were interrupted by a message coming through on her phone. It was Will.

Oh, she couldn't help but feel a buzz of excitement as she opened the text to find out more. It went up a further notch as she read:

*Brunch on the beach tomorrow? And a walk? Weather looks
to be fine for another day or so. Let's make the most of it.*

So, the going slow wasn't to be *too* slow then. Phew. She was
warmed by a huge inner smile.

Instead of messaging back, she dialled his number. Yes, he
might be at work, but she'd take a chance. She'd really love to
hear his voice, with that warm Northumbrian lilt.

'Hi,' Cath started when he picked up.

'Hey.'

'Yes, that sounds wonderful: the walk, the beach, brunch.
Thanks.'

'Ah, great.' There was a hint of nervousness in his tone. This
was still evidently a big deal for them both.

'Umm, can I bring anything? Help with the food, perhaps?'

'Nope, I have it all worked out.' He sounded adamant. She
could hear a smile breaking through in his voice.

'Perfect. So, what time are you thinking?'

'Leave at ten-ish, if that works for you? It's a Sunday, so I'm
a free agent.'

'Great. The lads don't need me to help in the shop this week.'
Cath had been helping out in the stores on the odd Sunday
morning, giving Andreas and Dan a well-earned break, as well
as helping her slightly stretched finances. 'And my first tuition
isn't until early evening, so I have all day too. Uhm, can I drive
us to the beach?'

'Ah, well I imagined I would, but yeah if you'd like to.'

'Yep, the Mini could do with a little action. Haven't been far
lately. The battery'll be getting flat.' It was more than the Mini
that had been out of action for a while, she thought. 'I'll pick
you up at ten then – look forward to it.'

'Me, too. See you in the morning.'

Ah, that was lovely. Her anxiety settled a smidge. Since last
night, she'd been wondering if he wanted to see her again, or how

things might develop. This later-in-life dating came with the same level of angst as the teenage stuff, she'd realised. Putting yourself out there again was hard, even if it was lovely, too. Laying your emotions on the line again took a huge leap of faith, especially when you'd recently had them steamrollered. All she could hope was that they weren't about to get flattened again.

Chapter 9

Cath pulled up the Mini on the main street, right outside Will's house. And there he was, coming out of his door, wearing black jeans, a Fair Isle grey knit jumper, and his black-padded puffer jacket. He was also sporting a grey beanie hat. He looked cool in a country-style way, dressed warmly yet ready to walk.

He gave a gorgeous smile as he reached the car, where he unloaded the large rucksack he was carrying onto the back seat, along with a red-checked tartan cloth roll. 'Morning.' He then hopped into the front. 'That's the brunch bag, and a picnic blanket.'

'Morning, Will. Oh, and you *are* prepared.'

The day had started bright and breezy, and that was how Cath was feeling inside too, glowing yet rather aflutter. And also, filled with promise.

'So which beach are you thinking?' she asked.

A short drive away was the scenic Northumberland coastline, and they were spoilt for choice with beautiful Bamburgh with its castle, fish and chip fun at Seahouses, the sweep of Beadnell Bay, golden sands from Newton to Embleton, and farther south, Craster village, with its quaint harbour.

'How about Low Newton? It's a great place to walk, and we could always stop for a pint at The Ship afterwards.'

'Sounds good to me.'

'You know the way?'

'I do indeed.' Memories of summers past, family days spent on holiday with Adam and Trevor were there in her head. There was still an inevitable soreness that all that was past, but Cath also felt more accepting that life had moved on. She had moved on.

And with that, she put her Mini into gear, and she and Will were off on their way. With the radio on, they were accompanied with chat, music and memories.

Nestled in the dunes, with a fabulous view over the golden sands and pewter-blue waters of the bay, they sat together on a picnic rug.

'Right, there's coffee and I have bacon butties.' Will smiled, with a hint of nervousness. 'You can tell I've gone all out. I've even brought sauces. Red or brown?'

'Hey, bacon butties sound great.' Cath grinned. 'And it's ketchup all the way for me.'

'Ah-hah, well, I'm a brown sauce kind of guy.' Will quirked an eyebrow, which made him look cheeky and kind of sexy, sending Cath's stomach on a helter-skelter. He dug into his rucksack, took out some foil-wrapped sandwiches and then opened them to top with sauce, passing one across to Cath. 'Here you go, madam.'

'Thank you, sir.' The first bite was scrumptious, as they were still a little warm. The bacon moist and salty-sweet with a crispy rind. Perfect, in fact, served with a mug of freshly ground coffee, from the flask. 'This is great.'

'The coffee's a Colombian blend, by the way. I ground the beans myself at home.' Will was evidently a bit of a connoisseur.

It tasted rich with a hint of nutty chocolate. 'Delicious. And brunch with a sea view, how wonderful.' The company wasn't half bad either, she mused.

They looked out over the bay towards the rugged rocky ruins of Dunstanburgh Castle, which stood out from the headland on the horizon. The sea rolled in to the bleached-wheat-coloured sands before them, foaming as it broke on the shore, where a group of white-and-grey sanderlings busied themselves scurrying as they foraged for marine worms and crustaceans. A couple walking a spaniel meandered below them on the beach, followed by an elderly chap with a cute border terrier, the dog happily chasing a ball to and fro. Will and Cath nestled in their vantage point, sheltered by the dunes. It was lovely to be sitting close together – though they weren't quite touching – watching the world go by.

'Oh, I nearly forgot. There are chocolate brownies, too.'

'Ooh, lovely.'

'Made by myself.'

'Really?' Cath quizzed. Will wasn't known for his baking skills.

'Yep, I messaged Lily – our baking queen – with a plea for help, and she sent over her foolproof chocolate brownie recipe. I needed to make some kind of an effort, after all.'

Aw, it was so sweet, that he was trying to make it special for her.

Opening a plastic tub, he revealed thick, slightly gooey chunks of brownie.

'Well, they certainly *look* good.'

'But the proof of the pudding …' He grinned.

'Okay, I'm going in, and …' Cath paused to chew and taste '… the verdict is … bloody delicious. In fact, I might need another just to check.' She smiled broadly, the chocolate all melty-brown over her teeth.

Will shook his head at her. With that goofy face, she looked so like the young girl he'd met and fallen for when she was only sixteen. How had he missed recognising that look when they'd met again six months ago? But thirty-six years was a long, long time.

A few minutes later, a young couple, perhaps in their early

twenties, walked by on the sand, their hands laced together affectionately. Cath began thinking back to all those years ago too, and their own youthful romance that was destined not to be. Their first ever kiss in the dunes at Bamburgh Beach, falling for each other, yet knowing there were only a few days left to be together.

She found Will watching her intently. Was he reminiscing too? Or looking forward, to where they might go from here? Might there yet be a future for them, together as a couple? How strange, how lovely, how scary. Cath hardly dared to imagine what lay ahead, preferring to take one day at a time for now. There were far too many dreams to be broken.

Yet, all she wanted to do right now was to lean in against him, feel the warmth of his body next to hers. Hoping his arm might come to gently rest around her, as they sat side by side, soaking in the view of the blues and golden hues of sea, sand, sky. She shifted an inch or so towards him.

'Right, let's pack up and go for that walk, hey?' Will was already rising to his feet, putting away the flask and food boxes. 'Shall we head along the beach towards Dunstanburgh and then back by the golf course to Low Newton village?'

Had that closeness been too much for him? 'Ah, yep, sounds good to me.' Her dreamy bubble of a balloon had burst. The moment had evidently passed. But a walk on the beach would of course be nice, too.

'Oh, and the brunch was delightful, thank you. Ten out of ten for the brownies.'

'My pleasure.'

Cath stood, then shook out and rolled up the rug, with Will taking the rucksack.

They strolled the sands, content in each other's company, chatting away about the fine weather, their grown-up children, village life, work. The urge to be nearer, to feel his touch, still wouldn't leave her, so she reached for his hand. He'd asked her out for this walk, after all. Surely, he was looking to get to know her more. And phew, yes, he took her hand in his, their fingertips lacing. And it felt natural, a growing tenderness there between them.

He turned to give her the biggest of smiles.

Whoop!

After a thirty-minute stroll, a pint at The Ship was in order. The historic white-walled pub was tucked in the corner of a 'square' created by three rows of stone-built fishermen's cottages, giving a courtyard feel to its grassy centre. Cath ordered an apple cider, which was cool, crisp and sparkling. Will chose a pale ale, which had been brewed on site at the microbrewery there. They sat outside on a wooden bench, looking towards the sea.

They chatted easily, saying how beautiful the coast here was. And talking of other places worth a visit: Craster with its quaint harbour and kipper smokery, historical Holy Island, Alnwick with its castle and gardens, Will telling her that the cherry blossoms there were stunning in the spring. Cath realised there was so much yet for her to discover, in her new home area and with Will. Might there be more trips together, a walk hand in hand under that cherry blossom, she dared to wonder?

The day had been gorgeous. The weather fine until now, they'd been lucky, but then the skies darkened, the air cooled and the plink of raindrops started. Becoming louder, drumming on the table, and leaving spots on their clothes. Heavier now, and oh crikey, a crack of thunder that vibrated through Cath.

'Uh-oh.'

'Quick.' Will was up off the seat, with Cath swiftly following him.

They dashed to stand under the eaves of the old pub, but the rain just got heavier. Their near-empty glasses, abandoned on the bench, were beginning to fill with water.

'Oh my, we're not getting away with this, are we?' Cath observed wryly.

'No way, José.' Will pulled a woeful face, but he was smiling through his eyes as he did so.

There was only a foot width, or so, of eaves covering them, and so much rainfall that it soon began to cascade from the overflowing gutters, getting them wetter than ever.

'Well, that's me soaked through already,' said Cath, the rain dripping from her hair into her eyes.

'No point lingering here really. Are you ready?' Will looked primed to set off.

'As I ever will be …'

He grabbed her hand and they made a dash back to the car, laughing all the way up the hill, with shoes and socks squishing beneath their feet.

Back at the parking area, she could hardly open the Mini's doors quick enough. Damp and steamy, with clothes sodden, and the car heaters noisily blowing warm air at them, they sat and stared at each other, with a look filled with surprise and humour and a trace of something more …

Will leaned towards her, and they met above the handbrake, where they shared a gentle but gorgeous kiss. And despite being soaked to the skin, Cath felt happier than she had in a very long time.

Winding their way down the hill, with Tilldale nestling below them in the valley, with its cluster of cottages, the old stone church, tall trees, the country pub, and characterful stores, she realised this village – and one of its inhabitants – had already captured her heart.

'It's been a lovely day, thanks, Will,' she said, as they reached the bridge that led them home.

'Yeah, other than getting a soaking there at the end.' He gave a grin.

In reality, that had all been part of the fun. Cath glanced at the time on her dashboard; it wasn't yet four p.m. She felt a tug in her stomach, loath to let the magic of the day end so soon. 'Ahm, do you fancy a coffee? At mine? Come on in, and we can warm up and dry out.' Why did that sound like a leading question? Did she, in fact, mean it to sound like one?

'Ah yeah, why not. That sounds good.'

Neither of them seemed in a hurry to part ways after their wonderful day. So, coffee at Cheviot Cottage it was. Standing in her hallway, Will looked rather soggy, his coat damp, and his dark hair stuck out at odd angles. And, she daren't think what *she* might be looking like. She took his wet coat and hung it over a door to dry, then said she'd fetch a couple of towels from the airing cupboard upstairs, taking a quick check in the bathroom mirror there. Her hair had gone super-curly, but didn't actually look too bad, so she merely towel-dried then tousled her fingers through it, wiped off the mascara smudges below her eyes, and quickly smoothed on a little lipstick to perk up her pale face. She was soon heading back down the stairs offering Will a towel too.

A warm shower together might have been a better option, but despite her minxy thoughts, she wasn't quite ready – or body-buffed enough – for any of those shenanigans. They could stay in her head for now. But hmm, Will in a shower … She'd happily keep that vision in her head for a while longer.

Still feeling the heat of her vision-inducing blush, they sat and chatted at the snug table and chairs at the far end of the galley kitchen, warming themselves with steaming mugs of hot coffee.

'Well, I'm making an easy supper, some chicken tagliatelle. There's plenty for two,' she said leadingly. 'I was going to freeze some of it, anyhow.' She'd learned that batch cooking was the way to go as a single person. She was still making family-sized meals, and couldn't seem to break that habit.

'I was on a frozen pepperoni pizza tonight. All my culinary skills have been used up on the brunch. You've absolutely won me over with the prospect of homemade pasta. If you're sure?'

'Great, of course. Oh, I do have a tutorial at six, just for an hour, so if you don't mind waiting until that's done? You can stay and chill here, if you like. It's fine.'

'Ah right, well, if you're okay with that.' He seemed quite settled there in her kitchen. Perhaps the thought of going home, once again, to an empty house wasn't an appealing one.

'I'll get you a glass of wine, if you'd like. Red okay? You can chill here and relax, or in the lounge, if you'd rather. I'll be working upstairs.'

There was half a bottle of red left on the kitchen side from last night.

'Thanks.'

This seemed very domesticated, very 'coupley'. It felt like a glimpse, perhaps a promise, of how their future might be.

'Right, well I'll just head on up. I work from the spare bedroom.' Why did the mere mention of a bedroom make her blush once again and feel a bit tingly, dammit?

She sped upstairs, and quickly changed out of her damp clothes.

She set up her laptop, and logged on ready for her Zoom tutorial call. She greeted her student, Charlotte, and had a brief, friendly 'how's your week been?' chat, then deftly switched to the subject for tonight: algebraic equations and formulae. Oh my, Will was downstairs in her living room, the thought kept thrumming through her mind. She was finding it hard to concentrate. Right, focus. She needed to stay professional for the sake of Charlotte, and her reputation as a teacher. Think maths, think algebra, think about anything but Will. What kind of equation did Cath and Will make, in fact? Simultaneous, linear, rational … there was no bloody rational about it! She'd never had these kinds of issues before. She was a solid professional in her work. But hey, Will hadn't been sat there in her lounge, all damp sexy hair and filled with wantonness, waiting for her, before. (She'd actually thrown that in for good measure; he was probably checking emails on his phone or something.)

She refocused and went through her worksheet, step by step, ensuring Charlotte was keeping pace with her; luckily she had planned the session yesterday. And that helped her attention somewhat. But blimey, her teacher head was doing one thing, and the minxy monkey on her shoulder kept throwing in Will-based reminders. Crumble kisses in the kitchen, for one. It was a relief when five to seven came, and she began to wrap up the session. Cath said a cheerful, 'Bye, see you next week', hoping to goodness that Charlotte hadn't spotted her several lapses in concentration.

When she finally got back downstairs, Will had lit the log burner. It flickered with warming red and orange flames.

'Hi.' Those dark, sensual eyes were trained on her. 'Hope it was okay to light it, just felt a little chilly in here. I was feeling the cold, getting wet through like that.'

'Ah yeah, that's fine.' She did in fact feel more than warm enough, but it would certainly make it cosy there after supper.

They headed back through to the kitchen, where Cath began assembling the ingredients for her pasta dish, glad of a little routine diversion. She was feeling the heat in more ways than one.

Will seemed keen to try out his newfound kitchen skills, so whilst she chopped the chicken, she gave him an onion to slice. Working away beside him at the bench, she gave a sideways look and had to smile. He made a very tasty sous-chef indeed. She proceeded to make the sauce, frying onions with crushed garlic and adding tomatoes, roasted peppers and herbs; Will watching her every move. Stirring. Tasting. Adding a touch more seasoning. It felt very sensual. A final taste test, straight from the wooden spoon, with all those bursts of flavour, rich and warming.

'Ooh, can I have a try?'

'Ah, yes, of course.' She turned towards him, offering a spoonful, and as it passed his open lips, his eyes seemed to light up. 'Mmm, that is delicious. So simple, just a few ingredients, but I love it.'

She dished out, and they took their pasta bowls and a board with some freshly cut bread and butter down to the galley-end table. Chatting more easily now, with Will saying how he was taking to this cooking lark far better than he'd ever imagined. The Italian-style meal went down well, even if it left Cath feeling a little queasy. Her nerves were way too wired.

After their dinner for two, they found themselves back in the living room, and on the sofa. It wasn't that big, a snug two-seater, so they were close, close enough to feel the warmth between them. With the last of the red wine shared, some easy soul music from the Sixties playing, and the log burner aglow, the mood was relaxed and, yes, romantic. Cath leaned in to rest her head on Will's shoulder; it felt a natural thing to do. They stayed like that, quietly for a while, both lost in their thoughts. It had been such a lovely day, and she couldn't help but want to get to know him more.

Despite her earlier misgivings, and their talk of taking things slow, she shifted to look up at him, then reached an arm to gently cup his head, drawing his face, his lips, down towards hers. Her chest turned towards his. Her body yearned for this closeness. And she moved in for the most tender, and slowly lingering of kisses. A tease of pressure across his lips, then pressing closer, lips moving together. Cath parted his lips, with the tip of her tongue, testing, tasting. The newness of it all, so sensual. His response was gently insistent, the kiss growing deeper, their lips soon dancing with desire, spreading a molten warmth through her whole body. Her toes tingling. *Oh my.*

Where was this going? At this rate, somewhere pretty damned fast. His erection was firm now, as she shifted up kneeling over him, still fully clothed. Sod her slightly prickly shins and mismatched underwear, she could shimmy out of her jeans in seconds. Wow, who the heck was this new and wanton woman?

Don't think, just do. This is your time, Cath. But oh, did they in fact need protection? She'd been without periods for over a year now … hmm.

And just as all that was buzzing in her mind, Will shot up straight, bringing her up with him, and out of her aroused quandary.

'Oh God, I can't do this. I thought I was ready, but I'm not. I'm so sorry, Cath.' He was biting down on his lip, she guessed holding back tears, his hazel-brown eyes misty. 'I really, really like you, Cath … but it feels so wrong.' He puffed out a sigh.

'It's okay, it's okay,' she soothed, sensing the weight of his grief, whilst smothering her own feelings of disappointment. Surely it wasn't wrong, trying to find some comfort, some love after all that hurt. 'We can put that side of things on hold.'

Hey, she tried to cheer herself up with the thought that it'd give her chance to buff, depilate, exfoliate and perhaps even lose that extra pound or two that seemed to be happily set like an inner-tube ring around her waist. She could absolutely wait on that front. And Will was so worth waiting for.

But oh, as long as he didn't mean he didn't want to see her in a personal way *at all*. That would be crushing. She felt a dull ache within just at the thought. She already felt so attached to him. She knew he needed time, but couldn't cope with the idea of just stopping what they'd finally begun. 'We could still see each other, do the normal stuff, go for walks, cooking lessons.' Was she clutching at straws here?

She couldn't read those dark, soulful eyes as they gazed at her.

'I need a little time …' he said. Then, he looked away, out of the window, as he scratched at his temple.

Cath mentally kicked herself. Why had she pushed things physically? The man was clearly struggling and she'd added to the pressure – not to mention put herself out there for further hurt. Clearly the walls had gone back up, and whilst she'd love to talk things through, she sensed that now was not the time to probe the emotions that lay behind his need to withdraw. He'd shut her down. He wasn't ready to talk about it. Seeming protective of his feelings, of his grief, avoiding any mention of his wife in their conversations, which Cath felt pretty sure was behind all this. It was like whenever she was getting near to the real him, it was all too much. But if he couldn't open up, expose the part of him that held his grief and of course his love for Jane, could they ever truly get to know each other or have a proper relationship?

'Okay.' The word was meant to reassure Will, but Cath felt anything but okay.

She tried to settle her fears as she rested her head gently back against his chest, but he felt so very tense beneath her now. She took a moment to breathe in the woody-fresh scent of him, the solid warmth of his body beneath her. She had to, just in case it might be one of the last chances she'd have to do so.

Chapter 10

'Are you all right?' Andreas asked, two days later, with a crease of concern across his brow. 'It's just, you're walking a bit funny.'

Cath had just arrived in the shop. The short walk over had indeed been testing. 'Oh yes, and don't I know it.'

'Well, I knew things were ramping up with Will, but really, I didn't think you'd leap in quite that quickly.' He gave the cheekiest of winks.

Cath blushed like a beacon as his comment was so near the mark in a sadly ironic way. She darned well wished she had been given a good rogering by Will. 'Pilates – had my first ever class last night,' she explained. 'Feel like I've been kicked all over by a donkey. I think I may have found my waist muscles for the first time in twenty-two years.' She chuckled, then winced as even laughing made her a little sore. 'They weren't up to the task.' The class had at least been a good diversion from her dilemma with Will. The timing now a bit out, however. After chatting with her sister, who was a Pilates fanatic, and wondering if things might soon ramp up with Will, Cath'd booked herself in for a batch of lessons. The thought of revealing her flesh for the first time in years had filled her with dread. Her new slimmer and hopefully toned body in a few weeks' time, sadly now likely wasted.

Andreas smiled. 'Well, no baklava for you then, young lady. If you're on some kind of a health kick.'

'Hey, I wouldn't go that far. I need some pleasures in life.' Cath tried to smile.

It was hoping for some pleasures in life, or more precisely, what she hoped might develop pleasure-wise between her and Will, that had got her signed up for this batch of exercise classes in the first place. But hey, all that had changed. She'd be back in her comfy undies and cover-all loungewear, and her suppers for one. Oh well, she rallied, it'd do her good to be a bit healthier. *Cling on to that silver lining, Cath.*

Andreas was standing, smiling at her. Oh, she must have gone off into a little world of her own.

'OMG,' she continued, 'that class: the "hundred" – that's a killer – felt like a bloody thousand to me. Then there was "downward dog", and the "saw" – the name alone should have been a clue – and she had us doing "bridges" and "bananas". It was enough to send you bloody bananas.'

'Hah, sounds like you've done some monkeying around,' Dan quipped, from across the stores, having finished stacking a shelf with boxes of tea and biscuits, whilst listening in on the conversation.

'Pilates, so she says,' Andreas jibed. 'Sounds fun.' He gave a wink.

'Well, if it shifts my spare tyre, it'll be worth it. And I really do need to get fitter.' She was well aware that middle age was creeping up on her, her body drifting south and getting creakier by the day. She needed to use it or lose it. But bloody hell, she'd been hoping to use it in a far more exciting way than by striking painful poses, on repeat, in a hall full of gym-kit-clad middle-agers.

Andreas was chuckling. 'So, are you going back? For more torture?'

'Well, I've signed up and paid for a six-week block, so I may as well get my money's worth.'

'Eeh, you'll be sporting abs of steel by then,' said Dan.

'Or I'll not be able to walk.' She laughed.

'It is meant to be good for your core, and supporting your back,' he added more seriously.

'I'll keep you posted on that. But yes, I'm sure it'll do me some good at some point. In the meantime, I'll try and be healthy and stock up on some fruit, veg, a couple of slices of your delicious ham, and a loaf of wholemeal bread. And I will, in fact, forgo your baklava for this week,' she announced. 'Though I can't promise to hold back for any longer than that.'

'Shame. A little of what you fancy and all that,' said Andreas. 'You know you want to.'

'Don't even try and tempt me.'

Another distraction for Cath over these past two days had, in fact, been this community event. She'd been feeling a little lost sitting alone in her living room of an evening, and wondered about others locally who might well be in the same boat. It wasn't only the elderly of the village who might feel a touch lonely, especially on these long, darker nights.

She'd come up with a couple of ideas, which she was quite excited about, tying in with Christmas festivities, but she'd love some feedback from her fellow supper clubbers on this, and hopefully some practical support. It was time to reach out. 'Lads, with you talking about Maria the other night, and her loving Christmas …' She glanced at Andreas, not wanting to upset him. 'I've been thinking of the elderly, and those living alone, and been wondering about hosting some kind of community event. In the run-up to Christmas.'

'Ooh, sounds interesting. What are you thinking?' Andreas asked.

'Well, I have one or two ideas I'm fine-tuning just now, but how do you fancy a supper club brainstorm on this?'

'Oh, fabulous,' launched in Dan. 'Nibbles as we natter, perhaps.'

'Perfect.' Cath smiled. She was more than happy to host again.

They hadn't registered the jingle of the bell, but turned towards the door as they heard a cheery voice add, 'Prosecco as we ponder?' Nikki was there, with a big smile. 'Couldn't help but overhear. Sounds fab. But what exactly are we brainstorming?'

'A community Christmas event.' Cath's heart lifted with the thought. It was going to be lovely, full of all the festive feels, and she felt very much that after the warm welcome the village had given her, it was time to give something back.

'Nibbles and Natter – now that sounds just my sort of thing. If I can sort the boys out for the evening, I'd love to hold it at ours,' offered Nikki.

'Ah, well, that'd be great. If you didn't mind?' said Cath.

'Not at all. You had us all over last, and hey, nibbles don't sound too daunting. And well, I love a get-together, me.'

And that's exactly what this event was going to be about – getting people together.

'Oh, that sounds lovely. Thank you.' Cath smiled again, but then realised that this would also mean her seeing Will, who'd definitely been lying low since their rather mortifying evening. Another bridge to cross.

Jeez, why was getting to know someone so damned difficult? And why couldn't she have fallen for someone without the huge amounts of emotional baggage that Will was lugging around with him? Or even simpler, not fallen at all? But this was Will, gorgeous, grieving, tousle-haired, sexy-eyed Will … and she knew there was no way she could switch off her feelings for him.

'I'll help out with making some snacks, too,' offered Andreas, knowing full well that Nikki had plenty on her plate with her busy family life and her cleaning work. 'So, darling Cath, there'll be no need to be calorie counting then.'

'Okay, you can tempt me then, but not before.' Her health kick wouldn't last long at this rate. But perhaps a night off once in a while wouldn't be the end of the world.

And of course, a little voice in her head rang out, *with Will there, too: a little of what you fancy ...* Well, baklava and nibbles were the least of her temptations, or her concerns.

The invites had gone out. The following Friday it was to be. And a full house of supper clubbers had answered back with a 'yes'. Oh, she and Will still hadn't met in person since their stalled moment of passion, and Will's words about needing more time were still ringing in her ears. They had been messaging these past couple of days, with some 'How are you doings?' and 'Hope you're fines'. The lines of communication were still thankfully open, but almost too polite. With trepidation, half of her looking forward to a social evening with the chance to voice her event plans, the other half scared that Will would be cool with her and it was going to be awkward for them both, Cath made her way to Nikki's place.

With greetings made and glasses filled, a few minutes in and they were all sat in Nikki's comfy lounge. The nibbles selection looked divine. Cath had no chance of holding back on those tasty delights. Nikki had made sticky chipolata sausages in a honey-mustard drizzle, and had put out bowls of crunchy kettle chips. There were delicious cheese straws made by Lily with strong Cuddy's Cave local cheese, plus some sweet treats for later in the proceedings. Andreas had brought along a gorgeous meze of warmed pitta breads, cumin-and-mint-spiced whipped feta, a charred aubergine and garlic dip, along with marinated olives and caramelised spiced nuts. And Cath had brought her own offering of chocolate tiffin, which she'd made with a tipple of Baileys in, for a sweet calorie-laden surrender later.

The snacks were served around the wooden coffee table. The lads and Will were on one velour navy sofa, the girls on the other, which was a bit of a relief for Cath. With Will dashing off from her cottage that night, to be sat right next to him here would have felt very strange, and would surely have been difficult for them both. Whilst trying to be understanding and reassuring all was fine, inside she felt anything but calm. Especially as it had left her wanting more – so much more.

The room filled with noisy chatter, as the group sipped white wine and enjoyed the nibbles. Now it was time for the 'natter': getting down to business to brainstorm the best Christmas community event they could afford and manage to do well.

'Right, this is all rather lovely, and the nibbles are absolutely delicious, folks, but it's time to get our thinking caps on.' Cath put on her best, most officious teacher voice to rally the supper club troops. 'So, part of the reason why we are here this evening, is that I'd like your thoughts on my Christmas community event idea. And, if you'd be up for getting involved.' She smiled at them, with a look of hope. Without their support she knew she'd never be able to pull off the kind of lavish festive occasion she was hoping to host.

All eyes were now trained on Cath. Nikki had paused mid-bite on a cheese straw, and Dan held his glass aloft, delaying taking a sip, until he heard the news.

'Okay, since our last supper club, when we talked about Christmas and Andreas's lovely mum, I've had several ideas kicking about in my head on how we can celebrate as a community. Ideas such as coffee mornings, carol singing, but one has stuck with me and seems absolutely perfect for us as a group. If you're on board that is …' She was crossing her fingers and toes, realising it was a lot to ask of them. 'So, my community event idea is to host a super-sized Christmas supper party.'

There was a second or two of silence whilst they digested the news.

'Well, I think it sounds marvellous. I agree it has to be about food,' said Dan, much to Cath's relief. 'That's what we're good at, after all.'

She hadn't realised, but she'd been holding her breath up to that point.

'Speak for yourselves,' piped up Will wryly, still evidently nervous about his cooking skills. 'But yes, I do think it sounds a nice idea. Though it might prove a big thing to organise.'

'Oh, and can we make mince pies for it? The best-ever crumbly buttery sort. With carol singing, and everyone gathered around a Christmas tree?' Lily was getting enthusiastic about it already.

'Oh, I can picture that. Very festive,' said Nikki.

'Lily, are you serious? About the singing, I mean? How do we know we are any good?' Dan queried.

'Well, I love singing,' Andreas announced.

'In the shower. It's a bit different singing in a choir and being in tune,' Dan said, dashing his George Michael moment.

'It's a lovely idea, guys. And I'll note it down, Lily. I've already started making a list,' said Cath, taking her phone out to add to it.

'Wow, you have been thinking about this a lot,' commented Andreas.

'Oh, and Andreas,' added Cath, 'as well as people from the village, I think we should invite some of the residents from the care home, too.'

'Oh, how wonderful, yes.' He clapped his hands together. 'They did so much for Mama there, after all. And, she so enjoyed a little trip out, back in the day.'

Cath had further news on this. She'd missed visiting Maria and the home and had time on her hands that she could put to good use. 'I've just signed up for visiting at the home too, once a week. I really enjoyed talking with Maria there. It will be lovely to give some of my time, hopefully spread some joy. And, the elderly are so interesting. All those stories and life experience.'

'Aw, that's so kind of you, Cath. I'm sure the residents will love chatting with you,' said Andreas.

'So, when I'm next there,' Cath continued, 'if we're all in agreement, that is, I'll mention a supper trip to the manager, Julie. Moot it as a possibility, at least.'

'Thank you, petal,' said Andreas.

'Hmm, if most of our target audience are elderly, isn't supper a bit late in the day?' The room filled with a group sigh at Mr Sensible's words. 'Sorry, to put a spanner in the works, guys, but just thinking about my own mum and dad, well, their supper's at five o'clock sharp. They're nodding off in their easy chairs by six. Just saying.' Will quirked an eyebrow.

'Well, let's do a daytime supper then,' Nikki chipped in merrily.

'Auntie Niks, I think you'll find that's lunch.' Lily's heavily kohled green eyes creased with mirth.

'Okay, smarty-pants.'

'Now, we're talking.' Cath's face lit up at the banter, despite her anxiety. 'That's fine and works really well with my thinking. Many of those living on their own find cooking a roast dinner a chore, even though they enjoy eating one. Let's do a proper Christmas lunch, with all the trimmings, and yes, Lily, a Christmas tree with tinsel, festive music, carol singing, the works.'

'Cool,' said Lily.

'Yep, sounds gorgeous,' Nikki agreed.

'Fabulous,' Dan added.

'When?' queried Will.

'Oh, perhaps in the week or so before Christmas?' Cath suggested, having already thought of this. 'Most people will have their own plans for Christmas Day, of course.' Though Cath still wasn't sure what hers would be, perhaps flying solo festively for the first time ever. At least this project would help give her a focus for the coming weeks. 'And those from the home can still enjoy their roast turkey dinner there too, on Christmas Day.'

'Crackers,' Andreas called out.

Cath at first thought he meant her plan, and felt a nip of disappointment. It was a big challenge, admittedly.

'Games,' added Dan.

Cath then realised they were adding to her list of event activities and gave a grin, suddenly having a vision of a tangled game of Twister, with various elderly joints seized in place, which made her smile.

'And hopefully lots of fun, friendship and laughter.' Lily was beaming.

'I think we've hit the jackpot,' said Nikki.

'Are we in?' Cath asked with apprehension. It all rode on this. Was her tribe ready to forge forwards as a team, out of their cosy home-supper zone and into the world of event catering? 'I know there's a hell of a lot of planning yet to do. And I'm happy to take on the brunt of it. But in principle – and there's no pressure here on any of you as individuals – are you happy to do this? To be a part of the next big community event?'

Andreas stood up immediately, as though swearing an oath. 'I'm in.'

Dan was then standing beside him. 'Me too.'

Lily followed with 'Yeah, why not, sounds fab. Though I will have to balance it with all my studies and hopefully the restaurant job.'

'Of course, and thank you,' said Cath.

Nikki then shrugged as she gave a smile. 'Ah, go on then, in for a penny, in for a pound. I've a lot on, but haven't I always. It's to help the village folk and the elderly, and Christmas is a time for helping others, so yes, count me in.'

It was down to Will, the last one left to respond. The last one still fixed to his seat.

Cath realised that whilst questioning the project, that wasn't actually a 'no' to helping from Will. She was still hanging on to a hopeful outcome here. It would be such a shame if he felt he couldn't join them in this, if he withdrew from their group. After recent mortifying moments, Cath was worried the main reason might be more about the issues between the two of them than having anything to do with the event.

'It does sound a really lovely idea.' Will at last was positive. 'All right then, I'm in.'

Phew. Cath was delighted and very thankful for all their support.

'Well then, after all that brainstorming, I think I need another glass of wine,' announced Nikki. 'Anyone ready to join me?'

'Would be rude not to.' Dan grinned, reaching for the bottle in the wine cooler.

And just like that, plans were afoot for the Christmas event. At least something was making progress, Cath mused. Whilst she and Will had both made it here to the supper club meeting, the recent closeness they'd shared as a couple had evidently been halted. Will was keeping his distance this evening, avoiding eye contact, seemingly unsure of how much of himself he was prepared, or able, to give to any new relationship with Cath.

Finally catching his eye across the coffee table and seeing a mere ghost of a smile from him, it was like he'd retreated from her all over again. She understood it was grief he was battling with, and it was a tough journey for him. But it hurt Cath too. All she wanted was to be able to go over, take him in her arms and soothe away his pain, but life and loss were never that simple.

They felt a million miles away, not a mere metre or two apart.

Chapter 11

With a head full of plans, and a heart heavy with dashed hopes and dreams, Cath decided to keep herself busy and make a cake. Something creative and comforting. She flicked through the pages of her baking book looking for inspiration and came up with a coffee and walnut; happy that she had all the ingredients in her store cupboard.

In tandem with the simple acts of weighing out, sifting and beating, her thoughts began to align more logically. It was already late October, and this community event was not going to organise itself. They needed to get going and fast.

With the two halves of the sponge now baking in the oven, the washing up done, and warm, sugary-sweet aromas filling the kitchen, she wondered if she ought to invite the group around for afternoon coffee? Cake, with the ulterior motive of discussing the next phase of her plan. It was Sunday afternoon, nearing three p.m., the village stores now shut, and lunch in the various households most likely over. She fired off a message and waited.

By the time the two sponges had cooled on the rack and been creamed back together with delicious coffee butter-icing, all five of the super clubbers had replied. Four of them were due within half an hour, and Will, who'd finally responded from a remote hillside in the middle of the Cheviots, was on his way back from a cycling trip and would arrive in the village in around an hour.

They were standing in her cottage kitchen with coffee mugs to hand, the cake slices having been polished off within minutes.

'Watch out, guys, the MAMIL's here,' said Lily, with a hint of mirth.

'What?' queried Dan.

'What do you mean, Lils?' Cath looked out to the garden, expecting to spot some kind of warm-blooded furry creature – stoat, rabbit, squirrel? – sat on her patio staring back at her.

'Mammal?' asked Nikki, her forehead frowning in confusion.

'Middle Aged Man in Lycra,' Lily deadpanned.

And in through the back door strolled Will in full cycling Lycra, all tightly stretched against his muscles, oh blimey, Cath wasn't sure where to look. He'd snuck in the back gate, with the intention of propping his bike out of sight against the cottage's rear wall. It was an expensive road model, after all.

MAMIL … Cath stifled a snort, whilst Nikki almost spat out her coffee. Andreas and Dan were now in fits of giggles. 'Oh, never heard that one, but I love it,' said Dan.

'Hi, all,' said Will.

'Hey, Will,' said Lily.

'Hi.' Cath felt suddenly shy.

'Umm, why all the laughter? Dare I ask?' He quirked a dark eyebrow.

'Just our Lily, apparently you're a MAMIL,' advised Nikki.

'Ah, right, well I have heard that one recently. Pretty accurate, I suppose. Comes with the hobby, and having the right the gear.' He took it all in his stride, with a warm sense of humour.

'He's certainly got the right gear and it's all on show,' added Andreas, to another burst of the giggles.

'Coffee? Cake. I've made a coffee and walnut,' Cath offered, trying to calm things down and shift her own thoughts to safer ground.

'Both, and that sounds delicious.'

'It is,' confirmed Andreas, a stray crumb still perched on his lower lip.

'Just what I need after a thirty-miler.'

'Wow, that's some effort,' said Dan, impressed.

'Just the usual.' Will was pretty blasé about it.

'In fact, I think I could manage another slice of that, lovely,' said Dan. He indicated the errant crumb to his partner.

As Cath deftly sliced more cake, she remembered how the Nibbles and Natter session had been so productive and supportive. She was absolutely thrilled that the whole supper group were engaged and on board, but she also realised this was just the start of it all.

She passed the slices over and poured a fresh coffee for Will from the cafetiere. 'Right, well, I have an ulterior motive in bringing you all over here.'

'Ugh, you mean it wasn't for our scintillating company, after all?' said Nikki.

'I knew there was more to it,' said Dan.

'Of course that was a big part of it. But, the other evening,' Cath continued, undeterred, 'we all agreed the community Christmas lunch event was a good idea, and that's brilliant, but there's a whole lot of planning to do. And initially, there's one crucial thing we need to decide on, and that is *where*.' She wanted to pick the brains of these fantastic people with the local knowledge.

'Hmm, I take it you're thinking about holding this event in the village?' Will began. 'The pub would need to charge per head if we held it there. Though it's great in there, that'd work out expensive. And are we charging for this? Would many come if we did? And I hate to point out the obvious, but none of our homes are big enough, or ovens large enough, to take this on.'

'Yeah.'

'Hmm.'

A few seconds of silence fell over the room. Had they in fact been getting carried away with themselves and their big ideas, and already hit a ruck in the road?

'There are a couple of large halls in Kirkton,' Lily mentioned.

'Possibly, but I bet they'll already have events laid on for Kirkton folk at that time of the year,' warned Dan.

'And I really do want to do something *here* in Tilldale, for our villagers first and foremost. Give our little local community a boost,' added Cath.

'We do have a village hall …' broached Nikki.

That had been one of Cath's thoughts. She'd walked past the seemingly unused stone building many times.

'One that's cold and has dodgy electrics. Can't think why it's hardly ever used,' Andreas reminded them, with a frown.

'It was the village school up until twenty years ago, so the kitchen and ovens are likely to be big,' added Dan, more hopefully.

'If they still work,' Nikki responded pragmatically.

It wasn't sounding that hopeful, but Cath wasn't one to fall at the first hurdle.

'Well, let's go and take a look at the hall firstly. See what the facilities are like, and suss out the kitchen, before we run away with ourselves.' Cath was sensibly slowing things down – much like her and Will, she mused ironically – even though, in this case, she felt a lift of possibility running through her veins.

'And we ought to check out a couple of dates that might work for the event. Make sure it's not booked out, or anything?' Lily mooted.

'Ah well, that's easy – it's never booked out. It hasn't seen a party or an event for at least five years. We've not seen a light on in the place for a long, long while, have we, Andreas?' Dan asked.

'Oh, that sounds ominous. It'll be in need of a good clean-up then,' Cath observed.

'Bet it's full of cobwebs and spiders. Yuk.' Lily pulled a face.

'Okay, so we ought to check it out, at least. See what we're dealing with, or if it's even suitable,' said Will.

'Definitely,' agreed Cath, before taking a soothing sip of coffee.

'Yeah, that'll get things moving. Good idea, Will,' agreed Dan.

As Cath munched her last piece of cake, she wondered if they might already have bitten off more than they could chew.

The huge old metal key turned in the lock with a creak, then a clunk. Cath shifted the circular cast-iron handle, and then pushed the heavy oak door.

'Here goes!' she announced, feeling a sense of trepidation.

All six of the supper clubbers had gathered for a 'recce' of the proposed venue for their community Christmas lunch, and were now stood under the stone plaque, set above the threshold that read *1872*, the year it had been built and originally purposed as the village school.

Veronica Manners, the hall committee's chair and upstanding member of the community, had been surprised to receive the call from Will. She'd informed him that the hall hadn't been booked out since 2020, 'a casualty of Covid' – and Cath wondered, perhaps now a victim of neglect – which gave them all some misgivings. But if they really wanted to hold this event within the village, which they'd all felt was important, then there weren't really any other alternatives, financially or size-wise.

A musty smell hit them as they entered, along with some wisps of stray cobwebs. Cath, being the first in, swiftly pushed a strand away as it tickled her cheek. The shaft of light from the open doorway illuminated the trillions of dust motes drifting through the stale air. Crikey, it'd certainly need a good airing and sweeping, was the first thing that came to her mind, and they hadn't even got past the reception area.

As they stepped into the dark-blue carpeted hallway, through a glass-windowed swing door, a noticeboard faced them with an array of old posters, curling at the edges, detailing events long past. A talk on rural agriculture by local farmer Wesley Trotter – which made Cath and Nikki snigger, what a surname for a farmer – and the Tilldale WI meeting, first Thursday of the month at seven p.m. followed by tea and biscuits. The WI group in the village had been disbanded years ago, so she'd heard. There was nothing at all that appeared to be recent.

Dan enlightened the team that the last classes to be held here were carpet bowls and yoga, not at the same time of course though that might have proved interesting, which had both now moved to Kirkton's purpose-built new and well-heated community centre. Tilldale's hall had evidently not been used for events for many a year. Its use dwindling seemingly long before the Covid pandemic, though that appeared to be the final straw.

They opened a door and peeked into one of the original classrooms. Desks were piled on top of one another to one side of the room, along with stacks of tiny grey plastic chairs. Wow, there was still an old-fashioned black chalkboard set on one wall, a wooden padded hand-held eraser still there at its base, and a half-piece of white chalk next to it.

Cath wondered what the last words were that that piece of chalk had written; perhaps 'The End' or 'Goodbye' or more positively 'Good Luck'. She couldn't resist picking the chalk up. Back in the day, she'd used the same tools herself early on in her career – the use of interactive whiteboards and laptops now taking over, of course. And she wrote in her best teacher script: 'Tilldale's Christmas Community Event' and drew a festive holly leaf. It felt like an announcement. A promise to her supper club friends and her new local community. It was going to happen, and she really hoped it would be here in this hall.

'Blimey, I feel like I've stepped back in time,' said Nikki.

'This is just like my primary school from years ago,' added Will, gazing around. 'I didn't imagine this would all still be left in here.'

'It's like Beamish or something,' quipped Lily with a smirk. 'It's actually a bit freaky.'

'Quit the nostalgia, folks; we need to suss out if this place is actually capable of hosting a Christmas lunch for twenty or more people.' Dan brought them back to the present, with his serious head on.

'And be warm enough,' added Andreas, feeling the chill already.

It seemed sad to see the building empty and neglected. Having been a teacher in a school for many years, Cath could almost hear the echoes of children's chatter, their laughter and play, the steady voice of the teacher filling this classroom as lessons were learned.

'Oh, look, what's this?' Andreas pulled Cath from her reverie as he discovered a long, thick white rope dangling tantalisingly all the way down from the ceiling. He gave it a tug, and a loud *clang* rang out from up above them. The old school bell. Like a naughty schoolboy, Andreas gave a cheeky grin. 'Oh, it still works then.'

'Yes, and the whole darn village will know we're here now,' Dan scolded, though he didn't look particularly concerned or surprised by his partner's behaviour. 'Right, let's get on with the job to hand. We need to go and assess the hall space. That'll be the main area for entertaining, after all.'

'And the kitchen,' chipped in Lily theatrically. 'If that's no good, then dinner is doomed.'

They trooped out from the classroom, back through the central corridor, past the entrance hall and reception, heading down to navy-painted double doors, and into the hall.

Cath gazed around her. It was big enough, certainly. High walls to three sides, a spacious parquet floor, with a rather tatty olive-green curtain half drawn across a stage area at the far end of the hall. There were three large arch-shaped windows that overlooked the tarmac playground, which had more recently served as a car parking area. Plenty of light coming in from there.

But she gave a shiver – it was darned chilly. 'Not a bad room …' Cath tried to stay positive.

'Bloody cold in here,' said Nikki.

'Well, I doubt it'll have been heated for years,' said Dan.

Cath scanned the hall, looking for radiators. There were some electric panel heaters fixed to the sides of two of the walls, in addition to several historic-looking Victorian-style cast-iron radiators.

Will went over to touch one of the Victorian ones, which was, of course, stone cold. 'So, there must be a boiler somewhere,' he pondered aloud. 'Most likely oil-fired, like the rest of the village.'

'Let's just hope the system works, or that we can at least get the electric ones going,' said Andreas, wrapping his coat tighter around him.

'That'll be crucial. We'll need to test them out, and soon. No point bringing a group of elderly people into a freezing cold hall,' said Cath.

Everyone nodded in agreement.

'Right, I'm on with an action plan. I'll be making notes on my phone.' Cath then began tapping away on her mobile.

'Thanks, Cath.' Dan gave a thumbs-up. 'Oh, and add sweep, clean, and remove the stage curtains. They look like they're about to fall down anyway.'

Despite the mounting to-do list, Cath couldn't help but feel a glimmer of hope, of possibility – excitement, even. Looking around her, she realised the hall was light and airy. The paintwork seemed to be okay, a standard cream on the walls with a wooden dado rail trim. There were, admittedly, plenty of crusty dead flies and insects lying on the window sills and the floor, but nothing a good hoover and mop couldn't sort out.

Veronica had advised the original trestle tables, originally used for the school lunches, were stored somewhere here, too. Cath had already spotted several stacks of large green-plastic chairs positioned to one side of the stage.

Whilst Will and Dan went to check on the boiler situation, the

102

girls and Andreas were keen to find the kitchen space. A working kitchen was also vital to their Christmas lunch plans.

Lily marched on ahead, excited to see the cooking facilities. 'It must be in here.'

There was one more door – other than the signposted loos – off the corridor which they hadn't yet tried. Lily turned the handle. Cath was hot on her heels, finding herself feeling nervous. This could be make-or-break time.

'Ooh, look.' Lily was pointing animatedly. 'There are two huge ovens.' She was in and opening the cooker doors, peering inside. 'Definitely turkey-sized! And pretty clean. Someone must have scrubbed them out before they shut down the hall, at least.'

'That's good,' said Cath.

Nikki took a look in the other one. 'Hmm, nothing a bit of Mr Muscle won't shift, anyhow.'

Andreas was grinning. 'And look here, there's a massive school-dinner-sized hob to work with. Wonder if there are big pots and pans left anywhere? They'd be so handy.'

Lily was in her element, opening cupboard doors and peering inside the units. 'Gotcha!' And she pulled out two ginormous saucepans as an example. 'It's full of stuff like this. They'll just need a good wash.'

'Brilliant.' Cath's mood was lifting all the time.

Nikki had discovered a storeroom off to one side. 'And here's all the old crockery. There's cutlery, and loads of glasses. Teapots, mugs.' She shot her head out of the open doorway. 'It's an Aladdin's cave in here. They must have kept everything.'

'Well, that's a bonus. It's all looking promising, Cath.' Andreas couldn't hold back the excitement in his voice.

There was also a microwave, kettle and a tall stainless-steel hot water urn on the side, ideal for filling pots of tea and coffee. Perhaps these were a later addition to the kitchen, when it became the community hall. Cath didn't imagine the main cooker with those ovens would have been used for quite some time … and that could prove to be a problem in itself. The basics they needed to cook a meal for twenty-five or so people (Cath's 'guesstimate' of likely numbers; thinking of the elderly she'd seen about in the village, plus a small group from the home) were all here. But the real question was, were they still in working order? And if not, that could prove quite an expense to fix, even if it was at all possible. Some of this equipment must be many years old, after all. And at this point, she didn't dare let her mind stray to health and safety issues – that could be a minefield. But it would all need to be addressed before the event could become a reality.

'Well, the kitchen's pretty well equipped,' Cath said aloud, trying to reassure herself.

'As long as it all works.' Lily was evidently thinking practically, too.

'No worries,' Nikki piped up. 'The ovens are electric, so I'll get my Kev to check them out. Free of charge, of course, community spirit and all that.' Thank goodness Nikki's husband was a qualified electrician. 'And he can check out those two heater things in the hall.'

'Are you sure he won't mind?' asked Dan, who'd reappeared with Will. 'There might be a lot of work to put it right.'

'Yeah, we'd have to at least pay for any parts,' acknowledged Cath, wondering where all the money to stage this event was going to come from. She needed to sit down and work out the likely costings. She couldn't expect her supper club team to fork out a fortune, after all.

'Well, perhaps,' Nikki conceded, 'but I'll make sure Kev's labour costs will be free. I'll sweetheart him with a steak supper. Works every time.' She grinned.

'Well, that would be amazing, thanks. And yes, let's get the cooking equipment in here checked and tested, as a starting point.'

Cath thought again about the original school hall. There must have been assemblies, school plays, Christmas shows, all sorts here since it began. 'Ah, it'd be so lovely if we could give the old place a new lease of life. Bring it back to life, and make it somewhere that can be used for the village in the future, too. I feel strongly that we should at least try to take this on as a project.' It was ambitious admittedly, but something in her soul had been sparked.

'I agree. We move forward, for now at least.' Andreas stood tall, sounding as though they were about to make a battle charge.

Lily giggled, as the others grinned.

'I'm happy to get stuck in and clean. I have all the gear,' added Nikki.

'I'll help with that, of course,' offered Cath. 'Let's set a day.'

'I'll help too,' said Lily. 'Count me in.'

'And I'm a whizz with a hoover,' added Will.

Cath raised her eyebrows at that. Hunky *and* handy with a hoover. And off limits for now, she reminded herself.

'It sounds like we have an initial plan, at least,' said Dan. 'And we found the boiler. Will was right, it's oil-fired, with a tank outside with just a little oil left in. I might need to persuade the hall committee to buy in some kerosene, then we can try and get the central heating up and running. If it's mid-December for the event, then I'm not sure that a couple of electric panels in the hall will be enough.'

'A service would be essential, too. We've got to know it's all safe,' added Will sagely.

'True.' Cath's initial flicker of hope was wavering. Costs were mounting, and that was without even considering the large amounts of food and drink they'd need to buy. Once her costings were made, they'd have to have a chat about where this was all coming from. Cath could foresee a big dent in her not-so-large savings. Perhaps she could think of some fundraising ideas. But whatever it took, she was determined to give something back to help her community. It was such a lovely idea. And it might well prove a welcome distraction from the 'will he, won't he' Will situation and her own likely quiet Christmas. 'So, in a few days' time,' she continued stoically, 'once we've been able to check the essential utilities are working and safe, we'll have a group clean-up. And hey, folks, by then, we might just have ourselves a venue.'

'And a whole heap of work.' Andreas raised his eyebrows. 'But if it's going to help lift the spirits of our little community here in Tilldale, as well as some of those from the care home, then I'm ready to roll up my sleeves right now.'

'Hear, hear,' agreed Dan.

Crikey, thought Cath, this was like her supper club shed renovations when she'd first moved into the cottage, but on a *gigantic* scale. This time, though, she had the wonderful supper club team on her side. She just hoped they hadn't taken on too much with this grand plan. They'd certainly have to put in a lot of graft to make it shipshape.

They had a lot of work to do, and not a lot of time to do it in. Cath prayed they could pull it off and make her first Christmas in Tilldale a special one.

Chapter 12

A few days after the village hall viewing, Cath was busy stripping off her bed linen, ready to take advantage of a fine, blustery day. She loved getting the laundry outside on the line in the fresh air and seeing it blow in white billows.

As she was crouched down in the kitchen, with her head virtually in the washing machine, pushing the duvet cover in, the doorbell rang. Then, with hardly a second to respond, she heard footfall in the hall. Standing up, on alert, she faced the hallway and in came her grown-up son.

'Adam? What are you doing here?' She was grinning away at the sight of him, but was astonished – it was a long way from his flat in Leeds. 'Are you okay?' Her maternal instincts were on high alert after his recent mental health issues. This was so out of the blue as she'd only taken a day trip down to Leeds a couple of weeks ago to check how he was getting on.

'Yeah, all good, thought I'd surprise you. Fancied that Sunday roast you keep harping on about. You said I was always welcome.' He gave a mischievous smile.

Cath found herself swiftly wrapped up in his bear hug. As she drew back, she replied, 'Well then, I'd better get over to the butcher in Kirkton fast. They close at lunchtime on a Saturday.'

'Sounds like a plan.'

'How did you get here, anyway?' It was a half-hour drive from the nearest station, the train his usual means of transport.

'I borrowed Dad's car. He and Steph are away somewhere this weekend, so it was just going to be sitting on the driveway. He seemed happy to hear I was thinking of coming up to see you, and let me have it. Got to be returned tomorrow night, so it's just for a couple of days.'

'Ah, that's great. How is he?' It felt easier to talk about Trevor now. The months that had passed since she'd moved here giving her that distance, a fresh perspective on things. The hurt about his betrayal had faded, if never quite healed.

'He seems pretty good. Happier now that Steph's back on the scene.' Their relationship had been a little on-off in the early months – Adam had told her that much.

'Ah, right.' The other woman. The office fling. It was what it was. It had happened, and there was no going back for her and Trev now. It had, at least, given Cath the kick up the butt (one mahoosive bruising kick) to go and find a whole new life of her own.

'She's not much of a cook, though,' Adam added. 'That's why they go out a lot wining and dining. I think Dad was actually a bit envious when he heard I was coming up for one of your Sunday dinners.'

Cath had to smile at that.

After unloading his large rucksack, and thoughtfully a bottle of red he'd brought to go with dinner (looking suspiciously like one of Trevor's favourite Riojas), she and Adam headed off to Kirkton. Adam had offered to drive. He was enjoying the novelty apparently, and building his experience. He was a good driver, steady on the country roads. You never knew what was around a corner here: quad, tractor, horse and rider, cyclists (hmm), a herd of sheep. She'd met them all since arriving here.

'So, what do you fancy? Beef, pork, lamb?' They were stood in the butcher's gazing at the meat selection. It was lovely to be able to spoil Adam this weekend, so Cath was happy to let him choose. She was confident about cooking any of the meats; roasts had been one of her fortes back at the family home in Roundhay. They'd all stop their busy lives for a few precious hours on a Sunday afternoon, and catch up over crispy Yorkshire puds, mounds of meat, and tasty veg, golden-crusted roast potatoes and cauliflower cheese being some of their favourites, around the family dinner table.

'Uhm, tricky, but I think it's gonna have to be your slow-cooked pork, the one with the crunchy crackling.'

'Sounds good to me. Okay, so can we take that belly pork joint, please.' She pointed to a scored rectangle of meat. She had just the recipe in mind, honey-roasted with a hint of chilli served with some tasty greens, a cauliflower cheese, of course, and crisp, yet melt-in-the-middle roasties. Better do some of her Yorkshire puddings, too. With a quick stop off at the local co-op for veggies, that was tomorrow's meal sorted.

That afternoon, between light November showers, wrapped up warmly in coats and scarves, mother and son took a stroll around the village and along the river. It was a bit muddy on the track through the fields, different from the summer months, but it was still lovely. You'd often see a heron down by the water's edge, or some moorhens, and the stream-side trees were still clinging on to their golden-brown autumn hues. The odd leaf swirling down around them in the breeze.

'It's great to see you.' Cath was still amazed that he was here. Her quiet weekend had suddenly been filled with chat, fun and possibility. Plus, the added joy of having someone to cook for, to share a meal with. That was one of the things she missed the most in her new solo life.

'So, how's the bar work going?' Cath asked. 'And have you

had any news on your other job applications?'

'Ah, the new place is fine. Nice and busy, and the team are much friendlier there, so it's working out okay.' He'd recently lost some previous bar work. 'And yeah, I keep looking, keep trying for different posts, but the right kind of jobs really are few and far between. I really want to get involved with something to do with nature, with wildlife. That's always been the dream and I'm not going to give up on that, yet.'

Cath was glad to hear it. She was worried her son might get disillusioned, settling for a job that would never inspire him. Since Adam had completed his degree in zoology at Leeds uni last year, then travelled in Asia for a few months, he had struggled to find any meaningful work.

'But hey, I'm volunteering for the Wildlife Trust now. They've various projects on. Just last weekend I was off planting trees in the Dales.'

'Ah, well, that sounds brilliant, Adam. And, that'll be good for your CV too.'

It was great to hear he was being proactive again. His recent low had worried her so much. She couldn't just pick him up, dust him off, give him a hug, and clean his scraped knees anymore. Adulthood wasn't simple at all. Though hugs, naturally, were always a must.

'Yeah, for sure. I'm far happier working outside in the open air. I don't know how the hell you and Dad managed, stuck away in a classroom and an office for years.'

'I suppose it's all about doing what you love. And for me that was teaching. Still is.'

'Yeah, s'pose. Don't know if Dad ever loved accounting, to be fair.'

'No, true.'

'I think it was the money he loved,' Adam added wryly.

They both smiled. They knew Trevor all too well.

They strolled on, making their way back via a country lane,

into the village and past the stores, spotting Andreas on his hands and knees in the window of the shop, arranging cards, crafts, and expertly placed baubles and tinsel. The Christmas display was taking shape. November already here, and December just around the corner. Christmas was arriving in Tilldale.

It made her wonder about Adam's plans over the festive period. It would be wonderful to have him here with her for Christmas Day. Perhaps she'd ask him over a cup of coffee back at the cottage.

She gave Andreas a smile and a thumbs-up, mouthing: 'It's looking good.'

'Me or the shop?' Andreas mouthed back through the glass with a silly grin.

'Both,' she responded, grinning too.

Dan then popped his head out of the door. 'I couldn't stop him. He's been itching to get the Christmas stuff out. I've relented now it's November. The shop's had a full makeover too. Gifts galore.'

'Sounds great. I know where to come to get some festive ideas then.'

'He's even planning a Christmas shopping night. Mince pies and Prosecco.'

'Even better. Count me in.'

'Will do. Hi, Adam. Nice to see you,' Dan added, recognising Cath's son. 'Up for a while?'

'Just the weekend.'

'Well, enjoy!'

'Thanks, mate.' Adam nodded. He'd met the lads back in the summer when he'd stayed with Cath for a few weeks post-travels.

'Back to the grindstone for me,' said Dan wryly. 'Stock-taking to do, whilst Laurence Llewelyn-Bowen here puts his creative touch on the window.'

'Just because I'm the one with the artistic flair …' Andreas responded wittily.

Cath and her son moved on, once more.

'They seem good fun, Andreas and Dan,' Adam observed.

'They are, and I love that they're a big part of our supper club group. They're like the glue that keeps everyone together.' In fact, she realised that's how she felt about the village stores, too. It was like community superglue. Andreas and Dan had made her so very welcome and been instrumental in getting her and Will together, after all – even though things on that front were a little dodgy just now.

Adam's white trainers returned to the cottage a shade of blotchy beige. But that was country life for you. Cath's walking boots had become her staple footwear, she realised, as she perched on a small wooden bench in her hallway to unlace them. Whilst chatting earlier, she was pleased that Adam seemed so much brighter than when she had last visited him in Leeds. This was a real positive and such a relief. Hopefully, he'd turned a corner, and was beginning to find his way in life again. He evidently had dreams and aspirations again. He was looking forward and wasn't that always the best way?

Though Cath knew all too well how hard that could be when life had knocked you down.

Supper that evening was a simple affair. Cath stretched her meal of spicy tomato and bacon penne pasta to make enough for two, and found a can of tinned peaches and some vanilla ice cream in the freezer for an impromptu pudding. Adam had always loved that as a small child, even picking up and drinking the remaining creamy fruit juices from the bowl so as not to waste a drop. It had made her and Trevor laugh. Life had changed a lot but she'd always remember their family times fondly. Be grateful for their joint history. Did Trevor get flashbacks of their life together too? she wondered.

Still sitting at the dinner table, enjoying a post-supper cup of tea, Cath's thoughts turned to Christmas. With the recent talk of festivities, and November now on the doorstep, she had an invite to extend. She hoped her son knew already that he'd be always welcome, wherever she lived, but it was better to make things clear. They'd never yet had a Christmas apart.

'Hey, I know it's a little way off, but have you got any plans for Christmas? If not, you are very welcome to come and stay here. Turkey and all the trimmings, of course. In fact, I'd love to share my first Christmas in the cottage with you.'

There was a telling pause. 'Ah, well thanks, Mum … that's really sweet of you, but I might well be staying down Leeds way.' He had the grace to sound slightly awkward, as he added, 'Steph's already mentioned spending Christmas Day with them. And well, I know some of my mates go out for a bit of a bash Christmas Eve. So, it'll either be that for me, or more than likely, I'll be working at the bar, if they need me. It makes sense to stay down there.'

'Oh …' Cath wasn't sure what to say. Yes, he was a grown adult with his own life. And after his recent low, it was good he had a social scene going on with his mates, as long as he wasn't planning on going on some mega drinking 'sesh'. Worry still nipped at her heels. She tried very hard to keep her tone light as she added, 'Well, the offer's there, should your plans change at all.'

And this might well be the first Christmas – *in her life*, she realised – that she'd be spending it on her own. And that was a very strange thought indeed.

'I bet it'll be lovely up here, though,' Adam continued. 'All quaint and very *Country Life*.' He made it sound a bit twee, that it was somehow not his thing at all, or was she just being oversensitive?

The real crux of her hurt might have been a touch of unbridled jealousy, of being left out, as she suddenly pictured him off to his dad and his dad's fling Steph's on Christmas Day, whilst she sat alone. Trev, who'd done the cheating, with Steph, who must have known he was married … and they were the ones who got to get the friggin' family Christmas. That did feel like a punch in the gut.

But Cath quickly chided herself. It was nice that they'd asked him. He was bound to be seeing more of them, living in the same city. She'd asked Trev to keep a closer eye on their son herself. She needed to be grown up about this, think about what was best for Adam and put their marital hurts aside. It was a good thing that since Adam's low, Trevor was being far more proactive in his son's life.

'Sorry, to disappoint you, Mum.' Adam's tone was gentle, considerate.

'Ah, I'll be all right, son. It's good that your dad's offered. I'm sure I'll have a nice day here, whatever happens. And I'll be busy enough on the run-up with that Christmas community lunch we're organising. If it all comes together, that is.'

'Oh yeah, tell me more about that. You mentioned it on the phone the other night.'

And off she started, describing her initial idea that set it all off, along with the village hall visit, the electrics and heating about to be checked (and fingers crossed for that), menu ideas and more.

'It sounds brilliant, Mum.'

Christmas was about giving. And she'd give her all to get this community event off the ground and make it a success, even if her own Christmas was to be somewhat quieter, and perhaps lonelier, than usual. Lots of people spend Christmas alone after all – that was the whole idea of her festive get-together.

To be fair on Adam, he'd been there for her last Christmas. Even postponing his world travels to spend the festive season by her side, making sure she wasn't alone. He was a good lad, bless him.

But her dreams of a cosy village Christmas, spent with her son celebrating in her new cottage, well they had just been dashed.

Later in bed, thinking about her day, and the lovely surprise of having Adam here this weekend, she realised she was luckier than most. She resolved she'd just have to do Christmas her way this year. The only problem was, she didn't yet know what *her* way was. Time to make some new traditions!

Chapter 13

'I knew I was missing something. The sauce! My apple and chilli sauce. It goes perfectly with this dish.' Cath was muttering to herself as she sat in the kitchen, munching on hot buttered toast with blackcurrant jam. She'd used up all the apples from her garden tree on crumbles, too.

The pork joint was on the side, salted, spiced with a little cumin, garlic and a drizzle of honey, and was about to go into the oven for slow-roasting. The cabbage was chopped, and cauliflower segments ready to parboil in a large pan of water. Preparation was key.

'I just need to pop to the shop, Adam. Anything you need?' Cath called up the stairs; now that took her back to his teen years. Adam was making the most of a lazy morning, and was only just out of the shower. She was fine letting him lie in, to be fair, as she'd bustled about in the kitchen. She was in her happy zone, back cooking for her family, well one of them. As well as prepping the pork, she'd baked a lemon drizzle cake. A slice each for them with morning coffee, and the rest of it to go back with Adam. Her healthy eating very much on hold for today.

She had to admit, the fear of a 'reveal' had been a major driving force in her dieting and exercise plans. Pilates hour was looming again, and her limbs and abs had only just recovered from last week's class. Though whether her body would ever see the light of day next to Will's was looking more and more uncertain. Other than a few friendly texts, he appeared to have backed off once again. Their budding relationship felt like a game of dodgeball at times. And though she tried hard not to let it hurt, wanting to protect her bruised and battered heart, it still did.

There was no response from her son's spare-room den, so she followed up with: 'See you in a few minutes, then.'

'Good morning, gorgeous,' Andreas greeted her with a warm smile.

'Hello, handsome,' Cath quipped back. 'Love the window display. Oh, and look, all these festive cards and gifts, wrapping paper, and the extra fairy lights above the counter. Love it. Christmas is here in Tilldale. Hurrah.'

'So glad you like it. I've put in so much time and effort with the Christmas ordering and the window, and Grinchy Dan's still saying it's too early. Never too early for business, my love,' he called out, Dan most likely being in the back of the store. 'Just wait until I get my first bauble sale. These are divine – take a look.'

They were indeed. Beautiful frosted-glass baubles, a set of six, in teardrop shapes, globes and stars, with just a dusting of sparkle, like ice crystals in the Alps.

'Ooh, they are. You might just have your first sale right here.' They were so very pretty. 'How much?' She daren't think. She was meant to be buying basic provisions, she reminded herself, but one small box of Christmas decorations to celebrate her new home. And they'd look so lovely on the real-fir Christmas tree she was planning on getting for herself.

'Only twelve pounds, the set.'

It wasn't extortionate, and they'd last a good few years, so that'd be, what, a mere pound per year.

'I'm in.'

Andreas grinned. 'And what else do you fancy today?'

A middle-aged cyclist in Lycra came to mind, but that wasn't going to be.

'Ah yes, a fresh red chilli if you have one, and some cooking apples. For my apple sauce with a kick.'

'That sounds great.'

'Better have some more milk, too. With Adam home, I'm getting through it fast.'

'Yes, nice to see him yesterday. How is he getting on?' Andreas asked kindly. Cath had shared a little of his troubles with the supper group, after having to make her dash to Leeds a while ago.

'Good thanks. He seems a lot brighter.'

'Ah, that's great to hear. He's a really nice lad. When he was in the village a while back, he popped in a couple of times, and we had a good chat. We loved hearing about his travels. Took us back. We did a bit of travelling too, back in the day. Send him our best.'

'Thanks, and I will.'

A thought was forming. She had more than enough roast dinner prepared for four people. 'Umm, do you guys have any lunch plans?' Cath asked.

'Nothing special. A toastie perhaps.'

Well, that was it. She knew Sunday was a short day for the shop, with it closing late morning.

'Well, why not come along and join me and Adam for our roast dinner? I got a huge joint of pork yesterday, and there's only the two of us. The veggies are already prepped, so it's not a bother. I bet Adam would enjoy your company, too.'

'Oh my, that'd be amazing. If you're sure?' Andreas's eyes had lit up.

'I'm more than sure. It'd be lovely. Say one o'clock?'

'Dan, we have a dinner date!' he called out to his partner with delight.

An echoey 'brilliant' carried from the back of the stores.

'Oh, and can Shirley come too?' asked Andreas. 'It's just with us both working this morning, we'll have left her virtually all day, otherwise.'

'Of course, she can. Might even save her a bit of Sunday dinner for a treat. If she's allowed, that is.' Cath smiled.

'Marvellous. You are a gem.'

Andreas and Dan, plus terrier Shirley who was sporting a pink-spotty neckerchief, arrived with a bottle of red wine and some gorgeous pink-and-white lilies for Cath.

'Hell-oo. Come on through.' Cath led them to the kitchen, where she poured out three glasses of chilled white wine, with Adam settling for a glass of fizzy water, as he needed to make the journey back to Leeds later on.

The slow-cooked pork was resting on the side, its mouth-watering honey-spiced aromas filling the kitchen, ready for Adam to do the honours with carving shortly. The savoy cabbage was simmering on the hob, the cauli-cheese in the oven, with the roasties and Yorkshires on the side, ready to pop back in the oven for a final few minutes of crisping. Shirley's nose was twitching with the overload of salivating savoury smells.

Cath had had a bit of a moment earlier, deciding where to sit them all, her galley kitchen dining area being tiny. In the end, she and Adam had pushed the living room sofa against the back wall, and they moved the bistro table set into the lounge, bringing a couple of extra chairs down from the summerhouse. For four people it'd work fine, any more would have been too much of a squeeze, and with the log burner on and a candle aglow, it actually looked very country-cosy for her lunch. She was happy with her plan.

As they settled at the table, ten minutes later, Cath brought through the temptingly loaded serving dishes: crackling topped tender meat, golden-cheese-crusted cauliflower, buttered savoy, rosemary roasties and a giant stack of crisp Yorkshire puddings.

Everyone looked eager to dive in.

Andreas then asked innocently, 'Oh, I thought Will might have joined us?'

Oh Christ, Adam knew nothing at all about her and Will being an item – admittedly, a bit of a lost item at the moment. It was all too early and uncertain to be involving her son. She flashed Andreas a silencing glare across the table. He caught the warning sign and nodded apologetically, with an 'oops' of a look.

Cath had actually thought about it too, mulling it over last night in bed. Should or shouldn't she ask Will along for dinner? He'd probably love a home-cooked roast. But she'd decided that things felt too difficult between them just now, and it wouldn't be the right way to introduce him to Adam, throwing poor Will into a family-style dinner.

And anyhow, how would she even begin to introduce him? What were they to each other? They were hardly partners, after all. Oh, Adam, meet my trial-relationship first-love buddy? In the end, not wanting Will, her, Adam or the shop lads to feel awkward, putting them all on the spot, she'd bowed out. They didn't need to be face to face with her and Will's latest hitch in the road to romance.

And her stomach certainly couldn't have handled it.

They were soon tucking into the tasty roast, the chat and ambience just right. Adam getting on well with Andreas and Dan, who were talking about their life running the village stores. He asked what they used to do before moving up to Tilldale. Dan surprised them with tales of being a sometime DJ, his chance to let off some steam apparently, weddings and parties being his forte, as well as his main career of marketing manager.

'That sounds really cool,' said Adam.

'Oh yes, move over Fatboy Slim, welcome Slimboy Fat.' Andreas chuckled. 'Actually, he was pretty cool back in the day. That's where I met him, when he was standing in, DJing at my local club. His beats were crazily cool.'

'And did you have a stage name?' Cath asked, full of curiosity.

Andreas and Dan raised their eyebrows. Dan stayed quiet, seemingly reticent.

'Go on, tell them,' Andreas egged his partner on.

'Do I have to? Honestly, it was years ago.' Dan appeared awkward.

'You've gotta share this now, guys.' Adam looked amused.

'Okay, I was Dan D Groove,' he said it quickly, wanting to get it over with.

Cath nearly spat out her wine. 'Oh my God.'

'R&B and hip-hop, that was my thing.'

'He still has the decks, out in the back of the storeroom,' added Andreas.

'That is so cool.' Adam was delighted with this revelation.

'It was *dope*,' said Andreas, making a peace V sign.

The things you learned, hey. These lads were such fun. Cath couldn't stop grinning at the thought of DJ Dan ... D Groove.

Having sat for a while, letting their dinner settle, with the camaraderie and chat still flowing, Cath headed out to the kitchen to make a pot of tea. It gave her space to think. It was lovely that the lunch had gone so well, but could she ever imagine sitting that comfortably with Will and Adam at the table? It seemed such a long way off. They had to get it right themselves, before including family in their romantic stakes.

'So, what's coming up next in the village for you folks, then?' Adam asked on her return.

'Well, we're organising a community Christmas dinner in the village hall here,' Dan started.

'Ah yes, Mum mentioned that last night.'

'Yep, bring the old place back to life, and give the elderly and anyone living alone locally a bit of a treat,' said Andreas. 'Your mother has been the driving force, actually.'

Adam looked to her proudly. 'Ah, that's the schoolteacher coming out. Always a key part of the school fete, weren't you,

Mum? Her organisational skills are tremendous. Kept me and Dad in check for years.' He gave a cheeky wink. 'And, I'll have you know, "Mrs Taylor" was a whizz on the coconut shy, too.'

'Oh, impressive. We'll have to watch our coconuts, then.' Dan laughed.

'Behave, you lot.' Cath couldn't help but smile.

'Oh, but we've had some news …' confessed Andreas.

'Yes, just as we came out, we heard from Nikki. It's on the WhatsApp supper club chat,' confirmed Dan.

'And?' She must have been busy cooking and missed the message. What exactly were they stalling on telling her?

'Do you want the good news, or the bad news?' Andreas pulled a concerned face.

'Bad first. Let's get it over with.' Oh no, was her community lunch about to fall at the first hurdle?

'Well, Kev's been to check out the electrics in the hall …' Dan started.

'And it's not good news,' Andreas continued.

'The ovens in the kitchen are both on the blink, and need new thermostats at the very least,' Dan followed.

'And though the panel heaters are working, he doesn't think the two alone will be enough to keep the big hall warm on a winter's day, either,' Andreas finished.

'So, there are some repairs to be done,' said Cath.

'Yeah, expensive repairs,' said Dan.

'And there's no guarantee the boiler will work properly,' added Andreas gloomily. 'We need a central heating engineer out to check that next.'

'Oh.' Cath felt like a balloon that had been popped. Was another of her dreams about to go by the wayside?

'Sounds like you've taken on quite a task, Mother.'

Cath nodded, absorbing the facts and her disappointment, whilst still desperately trying to formulate a plan.

She took a gulp of tea. Her thinking cap firmly on. 'Right,

well, we'll need to have a full list of costings,' said an undeterred Cath, ready to take the lead on this. 'I've already jotted down a few thoughts on the finances.' It had sent her head into a spin the other night, to be honest. 'So, I'll now get in touch with Nikki's Kev and find out the full estimate. And yes, the boiler will need checking and servicing as soon as, with the priority being to get ourselves a warm venue with a functioning kitchen. There's bound to be a few other practical repairs needed, too.

'And then we'll have cleaning costs – that's all in-house really with Nikki taking the lead on that – but we might need a few additional products, and any marketing costs, fliers and such like. The food will be a major expense, of course, and drinks on the day. Christmas decorations?' As she was speaking, she was adding to a list on her phone, and the weight in her mind.

'Wow, it's mounting up already,' observed Andreas.

'It *is* a bloody mountain,' Cath agreed. 'And hey, of course I don't mind chipping in, it's been my idea after all, but really this is too much for us to take on personally.' She paused, as they sat in a second of stunned silence taking in the reality of the large-scale event they'd committed to.

'Fundraising, that's what we need.' With that, Cath gave a rallying smile.

'See, I told you she was ace at organising,' Adam proudly told the lads. 'She'll have you lot sorted out in no time. You've absolutely got the best woman for the job, and she doesn't give up easily.'

'Well, that's good to hear,' said Dan. ''Cos neither do we. Not when it's for a bloody good cause. Look, if we can get our village hall back up and running, it's not just our Christmas event that'll benefit, it's the whole community. And think of all the other lovely things that might happen there in the future. Clubs, birthday parties, yoga, your Pilates. Once the building's fit for purpose again.'

'Absolutely,' agreed Andreas. 'We know it'll need a lot of

money, so let's start with some fundraising in the shop. A raffle to begin with. How about a luxury Christmas hamper with all the goods being donated by ourselves?' he offered generously. Shirley even gave a reaffirming yap from beside Andreas's feet.

'Ah, that'd be amazing.' Cath was touched by their kindness.

'What about if I do a charity run or something?' Adam was up for helping out, too. 'I was thinking of trying for a half-marathon. That'd be my incentive to crack on, do some training, and get it done. I could sign up for a JustGiving page for the Tilldale Hall. Mention the Christmas event. Maybe I could even run dressed as an elf or something.'

Cath beamed at that. 'That'd be brilliant, Adam.'

She felt her heart lift. It wasn't all down to her. These people she loved, and yes, she'd grown to love Andreas and Dan these past few months, were ready to put themselves out there, and do something to help. To help her and, more importantly, all those other people in their community.

The Sunday dinner had gone down well, which they followed with a slice of lemon drizzle cake and a cuppa. Glancing at her watch, from her prone sofa position, toasty warm with the log burner on and Shirley nestled beside her, Cath was surprised to see it was already past four p.m.

'Oh, I think it's time I cleared the plates.'

'We'll wash up, lovely. Just leave them stacked on the kitchen side,' offered Dan.

That was sweet of them. 'You sure?'

'Absolutely, you can make the most of your time left with Adam that way.'

'Fantastic.' Adam beamed. 'That gets me out of the drying up, too.'

Cath shook her head with a smile. Typical of her son to want to shirk the household chores. But yes, it'd be lovely to make the most of these last couple of hours with Adam around. All too soon, she'd be back on her own, after all.

Washing up done as promised and the kitchen left spotless for her – 'The least they could do after such a fabulous lunch and afternoon' – the lads and Shirley set off for home. A doggie bag for them all had been packed: with spare cake, some Yorkshire puddings for the lads – the best they'd ever had apparently! Well, she was a Yorkshire lass after all – and a juicy slice of pork with gravy for Shirley's supper.

Adam and Cath had a final hour of catching up before he needed to repack his bag and make the journey back down the road, to her old city, her old life. He had been chatting about his city days, about getting the bus that was always jam-packed and steamed up, to the bar where he worked near the Trinity Shopping Centre. She could picture the bustling grey-toned suburbs where he lived. It seemed a world away now, not a mere six months past. Saying goodbye to her son was never easy, but she didn't feel as heavy this time. It had been a wonderful weekend, and a lovely surprise. Her heart felt like it had been topped up. It was great to see and hear that Adam was on the up. She was so very thankful for that, and she had so much to keep her busy over the next few weeks.

Chapter 14

'Cath, can I call around?'

Her heart gave an involuntary lift. It was Will on the phone, that same evening.

'Ahm, like now?' This was unusual, especially after their cooling off.

'Yeah, if that's okay?'

It was almost seven o'clock, and Adam had set away in the car back down to Leeds an hour or so ago. That was timely, she mused. It was still a fragile path she and Will were on, after all. And by the tender sound of Will's voice perhaps a heart-to-heart was imminent.

'Of course. That'd be lovely.' Well, she hoped so. Unless this was another road to 'goodbye'. The thought of that made her feel bruised inside.

After ending the call, she kept herself busy, wiping over the kitchen surfaces which were already clean, and washing some mugs she and Adam had used. She felt jittery, uneasy. Finally, after what must only have been ten minutes, the doorbell rang.

She fluffed her hair with her hands and had just put on some lipstick. Perhaps she should have applied another coat of mascara, but it was too late for that now.

She gathered herself, taking a breath and raising a smile as she opened the door, with a 'Hi'.

'Hi.' His tone was gentle, cautious somehow. His smile warm, at least.

'Come on in. Tea, coffee? Something stronger?' Cath offered as she led the way to her kitchen.

'Ah, a coffee, I think. Thanks.'

'Everything okay?' she prompted, as she busied herself with mugs and the cafetiere.

'Yeah, fine.' There was an edge to his voice, however.

'Been a lovely day, again. Nice to see the sun.' She turned to pleasantries, taking the pressure off for a moment. He wasn't here just for the coffee; she was certain of that. 'Adam turned up out of the blue too, this weekend, which has been great.'

'Ah, great, how is he?'

'Good. He seems so much better, actually.'

'That's really good to hear.'

'Shall we take these through to the lounge? I've got the fire on.'

She and Adam had taken the bistro table back out to the kitchen. The spare chairs were out there now too, so her living room was back in order.

'Good idea.'

She felt like they were skirting around the real issue as to why he was here. It was unnerving. With the heat from the log burner feeling a little too warm, Cath tried to settle on the sofa but she felt antsy. Will was politely distanced in the armchair.

After a few sips of coffee, Will began, 'Cath, I'm so sorry I freaked out here the other night. I thought I was ready, to take that step further, you know ... but I guess I'm not.'

So, this was what was worrying him.

'Hey, there's no pressure. There's no rush.' She held his gaze, saw the pain in his eyes. 'You've done nothing wrong, Will. You've had – still got so much to deal with, you're bound to feel conflicted. It's only natural. We can take our time. We're in this together.' At least, she hoped they were.

'It's just, everything with Jane …' he continued, 'tackling the cancer, clinging on to hope at that point, trying to help her through it, care for her. Then the despair. I've seen some things in my time as a firefighter, but argh, seeing the pain she was in towards the end. It still haunts me.'

'Oh, Will.' She shifted to the end of the sofa to be nearer him, and reached out to lay a hand over his.

'I feel so bloody guilty, Cath. It's like she's lost everything. She's been robbed of our girls, their futures. And they miss her so goddam much.' He paused, staring into the flames for a few seconds. 'And fuck, I don't know where to go from here. I don't want to carry on hurting like this for always, but I think I just might. Cath, I don't want to bring you down with me. We should be happy, having fun, dating, going out and doing normal stuff, just getting on with it. But I don't know if I can do that yet. Or if I can be that person you need.' His dark-hazel eyes looked so troubled.

Was this Will giving her the chance to duck out? Or couldn't he cope with it? Did he not want a relationship at all? All of that hurt and the pain, so many jumbled up emotions, that he evidently couldn't tell which way was right anymore. She knew that feeling all too well. But grief, widowhood, that must be so much harder than coping with betrayal. At least she could be angry with Trev. Have someone to blame. The person who'd let her down and turned out to be different than she'd ever imagined.

She knew deep in her heart that this budding relationship with Will was precious to her, if still fragile. She wanted to help this gorgeous man through this grief. Not to forget Jane – of course he'd always love his wife; she understood that – just to learn to be kind to himself. To see that he deserved a life after his loss.

In truth, she wanted to be able to love him, openly, honestly. Was it too soon to tell him that? Was he still hurting too much to hear? Would it frighten him off?

'Will, I really do care for you.' She realised she had to choose her words carefully. 'And we don't have to make any promises that neither of us are sure, as yet, we'll be able to keep. We're just getting to know each other, after all. But please, let's not give up on us – not yet.' She gently rubbed his hand as it rested within hers. 'You're still grieving, and there's no right or wrong way to do that. There's no time limit. I learned that much when my parents passed – even though at their ages, it was less of a shock. But you've lost your life partner, and all too soon. You never expected any of this. We can slow things down if you need, of course we can. But if there's a way, can we try and face this next step together?' She smiled softly into his sad eyes, in a way that said *I'm there for you.*

But was this all still too soon for Will?

He gently nodded, taking in her words, but didn't respond, merely releasing a sigh that held a world of sorrow within it. Maybe, he didn't have the answer to reply with as yet. And maybe, she just had to accept that. She got up off the sofa, and went to him, reaching again to take his hand, to then give him a gentle hug, in a gesture of loving support.

He took a slow breath, registering that closeness.

She hoped she had managed to reach beneath his layers of grief, for a moment at least. And she knew instinctively that she couldn't rush this. He needed time to heal, to grieve of course, and he needed time to learn to love again.

Chapter 15

Cath pulled into the driveway of Kirkton's care home for the elderly.

Her hands involuntarily gripped tightly on the steering wheel. The last time she was here had been that fateful day where Maria had taken a turn for the worse and been driven away in an ambulance, along with a shocked Andreas. It was the last time Cath had seen her, was ever to see her.

But visiting Maria those few times had shown Cath just how interesting the elderly could be; with their stories, their sense of fun, their experience and advice. And she very much missed her parents, too. And that's exactly why she'd decided to contact the home and volunteer, to give a couple of hours of her time each week, and come and have a good old chat with the residents. With identity checks and documents now completed, she was ready for her first official visit and there was one person in particular she was very keen to meet.

Julie, the care home manager, greeted Cath warmly and gave her a quick tour. Leaving her in the day room with carer Linda who was on duty, along with several elderly residents sat in their high-backed chairs. A TV was on low, running the *Good Morning* show. Some of the guests were already taking a nap, and Cath was introduced to Betty, who had the most lovely thick, wavy white hair and smiling blue eyes. She was apparently hard of hearing to her left side, so Linda sat Cath on the green fake-leather armchair to her right.

'Good morning, Betty. I'm Cath. I'm here to have a bit of a chat, if you'd like that?'

'Oh, that'd be lovely, my dear.'

Linda had obviously set her up with a 'soft' target resident to start. Betty was easy to talk with, and the pair of them spent a happy half hour reminiscing about Betty's family, including six grandchildren and four great-grandchildren.

Some residents, as Cath was soon to find out, could be rather trickier, a lady called Joyce was getting crotchety and shouting at the television. Linda went over to calm her. Cath thought she ought to share her time, and moved to sit with a woman who introduced herself as Vera, who after a quick giggle about the animal antics on the telly – the presenters were struggling with a lively puppy in the studio – then proceeded to tell Cath about losing several precious items of jewellery (which Cath was soon to learn she'd never owned, or perhaps not for many years). Cath had felt quite embarrassed when the old lady's tone changed, and her finger was pointed firmly in Cath's direction. But after briefly mentioning the issue with Linda, Cath was reassured that these accusations of a jewellery heist were a regular complaint of Vera's, with a new culprit blamed each time. All a matter of the inevitable ageing of the mind, and frustrations of the ailing body, Linda had explained kindly. The carer was soon able to settle Vera and her anxieties; no doubt having done it many times before.

Time stole so many things, and getting old – if you were one of the lucky ones to reach those grand ages – seemed sadly to take away so much. But many seemed happy here in the home too, Cath conceded. They were well cared for, had plenty of activities should they want, and had company. There must always be someone around to have a chat with or share the crossword clues, after all. Remembering Maria, and her own parents, Cath wanted to bring a little extra joy to these people who were nearing the end of their days.

With only twenty minutes left of her initial two-hour session, and her latest conversational recruit now ready for a doze, she caught up with Linda again, asking if Reggie from Tilldale village might be here in the day room?

Linda pointed over to the corner where a sprightly looking chap, with a sharp short-back-and-sides haircut of light grey, was reading a newspaper. Cath explained to Linda where she now lived, checking whether she thought Reggie would mind hearing that she was there in his house, not wanting to upset him in any way. Linda thought he'd be more than happy to chat, and led her over.

'Reggie, this is Cath, kindly come to visit us. Guess where she's living now?'

'Morning, Cath. Nice to meet you.' He looked at her with twinkly grey-blue eyes, and reached out a wrinkled, age-spotted hand. He had a firm, warm handshake. Cath took to him straight away. Taking in his tidy appearance, the friendly smile, she decided he kind of 'fitted' her house and garden, and the potting shed. She wondered what he might make of its supper club makeover.

'So, Reggie, Cath is the lady who's moved into your cottage in Tilldale,' Linda explained.

Cath sat down next to the gentleman, leaning in a little to be able to chat.

'Ah, so how's the old girl doing now?' Reggie asked with fondness.

Cath furrowed her brow, trying to understand. Was he talking about his late wife? Was he confused?

'The cottage, my little Cheviot. She always felt like a "she" to us,' he explained. 'Looked after us, so she did.'

'Ah, well, she's doing absolutely fine. I'm living there on my own, and she's made me feel very welcome.' Cath took up the 'she' word, liking how it sounded so personal. She'd never before imagined a house as a he or she, but hey, ships were always a she, so why not?

'Well, tell me all about how you're getting on? When did you move in? How's the garden? Are those apples ready on the tree, yet? You can eat them straight off the branch, you know. Lovely and juicy.'

'Oh, yes, they are. They make a lovely crumble too.'

'That's grand. My Elsie used to make a wonderful apple pie with them, with a sugary-crisp shortcrust. Marvellous with her homemade custard.'

Now there was an idea.

The pair of them chatted animatedly. Reggie seeming to love hearing all about their old cottage, and a few 'select' details from Cath about her moving up and in there, with any tales of Trevor and that torment being brushed lightly over.

It was evidently getting near to the residents' teatime with the dining room being set up through a set of glass double doors, and Cath would soon be making a move to leave.

It was then that Reggie touched Cath's arm gently. 'There is something you might be able to help me with, lass.'

She wondered what he might be about to ask.

'Well, there were some letters. I've misplaced them somehow. I thought I had them here with me at the home. You see, my daughter, Sarah, helped me pack up the cottage, bringing what I needed across here. But there was one thing we never found after the move. I have to say it broke my heart a bit …'

'Oh?' Cath felt for him.

The twinkle in his eyes had dulled. 'There was a bundle of letters – some mine, some Elsie's – all kept together from my National Service days. They're pretty tattered by now, as you'd imagine. They were the ones I'd written when I was doing my service with the RAF.' He sounded very proud. 'Started my basic training in Watchet, Somerset, when I was eighteen, and then I got moved out to Egypt – 1955 that was. Bloomin' hot out there.'

'Oh, I bet. And you wrote to Elsie all the while?'

'Of course I did. We'd not long started courting when I had to leave Northumberland, but I knew she was the girl for me, right from the start. I wrote to my Elsie every couple of days.'

'That's so lovely.'

Reggie was on a roll about his service life, and Cath was enjoying listening. 'Next, was my Cyprus posting. I was batman to the Air Officer Commander in the Middle East Forces.'

'Oh, sounds very impressive.'

'Well.' He touched the side of his nose, as if in confidence. 'It had a posh title but basically, it was a bit like being his personal servant. I organised his kit, polished his shoes and set out his clothes, in the main. All good experience, mind.'

'Sounds like it. And getting to see some of the world, too.'

'Yes, it was a great experience, and I made some good mates, especially in Egypt. But it was hard for me and Elsie – and all those other couples. We didn't see each other for two and a half years, but I kept writing a few times a week, and Elsie always wrote back. I used to love seeing those blue airmail envelopes come for me. They kept us going those letters, so they did. Our link.' He gave a happy-sad sigh, which seemed to hold so many memories.

Cath felt a tug inside at his words, and at their devotion, the story also pulling her back to those gorgeous letters from a seventeen-year-old Will, her sweetheart 'Matty'.

Those letters had evidently been a lifeline for Reggie and his Elsie. It sounded so very romantic to Cath, happening at such a hard time for them and for the world.

'Anyway, we kept those letters all these years, bundled up in a navy velvet ribbon, one that Elsie used to wear in her long brown hair back in the day. I can picture her wearing it now. She had such lovely hair. My girl. My Elsie.' His smile was filled with nostalgia and love.

'They were separate at first, those letters, and then once I'd got back to her with my forces training over, we and the letters could be together again. I proposed. And we never spent a day apart until she died.'

Cath felt a tear mist her eye.

'They must be at the cottage somewhere. But I can't for the life of me think where. Me and Sarah had it all packed away, every box, every drawer. Oh dear, unless they got scooped up by accident in the rubbish. But if you could check for me … You haven't seen anything like that, have you?'

'No, I'm sorry, Reggie. The only thing I've found was an old mixing bowl in the kitchen. And I hope you don't mind, but I've used it to make a cake or two.'

'That sounds the best thing for it.' He smiled. 'Elsie would love that.'

'That's good.' Cath was happy to think she'd done the right thing.

'Now, where would Elsie have put those letters?' he mused. 'Hmm, there'll only be a few old Christmas decorations left in the loft, as far as I know. Me and Sarah left them up there. No use for them here. You might want to get rid of them. But maybe if you could double-check? If you didn't mind, that is? Don't know why those letters would be up there, though. Maybe when Elsie was tidying up or something? Neither of us had been able to use the loft for years. Couldn't get up the ladder anymore.' He scrunched his face, whilst thinking. 'Anyhow, you're welcome to have those decorations. Might be a bit old-fashioned, I suppose. No need of them here. Last Christmas when I first moved in, this place was teeming with tinsel and baubles. They had a big tree all decorated for us and everything.'

'That sounds lovely and festive. Thank you about the decorations. And yes, of course I'll check on those letters for you, Reggie.'

'Might be a long shot.' Reggie shrugged, but there was a fresh glimmer of hope in his eyes.

'It's no problem. I'm more than happy to look,' reassured Cath. It sounded really important to him, and it was the least she could do as the new custodian of Cheviot Cottage.

Just as Cath was pondering if she should risk going up the set of tall stepladders, having positioned them below the loft hatch on the upstairs landing, the doorbell went.

She'd been back from the care home for half an hour, and felt driven to find out if the letters were up there. Poor old Reggie had seemed so upset to have lost them. She was curious about them too, not that she intended on reading them, of course; they were private. But just to discover if they were in fact there, and if so, then to have the satisfaction of delivering them back 'home' to their rightful owner.

Down the stairs she trotted, wondering if it might be some sales call that had interrupted her. The latest seemed to be rugs, just passing, with a heap-load of rugs in the van, spare stock. *Really?* Out here in Tilldale in the middle of nowhere?

She opened the door. No salesman there, but one very attractive man: Will. Now that was unexpected. Her heart skipped a beat, firstly with longing and then another missed beat of fear … might he be here to really call things off this time?

'Hi.' Pushing her concerns aside, she realised this was in fact timely. Help with the ladders, and from the man … well boy, who'd sent her several love letters himself, back in the day.

'Hi, you okay?' Will gave her a warm smile, which after their last discussion was reassuring at least.

'Hey, yeah, good to see you. Coming in?' She wondered what might be behind it. Was he missing her company since they'd spoken so openly the other night? In need of some friendly advice, someone to offload to after a busy day at work?

'Yep, if that's all right. I was just at a loose end and thought I'd call by.' He sounded casual, but it seemed like he'd been thinking of her.

'Of course. Yeah, this is a nice surprise.' She found herself wanting to hug him, but held back. Had Reggie and Elsie's story stirred the old memories of hers and Will's young romance, too?

'Sorry, are you busy?' he asked.

'Well, I was actually just about to venture up into the loft for the first time.'

'Okay. So, what's up there, then?'

'That's what I'm hoping to find out.'

'It might just be cobwebs, and a resident mouse or two,' he teased.

'Hah, don't. I'll never get through the hatch if I think like that.'

'So why now? What's made you so curious?'

'I had my first visit at the care home today, and I met Reggie in person finally.'

'Ah, yes, I remember him, nice old chap.'

'Yeah, he was really lovely. He mentioned some lost letters, as well as some old Christmas decorations. And well, the letters sounded very special to him. They seemed to have been lost in the move to the home, so I promised I'd check the loft space, just in case.'

'Right, well, that sounds like a mission. No time like the present. If you're going to be up scaling heights, then I'd better stay around to secure the ladder.'

'Ah, thanks, that does make me feel a bit better. I was wary of getting stuck up there on my own.' Living a solo life wasn't at all easy, at times.

'Anything there?' Will's voice echoed from the landing a few minutes later.

'Not sure yet.'

There was no light connection up in the loft, so she switched on the torch of her phone. Eek, there were indeed masses of dusty cobwebs. Looking beneath her, she found she was stood on a boarded-out floor area of around four metres squared. The rest of the loft space then reverted to wooden beams, filled in between with rolled-out creamy-yellow lagging. A pitched roof, up above, revealed trusses of wood and the insides of the black roof felt that lay beneath the slate tiles.

She scanned the boarded area and was pleased to find some boxes. A stack, in fact, of sealed cardboard boxes. She'd been savvy, and had Will at the ready to pass her up a pair of kitchen scissors. Top box first. Someone had neatly written 'Christmas' on it in felt-tip pen. No prizes for guessing what might be in that one, then. She'd open that shortly, but moved on to the three other stacked boxes. Whoever had stored them, Reggie most likely when he was still in his prime, was evidently organised, as she then found 'Baubles/Tinsel' followed by 'Tree Lights' and 'Strands'.

Opening 'Strands' first, which seemed the more mysterious of the selection, she discovered reams and reams of old-fashioned festive paper chains, far too many for a single household. And then many flattened colourful tissue-paper and foil streamers. Hmm, perhaps enough to decorate a village hall …

She carefully sifted through them. But with no sign of any letters.

'Any luck?' a voice drifted up.

She'd momentarily forgotten Will was still stood at the base of the ladder.

'No, not yet. Bear with me. There are a few boxes here, all seemingly Christmas stuff, but I'd better open them up and check.'

'Okay. I'll wait here.'

'Yes please, I shouldn't be long. Actually, I could pass a couple of the boxes down, and you can look there, whilst I'll do the others?'

'May as well. It'll be quicker that way.'

With the stirring of decades of dust making her throat tight, she gave a cough as she shifted 'Tree Lights' down to him. As she carefully passed the taped box through the loft hatch gap, Will part-mounted the stepladder to receive it.

Cath removed some more of the contents of 'Strands', to make a further check. It'd be easy to miss something in there. It felt like she was taking part in a festive lucky dip. But it was soon apparent there was nothing but paper streamers, not the kind of paperwork they were looking for at all. Those decorations would be rather handy for dressing the village hall, however, so she gave Will a further shout, and got him to take this box down to the landing, too.

'Baubles/Tinsel' contained exactly what it said on the box. Cath worked delicately through those, spotting a large rectangular old-fashioned biscuit tin (which she'd hoped might hold the letters at last!). She opened it to find the most gorgeous Victorian-style baubles all wrapped individually in tissue. They were hand-painted with scenes of little girls dressed in dark-red cloaks with holly to hand, and featuring fir trees and robins. The baubles were beautiful with white lace tops hung on a red ribbon. Oh, if Reggie was still happy to pass his decorations on, then she was most certainly hanging these beauties on her tree. Along with Andreas's silvery glass globes, they'd look stunning.

She carefully wrapped them back up, returning them to their tin box, before checking the rest of the cardboard container. No letters, but lots of pretty tree decorations, which she'd look through when she got chance another day. One did catch her attention, however, a hanging Christmas tree with gaudy green paint that was plastered in glitter and stick-on jewels. It looked to be handmade by a child, and as she turned it over, the name S-A-R-A-H was written on the back in childish script. Ah, that was Reggie's daughter's name, she remembered. She kept that out, to go with her to the home next visit, thinking he might like to keep it.

'All okay up there?' Will was checking in again.

'Yep, just one box to go. I'll stay a while longer to look through it. Do you fancy popping the kettle on while I finish here? I'm parched.' The air was dry and dusty in the loft.

'Yeah, of course, but don't use the ladder 'til I'm back up,' he added cautiously.

His warning made her see that he did really care, aw. Sometimes it was the simplest of things that gave your true emotions away.

'Okay. Promise.'

She rescanned the rest of the loft area but the festive-labelled boxes were all that had been there. Sarah must have checked up here at some point, or perhaps even Reggie back in the day, leaving it orderly. The 'Christmas' box was the last to be opened and their final hope. Cath slid her scissors along the tape.

First out were some children's paintings from primary school age, perhaps. Thick splodgy paints, on curling-up paper, mostly in bold greens and reds. One picture was a big circle of red with another smaller circle of pink above it, with lots of white swirls roughly positioned as hair and a beard perhaps. Two black spots for eyes, a red hat with yes, a white blob at the end. Father Christmas. Cath gave a smile. That one was going to the care home, too.

There was a gorgeous small wooden nativity set, all hand-carved, with animals and a crib, a Mary and Joseph. And a rather shabby, well-used and loved angel that looked like a child's doll with white-lace wings. Cath realised poignantly that she was looking at their family history, and a host of past magical moments.

And then she dug down and saw a red-and-green-striped hat box. Feeling a glimmer of excitement, she unravelled the white bow that fastened it, and there was a bundle of letters. Just as Reggie had described, tied with the navy ribbon. Cath pulled them out carefully, filled with awe and anticipation. The first in her hands, a faded blue airmail envelope in the same neat writing as on the Christmas boxes, addressed to a Miss Elsie Davis. This was it, surely! She wouldn't read the letters – they were far too personal – but she flapped the delicate thin paper open just to check the start and the sign-off, to see if it was from dear Reggie.

She didn't want to give him that rainbow of hope to then discover they were some other letters. Though that was unlikely given his description. And there it was, starting with 'My Dearest Elsie', and she swiftly scanned to the bottom, ending with, 'Fondest love, Reginald. x'

A tear misted her eye, as a lump tightened in her throat. It felt like she had their love story, their youthful lives in her hands. Oh, Reggie.

'You okay up there?' She was still holding the letter, and Will's voice stirred up a whole heap of emotions for Cath. She remembered their holiday romance, the letters he'd sent her, including the one she had kept for over forty years. How life had moved on in separate ways for them both. And then, meeting again six months ago. How very strange that was, or perhaps it was fate. There was more to their story yet; she was sure of it. But for Reggie and Elsie their story had been told, had played out its precious course. And Cath couldn't wait to reunite the cherished letters with their rightful owner.

Her voice was croaky with emotion as she called down, 'I-I've found them.'

'Ah, that's brilliant. Come on then, I'll help you down.'

And his hand was there to guide her, as she made her way back to him.

Chapter 16

'In the Greek Midwinter'
You are cordially invited to a Greek-Cypriot-Themed
Festive Celebration
On Friday, 22nd November, 7 p.m.
at
Andreas and Dan's
RSVP
xXx

Cath picked up the card that had been popped through the cottage's letterbox. How wonderful, the lads had even designed a proper invitation. There were holly leaves, a Christmas tree, a glass of wine and what looked to be a plate of cookies drawn, one in each corner. And yes, of course, that Friday night she was free.

She was delighted that their supper club seemed to be going from strength to strength, and with the formal invite and theming, Cath wondered if there was perhaps an element of fun competition going on behind the scenes. She might have to up her own game next time. Oh, it might end up turning into a bit of a *Come Dine with Me* experience.

She messaged the lads straight away:

Thank you so much. I'd love to come along to your Greek-Cypriot evening. Let me know if there's anything I can bring to help out. x

It was just over a week away, so not long to wait at all. Before the fun to come of the Greek Midwinter evening, however, Team Supper Club had some work to do.

The Christmas hall preparations were about to go large. Cath had a central-heating engineer booked at ten a.m. tomorrow to check and service the old oil-fired radiator system. This was a big deal, they all knew, as no heating meant no event, simple as that. Cath had her fingers very firmly crossed for a good, and hopefully not too expensive, result.

And then tomorrow afternoon, with the lads busy working in the shop, she, Lily, Nikki and Will had agreed to arm themselves with mops, brushes, hoovers, soapy water, disinfectant spray and rubber gloves, ready to go and scrub up that community space.

Cath was also desperate to return those letters to their rightful owner, and hopefully to make Reggie's day. She had the morning free now, so gave the care home a quick call to check if it was all right to pop in and see Reggie at around ten-thirty.

Cath couldn't wait to get into her car and get over to Kirkton, knowing her personal delivery was a poignant one. She even had a fluttering stomach as she turned in to the care home's driveway and parked. She could only imagine how important this was to him. The hat box of letters was held tightly in her grip as she mounted the steps, and rang the reception buzzer.

'It's Cath here to see Reggie.'

'Oh yes, come on in.'

Linda was stood at the reception desk, giving a friendly smile. 'He's in the day room. Go on in.'

And there he was in the same seat in the corner, with what looked to be a jigsaw piece in his hand. As she approached, she

143

could see the table set before him had a two-thirds-completed jigsaw, the scene being of the Tyne Bridge with a cityscape. It looked to be a complicated one.

'Hi, Reggie.'

'Oh hello. Yes, Cath, isn't it? Hello.'

'It is indeed.' She gave a broad smile. 'And I've got some good news.' She lifted up the hat box.

'I think I may have seen that somewhere before?'

'It was in your loft, Reggie, along with your Christmas decorations. Here, take a look inside.' She placed the box gently on his knees. She couldn't wait to see his face when he opened it.

'Oh … oh my …' He pulled out the large bundle of letters, and clutched them to his chest, his hands trembling. Then, he untied the navy ribbon, opened one out and began to read. Looking up shortly afterwards with the sparkle of tears in his eyes, he said, 'I-I can't believe it. You found them.'

Cath grinned, delighted to have reunited him with these love letters.

'Thank you. Thank you so much.'

'What's all this then, Reggie?' Linda came over to join them. 'Mementos from your misspent youth?'

'Something like that, though I think it was very well spent, actually. Me and Elsie had over sixty wonderful years together after these letters. They were probably what kept us going, waiting for each other.'

A lifeline of love across land and seas, even the desert, Cath mused, and now, even in death.

Seeing Reggie filled with delight at the return of his letters made it seem all the more important to invite those who were able to come along from the home and join in with the Christmas lunch event. To brighten a few more lives. The village community wasn't that big, after all, so numbers would likely be light. She reckoned, the more elderly regulars she'd seen coming into the shop probably numbered no more than fifteen or so, and it was hardly likely that every one of them could make it. The home had twenty-two residents when full; she'd already checked. And after chatting with Julie last time, when she'd first mooted a Christmas event in principle, she'd been told perhaps only half of those would be able enough to make an outing. So, that made no more than twenty-five in total. It was a large group admittedly, but she'd not batted an eyelid on cooking single-handedly for twelve for dinner parties in the past, and this time she'd have her supper club team to hand, so it was not out of the question. As soon as they had the all-clear on the heating in the hall, and got the kitchen equipment up and running again – with Kev already on the case and sourcing parts for the ovens – she could then confirm the date with the home manager. Plans were in place.

Rubber gloves at the ready. And they were off!

Nikki had given Lily, Cath and Will one of her The Canny Cleaning Company sweatshirts to wear, figuring it might be good publicity for her business if they got a few mug shots of them in action to send to the local press, whilst also raising awareness. In addition, they were hoping to plug the new donation site thanks to Adam's half marathon Just Giving page and the shop's Fabulous Festive Raffle, all to help the cause for the hall's renovations and this amazing Christmas community event.

The hot water system hadn't as yet been fixed – that was one of the engineer's jobs – and he was *still* working away in the boiler room. It was proving to be a difficult task, with many trips in and out to his van for parts. As an ex-pupil of the school and a local himself, he was determined to get to the bottom of the ancient system's unique ways. The trusty kettle and old-fashioned urn were on and bubbling to a boil. A cup of coffee and some chocolate digestives were wending their way to Central Heating Colin, but for the rest of them, buckets were about to be filled.

Will had already swept the floor of the main hall in readiness, and was now hoovering the heavy-duty carpets of the corridor and reception office. Dan and Andreas were currently busy in the shop, but had promised to call over as soon as they finished should the cleaning work still be going on, which was more than likely.

Cloths and disinfectant to hand, plus mops and buckets at the ready, the four of them set to it, after taking a group selfie inside the hall. The 'Super Supper Club' team were in action. No shirkers here. It was going to be hard work, but so worthwhile. Will had brought a mini-speaker to play some music through, and the foursome were currently mopping to the beat of 'My Girl' by The Temptations. Lily had initially slipped in her own AirPods saying she'd prefer her own Charli XCX tracks, but was now tellingly swaying along with the rest of them to the exact same beat. Cath was humming and Nikki singing along as they reached the chorus. They were hoping to bring some sunshine to their community for sure.

The song also made Cath think of Elsie, Reggie's girl. And, of course, Will – there working away with them in the hall. Had he once thought of her, Cathy, as 'my girl'? Memories were rolling in. Holding hands in the dunes, a holiday romance. They must have been tucked away in a corner of her mind. She glanced over to look at him, hoping so much that he wouldn't withdraw from her once more. When he'd shut her out emotionally, it had weighed so heavily on her fragile heart. But they were moving forward with slow steps. Finding the letters weaving not only Reggie and Elsie together, but perhaps them too.

A little while later, the water in the bucket she was using began to look murky. Time to swill it out and start afresh. Back to the kitchen Cath went. In there she bumped into Will, managing to look gorgeous even with a Henry hoover to hand.

'How's it going, Mrs Mop?' He smiled at her, which was lovely.

'Good. We're cracking on, aren't we? The parquet flooring is cleaning up well. And what about you, Herr Hoover?' she quipped back.

'Marvellous, I'm emptying my second cylinder of dust and dirt.'

'Exciting times,' she said with a mocking tone, but actually it did kind of feel they were exciting times, for the hall … and hopefully for the two of them. It did indeed feel good to be cleaning this place up. Giving it, and fingers crossed them, a new lease of life.

They'd scaled the heights with dusters on extendable sticks, and brushed off windowsills, with Will following them about with the hoover hose, like a fly-sucking version of *Ghostbusters*. With all surfaces in the hall now wiped, mopped or disinfected, it was time for the loos to be cleaned and bleached.

She discovered some of the toilets were still the tiny ones for the schoolchildren. That'd be interesting when the oldies sat down; they might never get up again. Actually, with her own post-gardening/cleaning creaky knees, she might not either. She wasn't yet sure if the Pilates was helping. Everything seemed to ache for days afterwards, but hey, perhaps she just needed to give it time. Here in the hall, if it all went off as planned, some notices on the doors might be helpful with 'Child' and 'Adult' loos clearly marked.

'Hell-loo!' As she had her head down a pan, squirting toilet cleaner around the rim, in came Andreas. 'Did you like that? Hell-loo.' He re-emphasised the 'loo', and she had to grin.

'*Now* you decide to turn up, when all the work is nigh on done.' Cath straightened up, somewhat stiffly, and gave her neck and back a jiggle.

'We've been working hard at the shop; we'll have you know. And, I've had to deal with Veronica Manners, quizzing us about our project. But the good news is, I've twisted her arm, and we've got a chunk of money coming our way from the village hall funds, to help cover the boiler and heating repair costs. A jazzy three hundred pounds, no less.' He seemed very pleased with himself.

'Ah, well, thank you – that's great news. The engineer's not finished as yet, though. Been away on another job he had booked in, and is now back with extra parts, so I hope that donation doesn't prove to be a drop in the ocean.'

'Oh, I see.' His shoulders sagged.

'But that is brilliant. It'll make a big difference to the budget and everything helps. And hey, we've got lots of time to get going with the fundraising.' Whilst being realistic, and knowing just how much those big school-sized boiler repairs might cost, she didn't want to dampen everyone's spirits.

'Well then, we are here, present and correct. What's left to do?' Andreas perked up.

Will came out of the gents' toilets at that point, rubber-gloved and looking relieved to have finished that particular cleaning task. They met, along with Dan, in the corridor. 'Blimey, the things we get roped in to,' Will said. 'I don't remember signing up for that job. Hi, guys.'

'Hi, Will. Oh, Lycra, now rubber … heavens above.' Andreas chuckled.

Cath shook her head. 'Right, well the girls are wiping down the plastic chairs in the hall.' Cath called them to action. They'd shifted the lot down from the stage in order to give it a good sweep. 'And there's rather a lot of them, so that seems a good place to start.'

'Disinfectant spray at the ready, Daniel,' said Andreas, fishing a spray bottle out of his hessian shopper.

'Seems you've got off lightly,' commented Will wryly, whilst doing jazz hands with the rubber gloves.

'That's it. I'm jiggered. We can leave the kitchen for another day,' announced Nikki.

'Agreed. That was a busy afternoon, but we achieved so much! Thanks, all,' said Cath as she squeezed out her mop for the last time today.

They'd regrouped back in the hall, where the parquet flooring and stage area were now thoroughly cleaned, with every chair having been wiped down. Nikki had mentioned giving the wooden floor a polish to bring up the shine, but again that could wait. Cath was about to check off her event to-do list, and then of course add some more.

'I'm dead,' added Lily dramatically, giving a yawn and a stretch. 'How do you do this all week, Auntie Niks?'

'Well, I'm not just mopping and scrubbing. Ahm, well, that *is* a lot of what I do, actually.' She managed to smile.

'Anyone fancy a coffee before we go?' offered Cath, thinking it'd be a nice way to wrap up the day's work.

'Absolutely.'

'Sounds great.'

'Oh, and I have shortbread from the shop,' said Andreas. His holdall was seemingly a Pandora's box.

'Delish, yes please.' Cath'd worked off more than enough calories this afternoon. 'Well, if you wouldn't mind restacking the chairs in here,' she added, 'I'll go pop the kettle on, and then see how Colin's getting on in the boiler room.' Fingers crossed he'd had a breakthrough. She had, in fact, heard all sorts of promising creaks and groans emitting from the hall's pipework a short while before. And was that a hot flush coming on, or was there indeed some warmth coming from the radiators? Hope springs eternal ...

A few minutes later, and Cath was spooning instant coffee into decades-old WI mugs. 'Hellooo!' She heard a booming voice calling out from the corridor.

A head of stylishly cropped grey hair popped around the kitchen door. 'Afternoon. How are we doing?' The woman's tone was confident if slightly abrasive. 'Veronica Manners, Chair of the Village Hall Committee,' she introduced herself.

'Hello, I'm Cath. Lovely to meet you.' Cath held out a hand ready to shake, somewhat formally.

'Saw the door was open so I thought I'd pop in. Well, we're delighted you're taking such an interest in the old place.'

'Well, if we can get it up and running in time, it'll make a lovely local venue for the festive lunch we're planning.' Cath gave a hopeful smile, adding, 'We're just making coffee. Would you like one?'

'No thanks. But I'll help take them through. I'm guessing the others are in the hall?'

'They are indeed.'

The pair made their way through with the tray of coffee and biscuits.

'Now I'm here, is there anything I can do to help?' Veronica addressed the group. 'Practically today, or in any other way?'

'Well, that's great, but we're ready to finish up for the day now.' It was already past six p.m., and had been dark outside for over an hour already.

Nikki piped up, 'Ooh, I tell you what, you don't happen to have access to one of those old-style floor buffer machines, do you? Like the caretakers used to use back in the day at school? That'd really help bring the parquet flooring back to life.'

'Well then, I may have one or two contacts. Leave it with me,' said Veronica in an efficient tone.

'That'd be brilliant,' said Nikki.

'And,' added Dan. 'Thanks so much for that generous donation from the hall funds. I've also started looking into some rural grants that are available. There might be a way we can get some extra cash. The costs are adding up, especially for the hall repairs, and whilst we're fundraising and happy to chip in ourselves initially, well, we have to be realistic; we're not made of money. We'd need to go through the proper channels, of course. So, it's likely the hall committee would need to sign off any relevant paperwork. But it's exactly what these grants are here for, to help support local communities and causes.'

'Sounds a great idea, Dan,' agreed Cath, knowing full well the costs were mounting.

'Certainly,' was Veronica's response. 'If I can do anything to help get the hall back to its former glory, I'm all for it. I have to confess it's been a worry these past few years. But myself and the committee just don't have the energy, or time, to put into it like we used to. And well, to be honest, no one seemed particularly interested in using it either, so it felt a little like a lost cause.'

And with that Colin came in, his mug raised in a 'cheers' gesture. 'We're back in business, folks. The heating and hot water are fixed.'

The small group cheered, clapping their hands.

What great news. There was still a heck of a lot to do, of course, and November was disappearing fast. They had to get things moving if they wanted to send out invites in time.

But with that warming development, Cath's hopes of turning this lost cause into a great cause were at last looking up!

Chapter 17

Talking of invites …

The air was chill, the night air dark and frosty, making the tarmac pavement she walked on glint with starry ice crystals. It was indeed a perfect midwinter evening: A Greek Midwinter Evening. Cath was wrapped snugly in her thick woollen winter coat, over a sage-green woollen dress, which she'd teamed with thick tights and her brown knee-length leather boots. She pulled down her pine-green bobble hat, which she wore with a stripy green-and-cream knit scarf.

Thinking about it, she may in fact look rather like a Christmas tree. Had she unintentionally themed herself? Thank heavens, she hadn't worn any large bauble-like earrings. Or perhaps, she ought to go back and do *exactly* that; the lads would absolutely love it. She did in fact have some bauble earrings that she used to wear for the Christmas jumper day at the school where she taught, yes, with a tinsel wrap for a scarf. She still had a few minutes in hand, so why not? Life was too short not to grab some fun where you could. So back she trotted, found the box of Reggie's tinsel, helping herself to a silver strand, and found the earrings from her jewellery box. Seeing herself in the dressing table mirror she gave a silly smile. Perfectly festive. And off she trotted once more.

The side door that led to the flat above the village stores was adorned with a beautiful wreath of fir, pine cones, eucalyptus and pretty white wooden stars. She rapped out a cheery knock and rang the bell. As she waited, she heard footsteps tapping up behind her and turned to see Nikki, who was also wrapped warmly in a dusky-pink woolly hat, gloves, pink scarf and a long, padded black winter coat.

'Brrr, it's bloody freezing out tonight.'

Winter was here, in its full frosty glory.

'Ooh, I quite like it,' replied Cath. 'Time for cosy fires and candlelight, and snug winter coats.'

'Oh, get you, all poetic! How are you, hon?'

'I'm good, thanks. And I'm so looking forward to tonight. Sounds like Andreas is going all out. Such fancy invites!'

'I know, he loves a theme.'

And with that, the door opened to reveal the man himself. In chunky jumper, jeans and with his Naked Greek Statue apron. 'Good evening and welcome.'

The girls' grins were wide; he was such a bloody character.

'Or should I say *kopiaste!* in Greek. Come on up, ladies.'

'Thanks, and oh, Lily's running a few minutes late,' explained Nikki. 'Says sorry, she's just back from a busy day helping at the restaurant.'

'That's no problem at all. Sounds exciting for her, and she must have got the job then. Can't wait to hear all about it.'

They followed Andreas up the stairs, as he added, 'Will is already here.'

Cath felt a lift at the prospect of seeing him tonight, but also wondered how it might pan out for the two of them. She hoped Will would be more relaxed with her than of late. It was proving to be a slow, well more of a stop-start, process relationship-wise. Will definitely had the brakes on, as though he was afraid to let himself feel or reveal too much of himself. He was still very much in the grip of grief. She knew that, but she wanted so much more. She had to let him lead this, however, or she was afraid she might push him away altogether.

With coats now off, Cath's earring baubles and tinsel adornments were spotted. 'Look at you, all festive and fabulous!' Andreas exclaimed.

'Thought I looked a bit like a tree in this green dress, so went all out with the Christmas tree trimmings.' She gave a grin.

'Hah, I love it.' Dan appeared from the kitchen, smart in a dark stripy shirt and indigo jeans, ready to give the girls a warm hug.

'Mulled wine, anyone?' Andreas asked.

'Oh, yes, please.'

'It'd be rude not to,' said Nikki. 'I'll come and give you a hand.'

'Hi, Will.' Cath wandered over to where he was standing at the open door of the living room. She still didn't know quite how to greet him, plumping for a kiss on the cheek. His aftershave smelt gorgeous, all spiced wood.

'Hey, how are you?' His smile was warm and affectionate.

'Good, thanks. You?' She felt a fuzzy buzz inside.

'Yeah, fine.'

And she couldn't help herself. Fed up with holding back, she moved in to give him a hug. The others were still in the kitchen, after all. And, nestled there momentarily against his firm chest, feeling the warmth of his embrace, his arms briefly but tenderly around her, felt so damned good.

They pulled away, just in time, with terrier Shirley soon arriving at their heels, and Andreas coming through with two glasses fragrant with the cinnamon-orange spiced mulled wine.

The log burner was on in the stone hearth of the sitting room, and candles glowed from glass votives on the coffee table. And there, to one corner, wow, *how* had she not noticed yet – Will must have had her full attention for a few seconds there – a huge Christmas tree fully decorated; with silver tinsel, baubles in red and silver, red velvet bows, and gently twinkling lights.

'Well, I see Christmas has arrived early here,' Cath commented. 'Your tree looks stunning.'

'Thought we may as well get it up early, with you all coming around. It's not a real one, so we won't be bothered by any needles dropping. So, hey, why not? Christmas comes and goes all too soon as it is, so why not make the most if it.'

'True, and it does look gorgeous.'

'As do you.' Andreas smiled, as he handed Cath a glass of mulled wine.

She took a warming scented sip. 'Oh, that's delicious. Thank you.'

They'd certainly set the scene.

'So, traditionally we'd have some cookies to go along with your welcome wine, so here we have either *kourabiedes* or *melomakarona.*'

Dan had followed his partner in with a platter of cookies, one side was icing-sugar-dusted and looked like mini snowballs, the others were golden and crunchy-looking with a nut-honey drizzle.

'Oh, how wonderful.'

'Both are delicious,' Nikki announced as she came through. 'I've just tested them in the kitchen. You'll have to have one of each.'

'Oh, Lily will love these,' Cath said as she bit into a crunchy honey one. 'We'll have to save her some.'

'So, back in the village near Paphos,' Andreas elaborated, 'Mama Maria would have had plenty of these cookies made ready for any guests in the run-up to Christmas. Perfect with a festive drink for any casual callers. The cookies were especially popular when the children did carolling from house to house on Christmas Eve. She still made them every year once she moved to London, too.

'The drink wouldn't have been a mulled wine in Cyprus,' he continued, 'more likely a *Commandaria* for the adults – a sweet dessert wine – but I think this goes really well too.'

'A bit of an Anglo-Greek hybrid welcome,' Dan added with a smile.

'Cheers to that,' said Will. 'And thanks so much for having us.'

'You are most welcome.'

'Cheers.'

Lily arrived soon afterwards, bringing a small box of homemade rum and raisin fudge, and some mini 'snow-dusted' chocolate truffles – petits fours that had been left over in the restaurant. Ones, she proudly announced, that she'd made there all by herself.

Soon settled by the log stove and given a mulled wine and *melomakarona*, Lily asked, 'What are the melo thingies?'

'Cookies, and they're delicious. You'll definitely want the recipe.' Nikki grinned.

'I think we all do!' added Cath.

'Wonderful. It's one of Maria's specialities,' Andreas added, his tone proud and nostalgic.

'So, how's life at the fast end of the catering industry, young Lily?' Dan asked.

'Great, thanks. I'm working every Saturday now. It's a proper job. They took me on after my week's work experience, which was so cool. I've been doing some waiting on, getting an idea of the customer service side of things, and I love seeing how the food is presented. And just this morning, I've been working in the kitchen. I got to make the petits fours under the watchful eye of Henri himself. Hence the goodies.'

'It all sounds wonderful, Lily. And a great experience for you.' Will was very supportive.

'That's brilliant, Lily,' added Cath. 'And how are your parents feeling about everything?' This had been a sore point in recent months, with Lily wanting to go straight into a catering college and career in hospitality rather than doing a more traditional university degree.

'Uhm, they can see how much I love doing this. And it's great that I'm earning some money now. I've been looking into college courses with hands-on cheffing experience. Though I have agreed to go and check out a couple of unis with Mum and Dad, too. I'm working on them – put it that way. They seem slightly more chilled about my choices than they were.'

'It sounds like you're moving together positively. That's great, Lily,' said Cath.

'Right then, folks, time to step into the dining room. It's meze time!' Andreas called out.

'On our way,' responded Cath, as they filed into the other room, where a large dark-wooden table was set out beautifully with white cloth napkins, shiny cutlery, glasses, and a candelabra no less.

Dan passed everyone a starter plate, as Andreas began to bring through a feast of Greek-Cypriot flavours that he placed to the centre of the table. Warm pittas, homemade hummus, whipped feta-mint dip, a dish of shiny black and plump green olives, and mini meatballs in an aromatic tomato sauce.

'Amazing,' said Lily, eyes wide.

'I had to stop him,' explained Dan. 'He wanted to make more, but the main course is yet to come and is positively massive.'

'Don't spoil the surprise; keep them keen,' said Andreas. 'Okay then, cheers, guys, and *kali orexi*!

'Bon appetit!' added Dan, enlightening them all.

'*Kali orexi*,' they chanted back to Andreas and Dan.

Cath raised her glass which, having now finished the welcome drink of mulled wine, had been recharged with a mellow and fruity red. Perfect.

They chatted and chilled, enjoying the treat of being spoiled by the lads, whilst trying some delicious, authentic Greek-Cypriot food.

The main course was served with a flourish, as Andreas brought in a huge dish of lamb Kleftiko, which came with sticky-lemony potatoes and a side dish of roasted Mediterranean veg. Yet more pitta breads arrived, ready to dip into all the delicious meaty juices.

Talk turned to the Christmas lunch event. With the boiler now fixed, the focus had shifted to getting the kitchen back to full working order; unfortunately the ovens were still very much a work in progress, with Kev finding parts tricky to source, apparently. Cath had spotted a leaky kitchen tap whilst making coffee on the clean-up afternoon, and Will had noticed a pooling of water beneath one of the porcelain pans when cleaning the loos. So many repairs still do to and tradespeople to find – the pound signs were adding up on the costs side of Cath's event balance sheet. There was still such a long way to go, to make the venue shipshape. And they were rolling on stormy seas.

'Hmm, we can't really go ahead and advertise the event as yet,' observed Will. 'Not until we know it's pretty much all sorted and in working order in the village hall. Especially the kitchen facilities. They're key to the whole occasion. Plus, everything needs to be safety-checked.'

'Right, well, you'll be the ideal man for health and safety. Being an ex–fire officer and all that,' observed Dan, hopefully.

'Okay, I'm happy to take that on.' Will accepted the role. 'I'll give feedback to the Village Hall Committee, too. There'll be electrical reports to come in from Kev, and a certificate for the boiler system.'

'He's on it, like a car bonnet.' Nikki gave a giggle. 'Now then, where's that red wine?'

'So, Keeper of the To-Do List and Kitty.' Dan turned to Cath with a smile. 'What's next on the event agenda?'

Cath had been pondering this, too, and whilst watching a property makeover show on the telly last night, had come up with a bit of a brainwave. 'Okay, time is moving on fast. We can't do everything ourselves, we haven't got the skill set for a start, so at this point, I think we put out a call for help. A bit like that *DIY SOS*, for any local tradespeople, keen DIYers, anyone who can give an hour or two of their time with some practical help to do up the hall.'

'Well, I'd be right up for it, if it means that hunky Nick Knowles turning up in our little village,' said Nikki.

'Me too.' Dan's eyes lit up, as Andreas leaned across to give him a playful punch on the arm.

'No chance for you, honey. But yes, I think the idea's brilliant, Cath,' said Andreas. 'It'd hopefully mean we can get a small task force together to move on with all those repair jobs, and perhaps we can freshen up the hall with a lick of paint too. I'll get a poster made. We can pop it up in the shop. Oh yes, a call to arms with a paintbrush or roller.'

'Oh, I can see it now. It'll be like Rosie the Riveter!' Dan grinned. '"We can do it!" Go on, use the catch phrase too, Andreas.'

'I like it! And it'll be going up in the shop's window first thing tomorrow.'

'We can all help spread the word,' added Will.

'Thanks, Andreas, Will,' Cath continued. 'Let's set a date and give everyone a bit of notice, but not leave it too long, either. So, Sunday, first December, at, say, ten a.m.?' Oh my, December was nearly upon then. They'd settled on a date of twenty-second December for the event. Flutters of panic hit her very full stomach. 'Or do you think a pop-in session throughout the day might work better? What do you reckon?'

'Well, a Sunday's a good day. Most people are off work then, and I do feel a pop-in rather than a fixed time might encourage more to come along; they can fit it around their plans,' said Dan.

'We can help do shifts at the hall,' said Will. Whatever might be happening between them personally, he was still here backing up the group, ready to give his time, and she loved him for that.

'And what if we push for the community spirit angle, how the hall will be here for generations to come as well as for this wonderful Christmas do?' ventured Nikki.

'Yeah, go for it.' Lily was on board. 'I'll see if I can get Mum and Dad on the case, too.'

There was a full house of affirmative nods from around the table.

'Brilliant.' Cath beamed.

SOS COMMUNITY CHRISTMAS DIY was a go!

'Well then, folks. It must be time for dessert,' announced Andreas soon afterwards.

'You mean there's even more?' Nikki gave a mock groan.

'It's a festive feast. If you're not absolutely stuffed to the gills at the end of a meal in Cyprus, then we've certainly not made enough!' He chuckled.

'Now bring on the Greek-Cypriot pudding!' Dan sang out, in the style of 'We Wish You a Merry Christmas' and the figgy pudding part.

Andreas brought in a platter of honey-and-cinnamon-oozing pan-fried thin pastry squares. They looked and smelt delicious. 'So, here are my *Pitta Tis Satzis*, served with my ricotta, honey and thyme ice-cream.'

'All homemade, of course,' added Dan proudly, looking to his partner. 'He's been working like a Trojan in that kitchen this week.'

'Oh my, we won't be able to move after this.' Will chuckled. 'You do realise we're all staying here for the night.'

'Wouldn't worry me in the slightest.' Andreas grinned. 'I'd feel my feasting mission was accomplished.'

'Blimey, we're not going to be able to say no to that, are we. It smells divine, all sweet and Christmassy,' said Nikki.

'That'll be the cinnamon and honey,' added Andreas.

'Bang goes my diet!' Cath shook her head.

'I think that was shot at the first course.' Nikki nudged her friend, as they chuckled.

So, plans were ahoy for the Christmas event. Cath was busy making her list, and by the end of the supper club Cypriot-style evening as well as the DIY SOS Pop-in being actioned, a rota had been drawn up, with the group having their various ongoing tasks to do.

They were about to set sail on the good ship *Festive Lunch* with jobs aplenty, but were they about to hit more stormy seas?

Chapter 18

With Lily and Nikki already making their way up the frosty village street, chatting merrily as they went, Will offered to walk Cath the short distance home.

'Thanks, that'd be nice,' she answered, feeling apprehensive yet excited at the thought of it being just the two of them for a while. 'What a wonderful night that was.'

'It was indeed. They really are amazing hosts. They make it look so easy, but there must be so much work behind the scenes to put on a meal like that.'

'Definitely. And they seem to love hosting and cooking so much; they make you feel so welcome.'

They'd come out still feeling that warm glow, having been spoilt with all the wonderful food. It had been so relaxed and sociable, even as they made plans for the Christmas event.

Will's arm slipped gently around her, in a 'more than friends' kind of way, as they walked side by side. Cath snuck a tentative glance up at Will, and her eyes met his.

Where were they going with this faltering romance? Cath couldn't help but wonder. And how was Will really feeling about her? And about life after Jane's death? It was the trickiest of roads to navigate. The only thing she knew was that she wanted to find a way forward with him.

As they reached her door, she smiled up at him, looking into those dark sensual eyes. 'Right, well thanks.'

'Ah, you're welcome …' He was gazing back in such a serious, heartfelt way.

Tension hung between them, like a question.

'Do you want to come in?' She wasn't quite sure why, or what she was asking, and she really didn't want to scare him off again. But there was something different about tonight, about this moment. She didn't want to lose the magic.

'Okay.' He nodded, still holding on to that earnest expression.

Her fingertips trembled lightly on her key as she unlocked the door. He followed her through to the hallway, where she took off her coat and hung it on the rack. Taking a slow breath, she turned back towards him, the tension still very much there.

'O-kay.' She resorted to chit-chat to take the edge off her nervousness. 'How are your girls? Sorry, I didn't get the chance to ask earlier,' Cath asked.

Oh crikey, was it okay to chat about your children in the same space you were planning to seduce their dad? And is that what was happening here? For all her 'I'll let you lead it', was Will in fact wanting, needing a gentle nudge in the right direction?

'Ah, they're doing well, thanks. Been chatting with Sophie today. She's fine. Full of her student life down in York. More parties than studies these past few weeks, by the sounds of it. Actually, that's not fair, I know she works hard. She always did.' He gave a smile. From the way he talked about his girls, she could tell how much he thought of them.

'And I popped down to see Maddie in Newcastle last week,' he continued. 'She had a couple of days off. Took her for lunch down on the quayside. There's a great new Indian restaurant there. It was nice to catch up.'

'Ah, that sounds lovely.' One day perhaps she might get to meet these young women. But hey, one step at a time. She needed to calm herself, and of course, she needed to get to know Will more, firstly.

'Yeah, we'll perhaps have to go down to Newcastle sometime, have a meal or something.' Will's words included her.

She smiled. It was lovely hearing Will talk as though they had a future together. That there would be things to look forward to as a couple from now on. And the tension unwound just a touch, as Cath slowly felt herself start to relax.

'I'll just pop the kettle on.'

Catching sight of the kitchen clock, she saw it was almost eleven-thirty. And strangely, it felt like time was closing in on them. What happened – or didn't – tonight might well change the course of their relationship.

She felt desire thrum through her. She wanted him, to know all of him. Holding back these past few weeks had made her body yearn for him, even more. Though she was scared, and the thought of revealing her fifty-something flesh naturally notched up her anxiety even more, she knew it was what she wanted. But would *he* want to? Might he say a polite goodnight, head on home once more. His heart and body still holding on to Jane.

The kettle began to hum to a boil.

'Ah, I'm not sure if I need any coffee, actually.' Will's voice was soft.

'Oh …'

And his arms came around her, turning her body gently but meaningfully to face him.

His lips were warm, sensual on hers. Kissing, so very passion-ately, with her back pressed up against the kitchen surface. Taking her back to their crumble moment. Nothing at all like the pecks on the cheek received from Trevor these past years. Oh crikey, when had she and her ex-husband in fact stopped kissing like they meant it? Many, many years ago. Anyway, this was no place for thoughts about bloody Trevor.

'Shall we …?' Will stood back, holding his hand out to her,

as if to make for the hallway, the stairs? The bedroom? *Yikes.*

'Ah, uhm, Will, are you sure about this?' She'd hate for this all to come to a back-to-reality halt again.

Will nodded. 'Yes, I'm sure. In fact, I wish I'd had the courage to carry on last time.'

Okay then, Cath chivvied herself. *It's now or never. Go, girl!* Even with her middle-aged body, a full tummy, her mid-range soft-pink underwear from M&S and thankfully at least, freshly shaven legs, she took his hand. A warm, hopeful, yet slightly nervous smile played over her lips.

This was it. Her heart was thumping in her chest. *And so to bed …*

Up the stairs, in a careful dash. Reaching her cottage bedroom threshold, together. Giddily crashing in through the white wooden door. The bedside lamp she'd left on was giving a soft butterscotch glow of light. Still far too revealing, for her middle-aged waistline and slightly saggy boobs. But hey, it was too late now.

'Are you sure, too?' Will looked so earnest, so bloody lovely, as they hovered just inches from her bed.

'Yeah. You?' *Please* don't say no now. If they didn't get their kit off right now, and *do* this thing, she feared they'd never find the confidence to go through with it ever again.

He nodded, adding a resolute, 'Yes.'

It was happening. Yikes! Yabba dabba doo!

They landed on soft plump pillows and her cosy duvet. The white cotton sheets had been freshly changed just that morning. Ooh, had she had some sixth sense about this?

Nerves jangled, as anticipation and anxiety hit all at once. Sex. Would it all come back to her? Was it like riding a bike? But with someone new and after all this time. With wrinkles and saggy bits, neither of them spring chickens anymore. And oh my God, her dress was off and Will was unfastening the clasp of her bra.

All the while, that sensual pressure and the lingering red wine taste of his lips on hers. The feel of his gentle yet passionate touch.

Fingertips brushing over her left breast, then his palm cupping the fullness of it. His mouth travelling down, leaving her lips lonely, now tracing her neckline in a trail of warm tender kisses, her collarbone, down to her chest, until oh, her nipple was firm and taut in his mouth. *Oh my.*

An ache for him formed deep within her. A pulse of longing. She felt sexy, and wanted – a feeling that had been lost to her for a very long time. 'Oh, Will.' Words were lost to her after that.

Her confidence was growing, however, with every pleasurable second. She reached beneath the covers to touch him, his erection firm within her hand. Wanting to return that pleasure, too. She heard his gasp, which sounded so damn hot.

He must be nervous too, being with someone new after all this time, yet their bodies seemed to be bypassing that. And all those wonderful feelings from her youth, their young adulthood, swirled with the present in her mind, through her limbs.

Kissing once more, with abandon, delight, desire. The contours of Will's muscles defined in the lamplight as he moved up and over her … and, oh my. Nothing was going to stop them now.

Chapter 19

Waking with a ray of morning sun and a big smile across her face, Cath knew from the weighted dip in the mattress, the extra body heat and the arm that was stretched snoozily across her, that Will was still there beside her in bed. Also, from the way her body felt tingly and kind of well used this morning.

So, it was all real. Not a very sexy act of wishful thinking.

Watching Will stretch and then get out of her bed felt incredible yet surprisingly natural. As he padded towards the bedroom door, she greedily took in the V of his broad shoulders that slimmed down to his waist, above those well-defined cycling muscles of his buttocks and thighs. Hmm, those buttocks that she'd held so close to her last night. Wow, had that really happened?

She lay in a softly sensual haze, not wanting to break the spell by getting up quite yet.

The sound of the flush, the sink running, in the bathroom. Her bathroom. Everyday sounds, yet miraculous in the circumstances. Will was here. Will had stayed over.

Walking back in, absolutely starkers, he grinned. 'Well, that was some night,' he said casually, as he slipped back under the covers beside her.

'Hmm, it was indeed.' And her smile was like the cat who'd

got the cream, and who'd very much enjoyed lapping it up. Who knew sex could be like that in your fifties? She actually hadn't thought she had it in her anymore, but was very glad to have been proven otherwise.

Leaning over, he gave her a gorgeous morning kiss, his breath all minty, having used a blob of her toothpaste. She was a little afraid her own might not be quite as fresh, but it didn't seem to bother him. His arousal a sensual reminder as it brushed against the side of her leg.

Unfortunately, as he snuggled close, he then added, 'Ah, I need to get to work. Shop opens in forty minutes. I don't think I can get away with wearing my evening clothes. Bit of a giveaway to my clients. I'm usually in a cycling top, sweatshirt and cargo pants at this time of year.'

'Well, that's a shame – I wouldn't have minded a repeat performance,' she said minxily, sounding very unlike herself, as she looked into his dark eyes.

Who the hell was this new woman? The battered, bruised and discarded Cath of old had been very much revived, and replaced with a new sexier model, all thanks to this gorgeous guy next to her. She felt amazing.

As he got up to go after one last, lingering kiss, she hoped to goodness that he was feeling the same way as she was this morning, and not now experiencing a sense of grief-fuelled guilt. She knew how gigantic a step this was for Will.

'Hi, lads.'

'Morning, Cath, darling,' Dan greeted her warmly, even though his slightly red-rimmed eyes were a clue to his having enjoyed several glasses of Merlot last night.

'Thanks so much for a fantastic evening,' said Cath. 'Just perfect, the food was a-mazing.'

'Ah, you're very welcome. And how are you today, lovely?' Andreas asked.

Feeling rather wonderful after a romp of a night with our sexy cyclist came to mind, but she merely gave a small knowing smile and said, 'Very well, thanks.' Though she couldn't stop the heat of a blush forming across her cheeks.

'Marvellous,' he responded, his own smile wide.

Had they guessed? Cath felt a touch embarrassed, feeling like a teen again. But hey, they were both grown adults so what did it matter? she reminded herself. The lads would probably break into a round of applause if they actually knew.

'Well then.' Andreas moved swiftly on, much to Cath's relief. 'I've been working on the poster for next Sunday's Village Hall SOS DIY and Paint-a-thon. What do you think?' Andreas lifted an A4 sheet from behind the counter. 'If you approve, I'll get it laminated and up in the window, forthwith.'

Cath had to smile. He'd done a great job, with a graphic image of a muscled Rosie the Riveter–style arm holding a paintbrush and spanner. With an army-style tagline of: *Tilldale Needs You! Bring along your brushes, tools, and any spare magnolia paint!* And a further line: *Refreshments provided – baklava and tray bakes for the troops.*

'I love it. I'm sure it'll draw in some helpers, even if only for the baklava.'

'That was my plan. And we'll mention it to everyone who calls in at the stores between now and then. It'll benefit the whole village, after all.'

'Exactly,' added Dan. 'And we need to be cracking on. Christmas is fast approaching.'

'I know. Do we risk putting out the flyers yet? The invites? There's been lots of talk in the village, but guests will need some notice. And the home will need to organise transport and staff.' This had been very much on Cath's mind.

'Yes, I think we need to. It's a risk, with the repairs ongoing and the ovens still to fix.' Nikki's Kev was on the case, but the parts were *still* proving tricky to source. 'But I suppose we'd just have to find another venue last-minute,' said Andreas.

'Would that be possible so late in the day?' Dan sounded unsure.

'Oh, ye of little faith,' said Andreas. 'We'd find a way. There's always a way.'

Despite Andreas's confidence, Cath's fears were nipping like a terrier at her heels. She forced herself to sound positive, however. 'But yes, the hall is pretty sound otherwise. And it'll be getting its revamp very soon. Fingers crossed for a good turn-out on Sunday. So yes, let's get Lily on the case with the invites and flyers.' She'd already mentioned to Cath that she was keen to help with that. 'And I'm off to the Kirkton care home for a visit again this afternoon. I'll confirm the date and time with them. We're going for a twelve noon arrival, yeah?'

'Yep.'

This was real. It was happening. There was no going back once the invites were out.

As she left the store with her groceries a few minutes later, Cath wasn't sure if it was excitement or trepidation she was feeling. Most likely, a huge dose of both. The anxiety terrier gave a big old yap!

Chapter 20

Big, little, bushy? Cath was stood sizing up the fir trees before her. She'd spotted a sign at one of the farms on the road to Kirkton last week. She'd always loved a real tree at Christmas. Though they dropped needles and were a devil to hoover around, they always looked so beautiful, with such a magical scent. She even liked the spiky feel of them. For the last couple of years together, Trev had insisted on a fake one, to save all the mess and bother. He wasn't worried about the bother and mess he was making of his own bloody marriage back then, Cath mused drily, but then let that thought go.

This Christmas was about the new, and Cath found herself excited at the prospect of having a real tree once more. With all this talk of festivities, and the calendar about to turn to December, it was time. It was her first Christmas in Cheviot Cottage, and she wanted to make it feel homely and festive.

But did she get one from the floor up to the ceiling? Or a smaller one to sit on a table? She had driven here in a Mini, after all, and she'd be solo putting it up. There were practicalities to consider. In her mind's eye, however, she'd envisaged a tallish tree stood in the space (she'd make by shifting her armchair) next to the hearth, where she could look at the tree every evening as she relaxed on the sofa. It would make the sitting room look oh-so-cosy and pretty with its twinkly lights and decorations. In fact, she'd need a reasonable size to be able to make the most of Reggie's vintage baubles, plus the gorgeous glass ones that she hadn't been able to resist at the village stores. A big one it was, then. She headed towards the seven-footers. And she'd ask if they'd deliver.

The fresh woodland pine scents all around her took her back to the years of choosing a tree in the outskirts of Sheffield, with Susie and their parents, the girls mulling over quite how big or bushy to go. Dad ready – with the boot of his estate car open – to hoist in whichever massive tree they went for. Memories of Christmas pasts, of times as a family with Adam and Trev, were close to the surface on days like these. There were so many traditions and poignant moments associated with these special celebration times.

This one looked good. She paused in the six-foot section. Tall, nicely even branches, and plenty of them for the all-important festive dangly bits. Hmm, nothing like a strapping six-footer. The farm lad turned up beside her. She must have been gazing longingly, giving out all the signs that this was the one.

'Umm, hi,' said Cath, with a hopeful smile. 'Do you deliver at all?'

'Whereabouts to?' He looked to be about eighteen, most likely the farmer's son.

'Tilldale.'

'Yeah, that's fine. We'll go up to ten miles or so. It'd be tomorrow, if that's okay. We tend to do a few at once.'

'Perfect.'

'I'll get it wrapped and labelled for you. Just leave me your address.' He took the tree easily under one arm, and walked to a machine with a metal chute that looked somewhat like a huge megaphone, where he pushed it through, turning the tree into a mesh-wrapped bushy pole.

Cath settled up, feeling pleased with herself. It wasn't too scary a price. And tomorrow was fine. It'd give her chance to get Reggie's decorations ready, as well as her own, and shift the armchair out of the way.

And thinking of Reggie, that was exactly where she was heading next.

After having spent a half hour with a resident called Phillip – a talkative chap who used to be a civil engineer, and had interestingly been involved with the design and construction of the Metro Shopping Centre at Gateshead back in the Eighties – Cath headed over to catch up with Reggie. She couldn't, of course, be seen to have any favourites at the home, though secretly she was keen to chat with the dear old chap again.

As she walked over, she could see he was holding one of the letters from Elsie. She later found out that since their return he kept one tucked in his top pocket at all times, ready to have a read whenever he felt the need.

'It's like I've got her back,' he said, his eyes a little rheumy. 'Thank you for finding those letters, Cath.'

'Like I said last time, you're more than welcome. So how are you doing this week, Reggie?'

The conversation rolled on, and she told him all about choosing her Christmas tree, on her way over, and that she had plans to put it next to the fireplace in the living room. Which, back in the day, was exactly where Elsie and Reggie had used to place theirs, he told her. It seemed very fitting that Cath had chosen to follow tradition.

'I missed the old cottage last Christmas. They did a lovely job here, but it wasn't quite the same. I suppose I'd only just got here then, moved in early December. It was all so very different. Might be a bit easier this year, hey, pet.'

'We'll be getting our tree and decorations up in the next day or so here too, Reggie,' Linda piped up, overhearing their chat.

'Oh, that'll be lovely,' said Cath.

'Love a bit of tinsel and baubles, and those pretty paper-chain garlands.' Reggie was enthusiastic.

'Yes, we have a big tree up in the day room,' Linda elaborated for Cath's benefit, 'and a smaller one in reception. We have a super event lined up one afternoon where a group from the local church come along and sing carols for us. There's tea and mince pies. It's lovely. A bit of a sing-song with everyone joining in by the end of it, too.'

'Oh, it was such fun last year,' called out Vera from her armchair, who'd been listening in.

'Yes, I remember that now. We had a good old sing-along,' agreed Reggie.

'Sounds wonderful.'

And that reminded Cath that she'd need to speak with Julie, the manager, before she left, to make their formal invite for the Christmas lunch event. She had one of Lily's fabulous fliers for Turkey and Tinsel in Tilldale in her handbag, ready to hand over with all the details. She just hoped the residents of the home would be keen to attend.

Chapter 21

Ten o'clock came and went. It was SOS DIY day, and the only tradesperson there was Nikki's husband, Kev, who was busy up a stepladder putting a new starter in one of the strip-lights in the hall, which was literally on the blink. Dan was stood at the ladder's base keeping him steady.

It had been a massive relief, at least, when Dan went to turn the heating on, and they heard the old boiler clunking to life and the radiators gurgling into action. In fact, Nikki and Andreas gave a whoop! of delight and high-fived each other at that point.

But as one job was fixed, another seemed to line up to fill its place. It was like playing DIY Whack-A-Mole. Cath already had kitchen tap, leaky gents' toilet, dodgy door handle to kitchen, plus paint the hall – a huge task alone – on her 'Repairs' list.

And, the more worrying news was that the oven thermostats were proving very 'challenging to source', Kev'd told them with a frown, being listed (unnervingly) as obsolete. He'd come in to check over the electrical equipment some time ago, hoping to get a head start, and had instead been given a headache.

Cath felt the nagging pulse of a headache too, what with the oven hold-up and no one as yet turning up to help today. Had the supper club group been too damn hopeful, unrealistic, naive?

Imagining the village were on board and ready to turn out in force? That the local trades might be happy to help for free? Cath felt annoyed with herself, for pushing for this idea in the first place. What had she been thinking?

Andreas looked at his watch one more time: twenty-five past ten. Dan shrugged, his face showing concern. What was going on? The list in the shop had had several names on. Volunteers, of all trades, apparently eager to help out for a good cause. So where were they? Why the delay? Had they found something better to do with their time? Realised that doing something for nothing wasn't the best plan business-wise? Or had they, in fact, felt pressured to add their names to the list, merely appearing to be doing the right thing, in a bid to exit the shop?

'Right then, while we're waiting,' Cath announced, 'I'm going to get our paint supplies and equipment ready, and organise the hall. There's enough paint to start us off at least. Once Kev's finished up there, I've got several dust sheets to lay out to help protect the parquet flooring. And then, does anyone fancy a cuppa?' she offered, needing something to keep her busy. She was feeling restless and a touch irritable, concerned that no one other than their posse was actually going to turn up.

Lily and Nikki had gone to fetch some spare tins of cream paint that were apparently lurking in Lily's parents' garage, and seeing the turnout was so low – read: non-existent – also try to twist Lily's parents' arms to come along and give them a hand. Even Will was AWOL – hopefully just running late – without a message or anything, which wasn't like him. Cath wasn't sure, at this point, whether to be cross or concerned about him.

The lads from the shop had come across laden with teabags, instant coffee, a large carton of milk, shortbread biscuits and as promised on the poster, a plastic tub filled with Andreas's sticky-honey baklava, to keep the 'workers', who were of course currently absent, happy.

Dust sheets put out, Cath was now in the old school's kitchen setting out mugs on the side. Kev was there now too, sporting a pale-buttocked builder's bum on the other side of the room, as he navigated the interior of one of the enormous ovens. Apparently double-checking model and serial numbers, and taking photographs, in his bid to find those elusive parts. Now that was a sight for a Sunday morning. Blimey, there was always a crack in the job somewhere, Cath thought, trying to cheer herself up.

'Cuppa, Kev?'

'Please, love,' his deep voice echoed from the oven.

There was time yet, Cath told herself. They had put *from* ten a.m. after all, and it was advertised as a 'drop-in' on the poster in the shop.

'Hey, sorry I'm a bit late. Sophie's here for the weekend.' Will finally strolled in, his tone seeming measured.

At last. She'd been feeling somewhat irritated by his absence. Actually, he looked a bit pale. Did she ask how things were? Had something happened at home?

But then he started talking again. 'Just popped in to the hall, uhm, it's pretty quiet, isn't it?'

'Yeah, ah ...' Her shoulders dropped and she couldn't hold back her sigh any longer. 'Well, it's just, I really hoped the village would get on board with this. Some DIY SOS this is; it's just the SOS bit right now.' She couldn't help but feel disillusioned, and rather cross with herself, to be honest, for leading them all down this path. There was going to be *so* much work for their little team now.

'Hey, come on, there's plenty of time yet.' Will's words were meant to reassure, but as Cath glanced his way, he looked kind of worried too.

'Ah, you're right, I think I'm just tired. It's early in the day. Things can change.' There was no point being down about it.

'Okay, so I've come to give you a hand taking the drinks back to the gang.'

'Thanks. And are you okay?' she dared to ask, more personally, wondering what might have caused his delay, his own disquiet. This might be the only chance they'd get to speak as just the two of them today.

His dark eyes were on hers. He merely nodded, adding, 'Yeah, I'm fine.' But Cath knew him well enough to know there was a cover-up going on.

They hadn't had chance to catch up in person since their steamy session, and that was a week ago now; that had been worrying her, too. Cath was trying to read the lines between their ongoing messages, giving him the space she knew he still needed whilst letting him know she was there for him, whenever, however. She was ready to give so much, yet seemingly getting little in return. Like the village turnout that hadn't happened, was she just expecting too much from him? One night of glorious sex didn't mean a lifetime of promises, after all.

'Mine's two sugars, please, pet,' bellowed a deep voice from the cavern of the oven.

Oops, they hadn't been alone at all. No chance for any heartfelt conversation now. That was the end of that.

'You okay, petal?' Andreas asked kindly as they stood side by side sipping their warm drinks.

The slice of sticky baklava only marginally lifted her mood.

'Yeah, I'm all right, thanks,' replied Cath, trying to perk herself up. 'Just hoping we can pull this thing off. There's so much work involved already. And we haven't even got as far as planning the food and the event itself.' There was far more to think about than she'd first imagined. As well as a lunch event, they had somehow taken on renovating a whole village hall. And it was snowballing.

'Yep, but we will once we get the hall and its facilities up and running, thanks to people like Kev here.' Andreas gestured.

Kev was stood with the gang, brew in hand. 'Cheers, mate.'

'Then, it'll be more straightforward,' Andreas continued, 'and we can get down to planning the event itself.'

'We'll darn well give it our best shot,' said Dan, who'd been listening in, next to his partner. 'But hey, where's a plumber when you need one?' he added wryly, scanning the hall as though he might summon one up. The tradespeople who'd put their names forward in the shop were still missing in action just now.

Thankfully, once the coffees were down to the dregs, the hall door creaked open and there stood the first of the volunteers. John and Mary, Cath's next-door neighbours, offering to help with the painting, John having been a keen decorator in his time, apparently. Bless them, they must both be approaching eighty. Cath'd find them some light tasks. Soon to be followed by – yes! – three of the hall's committee, Andreas introducing them as Nigel, Keith and Dorothy.

Nigel came bearing a two-thirds-full can of Dulux Magnolia. The supper group had purchased two large cans of Magnolia from the hardware store in Kirkton to start today's project off with the proceeds of the shop's raffle so far, but crikey, paint was expensive.

Slowly but surely, more volunteers began to arrive. Including, rather wonderfully, Lily and her parents, each carrying a five-litre tin of emulsion.

'Hi, guys. This is Mum and Dad, ah, Anna and Jason.'

'Hi.'

'Hello.'

'Nice to meet you.'

Anna gave a smile. 'Yeah, I got a bit carried away ordering paint when we did up the barn. Natural Calico, this is. It's pretty close to Magnolia. I heard you were on the hunt for that and well, there's plenty of it, as you can see. We should have taken it back really, but once we'd finished the job it got stored in the garage, just in case, as you do, and been sat there ever since. You're more than welcome to have it.'

'Ah, that's brilliant, thank you,' said Cath. 'And lovely to meet you both.' Cath was delighted for the paint, of course, but also to see that Lily's parents were interested in helping and supporting their fabulous daughter, too.

The family had also come armed with rollers, trays and brushes. Jason returned, loaded up, from their car, saying, 'Thought we'd come and see what's happening here, for ourselves,' as he placed the items down on a trestle table. 'And of course to say hello to your supper group that our Lily's been telling us all about.'

'That's wonderful,' said Dan. 'Thank you.'

'Yeah, I used to come to this hall for Lily's playgroup, many moons ago,' added Anna, with a touch of nostalgia. 'And now look at her, nearly an adult. Doing all sorts. Been finding herself a job in a restaurant and everything.' She sounded proud, if perhaps a little reticent to let go. Cath recognised that empty-nest feeling. It was so lovely that they were here, together as a family.

'Well, it must be time to set to work.' Cath's mood was lifting by the second.

And right on cue, local painter and decorator Allan, who lived in a hamlet not far from the village, arrived and he told them he had been a pupil at the school. He stepped into gear and took the reins from Cath, organising the DIY decorating troops, advising they'd used the Calico on two walls and the Magnolia, which he had also had spares of in his van parked outside, on the other two. 'You'd hardly know the difference, but best not to mix.' Volunteers and paintbrushes and rollers at the ready, and they were off.

Cath's heart was in her mouth as she watched the first brush-strokes go on, freshening the dull grey walls immediately, and Nikki, with roller to hand, gave a cheer. With the music on, coffee, stacks of biscuits – Lily had also brought tubs of rocky-road bites and some brownies that she'd made earlier that morning – and with a huge brushstroke of camaraderie, the workers got stuck in, and the old hall began to yawn and stretch itself back to life. It was great to see the whole supper club there getting all paint-spattered, and chatting away with the others. Her glance was drawn to Will every now and again, to check if he seemed okay. His emotions, as seemed so often in a public arena, were kept under lock and key.

Lunchtime was soon upon them, and apart from Mary and John who were no doubt shattered and ready for a sit-down, everyone else had agreed to continue. With two of the four hall walls completed in the Calico colour, and a small section of the Magnolia started, Cath nipped home and brought across a huge pan of homemade leek and potato soup to warm on the hob. At least that part of the industrial-sized cooker was working. She was soon carrying through a tray of filled mugs and a stack of bread buns halved and buttered, announcing there was 'soup for the troops'.

Whilst the act of painting had warmed the helpers somewhat, the hall was still rather chilly, having been so infrequently used. It'd take a while to warm the high-ceilinged room through, even with the radiators back in action. A mug of hearty soup would go down well for sure.

After passing out the lunch supplies, Cath realised she hadn't seen Will in the hall for a while. She asked Nikki if she knew where he was.

'Oh, he had to dash off just before, saying his daughter was up for the weekend, and that he needed to get home to see her for a couple of hours. I think he's coming back though.'

That sounded reasonable enough, but his muted manner before had left her concerned. He just hadn't seemed himself. And of course, with so many people buzzing about and jobs to do, it hadn't been the time or place to talk.

The next tradesperson to turn up was a thirty-something plumber, toolbox to hand, who introduced herself as Gemma. She was chatty and friendly, saying she was more than happy to look at the kitchen tap, and she'd check out the general pipe-work plus the toilet facilities, too. Cath had warned her about the leaky loo pan in the gents'. Oh, it'd be fantastic if she could sort those issues, then Cath could then tick several jobs off her list in one fell swoop.

Her Pilates teacher and a couple from her exercise group had rocked up, happy to lend a hand; mentioning they were keen on getting a class set up here in Tilldale, if the hall revival worked out. And a tall, rather good-looking joiner in his forties called Mick arrived; he was able to help with the dodgy door handle, and thereafter more than happy to turn his hand to painting. It had been a heartwarming day after all, and so good to see the community coming together.

At the next tea-break time, Andreas whispered to Cath naughtily, 'Ooh, I haven't seen such a hunky gathering in a long while,' as he helped himself to a chocolate brownie. Other than Gemma, the majority of the tradespeople who had turned up seemed to be canvas-trousered males, with rather muscular arms and torsos.

'Behave,' Dan whispered back at him, having overheard the comment, as Cath gave a giggle.

That fact hadn't passed her by either, actually. They were indeed a good-looking bunch, perhaps it was the tool belts and the air of practical authority they brought with them. But there he was, back again and over the way, her own chunk of hunk – well, one fine day she might get another chance to find out – holding the stepladder for Allan to reach a tricky part with his roller above the stage. She gave Will what she hoped was a foxy smile. She was a bit out of practice with such things, to be honest. He managed a small, somewhat cautious smile back.

So close and yet so far – both with Will and the organising of the event. There was still a mountain to climb to pull this Christmas lunch event together. As the afternoon drew to a close, with the sky already darkening outside, some of the helpers drifted away, to huge thanks from the gang, armed with takeaway portions of rocky road, baklava and chocolate brownies. These guys really were local heroes.

The painting of the main hall walls was now complete, looking great in that fresh calico-cream shade, with the final detail, suggested by Allan, being the old dado rails touched up with a classic navy. In the end, everything had gone far better than Cath could have hoped for, that was other than with Will.

He hadn't seemed himself at all. And he'd only gone and nipped away again before they'd had chance to catch up. Him disappearing like that had left her even more concerned.

A while later, Lily filled her in further saying that before he'd left, Will had asked if he could take a couple of chocolate brownies for Sophie, muttering something about them being her favourites and a 'peace offering'. Cath couldn't help but wonder what had gone on between father and daughter, but was all too soon caught up in the melee of thanking and helping the various tradespeople and helpers to pack up.

Dan must have spotted something was amiss too, and before he and Andreas left, came over to put an arm gently around Cath. 'You okay, lovely? The day's gone off brilliantly in the end, hasn't it?'

'Yeah, it has. Everyone's been great.' But her wistful tone gave her concerns away.

They'd definitely been aware of a situation, with Dan adding, 'Uhm, we couldn't help but notice that Will wasn't quite himself. And then dashing off like that ...'

'I know. I'm a bit worried about him. He wasn't right, was he? It's annoying that we never got chance to talk ...'

'Lily mentioned about the chocolate "peace offering",' he shared. 'And in my limited experience, chocolate is one way to a woman's heart, so perhaps it's all sorted by now.'

'Yes, I hope so.'

Whatever was wrong, Will seemed to be trying to patch it back up with Sophie, one small gesture at a time. Cath so hoped they'd get the chance to talk about it together at some point. Will might well need a shoulder to lean on.

Cath left Veronica, the very last of the lot, and as it turned out a real trooper, buffering the hall's parquet flooring. The committee had pulled a few strings, apparently, and managed to get the floor-polishing machine on loan for the weekend from the primary school in Kirkton.

Wow, what a day! Cath hadn't stopped and now she suddenly realised how knackered she was.

'You get away, Cath,' called a smiling Veronica. 'I'll finish here and lock up.'

'You sure?'

'Absolutely.' She switched off the machine for a second to be heard. 'And I can't thank you all enough.' There was a glint of tears in the eyes of the very upright and upstanding Veronica. 'It was so lovely to see it filled with people, and bustle and chatter again. You've absolutely brought this old hall back to life.'

And they had. They'd only gone and done it – other than the two dodgy ovens, anyhow. And Cath felt a swell of pride, and the glisten of a tear in her own eye. She might pull this off, after all.

Chapter 22

It was Tuesday once more, time floating by like a leaf caught in a swift breeze, and it was time for Cath to do her visit to the care home. Entering the reception area, she saw that the place had been festively decorated throughout. Metallic streamers and garlands caught the light as they danced from the ceiling, a small fake fir stood on the table in the entrance area, adorned with colourful twinkling lights.

In the day room was an even bigger tree, almost to the ceiling, glowing prettily with warm-white lights, lots of silver and gold tinsel, and literally a hundred baubles and bold-red bows. Christmas had landed at the care home. It gave the place a celebratory atmosphere.

Today, it was Joan's turn to chat, a lovely lady in her nineties. Cath took the seat beside her. The elderly woman's back was so bent over she had trouble straightening enough to make eye contact. But the two of them talked easily, Joan telling Cath all about life in Kirkton in her land army days, yet a little later on not being able to remember what she'd had for lunch.

She hadn't known anything about farming when she'd volunteered at eighteen for the Women's Land Army in the Second World War, she told Cath, and had been sent up from Newcastle in the late 1940s. Back then, the youth hostel in Kirkton had been used as a dormitory and base. The camaraderie and friendships struck up sounded wonderful, even though the work was tough and could be back-breaking especially when 'shawing' turnips – Joan explained that was removing the greenery and root stump – and harvesting the corn. A six a.m. start every day was the norm, and off to bed by ten p.m.

Joan's eyes sparkled as she told of dances over at Milfield camp, and how they even had a cinema in Kirkton back then. They were allowed two late passes out per week until eleven p.m. Joan finished her reminiscing by telling Cath how she'd never returned to live back in Newcastle again, having fallen for a handsome young farmer. Marriage and two children had followed, and a hard-working but fulfilling and happy life spent in the Northumbrian countryside nearby.

The old lady seemed rather tired after recalling all those magical memories, so Cath said how lovely it had been to hear her story, but that it was time to move on and give someone else a chance to chat. Cath gave Reggie a cheery wave from across the room, but thought it only fair to give her time to someone new for her second half hour. She was just going to ask carer Linda who she felt might best benefit from a bit of company, when in bustled the manager, Julie, sounding rather flustered.

'Linda, I've just had a call. The church group have had to cancel the carols.'

'Oh crikey, no! What a shame. Everyone's so looking forward to it,' responded the carer.

'They're all down with flu, apparently,' Julie explained.

'Oh, dear,' added Cath, imagining how they'd be missed. The sing-along had sounded so lovely when Linda had told her about it last week.

'I know. The residents always love it, too. Carols around the Christmas tree. Mince pies, the works. We do it every year,' added Julie.

'Can't risk anyone getting the flu here, mind,' said Linda.

'Absolutely not,' confirmed Julie. 'Josie, the group's leader, sounded terrible. She could hardly speak, let alone sing.'

Cath knew how much the carols meant to some of the residents here and it set cogs turning in her mind. And Lily's idea, many weeks ago now, of carols and mince pies around a Christmas tree felt like the hand of fate. And then she remembered how Dan had wondered if they could actually sing as a group. But company, they could certainly give a bit of chatty company, along with some homemade mince pies. It had been lovely talking with Joan here today. Andreas would be up for it, for sure, his mother, Maria, having been a much-loved and well-cared-for resident until her recent passing.

Could she? *Should* she venture their help as a group? They'd given so much of their time already.

But it'd be nice for the group to get to know some of the residents before their village lunch event. Cath had yet to speak with Julie and find out definite numbers for that. But it would be such a shame if they had to miss out this week. The festive decorations were up, and the big Christmas tree was looking so pretty. It wouldn't be hard to do a short festive visit. Just a little time and conversation, and perhaps one quick carol to end.

She couldn't stop herself. Even if it was just her and Andreas, so be it. 'We could do it. I mean it wouldn't be anything like a group of practised singers. More conversation and mince pies, really.'

'You'd be prepared to do that? Really? Who do you have in mind to come along with you?' Julie looked rather gobsmacked.

'Me and the group who are organising the Christmas lunch in the village. You know Andreas, Maria's son, and his partner, Dan.'

'Ah yes, of course.'

'And there's a couple of others from the village: Nikki and her niece, Lily. Oh, and Will.'

Fingers crossed, they'd all be up for it and that she could get them here.

'When's it scheduled for?' Cath checked.

'Thursday at four p.m.' That was only two days away.

Oops. Andreas and Dan had the shop. Will had his cycling store. Lily was at school. 'Could we possibly make it for five-ish?'

'Of course. We can shift teatime a little earlier, I'm sure.' Julie gave a warm smile. Linda was beaming. Joan was having her well-earned nap. Philip, whom she'd met last week, gave a nod from across the room, and there were Betty and Vera settled watching TV, as Reggie gave her another cheery wave.

There was no way she was letting them down now.

They arrived at the care home, laden with tubs of freshly baked goodies. Homemade buttery shortbread care of Cath, always a treat, and Lily who hadn't had so much time for baking with her studies and restaurant work, had got up super-early, desperate to try out her idea of mince pies three ways: traditional with buttery, crisp pastry, star-topped flaky with a hint of sherry, and some with a sprinkling of marzipan that gave a taste of stollen.

The group had come in two cars, and yes, they'd come up trumps, being a full house of fabulous supper club volunteers. Andreas and Dan had even closed the stores slightly early, with Will coming straight across from the cycling shop.

It was just before five p.m., and the residents had finished their early supper. The idea was that the six volunteers would sit in the lounge with the elderly and engage in some chat.

Cath was looking forward to seeing Reggie and her new friends from the home again. The day room was busier than ever, with an eager gathering waiting to be entertained. Lily's mince pies had been plated up and were now being passed around. The residents hadn't been served any dessert today on purpose, which had apparently resulted in one or two grumbles at the dinner table but Cath had advised they were bringing along some festive sweet treats.

After them touring the room to chat for around fifteen

minutes. One elderly lady seemed to be somewhat agitated, rocking in her chair as she said, 'Why aren't they singing? You said there'd be singing.'

'Oh, that's not happening today now, Gladys. The carol singers are down with flu. They've had to cancel,' Linda, who was handing out cups of tea, explained.

'Oh …' The rocking got more persistent.

'Well, that's a bloody shame,' chipped in Philip. 'I like a bit of singing, me.'

There was a chorus of disappointed voices. Oh dear, this wasn't the reception or impact they'd hoped for.

'Well, what *are* they here for then?'

'They've made and brought in all this lovely food for you all. The mince pies and biscuits you're eating. And they've come for a chat,' Linda explained.

'Oh, but the carols were the best bit.'

'It's not Christmas without carols.'

Andreas and Dan looked to Cath. Will shrugged, and Nikki tried a weak smile. Lily wasn't sure what to say, when the old chap beside her piped up, 'Well, do you like singing, love?'

'Umm,' was all she could muster.

'Do you know "Rudolph the Red-Nosed Reindeer"?' asked another.

'Right then, that's enough about singing, you lot. These lovely people have given up their time to come and chat with you, and they've brought you all these goodies. You're very lucky to have them here.' Julie stepped in, trying to appease the situation, mouthing, 'Sorry,' across at Cath.

Andreas then whispered something to Dan, who motioned to Cath and Nikki to come over, who then went back to pass the word to Will and Lily respectively.

Dan fished his mobile phone from his pocket, and quickly did a search on his Spotify. Soon, the opening bars to 'Jingle Bells' started and the supper clubbers stood up, one by one, shuffling to make an informal group at the centre of the day room. The first notes came out somewhat shakily, then Dan and Andreas began to pair in unison. Cath joined in enthusiastically being well used to school assemblies, with Nikki half-humming half-singing whilst performing some actions with gusto – her own made-up ones – to counteract her lack of vocal skills. Lily started shyly but then got into the swing of it, with Will at the last, surprising them all with a rather good tenor voice.

Soon, some of the residents began swaying in their seats and clapping their hands, and a few joined in with the singing, warbling away merrily.

'Jingle Bells' finished to a round of staggered applause, and a cheer from one old lady, which woke up a male resident who'd managed to miss the whole event up until this point.

'Oh, what was that then? Is Father Christmas here?' His eyelids batted open.

'Not yet, Leonard. We're just trying to sing to wake up him and his reindeer.' One of the nursing assistants smiled.

'Oh, lovely. Tell him I'd like a new hearing aid. This one's knackered.' He gave a toothy grin and chuckled to himself.

'Another tune?' Dan asked, scrolling through his phone once more.

'Why not?' Will smiled.

'In for a penny …' Nikki added.

'Rudolph?' Lily suggested. 'With his very shiny nose? We all know that one.'

And off they jollied, with a rousing rendition, now both old and young were finding their voices.

It turned into a volley of requests being launched from around the room. They got away with a couple of verses of 'Away in a Manger' but struggled with some of the words. And 'Silent Night' was extremely high-pitched, causing Vera to heckle them, calling out that they sounded like a load of wailing cats. They had a chuckle at that.

They wrapped things up with a cheerful 'We Wish You a Merry Christmas!' with the whole audience and carers joining in. Receiving hearty applause and a couple of 'hurrahs' from the gathering.

Phew, it was time to collapse on a high-backed chair and partake of a cup of tea and a mince pie themselves.

'Thank you so much. That was brilliant.' Julie came over to them, grinning widely.

'Aw, that was so good. Hidden talents, you lot. They loved that,' added Linda, bringing over the tea trolley and serving the newfound choir a well-earned cuppa.

Reggie then came over to thank them. And, helping himself to another mince pie, he added, 'These are almost as good as my Elsie used to make.'

The mince pies were crumbly, festive-spiced and delicious. Cath especially loved the marzipan-laced one. 'These are amazing, Lily. Thanks for all that hard work. Well done, you.'

'Yes, those mince pies were delicious. Might need to get the recipe off you to make them at home,' added Julie. 'Oh, and Cath, I'll catch up with you by email on the Christmas lunch event. We have a few interested in going. And I'll check times with you for the minibus transfers. But we can sort that another day.'

'Ah, that's great. I'll look out for your email.' Aw, she hoped Reggie would be amongst them, and have the chance to come back and enjoy the newly spruced-up hall and the village that was his home for so many years.

'Oh, and Lily here will be happy to share her mince pie recipe, for sure,' Cath continued. 'She's our budding chef.'

Cath felt proud of their youngest group member and, in fact, the whole lot of them. What a lovely couple of hours it had turned out to be. Who knew they could even sing like that? And what they lacked in talent, they more than made up for with enthusiasm. It felt like they'd sprinkled a bit of 'joy glitter' over the home and its residents.

Chapter 23

'Well, our event poster's drawn some attention in the shop,' announced Dan. 'We've started a list of those interested in coming along to the Christmas lunch, and there's eleven on it already.'

'And my Turkey and Tinsel in Tilldale fliers that I've posted through the village doors are working well, too,' Lily added. 'I've had nine interested and loads of enquiries coming in daily. My mobile's been buzzing.'

'That's great,' said Nikki.

'Oh, and six of them are definite,' added Lily. 'I've saved the names in my phone, so Dan, if you can add them to your list ...'

'He's making his list, and I bet he'll be checking it twice,' Andreas couldn't help himself chanting.

'Oh yes.' Dan ignored his partner's silly grin. 'I'll get on to that straight away. And Lily, keep me up to date on any future bookings, too. A definitive list is what we need.'

'Of course.'

Tonight was the night for the Turkey and Tinsel planning session. Cath had been feeling a touch unsettled about seeing Will again. He had definitely been lying low since the Paint-a-thon, and she still hadn't discovered what had happened last weekend between him and his daughter.

They were sat with glasses of mulled wine to hand around the large oak dining table at Lily's house: a beautifully converted barn, set on a side lane in Tilldale village. After joining in with the Paint-a-thon, Lily's parents had at last conceded that the supper group seemed to be a good thing for her, and agreed to let them use their home for tonight's planning meeting, whilst they headed off out to the theatre in Alnwick. They'd seen for themselves how many mince pies Lily had managed to produce that day before school for the care home carol singing. And they could tell how hard their daughter was working, juggling the restaurant weekend work whilst keeping up with her A-level studies. She was indeed a girl on a mission. A big baking, cheffing mission.

'Hmm, I wonder how many we'll have at the event in the end?' Nikki mused. 'Well, seventeen.' She'd done the maths. 'That's very doable for a big Christmas dinner, but it's bound to grow a bit more yet.' She glanced at her phone, slightly uneasy that she'd had to leave the boys home alone for the first time, with her eldest Hamish in charge.

Kev was off taking part in a local darts match, and the three boys were left for the next hour or two. Their mother for once was glad for the diversion of the Xbox and a family bag of Doritos to keep them occupied. Well, they'd had a healthy tea and done all their homework earlier, and she was only just down the road, she'd reasoned.

'Umm, I may just have added to those numbers ...' Cath gave a small cough and an apologetic smile. She'd just this afternoon received the email from Julie at the home. 'Hmm, well, kind of in a big way.'

Five sets of eyes were trained on her, with Dan piping up, '*What* have you done now, our Cath?'

'Well, remember we agreed to invite some from the care home in Kirkton.'

'Ah yes, of course.' Dan nodded.

'Well, I didn't think to limit numbers when I first mentioned it. Didn't think that'd be fair. But after the great success of our carols and mince pies afternoon, it seems rather a lot of residents would now like to come. Julie said some of the shyer souls have signed up too, after the fun of the sing-along and meeting us all. Well, it's run away with itself a bit.'

Cath took a bite of a Stilton-and-walnut-topped crostini, one from a selection of tasty treats Lily had prepared, plus a sip of Merlot, thus postponing the inevitable confession.

'Okay, so it's kind of snowballed,' Cath had to admit, the anxiety twisting in her gut. 'When I got the email from manager Julie today, they've already booked the date, and reserved transport for it. So, apparently there's a group of sixteen residents—' she said it quickly '—coming along, as well as two members of staff. So, I guess that's kind of doubled the numbers.' She'd in fact spent the last few hours worrying about the revised costs, which was way beyond the fundraising from the raffle and donations so far.

The others stared at her for a second or two.

'*Eighteen* extra people. Wow.' Nikki's eyes widened.

'I'm sorry, I never imagined …' Cath floundered. 'It seems our carolling doubled the numbers.'

'Oh, that *is* a lot more. Plus, the extras we're bound to get from the village from hereon in,' remarked Dan, as he processed the news.

'Ah, but look on the bright side, just think how much Mama used to love coming over for a Sunday lunch at ours,' Andreas reminisced, a gentle smile playing on his lips. 'It'd be a lovely tribute to her, to help the home and its residents, and after all they've done there for Mama …' His eyes glistened as he spoke.

'We're just spreading a little festive joy. It'll be fine. We'll work it out,' said Lily positively.

'It'll be manic … but great if we can manage to pull it off,' said Nikki.

'We can't really say no now, anyhow,' added Will. 'I'd hate

to let them down. That's the opposite of what we're trying to achieve.'

'I know, we can't disappoint anybody by capping numbers at this late stage. It's just being kind, giving our time, and doing a bit of cooking.' Cath was trying to convince herself as well as the others. 'And gosh, I know the extra numbers will make it more expensive, but I'm happy to shoulder the extra costs.' Cath didn't have a lot of cash to splash, but it was for such a good cause, she'd willingly dig in to her savings. She didn't need to be spending on a roast turkey dinner for herself this year, after all.

'No need for that, petal,' Andreas jumped in. 'We can share the expense. I can't complain at all about giving some of those elderly residents a nice day out. And I do believe inviting them may have been my idea in the first place.'

'Hey, I'm happy to help out financially, too,' Will added.

'And I've got some savings from my work.' Lily was ready to donate to the cause.

Cath felt a lump form in her throat. Their kindness, their team effort, catching her emotions. 'Oh, thank you so much. I've been so worried about telling you that.'

'And I'll raid the boys' piggy banks,' Nikki added with a chuckle. 'No, it is an expensive time of year, but seriously, me and Kev'll help share any extra costs.'

'With more donations yet to come in, and perhaps the rural grant, we'll hopefully not be too far short anyhow,' Dan reminded them.

'My Adam's still got his sponsored run to do next Sunday on the fifteenth, too,' added Cath, brimming with pride that he'd trained and committed to it. 'He's signed up for the "Christmas Bobble Hat Run" in Leeds, half marathon. I'm going to go down there to see him off, and cheer him back in.'

'How fantastic,' said Andreas. 'We were chatting about that, weren't we? Good for him.'

'Ah, that's great,' agreed Will.

'Brilliant.'

'Hmm, our bash'll definitely need a bit more co-ordination, being a bigger event now. The catering side of things especially …' Nikki let that sink in. 'And, we still haven't got those ovens up and running as yet. But Kev's still trying.'

They took a sip of wine in unison. That was a big issue, the hitch that might trip them all up. The planning session had just gone up a gear.

'Don't worry, I'm sure he'll find a way.' Nikki saw the panic in Cath's eyes.

'We still have a bit of time to sort them out. And everything else is in place,' Dan tried to reassure them.

In the lull thereafter, Cath caught Will's eye across the table and gave a tender smile. His own smile back seemed cautious, measured. It felt bittersweet to be acting normally, chatting as part of the group, whilst their emotional distance weighed so heavily inside of her. They'd been messaging, but he still hadn't opened up about what had happened with Sophie. Cath hadn't held him close, not properly, for what seemed like a long time, their night of passion becoming a memory. This holding back on his part was hurting her; but his situation was complex. Was he hurting too? *What are you thinking, my love?*

'Blimey, so there's at least thirty-five to now cater for. We're going to need a few extra turkeys to cook, aren't we?' Dan's words brought her back to the Christmas dinner dilemma.

Cath had already been doing the sums, and the shopping list.

'And we'll have a mountain of veggies to peel.' Nikki was thinking practically.

'And we'll need gallons of gravy.' Will was in the zone, too.

'And plenty of pigs-in-blankets,' added Andreas.

'Stacks of stuffing.' Dan picked up on the alliteration. It helped ease the mood.

They couldn't help but raise a smile at that point, as well as their glasses. 'In for a penny, in for a pound,' said Nikki, pulling out one of her nana's old phrases.

'Oh, and are we doing a pudding?' Lily asked. 'Or some kind of sweet treat for afterwards?'

'Piles of pudding,' quipped Nikki, which was followed by a group groan.

'That could be your domain, our budding young pastry chef, if you're happy to?' suggested Andreas, quirking an eyebrow.

'Seriously, we need a detailed event plan, gang. That'll be key to our success,' announced Cath. 'Allocation of tasks and responsibilities that we can do ahead of time, and then for the day itself.'

'Oh, get you.' Dan grinned. 'Getting all bossy and masterful there.' He gave her a wink.

She felt the heat of a blush, and daren't look at Will. *If only.* 'You can never be too organised.' The schoolteacher in her was back at the fore.

'And yeah, I'm happy to get a pudding sorted,' agreed Lily. 'A little something to rustle up for a mere thirty-five guests, lol.'

'Well then, before we get in full planning mode, top-ups, anyone?' Nikki passed the remaining bottle of red around the table. 'This calls for refreshments.'

'Mmm, these are good.' Will was tucking into a crostini topped with smoked salmon, cream cheese and chives.

'The brie and cranberry ones are lovely, too,' said Nikki.

'Simple but effective.' Lily gave a grin. 'I've been at school all day, so this was rather last-minute, I have to say. A quick trip to the village stores and I soon got sorted. Didn't I, guys?' The three of them shared a smile. 'And Andreas here has helped me create a festive foodie wreath board with crackers, grapes, olives, cheese and chutneys. I'll just fetch it through. It looks ace. I took a couple of photos, and I'm going to show the guys at the restaurant. It's such a fab, yet simple idea.'

'Oh, I can't wait to see it, Lils,' said Nikki.

Lily was soon back. 'Ta-dah!'

It looked amazing: a circle of savoury treats on a dark-green rocket base.

'Wow, how clever. Love it!' said Cath. 'It's almost too good to eat.'

'Almost …' Dan helped himself to some grapes and a chunk of blue cheese.

'Well then, twenty-second December is going to be one hell of a busy day,' observed Nikki.

'It is indeed, and the few days leading up to it, too, what with the food shop, all those veggies to peel,' said Cath, adding to herself, *and probably most of the next two and a half weeks building up to it.* The call to action had begun.

It was past ten o'clock, and time for the short walk home. Andreas and Dan were chatting away at the threshold to the barn, thanking Lily for her and her parents' hospitality. Will was loitering outside in the frosty night air, along with Cath and Nikki. Waiting to say their group goodbyes. Will should, in theory, head off in the opposite direction to Cath from Lily's place, but Cath was hoping he might offer to walk her home, wanting to claw back some intimacy between them.

Will seemed to be hanging back, but then of course, the lads stepped in, offering to see the two ladies home. It made sense geographically, but no sense at all to Cath's hopeful heart. The evening had been a busy one with lots of group chat, and all the event organisation, so there hadn't been much chance for personal talk.

'Night, then.'

'Night.' Leaving Lily's frost-dusted front garden, and back at the main street where they'd split off to go home, she and Will shared a careful hug. Cath could sense that something was off kilter. He had a heaviness about him. Will then gave the hint of a sigh as Cath turned to go, catching at her heart, before she then caught up with the others.

Chapter 24

Cath woke feeling S-H-I-T. She had the aches, a runny nose, sore throat. She knew she needed paracetamol, but hadn't the energy to get out of bed and get herself down the stairs to take it. The glass of water she'd had by the bed was almost empty, too. Drat.

It was the morning after the planning session, and this was no hangover. She'd actually been quite measured last night, what with Will and the to-do list. There was enough on her plate without feeling jaded. Argh, this was the last thing she needed. She had *sooo* much to do. With only a little over two weeks to go until the Tinsel and Turkey bash. Damn it, what if this was flu or something? How could she even cook or host a lunch for a group of fragile OAPs? She'd bloody well end up giving them a dose of flu as well as a Christmas dinner. No, no, no, no, no …

Even her eyeballs ached. She lay back on the sweaty pillows, with a sense of impending doom. She needed to rally, to get up, get on. But she was just so tired, so very tired. If she just closed her eyes for a bit …

The 'bit' was actually well over two and a half hours, and when she came to it was almost eleven a.m. She was meant to be finalising the event shopping list, she thought, and had two tutorials to prepare for this evening, but instead all she managed to do was to stagger to the bathroom, then creep downstairs, clinging on to the handrail like a ninety-year-old, find the paracetamol packet, fill her water glass, guzzle down two of the tablets and head back upstairs. She lay back on her pillows in relief, and thought to send a short message on the supper club WhatsApp. Her head was so damn fuzzy, she wasn't sure which jobs she had promised to do next from the to-do, or if she was indeed meant to be helping someone, somewhere with something. Also, she mused, if it was a touch of flu, and she was missing for too long, someone might possibly pop to check if she was all right.

Then, she gave in to the heady fuzz and shut her eyes again. There was no way her body could do anything else.

With her online tuition, the stress of the hall renovations, the impending festive event, her ongoing concerns about her relationship or not with Will, and a host of winter bugs doing the rounds, she'd been well and truly floored.

The sky, from the square of her window, was a watery grey-gold when she woke again, having missed lunchtime and the whole afternoon. She couldn't function properly, she knew, so managed to reach for her phone on the bedside table and message the two tutorials she had booked in for this evening. She hated to let her students down, but she'd reschedule as soon as she could. She also saw there was a message from Nikki:

Get well soon and shout if you need anything x

And from Andreas and Dan:

Let us know if we can help at all. Take care, honey xx

Feeling marginally better after that big dose of sleep, she put on her dressing gown and wandered downstairs to make a cup of tea, and perhaps try a small bowl of porridge, which was all she felt she might stomach. On her way to the kitchen something caught her eye on the doormat. She bent down to collect the post.

There was an envelope which might well be a Christmas card, but also, a pack of paracetamol, a box of Lemsip, four sachets of hot chocolate, and a message written on the back of a business card. The card was for The Cycle Man repair shop, and the note read, *Hope you're okay? Couldn't get an answer, so posted these. Get well soon. Call me. W x*

Aw, whatever was going on with Will, he did care.

Cath's snotty snuffle might well have been the head cold hitting, or something more emotional.

All her energy was used up getting to and from the kitchen. It was time to sleep it off again. To get back to the haven of her bed, now with a soothing mug of Lemsip by her side. And though she felt damned rotten physically, knowing Will was thinking of her gave her soul a much-needed boost.

Cath sent a thank-you message to Will the next morning. And after giving herself a quiet day, later that evening, feeling a bit wiped but generally much better, chanced a further text to him: *Do you fancy a short walk tomorrow? I think some fresh air might do me good.*

What she really wanted to do was to try and restore some of their closeness. This relationship was taking more than a little working on. Trying to seam together two separate lives after gutsful of heartbreak was never going to be easy, after all.

Yeah, okay, if you're sure. x came back soon afterwards.

Cath was more than sure. They needed to find a way back, and this might be a good place to start.

They'd agreed to take a stroll down by the river, the next day, squeezing in a quick half-hour after Will finished work and before it got dark.

Cath felt a little dizzy as he arrived at her door. She blamed it on the virus that was no doubt still in her system. But her emotions were all whizzed up like they'd been put in a blender.

'Hey, how are you?' He was there all handsome in his jeans, boots and a thick red-and-black-checked winter jacket. Even the bobble hat he had on looked sexy on him. 'You sure this isn't too soon? Should I be tucking you back up in bed?'

I wish ... ran through her mind. 'Hmm,' was all she actually responded, but she couldn't help the quirk of her eyebrow, which resulted in a cheeky smile from Will, as he realised what he'd just said. Hah, she wasn't even sure she could cope with the physicality of sex, right now. This walk might prove testing enough. There was still the echo of a viral ache throughout her system. 'Just a short walk will be fine,' she followed up.

Wrapped up warmly in her black winter woollen coat, pink-and-grey tartan scarf and pale-grey knitted woollen hat, with her walking boots on, they set off.

'Sounds like you've been floored by this bug.'

'Yeah, it was a nasty one. Like a forty-eight-hour thing. Thanks so much for your thoughtful gifts, too. They were great. The Lemsip was a godsend. Honestly, the first day, I couldn't keep awake, and I was aching all over.'

'Well, let's take it easy, hey. We needn't go far. You need to make sure you've got your strength back.'

'Yeah, and once I do, the Big Bash to-do list is waiting for me.'

'Remember we're all here to help, too.' Will gave her a serious look with his dark toffee eyes.

They walked slowly, taking it steady, which was just what Cath needed. Wisps of smoke were coming from the cottage chimneys they passed. Lights on, and as daylight began to dim, the coloured strands of festive lights and Christmas tree lights were twinkling at some windows. A sparkly reminder that time was racing on. Less than two weeks to go ... The monkey reminder system was back on her shoulder. But there'd be no racing today, just a steady stroll.

As they reached the grass pastures down beside the river the ground was a little uneven, Will took her hand, and she leaned in to him. She was a bit weaker than she'd realised, the virus taking it out of her; but feeling him close like this was all she'd been wanting to do for the past few weeks, if she were honest. They watched a pair of mallard ducks paddling through the chilly swirling winter waters. The willows and silver birch trees on the banks were now bare. The hoot of a cock pheasant echoed through the valley.

'How are the girls?' Cath asked, hitting his soft spot unwittingly.

'Ah, fine. Sophie's coming home again this weekend, actually.'

'Ah, that'll be nice.'

Will puffed out a small sigh. 'Things have been a bit tricky, to be honest. And I'm sorry if I was a bit off-hand there in the hall, on the painting day. It's just ... as we'd been getting on so well before that, me and you, I got the courage up to mention to Sophie that I'd been seeing someone. I made it clear that it was early days, but that we were becoming good friends. I tried to explain that it wasn't about replacing her mum. It didn't go down too well – put it that way.'

'Oh, crikey, Will. That must have been a tricky conversation.'

'God, Cath, sometimes I feel like I'm navigating a minefield. I don't want to hurt them, the girls. They've been through enough already but ... ah, I don't know. I thought maybe it was time to let them know ... about you. But it's just upset them. Of course, Sophie's now told Maddie. I had wanted to tell her myself, but it got out before I ever had the chance. So, she's being off with me now too. And I can see you getting caught up in it all, and that's not right, either. Sorry, I shouldn't be worrying you with all this stuff.'

'Yes, you should. It's fine. I want to help, Will. Even if it's just a matter of letting you air some things, that's okay.' She was pleased he was finally opening up, that he felt comfortable and safe enough to tell her the truth about his daughters. It meant that they were slowly but surely building that trust together. 'And, hey, it was bound to be a bit of a shock for Sophie.'

'I guess. I messaged once she'd got back to uni, saying I understood that she needed time and that I'm always there for her. Then, last night she finally called saying she wanted to come home again this weekend.'

'Well, that's good. She's probably been thinking things over. Hearing that must have been difficult for her.'

'Yeah, it must have been. Anyway, we'll see what this weekend holds ...'

They strolled on, still leaning in close, and decided to turn around before the arches of the stone bridge. The grey dusk was creeping in. And to be honest, that walk had probably been enough for Cath today. Blimey, she'd be needing to get her batteries charged up again, and quick. So much to do, so little time.

'You know, I really feel like I should be making more of an effort to make it Christmassy for the girls this year,' Will said. 'It looked so lovely and festive at the care home last week. The past two Christmases have been pretty dire, to be honest – both a bit of a write-off.'

'Well, that's only natural.'

'But I can't go on acting like The Grinch forever.'

Cath raised her eyebrows at that, giving an empathetic smile as she remembered the grumpy chap she'd met and reversed into in the supermarket car park all those months before, when she'd first arrived in the village.

'I feel like I've been making them miserable, too,' he confessed. 'We need a little sparkle back in our lives.'

Cath nodded, listening to Will speak, as they strolled on. They were still walking hand in hand, she noted, even though the ground was steadier here. This was Will's call, which steps he wanted to take with his girls, and his life, as he pondered how he might be able to once more discover some Christmas magic. Cath walked, nodding, smiling softly as he continued. Listening was as important as talking at times.

'Hmm, the Christmas tree must be still up in the loft. Jane bought a big John Lewis one, a few years back. It was a fake but a really good one. Looked real enough, and not a needle to have to hoover up.' He paused, remembering. 'That was always Jane's job – getting it all decorated. I'd probably go and make a right pig's ear of it, even if I did put it up.'

'Might provide some humour for the girls? The new-look Will-style tree …' Cath commented, with a gentle smile.

'Yeah, with some hanging bicycle parts: clips, a pedal or two? Inner tube for tinsel. But nah, seriously, I do want to do it right. I'd love the house to look festive when they walk in.'

'Okay, well, whenever you're thinking of doing it, let me know, and I can pop by and help you to decorate it. I love a bauble or two.'

'That'd be great, honestly. You're a star.'

'A Christmas star?'

They grinned at the festive puns.

'I'm picking Sophie up from her train, Saturday morning,' Will explained to Cath on a call on the Friday late morning. 'She's going to text me the time once it's booked. Maddie's coming up on Sunday too – a family gathering. So, let's do the Christmas tree this evening, so it's all ready for her and Maddie. If that's still okay with you?'

''Course it is.' Oh, it was lovely that he wanted her help with this, that he was beginning to share his thoughts with her. This felt like such a breakthrough.

'I might even open a nice bottle of red, and we can make a chilled night of it.'

'Sounds perfect.' Cath was looking forward to it. It was heart-warming to be included in Will's life, to be doing things together once more. Slowly, but surely.

'I've got the tree down. It's in the lounge.'

'Oh, have you been up in the loft by yourself?' Cath was concerned.

'Yep, it was fine. I kind of slid the tree box down slowly.'

'You should have waited 'til I got here,' she scolded, her tone caring.

'You get used to doing things by yourself. You just have to crack on with it most of the time.'

'I suppose so.' And she knew all about that, since starting a single life. The teetering stepladder moments, both physically and emotionally.

'There's a box of baubles, and a storage tub filled with all sorts of decorations – bits we've gathered over the years. I found a sack of tinsel up there, too.' Will led her into the lounge where he'd set it up; the tree on its stand but its branches still mostly upright and box-shaped. 'I'll go pour us that wine.'

It seemed like he might need a bit of Dutch courage to start. Christmas, with all its traditions and memories, was such an emotionally loaded time. Cath's heart went out to him. There'd been a whole host of memories, ready to ambush her, snagging at her heart, when she'd done her own tree.

Setting to work, she busied herself, gently pulling down and tweaking the fir branches from the bottom up to the top to shape the tree.

'Ah, that looks way better. How have you managed that?' Will came back in carrying two glasses filled with ruby-red wine.

'It just needed the branches adjusting. They fold back up to fit in the box.'

'Ri-ight.'

'It really wasn't your domain, was it?' Cath smiled.

'Nah.' And he took a breath, then gave a half-smile back. 'Lights first, I guess. I found two strands of fairy lights in with the tinsel.'

Cath nodded. 'Okay, let's test them out first. Where's the nearest socket?'

Will took out the tree lights, finding the plugs, and then tried them in turn. Both strands lit straight away. They were a warm white and softly glimmered; very pretty and tasteful.

Will couldn't stop his hand trembling as he took up a strand of lights. 'Jane must have done this three years ago, held these lights in her hands. The girls would have been so excited; they always liked to help her. Jeez, none of us had the slightest idea of what lay ahead.'

Cath lay a hand gently on his shaking lower arm. 'So, let's do it right for her.'

The words sank in; they were together in this. With the girls, of course. They needed to remember Jane, and do her proud. 'Here, unravel them slowly, and we can layer the tree.' Cath was kindly giving instructions, gently helping to pull him back to the present and the task in hand.

'Okay.' Will's voice was thick with emotion.

And they worked together, encasing the tree in even swirls of twinkling light.

Gold and silver baubles, and sparkly hanging stars came out next, and then they were sorting through the tub of all sorts. Oh, Jane had kept decorations that the girls had made at nursery – a red-painted hanging stocking, a glitter-encrusted pine cone on a string, and a Father Christmas figure that Will recognised, telling Cath with a tear in his eye that Maddie had bought it for them once she was old enough to save some pocket money. Their family life was here in festive mementos.

Will pulled out a small cone-shaped angel splattered with daubs of white paint with wings made from cardboard, stuck-on white tissue and tinsel. 'This one was made by Sophie,' he remembered, his voice somewhat hoarse, as he dangled the doll between his finger and thumb.

'It's really sweet.' Cath looked across at him. 'Will, are you okay? We can stop here if you like? There's plenty on the tree already.'

207

'It's okay. I'll be okay. It's just, well … Shit. It should be Jane doing this – she and the girls. It seems so cruel that they've had so much taken away.'

Cath nodded, her own eyes misting. She rested her hand on his shoulder for a few seconds. Hoping to show how very much she cared for him.

'Let's do the job properly.' Will stood up tall, sounding surer of himself again.

'Okay. Pass me another then; there's a nice branch to hang something on here.'

He passed her a hand-crafted glittery snowman.

They were so invested in their task they hadn't heard the footsteps coming up the front path. There was a brief knock on the door, but before Will had chance to go and answer it, it more or less opened immediately, and soon afterwards so did the lounge door.

'Hi-i! I'm home.' A young woman with long blonde hair strode in, the excited smile on her face dropping instantly as she took in the scenario before her.

'Dad? What's going on? Who the hell is *this*?'

Cath stood upright, still dangling the childish decoration before her. 'Hi,' was all she could manage, as the situation began to register. This really was not how she'd have wanted to be introduced to one of Will's daughters.

'Sophie, love! You're a day early? Or did I get that wrong?' Will's tone was puzzled.

'I thought I'd surprise you. My afternoon lecture was cancelled, thought I'd jump on the train and get home and keep you company, but, well, you're obviously not sitting here all lonely.' Sophie looked about her, taking in the Christmas tree, the decorations.

'What the hell is going on here, Dad? This was always Mum's thing.' Her eyes cast angrily over to Cath. 'Who is this woman? I suppose it's your new bit of fluff.'

'Uhm, Sophie, this is Cath. She's the woman I mentioned to you the other day, yes.' He sounded so damn awkward.

'You said you'd made a new friend, but jeez, Dad, what is this? She has no right to be getting all cosy here and putting up our bloody Christmas tree.' She sounded close to tears.

'I just wanted it to look nice for you and Maddie. To have something festive for you to come back home to,' Will floundered.

'Are you nuts? It's the last fucking thing I want to come home to. Some other woman in *our* house, doing the things that Mum should be doing. These are Mum's things. And mine and Maddie's. Nothing to do with *her*. It's been two years, Dad. She's only been gone two fucking years and you've already replaced her.' Anger and tears made his daughter's voice brittle.

'Sophie, that's not true. I could never … That's enough of the language, though. And don't be so rude to Cath. She's only helping me out.'

Cath felt like piggy in the middle. Perhaps they'd got this wrong, her and Will. Maybe it was all too soon for the girls anyhow. Father and daughter needed time alone to talk this through. It wasn't her place to stay. Cath was ready to pop on her shoes and grab her coat.

'I'm sorry this is upsetting for you, Sophie. I was just trying to give your dad a hand,' Cath tried to explain, as she gently placed the festive treasure she was still holding on to the arm of the sofa and gathered her things.

'Yeah, I bet you were.' His daughter's tone was razor-sharp.

This was not the time to try and make friendly pleasantries. 'Look, you two need some time together, to talk things over. I think I'd better go.'

'Yes, you had,' Sophie snapped, like a terrier at Cath's heels.

'Really, there's no need, Cath. She'll calm down in a minute,' Will intervened.

'I damn well won't. I'm not a toddler, Dad.'

'Well, you're bloody well behaving like one!'

Cath started making her way towards the door. It seemed wrong to say, 'Nice to meet you,' to Sophie, after the young woman's outburst, so she didn't. Cath could see how walking in on that 'cosy' scenario unexpectedly could hurt way too much. Emotions were riding high all round. So, instead, Cath said, 'Perhaps we can meet again sometime, Sophie,' in a calm enough tone to take some of the wind out of the young girl's sails.

The only reply she got to that was a huff.

She'd dealt with enough teenagers through her teaching and life to know it was time to exit calmly. And this wasn't just some stroppy, rude girl. This was a young woman struggling with the rawest of grief. It was time to let father and daughter work this out for themselves.

'I'll catch you soon, Will.'

'Bye, Cath. I'll call you. Thanks for your help.'

'No worries.'

As she closed the door gently in her wake, she heard, 'I can't believe you were that rude. Cath was only helping me out.'

'And I can't believe you've got some other woman here, doing the tree together like some bloody Christmas romcom, acting as though Mum never existed.'

Cath had a feeling the argument was going to roll on for some time. Will's thoughtful gesture of getting the Christmas tree ready as a lovely surprise to cheer his girls had just backfired spectacularly. But whatever had just gone on, Cath could see the situation for what it was – an explosion of grief.

Dammit, that was not how she'd have wanted meeting one of Will's girls to have gone at all. Yet, Cath could empathise with them all. She still felt as strongly for Will as ever, and she knew she'd be there for him just the same.

But if navigating the girls' grief was proving a minefield for Will, then she felt like they'd just stepped on a bloody bomb.

Chapter 25

A morning working in the shop was just the salve Cath needed, after that extremely difficult evening. She'd arrived home last night feeling frazzled, gutted for them all how things had turned out, and rather unsure as to how to best to help Will. The situation with his girls was delicate to say the least. And whilst she knew no one had done anything wrong, she couldn't help but feel like the bad guy in all this, the one who was stirring things up. She couldn't stop thinking about the hurt in poor Sophie's eyes as she'd walked in.

Cath'd messaged Will last night before going to bed, with a *Hope you are both okay. Not an easy situation for either of you. Sending love, C xx* All she'd got back was *xx*; Will was evidently finding the whole episode tough. Cath understood that sometimes words were just too hard to choose or voice.

And today she was helping the lads out by covering their shift until mid-afternoon. Andreas and Dan hardly took any time out for themselves, and with all the volunteering for the hall lately, even their precious Sunday afternoons had been filled. So, hearing they wanted to have a day in Newcastle this Saturday to do a bit of Christmas shopping, Cath had jumped right in and offered to mind the shop. She'd done it over a weekend back in the summer, plus the odd Sunday morning, and felt far more confident taking the reins nowadays.

She was there at seven-forty-five sharp, ready to open up, armed with the key and alarm codes they had left her. First up was sorting the morning newspapers and popping them on the shelves, then she'd check the fresh fruit and veg display was well topped up.

Her first customer of the day was Kenneth. 'Morning, Kenneth. Crikey, you're in early.' It was eight o'clock on the dot. Opening time.

'Didn't sleep so well. I don't know, I can nod off in the day just like that and at night, it's such a battle at times. I think I miss my Dot there next to me. Two in the bed was far more fun.' He gave a cheeky wink.

'I bet you're ready for a cup of tea, then?' Cath offered, knowing his routine after the last few shifts she'd done. 'Milk and two sugars?'

'That's my girl.' He took up his usual seat – the one that was next to the counter, ready for anyone in need of a rest and in want of a natter.

Cath went out to the back of the stores to pop the kettle on. She'd join the elderly gent in an early cuppa, as it was bound to get busy thereafter.

They just had time to talk about the latest cricket match in New Zealand, a bit of a belter apparently, with England all out for four hundred and twenty-seven, and about his concerns for his old cat, Tabitha, who was starting to lose her once-beautiful tortoiseshell fur and looking a bit patchy, before a flurry of early customers came in for their morning croissants, deli bakes and weekend treats. Andreas had left a tray filled with freshly baked goodies, with more supplies in the store area, knowing what Saturday mornings were like. As she served the pastries out, chatting to the customers as she went, the honey-oozing nutty baklava was calling her name. Perhaps she'd keep a slice back to go with her late-afternoon cup of coffee when she'd inevitably crash out ready to put her feet up, back at the cottage.

When there was finally a lull, Cath managed a sip of her now lukewarm tea. Kenneth was still in situ, looking very content. He'd been making conversation with those in the queue. It was like he was the shop's mascot. They all seemed to know him.

'Oh, Kenneth, by the way, have you heard about our Christmas lunch event on the twenty-second of December?' Cath asked.

'Oh yes, it all sounds rather wonderful. My name's already down. And I've been telling everybody about it.'

Cath spotted Dan's A4 list poking out from a shelf under the counter. She took it out and scanned the names. Yes, of course, there right at the top, in pride of place, was Kenneth. There were several names recorded under his, then the batch added as eighteen in total from the care home, and below those now a further one, two, three, four, five … six. Her maths teacher mind turned out a result in seconds, ooh, a total of forty-one so far, with just over a week to go! They had their work cut out, for sure. Her stress levels notched up. Tomorrow was Adam's charity run, and she was heading down to Leeds to support him. There really wasn't much time to get everything sorted and there was a lot of work still to be done.

It'd be fine. It was just more people to make happy, she thought, trying her best to turn her worry around. Seeing how much joy Kenneth got from his social time in the shop, it was easy to see how much good they'd be doing. Christmas was about giving – time, friendship, food, love and laughter – and about bringing people together. They were going to be doing that in bucketloads.

After Kenneth had left, an hour and a heapful of memories later, in came a smartly dressed lady, wearing a navy woollen coat over a black skirt, thick tights and a cream polo-neck woollen jumper.

'Oh, what's this about a festive lunch in the old school hall?'

She'd spotted the poster for the Turkey and Tinsel lunch in the window.

It soon came to light that she'd been a teacher at the village school in the Nineties. There had been two classrooms back in the day. This lady, who introduced herself as Janet – Mrs Jones – had taken the older children aged seven to nine. She'd taught everything bar PE and music, for which they had visiting teachers. It was small but so lovely, she remembered fondly. Memories of school plays and Christmas dinners, carol singing and fetes, fundraisers, tombolas and raffles. It had all happened there in the past. She was delighted to hear the hall was going to be given a new lease of life. Adding that she thought it would make a wonderful place to host their festive lunch.

'I'm don't live locally anymore,' Janet explained, 'just calling in on my way through to visit a friend in Kirkton, who's sadly not well. Thought I'd come the scenic route. But is there any way I can help at all?' she asked kindly.

Cath had to think on her feet. She spotted the book of raffle tickets there on the counter. 'Oh yes, thank you. We've launched a raffle to help the village hall funds. It's a pound a ticket. Five for a strip,' she added with confidence. It was all coming back from her school fundraiser days. 'There's a gorgeous hamper from the village stores with a bottle of fizz in.' The lads hadn't put it together as yet. She wasn't sure about the fizz being part of it. She was going to have to twist somebody's tanned Greek-Cypriot arm here.

'Lovely, I'll take ten pounds' worth.'

'Thank you so much. I'll just jot down your contact number. It's going to be drawn on the day of the festive lunch.' She took down the details, passing the lady two strips of five tickets. How marvellous.

'Oh, with all the chat, I'd forgotten! I've come in for two pieces of cake, and something for our lunch. It'll save dear Brenda having to cook.'

Cath recommended the large Mediterranean roast veg and feta quiche, which she knew Andreas had freshly baked this morning. He'd had an early start cooking before his shopping day. Janet then chose two slices of Dan's dark-chocolate orange cake to go with their morning coffee.

'Thank you. That all looks delicious.'

'It will be. I've tested them all over time.' Cath smiled. 'Well, I hope you have a lovely time with your friend, and that her health improves,' she added kindly. 'It's been lovely to chat. And I can picture the school in its heyday now with all those children chattering and dashing about.'

'Yes, it had a wonderful feel about it back then. It was a happy place. Perhaps I can bring in some old photographs. I'll have a look when I get home. I'm not often passing this way, but I could make a special trip and drop them here at the stores, I suppose.'

'Oh, that would be so kind, thank you. And if it's in time for the Christmas lunch, we could make a little noticeboard of memorabilia.' The idea popped up in Cath's head. 'A memory board, in fact.'

'That sounds a fabulous idea. I'll definitely have a hunt when I'm back at home.'

Cath could picture it. A big corkboard, pinned with old photos of the school, some of the children who'd once attended (there were indeed some ex-pupils coming along to the lunch), perhaps of the groups that once used it as the village hall, too. They could add the best of the old posters they'd spotted when they'd first visited the hall. And, she could ask around in the village, see if anyone else had any keepsakes or photos. There must be several people locally who'd been pupils at the school. A heartwarming display of memorabilia, indeed.

Another job for the ever-growing list, she realised, but it shouldn't be hard to organise.

As Janet left the stores, a message pinged on Cath's phone. It was from Will.

Thanks for your message. We'll be fine, I'm sure. It may just take a little while. Tricky times. x

She hoped this wouldn't make him shut her out once more, she really wanted to talk to him properly. She had limited experience of grief, her parents being of an age where it had been expected, even if it still hurt, but plenty of experience of motherhood. Perhaps she might be able to help, or at least listen and let Will get some of his concerns off his chest.

Two minds must have been thinking alike as his new message read: *Can we meet up later, once Sophie has got her train back? Be good to talk. x*

Yes, of course, do you want to come around to mine for say 7.30 p.m.? x Cath replied. Oh, wasn't Sophie meant to be staying until tomorrow? With Maddie coming up then, too. Had all those plans now changed? It wasn't a good sign.

A couple of customers came in and Cath had to refocus on the task in hand, but she couldn't help thinking about their meet-up this evening.

Whilst she was looking forward to seeing Will, and the chance to talk through some of the difficult issues he was facing, hoping to help him put some perspective on that, there was a feeling of misgiving growing inside Cath. He'd been known to cool things relationship-wise in the past. Would this give him yet another reason to pull away?

She'd already let the terrier, Shirley – who was home alone in the upstairs flat – out for a quick wee at lunchtime. But after finishing at the shop at four p.m. as instructed, and finding herself at a loose end, Cath took her doggie friend home with her, intending to head out for a walk. Perhaps clear her mind a little of those cobwebs of confusion, before seeing Will. It might go well later, and her fears might be unfounded, she reminded herself. But whatever she was about to face, the canine company

216

and a country stroll would definitely do her good.

Blue skies above, with mere puffs of cloud drifting on a crisp, chill breeze. Trees silvered and winter bare. December in Northumberland could be stunning. You just needed to wrap up warm and get outside. Nature and a blast of air did the rest.

Cath had driven the short distance from the village, with Shirley sat in the passenger footwell, to the nearby woods where she and Will had walked just those few weeks before. Back then there had been the promise of a relationship, the excitement of it all to come; now she knew his body, if only for one night, but having tasted his love – both physical and mental, she was greedy for more. She wanted to be together, be a couple, not be afraid to love but to shout it from the rooftops.

'Come on then, Shirley, let's go.'

She gave her furry white pal a pat, and clipped on her lead, ready to walk the two-mile track around the woodland. Small birds darted above, blue and coal tits, and gold, yellow and green finches. The winter birds were looking for berries and bugs in the woods, keeping themselves going through the harder months.

Looking at the bare branches around her, she saw that the nature of living, be it human or tree, was change and loss, but then ultimately renewal. Yes, the woods were stripped back now, but still beautiful. *Stripped back* – that was exactly how she'd felt after her marriage had broken down. Being hurt and betrayed left you vulnerable, of course it did. But you either shied away and lived a quiet, perhaps lonelier life, or you could risk the bloody lot, and go and grab life by the balls. Spring would come again, even if the buds, the seeds, were hidden for now.

Cath had found herself again, here in Tilldale, and discovered a fantastic new group of friends to support her whilst doing so. Her supper club team were her tribe. Renewal, that was the key – that, and hope. She thought of Will, of being in his arms, their tender kiss bringing them together on that fateful supper club night back in the autumn. She'd thought back then that making the move to find out if he felt the same would be the hard bit, but knowing now that he did, the impact and complications of his family's grief were proving to be even harder. She'd found the courage to love again, in the midst of all that pain. She just prayed that Will could too.

Chapter 26

'Hey, come on in.'

Will was standing at her cottage door. His breath misting in the cold evening air. There was an unmistakable air of sorrow about him.

Cath went to give him a hug. He must have had a difficult day of it, after all, with the drama and emotions of last night and saying goodbye to his daughter today. But even with her arms around him there was a distance, a stiffness about him.

She led the way through the short hallway to the kitchen. The safest port of call, she figured. 'Shall I make a coffee? Or would you rather a wine, perhaps?'

'Just a coffee, will be fine. Thank you.'

He took a seat at the table.

As she filled the kettle, got mugs, took out the cafetiere, Cath felt an uneasy prickle of fear. This wasn't going to be some cosy chat about how Sophie had been apologetic later on, how it had all seemed better in the morning. Nor how it was bloody awful between father and daughter but he just needed a big hug, a mug of coffee and Cath's support. It no longer felt like they were a team.

'How are you? And how's Sophie?' She put it out there, prepared to face the music, even of it wasn't a tune she wanted to hear.

'We're okay.' There was a heavy pause, then Will restarted. 'I've got to think of the girls in all of this. They are the most important thing, Cath.'

'Of course they are, I understand that.' Cath nodded. She didn't want to push him but felt she needed to say more. 'But Will, you've got to find a way forward for you, too. The girls will have been shocked, I understand that. And of course it'll be hard for them to get their heads around. But I really don't think Jane would have wanted you to be sad and on your own forever …'

Will gave her a sharp look.

Cath stopped there, worried she'd overstepped. She could see that he was trapped in his grief. Torn apart by guilt. How could he possibly take the blame for such a cruel trick of fate, for the randomness of cells going wrong, and the heartache of a deadly cancer? She wished she could make him see.

He still hadn't said any more.

'Whatever the girls think now,' Cath continued, filling the silence, 'surely they're old enough, and love you enough, to not want to see you unhappy for the rest of your days. You of all people should know how short life is—'

'It's not as simple as that.' He cut her short. The look he gave her was cold.

Cath tensed. She didn't want to give up on this budding relationship but, more than that, she didn't want this wonderful man in front of her to give up on himself. She could see the pain etched on his face and knew that pushing everyone away and feeling guilty for any glimmer of happiness he felt was not the answer – and wasn't fair – but she didn't know how to get through to him.

'Will, my love, you need to find a life for you.' Everything was easier to say, to see, from the outside. She knew this made sense, and that his blaming himself did not. But how did she make him realise that?

'The girls are my life.' The shutters were closed, along with the light in his eyes. Their beautiful sparkle diminished.

My darling Will. How can I help you? Those were the words that were loud and clear in her mind. But she knew that, right now, they wouldn't be heard.

'I'm sorry to upset you, Cath. I should have known better than to start getting involved with anyone. I don't want to hurt Sophie and Maddie any more than they have been. We need to call it a day on this.' He gestured vaguely between them. 'Let's just go back to being friends.' His decision was made.

Cath felt her stomach churn, followed by a deep dull ache within.

She had tried so hard to get him to realise that in all of this, he needed to think of himself as well as his girls. That he needed to find a life after loss. But Will couldn't hear it.

Chapter 27

'Come on, Adam!' Cath cheered him on, her voice loud and clear above the noisy chatter and clapping of the crowd, gathered near the finishing line in Roundhay Park.

The race had started and finished just down the road from their old house. It had felt strange coming back this way, driving the streets she knew so well. She even took a small detour to look at their not-so-long-ago family home – the smart brick-built suburban semi. Someone else's car, and life, parked there now. It didn't hurt anywhere near as much as she thought it would. And it certainly didn't feel like home anymore. A chapter closed. A drive-by salute.

Adam was red-faced and sweaty, and his run had slowed to an achy-looking jog. The race number, pinned to his T-shirt, askew. He'd heard her above the noise and looked up with a big grin that she captured on her phone camera. 'Well done! You're nearly there,' she cheered him on proudly. And she squeezed herself back from the front row of onlookers, managing to zigzag past the gathering of supporters and already-finished runners wrapped in foil blankets, to keep up with him for the last few metres.

He was in, after a few last wobbly steps over the line, and he took himself to one side, knees bent, hanging from the waist and panting like a dog. Another click of the camera, the pics might come in handy for his charity donation page. And she was there giving him a big hug, no matter how sweaty he was.

'Amazing. Well done, son.'

'Urgh, thanks.' His breath was short and sharp, making it hard to speak.

'Here, have some of that water they've given you.' She took the plastic bottle he was clutching, that they'd thrust at him along with a medal at the finish line, and unscrewed it for him.

He glugged it down, puffed out another big breath, and then stood up taller. 'Cheers, Mum.'

'You did fantastic.' Looking at him with a huge sense of maternal pride, relief and awe, Cath knew that Adam was definitely back on track.

She stayed into the early evening.

Adam had taken a quick shower back at his flat, whilst Cath made them a coffee, and they then went into the city centre on the bus, which was easier than trying to drive in and park. With her son now 'famished', they found a cute little Italian bistro. All red-and-white-checked tablecloths, and huge bowls of carbonara and penne arrabbiata pasta, with a shared garlic pizza. Leeds centre was looking extremely festive, with colourful Christmas lights strung across the streets, and shops with windows adorned with bows and baubles, and inside, packed to the hilt with gifts galore. She ought to make the most of this shopping opportunity, she'd mused, but other than quickly nipping into John Lewis and picking up a couple of Molton Brown bubble baths for her nieces, and a bracelet she thought would suit Susie, she'd found the sheer number of people, the city buzz, a little overwhelming. Tilldale Village Stores felt a comforting world away.

Tilldale, home … *Will.* Her heart dipped. She was glad she'd had this busy day already planned. Last night's announcement from Will had hit her like a truck, if she were honest. She'd had to be super-careful driving down this morning, forcing herself to concentrate on the traffic, emotions and a poor night's sleep making her brain feel fuzzy. She did feel a bit more herself now, her 'Mum Day' refocusing her. Life, as always, went on. It had to.

Back at the flat, they said their goodbyes, with big thanks to Adam who, at the last count, had raised almost four hundred pounds for the village hall funds. Yippee! With Trev and Steph stepping up to donate a hefty chunk and many of his uni and bar workmates getting on board too. Then there were the Christmas wishes as – oh, and it still hurt a little – they'd be missing the big day together. She'd brought down his wrapped gifts and left them here with him. It had felt very flat handing them over earlier. They shared a farewell hug, with an extra squeeze for good measure. It was time to get back in that Mini and head up the A1.

Her day with Adam complete, her brain moved on to the next priority – turkey and tinsel. Cath's head was once again swimming with her to-do list.

There was one mammoth lunch to organise.

With only one week to go, the community lunch event was steamrolling in. Cath's list was getting checked off, but there was one very crucial thing not as yet sorted. Kev was still on the case, but Cath was feeling extremely uneasy about it.

When she got back after her long journey from Leeds, she spotted a missed call from Nikki, plus a couple of others from an unknown number, and a voicemail message. It was from Nikki: 'Hi, Cath. Umm, hope you're okay? Sorry, forgot it was Adam's run and you're away down there. Hope it went well. Ahm, have you heard from my Kev, yet? He's been trying to get hold of you.'

Her friend's tone was definitely *iffy*. Something was up. Kev had news. And it didn't sound good. It had to be something to do with the oven thermostats that he'd been trying to source. Without those, there were no cookers, and without cookers there was nowhere to roast the turkeys. And without turkeys there's no Christmas dinner and no event. She felt a horrid black swirl of anxiety inside.

She called Nikki back straight away. She knew it was late, almost ten p.m., and she was knackered, but she had to find out what it was they were dealing with.

'Hi, are you back?' Nikki's voice came down the line.

'Yes thanks, it was a good day. Adam did great. So hey, what's this that Kev's been trying to call me about?' Cath was straight in there. 'You've got me worried.'

'Ahm, yeah, well, Kev's right here.' She sounded cagey. 'I'll let him explain.'

Kev came on and began to tell Cath how he'd tried every online site he could think of for parts. He'd even called up a couple of scrap merchants and the recycling centre, and drawn a blank. The ovens and their parts were seemingly obsolete. He still hadn't given up, however, but he wanted to warn her that it wasn't looking good.

Cath went quiet, racking her brain for a solution. There was only a week to go. Forty-one people were booked in. She couldn't cancel this event, not now, not when everyone was so looking forward to it, and all the helpers who'd given their time and been so invested in it, the kind donations. But she also knew that they couldn't afford two new industrial ovens, even if they could get them delivered and set up in time.

'Okay, well, thanks for letting me know, Kev.' She tried to sound calm – it wasn't Kev's fault after all – but her voice trailed.

'Hey, I'll keep trying for you, pet. I'll not give up yet. I'm just sorry I couldn't sort it out sooner for you all.' He was trying his best to sound cheery.

'Thanks, Kev.'

'Well then, here's Nikki back for you.'

'Sorry, hon. Not great news, is it.'

'I'm gutted,' Cath confessed, disappointment and weariness biting hard. 'What the hell are we going to do now?'

'I'm really not sure.'

'Well, it's a Sunday night and it's late. There's nothing much we can do right now. Let's sleep on it.'

'Yeah, we'll chat tomorrow.'

'Bye, Niks.'

Dammit. She'd only wanted to do something special for the community and its elderly, after all. Something to put a smile on their faces, fill their tummies and give them a wonderful day to remember. Okay, so she might have got carried away with the grand lunch scheme, and doubled the numbers with the care home guests coming. Taking on an ancient village hall that the real *DIY SOS* might have baulked at. And now she was worried she'd got their hopes up just to let them down.

Why on earth hadn't they gone with something smaller, more practical? Had she wanted it to be here in Tilldale Village Hall so much that she'd been blinkered? Then instead of having to cancel at this late stage, which now looked inevitable, they'd still have something lovely to enjoy. Was it too much to ask that it might go off smoothly?

Shitty McBloody Shitface.

Two days on, still no closer to an oven solution and with only five days to go, the local Brownies from Kirkton were at the hall doing a mega washing-up session of the crockery and cutlery to freshen it ready for the big day, plus a general tidy-up, including a quick sweep of the steps and entrance area. The organiser had heard about the event and the fundraising, and said their local group would love to get involved. Cath was worried all their hard work might be for nothing. Although at least they would all get their 'charity' badges and the leader had also mooted interest in using the hall's facilities for projects in the future.

She knew she had to rip the plaster off and be brave enough to make the decision and call the lunch event off, or perhaps at least scale it down to a coffee, tea and mince pies social. But she couldn't help wonder if there was any other way she could still make this work. Yesterday morning, she'd even phoned about a church hall venue in Kirkton to see if they could use that instead. She'd heard it had a reasonable kitchen facility, but it was already booked out – of course it was. Clutching at straws, she'd even wondered if the supper group might all cook one turkey and some roasties at home, and then carry it all over to the hall. But they couldn't risk the food hygiene not being right, especially considering the guests were nearly all OAPs.

An hour later and the dinner plates and knives and forks were sparkling, the children happy to have achieved their tasks, and Cath was thanking them all, and waving as she saw them out. Brown Owl saying again that she'd be in touch, as they had a craft idea that might work well for the lunch day, too. They'd been busy making robins and reindeer, apparently.

'That sounds lovely, and thanks so much.' Cath saw them out to their minibus, with her head mentally in her hands, whilst smiling all the while. She couldn't put off making a decision for much longer.

It was when she was locking up, just a few minutes later, that a call came in. She recognised that mobile number: Kevin.

He didn't speak, but was singing as she answered: 'Driving home for Christmas' in the style of Chris Rea, his voice getting louder. Honestly, he sounded odd and possibly slightly mad. There was a low hum like a vehicle engine noise, too. Was he pocket-dialling or something? Until she listened to the words, as he sang on, 'I've got thermostats in my van.'

'Kev?'

'Halloo, halloo. Yep, it's me, and I've made a mercy mission all the way down to Belper.'

'Belper? That's way down in Derbyshire.' Hundreds of miles away.

'It is indeed. Guess who's just sourced two still-in-working-order thermostats for your old school ovens?'

'You haven't?!' Cath was incredulous.

'I bloody well have, and I'll make sure they're fitted and tested out, tonight. How's that for you?' He sounded delighted with himself. And so he bloody well should be.

'That's unbelievably brilliant. But how?'

'Found an old primary school that had closed a while back. Traced and got chatting to the old caretaker online. Same cookers and everything, still working. They've no use for them as the old school's going to be knocked down and cleared soon for local housing. He's pulled a few strings, and I've given a donation to St Giles Hospice and Bob's your uncle. The internet is a wonderful thing!'

'You're a wonderful thing! Amazing, I think I've just fallen in love with you, Kev.'

'Hah, well, don't tell our Nikki that.' He chuckled.

'Wow, that really is just the best news. Well, safe rest of your journey, and thanks so much.' She still couldn't quite believe it.

'No worries, pet. And I'll message when I get them all fixed up later.'

'You're a star, Kevin.'

'Hah, I feel like one of the three wise men bearing gifts.'

'You are. You bloody well are.'

Chapter 28

It was time to deck the halls.

It was on! The ovens were in full working order. And today was the eve of the big Christmas lunch. Cath decided to get in early and make a good start before the agreed meeting time of ten a.m.

Time for setting up the tables, adding festive decorations and making the hall look the part. And this evening they were to have a Supper Club Peel-a-thon – a veggie-peeling extravaganza, no doubt accompanied by a cheeky glass of red. Though they had to keep focused as tomorrow was a BIG DAY. A team effort was required, and thank heavens her fabulous supper clubbers, plus a couple more recruits, were to be at her side.

But, and she couldn't help but sigh, even that would be difficult now. After seeing Will last weekend, and the devastating news that they couldn't carry on a romantic relationship for the sake of his girls, he'd shut her out, and that was that. How the hell could they go back to being just friends? How could she 'un-remember' the taste of his lips on hers, the feel of his gentle, sensual touch? And, right now with Christmas nearly here, every bloody film and advert on the telly seemed to show couples all loved up, too.

It would be so hard seeing him today, having to pretend that none of that had happened. But she'd do it for the sake of the supper club, and tomorrow, for the sake of the event. She felt like crumpling down in a heap, to be quite honest, but they'd got this far, and she'd damn well make sure this festive event was a success.

She had the hall's old door key to hand. Teacher Janet and so many others must have held that key over the years. The heavy oak door creaked open. Once inside, she walked through the reception area and then into the corridor. It was still chilly and slightly gloomy in there, so she found the switch panel and popped on some lights. She dropped down her bag that was crammed full of decorations and supplies. Time to turn on the central heating and bring this place back to life, ready for its big day tomorrow.

It was rather nice, having a few moments to herself in the old hall. Cath took a slow breath and gazed around her at the fresh paintwork, the buffed parquet flooring. She thought of the kitchen cookers about to spring back to life – thank heavens for Kev and his incredible journey, and all the hard work her fantastic supper club had put in up until now. Tomorrow was going to be another full-on day but she was sure they could, and would, pull it off; she had a good feeling on this.

The troops soon arrived armed with bags of vegetables, Christmas decs, extra oven trays and pans from their own kitchens, cleaning materials with Nikki, Lily with a stack of tea towels and a big smile, and Dan and Andreas having come straight from closing up the shop. Her wonderful gang, and whatever happened next – and personally, with her and Will – she knew she'd have them by her side. Then the man himself arrived, Will, ready to do his bit to help set up – and oh, seeing him as he walked in tugged so hard on Cath's worn and weary heart.

As they set about freshening up the school's pots and pans, ready for the big peel, they were joined by plumber Gemma in the kitchen.

'Hi, guys, I'm here to change that leaky kitchen tap. The new one I ordered has finally come in.'

'Ah, that's brilliant,' said Cath. 'Thank you.' They'd have managed with the old tap for tomorrow, but a brand-new one that didn't constantly drip would be so much better.

With the tap fixed, and some of the kitchen prep done, a tea break was due, with a custard cream or two – care of Dan who'd grabbed a pack from the shop's shelves as he left. Lily popped the kettle on, and made mugs of strong builder's style tea for them all. Gemma reappeared, after making a quick check on her new loo pan in the gents, which was 'working a dream', and the group propped themselves against the kitchen units for a quick breather and a brew. 'Well, that's me done,' confirmed Gemma, swiping back a wisp of auburn hair that had escaped her bandana-style headband. She took a gulp of her tea. 'Thanks for that. Hits the spot.' She nodded at brew provider Lily.

'Thank you so much for all your work,' said Cath.

'How much do we owe you for coming out and the parts?' asked Dan.

'Ah, no worries, it's not a problem. It was just the tap and a bit of my time today. I'm more than happy to help out, if it means we get this hall up and running again.'

'If you're sure? That's so very kind.' Cath didn't want to leave her out of pocket.

'I was one of the last pupils here at the school, you know,' Gemma told them wistfully. 'It'll be lovely to see it used again.'

'Ah really, that's amazing,' said Lily.

'In fact, would you like to come along tomorrow afternoon?' It was the least they could do, thought Cath. 'Come for the festive lunch, and there'll be plenty of mince pies and shortbread, too. Oh, and if you have any photos of your school days here that you don't mind sharing, we've started a board of memories.'

'That sounds lovely. I'll certainly have a look for some pictures, and I'll bring them in with me. Thank you.'

'Perfect. And thanks so much again.' Cath was delighted.

After their refreshments, and with Gemma now departed,

Team Supper Club were ready to crack on. Firstly, Cath and Nikki went to check that the kitchen ovens and hob were still working fine, and after several minutes coming up to temperature. All was in good order there. Phew! Check – one more thing ticked off Cath's list. It was actually getting shorter at last.

And it was time to go and 'deck the halls'. This place was going to look like the Christmas Fairy had been and had a ball, Cath decided. Trestle tables were taken out, wiped over, and set in two long rows. Seats were unstacked from the stage and placed in lines – eleven each side, making twenty-two per table. Forty-four in all. They'd figured a couple of spares wouldn't go amiss. Wow, there was a whole lot of cooking to do.

She brought in Reggie's attic box of paper chains and festive garlands from the car, and Will and Dan were already scaling stepladders and fixing them up. Cath had bought some silver tinsel strands, and found some cheap Christmas crackers in a last-minute sale at the supermarket, to decorate the tables with. She'd also been snipping off festive sprigs in her back garden where a holly bush was laden with bold red berries, and had made another trip to the woods, which brought back some moving memories of her and Will, trimming a few of the smaller branches from the plentiful pine trees there, to decorate the centre of the long trestle tables along with the windowsills.

Cutlery was set for each place, with a holly-patterned paper napkin and a red-and-silver cracker on top. The cutlery and crockery were all now stacked ready after the Brownies's washing-up session, plus they'd found several jugs, sugar bowls and tea sets saved from the old Tilldale Village Women's Institute group. All from the Aladdin's cave of the old kitchen storeroom.

With the school, the WI and lots more going on, Tilldale must have been vibrant back in the day, but like many rural villages, the community had grown smaller. Farming had become more mechanised, and generally people looked to the towns and cities for work. Only last week at the care home, Reggie had told

Cath that when he was a young boy, there used to be a tailor, a blacksmith, four pubs and two shops in the village. How life had changed. And yet, here they were, their supper club team, forging a new community, repurposing the hall and the old school once again, and most importantly helping to bring people back together.

Before they left, later this evening, they needed to be sure that everything was in order. Yes, the heating had creaked back to life; the hall had to be warm enough ready for tomorrow. The last thing they needed were chilly pensioners.

And boy, that had been some food haul yesterday. Cath and Nikki, Dan and Will, travelling in two cars for carriage space. With Andreas left minding the village stores, and Lily at school, Cath was in charge of the humungous shopping list, and off they set. It was like supermarket sweep at the local farm shop for the veggies: a huge sack of Maris Piper potatoes, stacks of sprouts, piles of parsnips, a bag of onions, and a container full of carrots. And the butcher in Kirkton had put aside four extra-large turkeys, at what must have been a specially reduced price for them, as the bill was less than Cath had anticipated. He told them he'd heard about what they were doing for the local community and was merely doing his bit to help. Dan also collected some huge packs of pork sausage meat ready for his stuffing balls, to be made to his special secret recipe at home. Chipolata sausages and streaky bacon for the pigs-in-blankets were on the butcher list too – a Christmas dinner must.

Next was a pit stop at the supermarket for kitchen foil, gravy granules, cranberry sauce galore and several bottles of celebratory sherry.

It felt rather odd and strangely domestic doing the 'weekly shop' (okay, a very strange week) along with Will. The pair of them chatting about which cranberry sauce looked the best, at one point. It also felt rather sad that they'd never get to do these kinds of things together as a couple. Sometimes, it was the little everyday domestic details that she'd missed since her relationship with Trevor ended, just chatting about what you fancied for tea, or whether to try a new shower gel for a change.

The lad on the till nearly had a heart attack when he saw the volumes that were loaded on his conveyor belt. And getting the supplies back into the trolley, in some kind of manageable order, took the skills of a speedy and logical mathematician – luckily, they had one to hand. As keeper of the kitty, Cath had taken a deep breath as she paid the various bills, with a big chunk coming out of her own credit card account – hopefully to be refunded from the still incoming donations and possibly the grant, if accepted, in the next few weeks.

Back to this evening, they needed to be sure they had all the food supplies ready and as organised as they could be to create the best ever supper club feast – Turkey and Tinsel in Tilldale–style. With pots, pans, knives and vegetable peelers lined up and ready for action, the Peel-a-thon was about to begin.

Lily set up Will's speaker on the kitchen windowsill, linking her phone and putting on a lively mix with a good beat. Cath was happy to go with the flow. Apparently, it was the soundtrack she used when out jogging to keep the motion flowing.

'Glass of red at this point, anyone?' Dan pulled a bottle and a corkscrew out of his shopping bag.

'Why not?' Nikki gave a grin.

'Okay, but just the one glass. We need clear heads tomorrow, chaps,' warned Cath. *Nothing* was going to wreck this event now.

'We know,' the supper clubbers answered, having had the lecture already. They all laughed. The camaraderie was clear in the kitchen, as the stainless-steel sink was part-filled with water, and piles of potatoes were put in. No leaky tap to annoy them either, hurrah! Peelers at the ready and they were off, with Will, Nikki and Lily removing the skins. Andreas chopping them to size, and Cath popping them into pans, production-line style.

Sprouts, carrots and parsnips were dispatched in a similar

manner. The biggest problem was deciding how much was enough. Seven bags of parsnips, eight, nine …? They decided to overestimate. More was definitely better than ending up short and coming a cropper at the serving-out stage.

Andreas began to sing out, 'Can you peel it?' in the style of The Jacksons's 'Can You Feel It' track. Then he asked Lily to put the song on loud on Spotify. The whole group were soon swaying, dancing and singing along to the catchy chorus, 'Can you peel it? Can you peel it? Can you pee-eel it?' Cath couldn't help but grin. What a crazy lot they were. Crazy to even think they could pull this off, more like. But hey, they were nearly there.

Lily pulled her arms out of the sink, waving her fingers jelly-jazz-hands style. 'Look, my hands are all white and wrinkling, eugh.'

'A sign of hard work and water osmosis,' said Will drily. 'You'll be fine. They'll be back to normal in a few minutes.'

'Well, I think that's the lot done,' said Cath, scanning the mass of very large, filled pots and pans. How the hell would they fit all of those on the hob at once? A wave of panic hit her. Her brain then answering her own question: potatoes first, then they'd go into the hot oven trays. The parsnips could roast, too. So, it was only the sprouts and carrots to boil together at the last. Cath's mind was still, not surprisingly, on overload. Before she left this evening, she'd jot down a cooking timings list. 'Well done, guys, and thank you all so much for your amazing help today.'

'And tomorrow, we go again,' observed Dan wryly.

'We do indeed,' added his partner. 'But it'll be more than worth it.'

'Aw, I can't wait to see all their happy faces,' said Nikki. 'The hall looks so lovely.'

'And all those empty plates,' added Lily.

With the rest of the fresh food safely stored in the hall's big refrigerator and cold store, (apart from a turkey each that Cath and Andreas had in their respective fridges at home to bring across first thing; they'd found they couldn't actually fit all four of the mega-birds into the school's fridge!) that was a huge chunk of the preparation done.

After the frenetic start to the evening, it had all come together well, other than Cath trying hard not to brush close to Will as they worked. At one point, she'd looked up and spotted him glancing at her with a pensive expression on his face. She knew she had to respect and abide by his decision, and yes, in some ways, she could understand it but she still wondered how much was guilt, and pressure from his girls, with his own feelings being put on the back burner for the sake of his family. She suppressed a sigh as she held his gaze for a second and gave a gentle, poignant smile. She found she couldn't be angry with him. She told herself to stay focused. Today and tomorrow were going to be hectic enough; no need to tangle them up with added emotion, too.

She had to remind herself that there was much to be thankful for in this new life of hers. There was no way she was losing this precious friendship group over their romantic split.

It was time for Cath to go home, grab an easy snack, collapse in the bath and then get some rest. Tomorrow was a big old day.

She took a while to doze off, though shattered, and instead of counting sheep, she found herself mentally checking her Christmas event to-do list, filled with a sense of nervous anticipation.

Chapter 29

Today was the day! The Turkey and Tinsel lunch had snowballed in a matter of weeks. What had started out as a small village lunch for perhaps a dozen elderly people, so she'd thought, had transformed into a gathering for the lonely, the elderly from the environs, *and* two minibuses filled with many of the residents from the Kirkton Care Home.

Well, Cath mused, Andreas's mother, Maria, had sadly never got her 'great escape' lunch, but this group were about to get theirs. And, amidst all the angst about getting a festive feast ready in time, plus renovating a village hall, remembering what it was all for warmed Cath's heart. In the old school kitchen full of pots, pans, veggies ready to boil and four turkeys basting, she just needed to hold on to this thought and know why it was all so very worthwhile.

Andreas was there beside her. They had decided that the pair of them would lead the cheffing – two was enough. It was no good having too many cooks in the kitchen. They seemed to be able to work well together: Andreas now lifting out one of the massive turkeys ready to baste it, while Cath was setting out her parboiled Maris Piper potatoes in goose fat–oiled oven trays, giving each other space and support at just the right time.

With her aproned friend (yes, the naked statue was out again!) bursting into a cheery blast of 'Four turkey's basting, three pans a boiling, two chefs a singing, and a Christmas pudding in a Christmas tree,' in the style of 'The Twelve Days of Christmas', Cath couldn't help but laugh.

And of course, it wasn't just the two of them; they had their trusty supper club support gang here, the others currently busy in the hall. Plus, a team of willing (and *not quite* so willing – in the case of Nikki's three boys) extras.

The turkeys had been in for almost three hours, as she and Andreas had got there super-early. The extra-large school ovens had coped with the four big turkeys; she was working on at least twelve portions per bird. And there was also room in the ovens for the trays of roast potatoes to go in for the last hour of cooking, which would work, in a rota at least. Once the birds were out and left to rest, the pigs-in-blankets – which Lily and Nikki had spent the last half hour making – rolling streaky bacon strips around mini sausages – would pop in along with trays of Dan's Special Stuffing Balls. All was prepared on that front, and Cath had a list of timings next to her, so nothing would be forgotten. It would be a full-on day of cooking, for sure.

Next, Andreas was on with the sprouts, having decided not to boil them. He was halving them, ready to pan-fry in a Mediterranean twist, with olive oil and pine nuts – he couldn't help himself.

Cath had baulked at making a pudding for so many people on top of the mountainous work involved for the roast dinner, and had originally intended on buying several packs of shop-bought mince pies, but baking queen Lily wasn't having any of it. Happy to organise that extra job herself, she'd brought in tubs of homemade spiced-cinnamon shortbread and mince pies galore, with Lily and her mum apparently having been in their element.

On top of that, yesterday, Lily's restaurant had got wind of her charity activity and encouraged her to cook some extra batches of mince pies there using their large ovens, and even providing the ingredients. The restaurant team had helped her to get creative with them, and there were stars and snowy icing-sugar tops, and some with a touch of cheeky Alnwick rum in.

Dan had also taken a phone call at the shop, just three days ago, and the wonderful young lady from Rachel's Pudding Pantry – part of a farm near to Kirkton – had stepped in, having heard of this kind community event through the care home, offering to donate a dozen of their large homemade Christmas puddings. She'd even come through and dropped them off at the shop. Her Granny Ruth had recently had some respite care at the home, and was now thankfully recovering well back at home. Cath had had a tear in her eye at all that. This event was proving to be a real collaboration.

With a blob of thick double cream, the delicious puddings and pies would be sure to go down a real festive treat. A truly scrumptious end to the meal.

Lily popped some Christmassy music on, and the preparations went up a notch. She headed into the storeroom to find some large platters to later display her biscuits and mince pies on. Nikki was still in the hall putting the final touches to the tables, now spacing the small white dishes of cranberry sauce at equal intervals. The Brownies craft session had come up trumps with a small handmade gift of a robin on a log or a stick reindeer with bobbly red nose, now set out for each guest. Freshening up the sprigs of holly, small branches of pine, along with fir cones, on the windowsills and tables, Nikki looked around her and was delighted with the decoration.

Back in the kitchen, Dan had joined them and was now laying out trays of long-sliced parsnips ready to roast, adding oil and a drizzle of honey and thyme leaves. And Cath found herself humming away to 'It's Beginning to Look a Lot Like Christmas' along with Michael Bublé, as she popped the water heater on to boil and set out rows of the WI cups and saucers ready to offer a welcome drink on arrival. Will was stood at the functional stainless-steel sink doing a spell of washing up.

After finishing her task, Cath thought she'd go and help dry up, and was at the draining area next to Will. It was the closest the pair of them had been since the supermarket, and Cath could almost feel electric strobes coming off him. She couldn't be sure if they were trying to send her away, or draw her back in. Whatever was going on between them was damn unsettling. She really didn't know what to say to him, so merely gave a small smile and kept herself busy.

Right, she needed to stop thinking about Will in that way. It wasn't to be. They'd tried and failed. He'd made that clear, after all. She had more pressing things to be getting on with today, she reminded herself.

Their stalemate hadn't gone unnoticed, however.

'What's up with you two?' Nikki whispered, cornering Cath in the storeroom a few minutes later. 'I notice Mr Frosty is back, and it's not the bloody snowman I'm talking about.'

Cath couldn't hold back her sigh. 'Ah, things have got a bit complicated, Niks. I'll explain more later … This really isn't the right time.'

'Okay, of course … but hey, I'm here if you need. Or, if you need me to kick someone's butt.' She gave a kung fu–style gesture with her foot and raised her hands, nearly knocking over a shelf of crockery. 'Oops.'

Cath laughed softly and then said, 'Well, I think we need to get back to the very important task in hand.' It was already ten-thirty. Their VIP guests would be arriving for teas and coffees at twelve o'clock. With dinner to be served at one p.m. sharp. A small yawn escaped her. She'd been up since five-thirty. But other than having one quick coffee break, there was no time to rest on their laurels.

In less than an hour, the turkeys would need to be taken out to rest and kept warm under foil, whilst the veggies were roasted or boiled, and the stuffing and pigs-in-blankets cooked. Dan and Andreas had offered to do the honours carving the meat, and then there'd need to be a production line to serve up. Cath actually had a tick list for each stage, to help stop her mind exploding with angst!

If it all came together as planned, it would indeed be a veritable feast. She'd keep her fingers crossed, that is if they weren't so bloody busy. The supper club team only had to finish cooking, and then serve what was essentially a roast dinner for, what, a mere *forty-odd* people. What could possibly go wrong?

Chapter 30

Where the hell had the time gone? Cath glanced at her watch. It was ten to twelve already. Her pulse rate zoomed. Dan had just nipped off in his car to go and collect Kenneth. They still had the final veggies and stuffing to cook. And very soon, they'd be busy making welcome teas and coffees for all. The big WI water urn was on, and she now filled a couple of kettles as backup. Lily and Nikki were busy plating up the shortbread, deciding to keep the mince pies as an option for dessert along with the Christmas pudding. If they put too much out, they figured their guests might get carried away and not have enough room for lunch. Cath watched as Nikki popped a holly leaf sprig onto each platter as decoration.

'They look perfect, ladies.' She gave a nervous smile.

It was exciting and scary all at once.

One of Nikki's sons popped a head through the kitchen door at that point. 'We're here!'

'Ah, good timing, boys.' Nikki beamed proudly. She'd been working hard to persuade them that helping out in the community was a good thing. Adding that it might also help to show Santa that they'd been nice this year and not at all naughty, thus upping the gift stakes.

Good old Kev had turned up with them, too. He'd already done more than enough with all the electrical work, but here he was ready to help once more. All four now appearing in the kitchen doorway dressed in festive jumpers. Kev as Father Christmas – he'd even put on red trousers – and the youngsters as elves. Nikki's eyes widened; she'd evidently had no idea.

'Well, we thought we'd better dress the part,' said Kev with a grin. 'It was Hamish's idea, actually. Thought it might cheer the guests up. And hey, it might let us off the hook a bit, if we happen to spill anything, being amateurs at this.'

They were under instruction from Nikki to help with the waiting on, serving the Christmas lunches to their guests at the table, and little did they know it, but any other jobs she might find for them before and after that important task.

Veronica arrived along with Dorothy ready to lend a hand, as well as have a nosy at how it had all finally come together, of course. 'Best foot forward, troops,' Veronica chanted, after thanking them for all their efforts. With a reassurance that after the event her hall committee would help with the tidying up, and check over the hall for them the next day. It seemed they might be ready to retake the reins, and carry the hall and its new life forwards for the village. And that filled Cath with so much hope and joy.

'Thank you.'

So, the moment of reckoning was here. Could they successfully pull off the big Turkey and Tinsel Christmas community lunch? The team were here, the hall was ready, the food was looking fantastic, and the guests about to arrive. *Deep breath, Cath.*

First to arrive, at five to twelve, was dear old Kenneth, of course.

'Oh, I haven't set foot in the old school in years.' He looked about him as he entered the corridor. 'Bit barer than I remembered.' But then, as he got to the hall, his face lit up. 'My, you've done wonders in here. And it looks so very Christmassy. The

243

tables all decorated so prettily.'

Cath felt herself brimming with pride. She looked around her with fresh eyes, remembering that day when they'd walked into the murky old hall with its dust and cobwebs. She'd been so busy in the kitchen this morning that she'd hardly had chance to notice the transformation. The fresh cream walls and navy trim. The tables laid out so beautifully. And Lily had even dashed home, saying they just *had* to have a Christmas tree, and that they had a spare one up in the loft. Her mum had bought a new bigger and better version for this year. Lily had carried it back down the street, set it up in the hall, and she and Nikki had done some last-minute baubling, whilst warbling merrily making up their own words to 'Oh, Christmas Tree'.

An elderly couple arrived next. It was Mary and John, Cath's neighbours. They had a brief chat as she ushered them through to join Kenneth in the hall.

And then, 'Hiya. Oh, how fantastic is this? What a great job you've all done.' A grinning Gemma popped her head round the hall's open doorway.

She'd called in with her school photos. A wonderful selection, showing the old classrooms, sports day out on the field, and the stage in action for the Christmas nativity show with Gemma dressed as a shepherd in a beige tabard with traditional tea-towel and curtain-tie-back headgear.

'That's brilliant. I'll add them to the board, if that's okay? Thank you so much. And I hope you're staying for the lunch?'

'Of course.'

Cath was delighted that Gemma had remembered. She added the pictures to the large pinboard she'd discovered in one of the old classrooms and had moved into the hall. The Christmas nativity scene took pride of place at the top. Then suddenly she thought to move the board into the corridor, just before the doors to the hall, so everyone had to pass by it. It would make a lovely welcome for everyone to the refurbished 'school' village hall, as well as being a good talking point, stirring old memories. And today was all about making some new magical memories, too. Oh, and perhaps if they took some pictures today, and everyone was happy with that, they could add those to the board too. History in the making!

Just as she and Gemma had shifted the picture board into place, the first minibus arrived from the care home. Out came Reggie, Vera, Betty, Joan, Phillip and several more, along with Linda and another carer to help with the group outing. They were all very much looking forward to their big day out.

Will went out to greet them, and Cath watched as he helped a frail old lady down off the bus. He could help others, Cath mused, but in his smothering loss, he really didn't know how to help himself. How could she be cross with him, when she just felt so very sad that he ... *they* might be about to miss out on so much, their wonderful second chance.

The new arrivals loved looking at the memory board, making comments, some mentioning that they had been pupils at the school back in the day and some that their children had been there, too.

'I think you were in the year above me, Reg,' said one of the gents. 'Always up to mischief, you were.'

'That'll be about right,' said carer Linda with a smile.

'Oh, I bet you'll have some wonderful stories from back then,' said Cath, delighted that her idea was already sparking conversations and connections. 'And, if anyone has any photos or any mementos they'd like to add to the board, that would be wonderful. We'd like to keep this memory board here in the hall for the future.'

Coats and hats were taken off and placed on the original school wrought-iron pegs, which had been moved up to an adult height several years ago.

'Come on through,' Cath announced to the newcomers. 'And welcome to the newly refurbished Tilldale Village Hall.'

245

'My, it looks wonderful in here,' said Joan, taking in the main hall and the festive displays all around her. 'All these marvellous decorations too, the streamers, garlands, and look, a gorgeous Christmas tree.'

Others began arriving from the village, including Terry, known as Mr T, who was one of Nikki's elderly cleaning clients, Agnes and her husband Frank, and Sheila from 'the lane', a single lady whom Cath had met from her times working in the shop.

It was time for coffee, chat and some buttery-spiced shortbread.

Dinner was now cooked, the mammoth feat accomplished, and the guests were now seated and waiting with anticipation.

In the kitchen, they needed some kind of dishing out and serving system. A production line was duly set up with Dan plating the sliced meat, Andreas on the roasties and parsnips, Lily on sprouts and carrots, and Cath adding the sausage wrap, stuffing and a good splash of hot, tasty gravy from one of the many jugs she'd just filled – it felt like she'd created gallons of the stuff using the meat juices and her trusty Bisto granules!

Waiting in the wings were the serving team. Will had been nominated as maître d', co-ordinating Nikki plus her three boys in elf jumpers, much to everyone's amusement, and Kevin in the Santa suit! Well, that had raised some smiles from the gathering.

Crackers had been pulled and party hats, in varying colours, were on at all angles. Chatter and laughter filled the room as the guests waited in anticipation for their hopefully delicious Christmas dinner.

Cath was in the throes of the hottest flush of her life, but kept on going. Plate one, two and three were done, looking very tasty indeed. Ready to be whisked away by elf Angus, who had managed to tear himself away from his Xbox for the day, and was actually wearing a smile above his elf top. Nikki was next, followed by Hamish, Scott and Kev. Two more helpers, from the care home staff, stood in line ready to take plates out, too. Bless them. Operation Turkey and Tinsel was a go! It was feeling very much like one of the *MasterChef* challenges.

Forty-one plates, fifteen minutes later and bloody hell, phew, they'd done it! Mission accomplished.

'Wow, well done, Team Supper Club!' Cath felt so happy. 'And jeez, does anyone have a large glass of wine at the ready?'

Cath stood for a few relieved seconds.

That was until Kev came back in looking serious. Cath's heart sank. Had they missed something? Was someone without a lunch? But Kev reassured her, saying that Reggie and his friends from the home were insisting the hard workers all came through and joined them for lunch. Cath hadn't even considered that. In all the planning, and with all that hard work to do, it hadn't crossed their minds what they might have for lunch themselves.

'Umm, right, well, Dan, Andreas, is there enough meat and veg for another six portions, do you think? Anyone feeling peckish?'

'Bloody ravenous. I thought you'd never ask,' said Andreas.

'And yes, there's plenty left,' confirmed Dan.

Cath felt the stirrings of a rumble in her tummy too, breakfast being one slice of toast and many moons ago.

Nikki nodded enthusiastically, and as Cath caught her eye, she remembered her fabulous elves and Mr Kevin Christmas himself, adding, 'Oh, and for Kev and the boys, of course.'

'Okay, we're on. Lily, petal, could you fetch us ten more plates from the crockery stack please? And it's back to your dishing-up stations, everyone.' Nikki whizzed off to the hall with Will, to set up some more seats, squeezing them in at the ends of the two trestle rows.

And as the helpers came through five minutes later, each carrying a cutlery set and a very tasty-looking plate of turkey dinner, the crowd started clapping and gave a huge 'Hurrah!' Reggie even got to his feet to give them a standing ovation, with Kenneth following suit.

As the last one in, Cath took a moment to pause at the doorway and gaze around the hall. She was so glad they'd made the extra effort with the strings of Reggie's paper chains looped along the cream-painted walls, the tinsel and foliage decorating the tables, the windowsills, with Lily's tree sparkling by the stage. And there, gathered at the old school trestle tables, she saw a host of party-hatted, smiling and cheering faces. A group of people making new friends, enjoying good food, and happily munching away as they chatted among themselves. Hah, it was like their supper club on steroids.

Nikki had joined her family at the end of one row of tables, and Cath took the last seat – ooh, right opposite Will – along with Lily and the lads. Which happened to be just a few seats down from Reggie and his care home crew.

'Absolutely marvellous,' said Reggie, who was sat back down, raising his sherry glass to them all, with that twinkle very much back in his eye.

Spare party crackers were passed down. The team soon sporting red and green paper crowns, and reading out the corny jokes.

'Okay, I've got one. How much did Santa pay for his sleigh?' called out Dan.

The ritual pause, as a few paper-hatted heads were shaken in thought.

'Nothing, it was on the house.'

Several chuckles were heard.

'Right, here's a good one,' said Will. 'What do donkeys send out near Christmas?'

'Mule-tide greetings.'

Giggles and groans came from the gathering. Cath was so pleased to see Will relaxed and having fun and couldn't help but catch his eye, and she gave a smile. His smile back was so damned beautiful, it hurt.

The food was indeed scrumptious. Cath tucked into tender turkey and luscious gravy. The veggies were tasty and not over-done – incredible considering the amount they'd had to boil and bake. She had to admit, they'd made a fine job of it.

Andreas gave a big thumbs-up across the table. 'I'd say we smashed that cooking, guys.'

'Yeah, we absolutely slayed it,' Lily chipped in with her teen slang.

'Sleighed it, more like. As in Santa's carriage …' Dan was harking back to his cracker-style jokes.

The conversation buzzing around their end of the table included several from the care home, or at least the ones who could hear them well enough. Some were merely smiling and munching contentedly, and that was fine too. Betty remembered one Christmas when her daughter was at the school and was a donkey in the school play, right in this very hall. She was the back of the creature and her friend the front. They'd got in a bit of a tangle at one point and ended up in each half at different ends of the stage, with her daughter Emily's head hilariously peeking out to sing from mid-donkey-torso. Other tales and memories were shared too.

These were magical moments not to miss, and Cath discreetly nipped off to fetch some sheets of A4 paper and some pens she'd spotted in the old school office, asking the lunch guests to jot down their memories of the place. More mementos for her precious board. Hamish, Angus and Scott swiftly devoured their food and were soon up again checking the guests were okay, and topping up glasses of water from the WI jugs. They seemed to actually (*incredibly* according to Nikki later) be enjoying their new role waiting. The old and young were getting on so well.

Nikki caught Cath's eye across the room, and pointed at her children, her mouth open. She then came over to join her. 'Well, I need to put these boys' new skills to good use at home. I'm going to make damned sure I get waited on now and again, and put my feet up!' She gave a grin. 'Good job, boys,' she called across the room, and the look of pride that spread across her face was wonderful to see.

Back in the kitchen once more, Lily set about making a quick reviving brew for their gang. The supper clubbers had brought back some of the empty plates with meals finished so far, and snatched a few minutes to chat.

'Well, I think we can count that as a real success.' Andreas grinned, his brow lightly beaded with sweat.

'Yeah, great teamwork, gang,' added Dan.

'Whoa, that was even more work than Saveur's kitchen on a full service. Been great experience though,' said Lily.

'I think most of the guests are very happy.' Will gave a small sigh, yet was smiling, as he leaned back against the kitchen surface.

'Only one complaint as far as I know,' added Nikki. 'That there wasn't enough gravy, but Angus was onto it like a shot, and found a little jug to pour some extra in for them.'

'Oh, and one old guy said the sprouts were too hard … mind you, it looked like his false teeth were on the move, so he'd probably need them pureed.' Kev chuckled.

'Aw, bless him,' said Lily. 'I've been chatting with lots of them about the school. One old chap was a pupil here over sixty-five years ago, and remembers having his school dinners right here. Says the quality has shot up today. He shared fond memories of the treacle sponge and custard, mind you. So, I hope my mince pies and the Christmas puddings come up to scratch.'

'On that note, I suppose we'd better drink up, and finish collecting the dirty dishes in. Ready for round two,' said Will.

'And we all want some figgy pudding …' Andreas started singing to jolly them along.

'Oh, don't start that again.' Dan pulled a face. 'The oldies from the home will be asking us to do carols next.'

'Well, it wouldn't be so bad, would it?' said Nikki.

'Maybe I'll go and set up my speaker in the hall with some Christmas tunes,' suggested Dan. He'd brought along some of his old DJ'ing gear just in case; it was just outside in their car. 'Dan D Groove at your service.' He doffed a pretend baseball cap.

'That'll add to the entertainment, and perhaps take the pressure off us lot needing to sing. But hey,' he conceded, 'one round of "Jingle Bells" and a "We Wish You a Merry Christmas" before the guests head off home might be sweet.'

'Yeah, I think we should do that,' Cath agreed. 'A few carols before home time. It'd be a lovely way to close the event.'

They needed to serve pudding before they could draw the raffle. Many of the guests had seen the lads' bountiful hamper prize displayed on the stage front, plus a new offering, with landlord Bill from The Star kindly donating a voucher for 'A Meal for Two with a Bottle of House Wine'. And after several requests, Lily ended up selling even more tickets whilst the gathering was served dessert.

Cath had warmed dozens of mince pies and heated the special Granny Ruth Christmas puddings. She was with Andreas ready to dish them out with a generous dollop of thick cream.

'I think I'd better make sure there're enough pots of tea on the go for any guests who want to have another cuppa, too.' Lily was acting as chief tea-maid.

'I'll sort some jugs of coffee out, too. The WI stuff has come in really handy,' said Will.

'Oh yeah, one of the old ladies here was on the original WI committee. She told me how they used to have coffee mornings, bake sales, village fetes and all sorts back in the day. They had to join forces with the Kirkton group, which are still going, when unfortunately the numbers here got too small,' Lily added.

'Bet this place was a hive of activity once. It's nice to think it's being used again,' commented Dan.

Out in the hall, more memories were stirring with Reggie now thinking back to the tea dances that were held here in the school hall as it was then, back in the Fifties, soon after the Second World War. When they were all full of hope for the future. He and his pretty Elsie swirling and twirling to the music.

Suddenly, Reggie was up on his feet and with a twinkle in his eye. 'Maestro,' he called over to Dan, who was now behind the decks, 'do you have any Fifties music? A little "Rock Around the Clock" perhaps, to get things going?'

Dan did a Spotify check and linked his phone to the speaker. 'Here we go.'

The first bars rang out jauntily.

Without his dear Elsie, Reggie gestured his arm towards the elderly lady from the village who'd been sat beside him. 'Mavis, would you care to join me?'

'Of course.' She stood up and brushed herself down, shaking mince pie crumbs from her skirt, before taking his age-weathered hand.

'Just take it steady, you two,' Linda, the care home assistant, warned gently despite the smile on her face. 'No jiving! We don't need any trips to A&E today.'

Reggie just gave a cheeky wink. 'No promises.'

The two of them claimed a space on the wooden parquet flooring in front of the stage, and did a slow-style jive with a few gentle twirls. Lily dashed out to the kitchen, telling Andreas and Cath to come on through. This was a moment not to be missed for sure. The end of the hall soon turned into a makeshift dance floor, as Dan and Andreas moved two of the top trestle tables out of the way to allow others to join in. Soon other couples and singles came to dance, or clap, as they watched or joined the spectacle, and tunes were called out as requests. The guests were soon swaying gently to the lyrical notes of 'Put Your Head on My Shoulder' by Paul Anka. Reggie's face was warm and tender, enjoying the moment, yet no doubt remembering his Elsie, too.

And then the track changed to an Elvis classic, 'Can't Help Falling in Love'. Even Andreas and Dan moved to the dance floor and began to waltz along together to this.

Cath hadn't meant to, but at the chorus, she caught Will's eye across the room, and her heart lurched. Oh my, she'd never meant to fall in love with him. She'd been trying hard to mend her already broken heart from her failed marriage. But oh, how she'd love to dance with him to this, to feel Will's arms around her once more. She dropped her gaze as a huge lump lodged in her throat, and she swiftly forced herself to move, starting to collect up dessert bowls, escaping to the kitchen once more, where she wiped a stray tear from her eye.

Despite her personal circumstances, Cath reminded herself that the impromptu dancing and the old-fashioned music, with the guests so obviously enjoying themselves this afternoon, was heartwarming and lovely to see. It made all the planning, the work, digging into their own savings so worthwhile.

As she began to wash the dishes, with a huge pile yet to do stacked beside her, outside a flutter of white began to fall gently beyond the windowpanes. And for a while, no one had noticed that it had started to snow.

The snow swirled and whirled silently, stunningly, along with the dancing.

It was Will who first noticed it from the main hall. The white flakes catching his eye as his gaze wandered from the happy scene before him, catching his breath as the Everly Brothers's 'All I Have to Do Is Dream' came on, stirring a memory of him and Jane. He'd tried to steady himself by staring out of the window.

It was almost four p.m., and around the time they'd thought to wrap the event up, anyhow. An early winter dusk was pulling in, and with the tricky addition of snow to deal with, Will thought to alert the team to the weather conditions.

'Oh, the minibuses are here!' Linda called out just then. 'It's a few minutes early, as Julie heard of the change in the forecast,' she explained to Andreas, adding louder for the benefit of all, 'And yes, the snow is already here, so we need to get you all home safe and sound.'

There was a mumbling of agreement, and the dancing slowed

as Dan turned down the volume on the music, followed by the sounds of several chairs scraping from amongst the non-dancing guests. Coats were gathered, loo trips made, with a flurry of activity much like the snow that kept on falling.

'Oh, Dan, we'd better offer to take Kenneth, and Agnes and Frank home safely then, too,' said Andreas. 'Our car's outside, anyhow. And then I'll come straight back again for another group of passengers. Don't want anyone trying to walk far in this, or to get stuck in the lanes in the snow.' Veronica, who'd reappeared with Dorothy for a cuppa and a mince pie later on – both being mightily impressed by the event – offered to taxi too, so a shuttle convoy was organised.

Gemma, who'd stayed for the duration and loved every minute, also volunteered to help see the guests out to the vehicles. The journeys weren't far at all, but it would be wise to tackle the country lanes now before the snow began to settle.

'Thanks, everyone,' said Cath.

'And we'll give anyone who has to walk back up the village a helping hand. The paths may be a touch slippery,' offered Kev, kindly. 'Me and the young elves here will gladly see you back.' Eyebrows were raised by those elfish-dressed youths, but they didn't complain. They'd actually had a good day in all, and were delighted when some of the folk there gave them a few pound coins as a Christmas tip for their hard work.

With preparations on the go for leaving, Nikki and Lily swiftly gathered together the clubbers for an impromptu carol-singing finale, starting with 'Jingle Bells' as coats and hats were put on, and a jovial rendition of 'We Wish You a Merry Christmas' as Zimmer frames and sticks were gathered up. The guests were then ready for home, with a supper club member or carer helping them make their way to the exit. The corridor now alive and echoing with sentiments such as 'Thanks', 'That was marvellous', 'Best bloomin' day I've had in years', 'Grand food', along with a host of smiles and waves.

Reggie paused before leaving the hall to catch up with Cath. 'It's been a wonderful afternoon, thank you.'

'You're very welcome, Reggie. It's been lovely watching everyone enjoy themselves.'

'You've all worked so very hard. Us old folk appreciate it very much.' He gave a warm smile, before adding, 'Oh, and I cannot think of a better person to take care of my Cheviot Cottage than you, dear Cath.'

'Oh, that's so nice to hear, Reggie. I'll be sure to look after her.' She felt a bit choked up.

Reggie leaned towards her, his own eyes a little misty, and they shared a heartfelt hug. 'Merry Christmas, Cath.'

'Merry Christmas, Reggie.'

And she led her elderly friend out to the care home's minibus, guiding his arm gently as he walked gingerly down the snow-dusted path. 'Your carriage awaits, sir.'

He gave her a wink as he turned to board the vehicle, his eyes filled with a cheeky, if moist, sparkle. She'd bet he'd been a right character back in the day. In fact, she realised, he still was now.

The remaining minibus was loaded carefully, with the driver and carers helping each traveller to their seat in turn. Then, it set off with a toot-toot, smiling faces, and a host of time-worn hands waving at the steamed-up windows. The supper club group stood on the hall's threshold waving back with flecks of snow drifting down on them.

With the lads, including Will, then on 'snow patrol' taxi and escorting home duties, the lasses set about the immense task of clearing up. There was no automatic dishwasher in the hall, so it was over to good old elbow grease. Music back on, with some cheery Christmas tunes to help them on their way, a sink full of hot soapy water in front of Cath, and Nikki and Lily with tea towels to hand, and they were off, chatting happily about the events of the day.

Almost an hour later, the crockery and cutlery, jugs and glasses were restacked on the storeroom shelves. Ready for any further events to come, with Veronica, Dorothy and the hall committee very much back on board.

With a little TLC, a lot of effort, including an amazing electrician who literally went the extra miles, plumber Gemma and the central heating engineer, the place had worked wonderfully. Cath had even taken a couple of photos of the Christmas party for the village newsletter and Facebook page, hoping to get the hall noticed, today's lunch being a showcase for how it might be used.

Soon afterwards, the 'snow patrol' group returned.

'Wow, you're almost sorted in here,' Dan commented, taking in the cleared kitchen zone.

'Yep, the dream team have washed up and put away.' Cath stifled a yawn, the long day seeping into her bones. But still, she felt happy.

There was only the hall to sweep and hoover. Trestle tables to wipe, fold and stack away. The decorations to gather together, and the tree to take back to Lily's. Fatigue was biting hard, but they decided to finish the job today, and leave the hall spick and span, and ready for its next purpose. There was already talk, on the grapevine, about some evening classes starting in to the new year. And a new booking system had been advertised on the hall's relaunched website. Hurrah! Their mission had been achieved and more.

Cath, Nikki, Lily, Andreas, Will and Dan were stood in the now empty hall.

'Woo-hoo! We did it!' Lily gave a smile.

'And we pulled it off with some aplomb.' Dan grinned.

'With DJ Dan D Groove on the decks,' said Andreas.

'And the Christmas choir.'

'Team Supper Club,' summed up Will.

'The very best team, and I couldn't have done any of this without you lot,' said Cath. And she meant the lunch event *and* her new second chance at life. 'Good job, gang.' She smiled at her supper club tribe – such a mix of personalities and ages that worked in perfect harmony.

They gave each other high-fives, and hugs, even she and Will – and that felt oh so lovely and fragile and she didn't want it to stop – before Cath turned off the lights, one by one, and then closed the hall's double doors, and went out through the corridor to lock the main door to the building.

Outside, the snow had stopped and was lying like a frosty-white carpet beneath their feet.

'Ah, time for a hot bath and a long lie-down.' Cath sighed, as the group gathered before going their separate ways. 'Thanks again, everyone. You've been brilliant.'

'Yeah, big thanks to you all,' said Andreas. 'It's been good to give something back today. And so lovely to see the residents from Mama's care home enjoying their day out.'

'It had a real party atmosphere, didn't it?' said Nikki.

'Catch up soon, everyone. We need to organise a Christmas drink together at the least,' suggested Dan.

'Sounds a plan.' Nikki smiled. 'Right, I'd better get back home to my lot. They've worked hard today. I think it'll be a pizza takeaway for tea. As long as Kev can make it out to Kirkton in the pickup in the snow.'

They were ready to head off in their different directions.

Cath's and Will's eyes met once again. Holding on for a few heartfelt seconds.

And then Cath turned to go, on her own, the short walk down the street to her cottage, and she couldn't help but feel a little subdued after all the excitement of the past few weeks. The fresh snow scrunched softly under her boots, in the silvered-indigo dusk of the December early evening. A white magical blanket had settled so prettily over branches and shrubs in the gardens that she passed. Lights were on in the houses, and Christmas trees twinkled behind the glass windowpanes.

As she strolled on, passing John and Mary's cottage, nestled next to hers, the smile returned to Cath's face thinking how the team had made it such a success. Her fabulous, generous supper club gang. They'd only gone and pulled it off, warming the hearts, tummies and souls of so many in their community.

Chapter 31

In the sanctuary of her cottage home, too tired even to make a cup of tea for herself, Cath headed straight upstairs, and ran a deep, hot bubbly bath. Boy, that was some day! She couldn't wait to take off her turkey-and-gravy-scented clothes, peel her slightly sweaty – she had to admit – socks from her aching feet and soak herself in the suds, like the many dishes she'd just washed.

She checked the water temperature, and then dived in, sinking down into the hot pool. Aah, it was *soooo* good, breathing in spiced-orange-scented perfumed popping bubbles, and letting the warmth wash over her.

All that planning, all that work. It had been hard, and a bit expensive, even with the fund-raising raffle and various donations, but she didn't begrudge a penny of it. Seeing those party-hatted smiling faces today, the many empty plates, hearing the stories of the hall, the games of charades and the impromptu dancing had all been wonderful. But lying there, the event over, Cath felt a little lost all of a sudden. What now? What next for her?

She'd had so much to keep her mind busy the last few weeks. It was like she'd put her own hopes and dreams on hold whilst she'd organised all this – and that was fine. But reality was now about to hit.

All those people she and the supper club gang had brought together today, that had been so lovely, but suddenly it seemed in stark contrast to her life living alone. With no Will in the picture now, she felt strangely adrift. Christmas was coming up fast, in just three days' time, and she shouldn't feel ungrateful. She had her supper club friends, of course, but they'd have their own festive plans and their families to be with. And there was no way she'd have put pressure on Adam to change his plans and spend this Christmas up here with her. It was good that he was feeling more settled down in Leeds, and supported by his dad. But that didn't mean it wasn't hard on Cath.

It was good that Trevor had invited his son for Christmas dinner with him and Steph. She'd heard from Adam that Trev's new partner had gone to a lot of trouble, ordering in a big fresh turkey and was going all out. Cath needed to sit with that, and keep schtum, even if it felt difficult to not be a part of Adam's Christmas this year. She was still, and would always be, a huge part of his life, even as he entered adulthood. If Adam wanted to stay down in Leeds for Christmas, then that was fine.

She'd bloody well miss him, of course, but perhaps he might just make it to Tilldale for a day or two between Christmas and New Year, or she could go down for a day trip herself. They'd chat tomorrow, and find a way to make things work.

Her new cottage home, even if she was to be on her own, was absolutely the place to be for her first Christmas in Tilldale. Maybe it was all that had recently happened with Will that had made things feel so unsettled, she mused. She slipped further into the suds with a tired sigh.

A mere week ago, thoughts of them going on romantic walks in the snow or snuggling up over hot chocolate or mulled wine had crept into her mind. She should never have let them in – have let *him* in. It hurt too damn much when it all went wrong

260

again. Whatever happened to her learning her lesson. Had she not heard once bitten, twice shy? She'd let her heart rule her head in a moment of madness and look where it had left her. Yes, she was missing Will and she knew it. But it wasn't going to happen now. There was no future for the two of them. He was still grieving, his family in pain, and she wasn't going to add to that. Time to step away, other than the occasional supper club event as a group. That was it. Simple.

Except in reality, it wasn't simple at all.

She was heading downstairs in her dressing gown, for a pre-bed camomile tea before a much-needed early night, when her phone buzzed to life.

It was Susie on the line. 'Hey, how did it all go, sis? Been thinking about you today, taking all that on with your big lunch.'

'Ah, it went off brilliantly. Really, couldn't have been better.'

'That's great to hear.'

'I'm shattered now though,' Cath confessed.

'I bet you are. Well, a big well done to you and your helpers.'

'Thanks.'

'Oh, and how are things going with Lover Boy? Are you still feeling it in your fingers and your toes?' she quipped merrily.

Cath hadn't even started to tell her sister anything that had happened recently. It had all felt a bit raw, and with the lunch event imminent, she'd had enough on her mind.

'It's not …'

'What?'

'Going anywhere.' There, she'd said it.

'Oh, Cath. What's happened?'

She took a deep breath, and then it began to spill out. The whole sorry tale of helping with the Christmas tree, of being there at totally the wrong time, of upsetting Sophie and no doubt Maddie too. Feeling like the Wicked Witch of the West in the middle of their grief zone.

261

'But the daft thing is, it's not that Will doesn't care for me. I *know* he does. I just don't know how to deal with all that hurt and grief. How can I compete with a ghost?'

'Oh, Cath.'

'Actually, I don't mean it like that.' Frustration had sharpened her words. 'I know it's not a damned competition, far from it. But dammit, I've really fallen for him. And I don't know how to break through his wall of grief.'

'I'm so sorry, Cath. It really sounded like you were getting on well.'

'That's the crazy thing. We were. We are. But ah, I feel so, I don't know … frustrated and *cross* about it all. It's not their fault, or mine. I do know that. But surely, they know better than most that life is too damn short. And I didn't know Jane, but I bet Will holing himself up and being miserable isn't what she would have wanted for him or her family, for the rest of their lives. Urgh, it's so damned complicated. There are so many feelings and so much hurt there.' Well, that outpouring let the cat spill out of its bag.

'Gosh. I'm not sure what to say, Cath. I'm giving you a huge hug down the phone right now.'

'Thanks.' Cath took a breath, holding herself together for now.

'And are you still up there for Christmas? Are you on your own?' Susie asked gently.

'Uh-hah.'

'You know you can come to us. It's not too late to hop in the car, come and stay here. In fact, we'd love that. I always buy far too much food. And it's only us and Mark's parents for Christmas dinner.'

There was a second where Cath was tempted, but she'd really wanted to be here in her own little cottage in her Northumberland village for her first Christmas, even if it wasn't going to be the easiest of times. In truth, she was absolutely knackered too.

'Ah, that's lovely of you, Suze. But I'm shattered, I think

all I need is a few quiet days here over Christmas. I'll be fine, honestly.'

'Are you sure?'

'Sure.' Well, if she said it enough times to herself, she would be.

Chapter 32

The next day passed quietly – which was a relief. A chance for Cath to catch her breath, and potter about at the cottage.

She was sat in the living room that evening, with the log burner on, watching TV, and still she couldn't shake off thoughts of Will. She missed him, wanted *him*, wanted *more*. There was a big Will-shaped hole in her heart and her life. She turned her mind to all the couples, all the families having fun at this festive time, but also all the lonely ones at Christmas – for so many reasons: divorce, loss, grief. It was like the festive season slaps it all in your face. The idyllic adverts – oh yeah, if she saw another happy extended family sat around a bloody table full of roasted turkey with all the trimmings, she was going to start firing her Quality Street at the telly. She took another glug of Baileys, and found the Netflix channel.

Sod it! A list of festive romantic comedies came up. Where was *Elf* or *The Grinch* when you needed them? She switched the TV off, deciding to put on some music. 'Alexa, play…' she began, not sure what to request. 'Ah, something Christmassy,' she blurted out, and Wham's 'Last Christmas' came on. Groan. She decided to pour herself another glass of this very delicious creamy-whisky stuff.

As she sat back down, a voice came through loud in her mind. Her teacher voice: *Enough of the self-pity.* She had so much more than most people, she reminded herself. She just had to find a life for herself. Work on that happy place to be. She did love her little cottage, her very own space. And she had already started to find her feet in this rural Northumbrian village. She just needed to keep on going, one step at a time.

Christmas Day was looming near, yes, but it wasn't the be-all and end-all of life, it was just a day, sometimes a special day and sometimes a tricky day. She'd get through it, and then move on. With a brand-new year ahead, waiting for her to get stuck in to her brand-new Second Chance life.

The snow had melted away, the sky this morning a dull, cloudy grey, but it was mild and dry out there. It was Christmas Eve, and Cath, in need of some fresh air and space, decided to head out for a reinvigorating walk. Even better, she thought as she stepped out, she'd call at the shop on the way and offer to take terrier Shirley along with her. Some canine company would do her good.

Ten minutes later, and they were stood outside of the stores. 'Now then, Shirley, which way do we head today?' Cath found herself speaking to the dog. And off they trotted, Shirley leading the way, along the street, through the churchyard and down towards the riverside. It was a walk she'd done many times since moving in. The scenery shifting with the seasons. The heron still there, perched on one leg, eagle-eyed in his search for a fish meandering in the shallows. The trees bare and skeletal, yet still reaching for the skies. She felt nature's balm as she walked.

Winter was a quieter time, a time for her to rest perhaps, now that the big event had happened. And she'd achieved so much, she could feel proud of herself. She'd gotten to know so many more people here in the local community since starting on that journey too.

Shirley sniffed about, happily trotting here and there on her long lead, as they strolled on.

And Cath took in the here and now. The smells of grass and the earth beneath her walking boots. The river flowing, ripples of light on iron-brown water. A pair of gulls swooping and soaring up above. The sound of a tractor, as it ploughed a nearby field, getting the soil ready to plant new seeds, for growth to come again.

Life could seem big and overwhelming at times, emotions drowning you from within. Two years of heartbreak had taught her that.

But there was still so much beauty in the world, even on a dull winter's day.

Enjoy the little things, Cath, enjoy the little things.

She dropped Shirley off back at the stores feeling far more settled in herself. The walk had done her the world of good, unwinding something in her soul.

Andreas was stood at the counter along with Dan, who was about to whisk the terrier back upstairs.

'Ah, thank you, lovely. I bet Shirley enjoyed that little outing,' said Andreas.

'She did indeed. And it did me some good, too. I don't know about you two, but I've been shattered ever since Sunday's big bash.'

'Oh, yes, we've been dog-tired too. Not as young and fresh as we used to be. Worth every ache and pain though. What a fantastic day for everyone,' replied Dan.

'And what a great idea it was, Cath, your community event here in Tilldale. We keep getting people in saying how marvellous it was, and look here, there's even a thank-you card from Kenneth.' Dan showed her a handwritten note on a card with a view of the village on. 'Actually, seeing as it was your bright idea to start with, I think you should take it. Pop it on the side in your cottage and feel proud.'

'Aw, thank you – though it was a team effort for sure – and pass my thanks on to Kenneth, too. With all the mobile phones these days, hardly anyone writes a letter at all.' And her mind was pulled back to Reggie and Elsie's bundle of letters and a love that lasted a lifetime. And her heart was tugged with bruised memories of Trevor, and her battered wings with Will.

'What are you up to tomorrow, petal?' Andreas asked, as if sensing her moment of angst. 'You're not still spending it alone, are you?'

'Well, that was the idea. I'll be fine. I'm going to buy a load of your tasty deli bits, and a treat or two from the bakery section, and I'm planning on a big chill-out.'

'Oh, it doesn't seem right. Not to be on you own all day on Christmas Day. And certainly not when there are friends just along the street,' said Andreas.

'I'll be fine,' she repeated.

'You may well be, but we'd love it if you'd call in for a festive drink, at least.' He arched his eyebrows in a plea.

Dan was there nodding vigorously beside him. How did they manage to make it sound like she'd be doing them a favour by coming? But just a drink, she supposed. 'Okay, and thank you. But only once you've finished your dinner and had your own time together.'

'Wonderful, well come for two-thirty. We can have a toast to Maria and then settle down in time for the king's speech. Ooh, sounds funny that, saying the king. Still seems a bit odd not to have the queen. Still miss good old Lizzie. Oh, and what was her Christmas tipple?'

'A "Zaza" gin and Dubonnet cocktail,' Dan responded with a smile.

'Oh, perhaps we can try one of those.' Andreas grinned.

'Sounds lethal.' Cath laughed. And being with the lads for a couple of celebratory drinks sounded a grand idea. She was bound to have some fun, after all.

'Right, I'd better get little missy up the stairs and out of the shop, pronto. Health and safety will be hot on my heels, otherwise,' said Dan.

'And I'll get choosing my Christmas Day nibbles. Thanks, lads, tomorrow for drinks it is, then.'

She felt a little lift. Christmas, with a little help from her friends.

Chapter 33

It was past eight p.m. and Cath was settled on the sofa. She should be watching a movie or something – it was Christmas Eve after all – but tiredness was seeping through her bones. She must have overdone it with all the work involved with the lunch event. That was only two days ago, after all. She wondered when might be acceptable to head off up to bed, then smiled to herself as she realised that it didn't matter; there was only herself to please.

Cath then heard a strange noise coming from the direction of the front door. And again, a rat-a-tat, this time followed by what she thought might be the creak of the main door opening. A draught of cold air blew in through to the sitting room. How odd. Had she not closed the door properly after coming back from the shop earlier? But that was ages ago. She hadn't yet locked up; she knew that much. Had the wind blown it open?

On alert, she stood up, ready to go and check it out, wishing she still had Shirley with her. She jumped out of her skin as a dark shadow appeared and a man walked into the room. *Shit.* Was she about to be accosted? There was nowhere to run. What could she grab to hit him with – the poker for the fire?

'Hi, Mum.' Her son's cheery voice rang out. He was stood there, with his hoodie up.

'Adam … what the hell are you doing here? You look like a mugger.' Cath was still in fight-or-flight mode.

'Ah, thanks, Mum. Lovely to see you, too.' He gave a wry grin, pulling down the hood away from his face. 'Man, it's chilly out there. And hey, I've just travelled three hours straight on Christmas Eve after working my stint in the bar today, that is.'

'But what *are* you doing here? I mean, what about Dad … and Christmas?' she babbled. Her mind was in a frazzle. Had he fallen out with his dad? Had Trev and Steph fallen out with each other? Was Christmas in Leeds cancelled?

'Ah, it didn't feel right not seeing you over Christmas time. Don't worry, it's still all on with Dad and Steph for dinner tomorrow as planned, but … well, I finished my shift at five today, and I figured that'd give me enough time to get up here and see you, too. Just for tonight, and first thing tomorrow. Dad said I could borrow the car, just as long as I get back there for two-thirty sharp. They're planning a three o'clock lunch. So here I am.'

Amazing. Instead of Santa arriving on Christmas Eve, here was Adam. And oh, that was the best Christmas gift. She wasn't going to be on her own, after all. And, what a sweet gesture of Trev and Steph, who had most likely pushed back their own lunch plans to help Adam spend time with both parents. 'Come here, then. Give me a hug.' Her arms were wide.

'Hah, I was frightened to get too close. Thought you might be about to beat me up.' He chuckled.

'That was actually what I was thinking. I was about to arm myself with the poker.'

And they both started laughing, proper belly laughing.

Once they'd settled down, after the drama of his arrival, Cath asked, 'Have you eaten? Can I get you anything? There're some cold meats and nibbly bits in the fridge.' Thankfully, she'd filled it with goodies from the stores today. Unsure of what she wanted to cook or eat for her solo Christmas festivities, she'd plumped for lots of delicious deli treats.

'Ah, yeah, that'd be great, thanks. I grabbed some crisps and fruit for the journey, but it wasn't much.'

As Adam brought in his overnight bag from the car, Cath sorted out a quick makeshift supper, including feta pastries, a cranberry-topped pork pie, sliced ham and local cheeses, mini tomatoes, rocket salad, chutney and olives.

'Oh, that's a right feast. Bang on, that is.' He gave a broad grin. 'A fitting Christmas Eve supper.'

And they tucked in, Cath having poured them a glass of red wine each, and rediscovering her appetite after all, they chatted and caught up. Her early night turning into a merry almost-midnight. And in the space of a few hours, between her fabulous friends and her son, her Christmas had turned from a solitary affair to a sprinkling of social magic.

'Merry Christmas, Mum!'

Her bedroom door swung open, and through just-opened eyelids, she made out Adam in shorts and a T-shirt, with a big smile on his face bearing a tray of steaming coffee, a couple of croissants and a silver cracker – one that had been left over from the community lunch. Last night hadn't been a hallucination, after all, then.

She'd only just woken, and wow, realised she had slept really well. And, she wasn't on her own for Christmas morning after all. How lovely.

'Aw, happy Christmas, Adam. I'm so pleased you made it up here.' She shifted herself up against her pillows.

'Me too. I hated the thought that you'd be here on your own. Anyway, Christmas lunch and tonight will give me plenty of time with Dad too.' He was going to drive back down later this morning to be there in time. 'And I figured they had each other this morning. I really don't think I could stand all the cute gifting and cuddly stuff anyway.' He gave a strained smile.

'Yeah, I can see that.' It was a vision Cath was finding hard to stomach, too. Her ex and his new partner all lovey-dovey. How many Christmases had she spent with Trev she pondered? Thirty-two – blimey. *Don't look back,* a little voice reminded her, *look forward.*

Adam rested the tray on her bedside table, and passed her a mug of coffee. She could see he'd taken the time to put butter and jam into little pots, set beside the croissants that he'd warmed. 'Found the croissants in the bread tin. I kind of hoped they were for this morning.'

'Yes, they were. Thank you. This is lovely. So thoughtful.' She'd bought two of the pastries from the village stores yesterday; one was plain and the other almond. Her little treat for herself for Christmas morning.

Adam sat down on the bed, his face suddenly looking serious. 'I wanted to thank you, Mum. You've always been there for me. And those few months ago, when I hit rock bottom ... well, you were just brilliant turning up like that, getting me through it, helping me see it all in a different way. I wasn't in a good place. It was like you put me back on track. So thanks.'

'Oh, Adam. No need for thanks. That's what mums are for.'

'Maybe, but they're not all like you. Guess I got lucky.' He nudged her arm playfully, like he used to as a little boy.

She gave a gentle bittersweet smile, remembering that recent difficult time. 'I was so worried about you and with me being so much farther away now. That was hard.'

'It's not so far really, and I'm glad you moved up here, Mum. I'm glad you did what was right for you ... after everything that happened with Dad. You're happy here, I can tell.'

'Yeah, it is a lovely place. I'm finding my feet ...' There was still the odd wobble, but she didn't need to share that with Adam right now. And he was right: where else in the world would she have found the space to heal? With the beautiful nurturing coun-tryside all around. The haven of her little cottage and its garden.

And the friendships that she'd already forged.

'Thanks, son. And I hope you're finding some happiness now, too?'

'I'm working on it, big time.' He gave her a wink, and she could tell the old Adam was back. Her cheeky, happy-go-lucky son. 'Got the new wildlife park job to look forward to next month.' He beamed at her as he casually slipped that into the conversation.

'You what?' This was news to her. 'Hang on … backtrack. A new *wildlife park* job? What wildlife park job? Why didn't you tell me?'

'I'm telling you now. That was another big reason to come up and see you in person. I wanted to share my news.'

'Wow, that's amazing, Adam. Okay, sit down.' She patted the side of the bed. 'And tell me all about it.'

'So, the *obscure* degree I've done in zoology …' His tone was laced with happy sarcasm.

'That was your dad's opinion, not mine,' Cath chipped in. Yes, Trevor had been pushing hard in the past for a maths, accountancy, or engineering course for their talented son, who happened to be an animal fanatic.

'Well, it's just landed me a role at the Yorkshire Wildlife Park. Meet the new research and education manager. *And* it means I'll most likely get the chance to travel a bit, too. They have links with zoos and ecology projects all around the world.'

'That's just brilliant, Adam.' She gave him a one-armed hug, almost spilling her coffee.

'Yeah, I'm buzzing, Mum. I didn't think I'd stand a chance. There must have been so many applicants, but they were really interested with the wildlife voluntary work I did whilst I was travelling, and my student placement at the Safari Zoo in Cumbria.'

'You obviously impressed them! I'm absolutely delighted for you. Sounds right up your street, too. Well done, son.' At last, a real break for him, and an opportunity that he'd love. This was better than any gift for Cath to open.

That reminded her. 'Oh, and have you opened your gifts yet?' She'd left his Christmas parcels when she'd visited for the run.

'Nope, I held back – amazingly – and left them at Dad's for later, but thanks.'

'It's just a few bits that might come in useful.' She'd picked up a sweatshirt, boxer shorts, some toiletries including a Boss aftershave that he liked, sweets – he was still partial to the strawberry pencils that he used to love as a kid – and a few other bits and bobs. If she couldn't spoil Adam, who could she spoil?

'No worries, and hey ...' He nipped out to his room, across the landing, coming back with a small white box with a silver bow. She opened it to find a single pearl set in a silver twist on a delicate silver chain.

'Oh, that's beautiful, Adam. But you shouldn't have ...' It looked expensive.

'Of course I should. It's the perfect way to say thank you. And thank you for sharing your *pearls* of wisdom with me ... and with all those other pupils you've helped over your years of being a teacher.'

'Oh.' She was lost for words. And she knew she would wear it every day, loving the idea that she'd be able to touch it now and again, and think of her son – it would be like he was there with her. 'Thank you.'

Adam slipped the necklace around her neck and fixed the clasp. The pearl dropped to lie gently in the dip of her clavicle, just above where she'd first ever held him as a newborn. She touched it, filled with a sense of gratitude and awe, and sat for a few quiet seconds.

'Oh, do you fancy one of these?' She then spotted the croissants that Adam had brought in.

'Yeah, thought you'd never ask. I've been eyeing up that almond one. Looks lush.'

'Go on then, I'll have the other.'

They sat chatting away, with croissant crumbs, coffee aromas, and a warm glow around them.

'There's a present or two under the tree, too,' he said proudly after polishing off the baked treat. 'Dad sent me up with a couple of things. And there's one from Helen down the road.'

'Oh, I really am getting spoilt this morning.' She grinned. Her old friend, who'd visited earlier in the year, had come up trumps. And crikey, even Trevor had thought of her. 'Anyone would think it was Christmas, or something.'

Mother and son had a lovely crisp walk through the village after breakfast, passing old stone cottages with wisps of smoke coming from the chimneys where real log fires burned below. All was quiet, with even less traffic than usual on the roads. The village looked pretty in the winter months, with gardens of berry bushes and shrubs now laced with a nip of white frost. Some of the houses had a show of twinkling fairy lights draped around shrubs and trees. Indoor lights were on, and festive trees glimmered, where friends and family would be gathered spending time with their loved ones; children going crazy on a sugar-rush adrenaline high, and the chefs of the household now busy in their kitchens.

She wondered about her supper club and what they might be doing. Nikki with her full-on family of five, all the gifts, the unwrapping, the early start. Lily and her parents going to visit Nikki's lot soon. The lads, having their own special day, sadly without the company of the wonderful Maria this year. She was looking forward seeing the pair of them later. And Will … gorgeous, distant Will – how was he doing today? His daughters were coming up to stay with him for a couple of days, so she'd heard from Nikki, who couldn't help from keeping Cath posted on his activities. But other than that, she'd heard very little.

Merry Christmas, Will. She sent him a silent message.

Cath and Adam wandered out of the village and along the hawthorn-sided lanes, taking a three-mile loop. They were contentedly strolling and chatting, and the walking seemed easy, so they'd just kept on going. But it left little time, once they'd returned to Cheviot Cottage.

All too soon, it was time for Adam to go, but Cath felt okay, she realised, as she watched him drive away. It was like her battery of love had been recharged. And knowing that her son was doing well now, that he'd a new job and a brighter future lined up, well that was all she needed.

Chapter 34

Lunchtime was approaching. Cath had enjoyed the impromptu roast at the big bash but certainly hadn't been able to face the thought of cooking another turkey dinner today. To be quite honest, it seemed far too much effort to sit down and eat a traditional Christmas meal all on her own. There would be too many ghosts of Christmas pasts lurking about, too. Her backup plan, other than the many delicious deli bits to snack on, was to heat up a 'Best of' fish pie served with some peas, broccoli and a very nice glass of chilled Chablis, which would have been her go-to wine for Christmas Day – some traditions were worth keeping whatever the circumstances!

And sitting at the small kitchen table, looking out at her frosty garden, that was okay. She still felt a glow within from Adam's unexpected visit, and touched the beautiful pearl at the base of her neck. The fish pie was really tasty, and as she hadn't had to make it herself, it felt like a treat with the delicious wine. There'd been a few of Lily's mince pies left over from the festive lunch too, so she warmed a couple of those, and took them through to the cosy sitting room where the log burner was aglow. A large dollop of cream was melting down the edge of the buttery pastry as she took a hearty bite. Scrumptious.

Her phone then buzzed with a notification. She'd already heard from Adam that he'd landed safely back in Leeds, and her sister had messaged earlier with a Happy Christmas. *Hope you're doing good. Chat later x.* Even Trev had sent a 'Merry Christmas.' So, who might this be? An old friend perhaps? She took out her mobile and saw 'Will' ... *Oh.* Her heart gave a little, well perhaps large, leap.

Opening the message she read: *Merry Christmas, Cath. Hope you're having a good day. xx* So, he *was* thinking of her.

She had wondered about sending him a Christmas 'thinking of you' message earlier too, but hadn't known quite what to say. It seemed too tricky, too hard, to be cool and polite, when all she really wanted to say was that she missed him and loved him. The 'just friends' was proving bloody difficult. Instead, she'd opted for a text to the supper group with a *Merry Christmas to all! x* Lots of festive replies had come back in from the gang, finally with a thumbs-up and Father Christmas emoji from Will.

But here he was, messaging her on Christmas Day. The pair of them sat in their respective homes, floundering in the festivities, and no doubt feeling at odds with life. Both trying to do the right thing. She wondered if his girls were there with him. Most likely. Had they roasted a turkey? Tried to do what they had always done in happier years? Will's cooking skills would seriously need brushing up to tackle a roast, she mused ... Boy, how she missed their lessons. Were Will and the girls soldiering on, pretending everything was all right, when the world around them had shattered into a million pieces? Or were they sharing a few tears, over stories of Jane?

Cath's heart went out to him and his family. It must be even harder to lose someone you loved to illness than betrayal. It all seemed so senseless, such a bloody waste.

Merry Christmas, Will. She typed the words she'd been wanting to say all day. Her fingertips hovering over the keypad. What else to say? Did she take a chance on telling him she missed him? Would that just make things harder for them both, or make him feel uncomfortable? *Hope your day is going well x* she added. And then, bugger it – perhaps it was the Chablis affecting her judgement, or her current romantic fireside setting – she typed *Miss you xx.* And before she could change her mind, pressed 'Send'.

Within seconds a heart emoji came back. Cath was touched … until no other message followed.

Whatever he had said about moving on and merely being friends, she *knew* he was missing her too. Will *was* trying to do the right thing for his family, and she had to respect that. But was keeping their distance just hurting them both?

Cath was glad she'd been invited over for festive drinks this afternoon with Dan and Andreas. It would be fun and would help take her mind off Will for a while, and hopefully stop her overanalysing his recent message. She wrapped herself up in a woolly Fair Isle scarf with a matching bobble hat (the gift from Helen) and navy winter woollen coat, then set off over frosty pavements and past twinkling festive lights, the short distance to the shop.

Andreas's gorgeous green-and-silver-toned door wreath, with its mini stars, pine cones, cinnamon sticks, dried orange circles and eucalyptus, greeted her at the side door to the stores, which served as the entrance to their flat above. She pressed the doorbell with an air of expectancy. It was always good to see Andreas and Dan, and whatever they did, be it a simple drink or full supper soiree, they made you most welcome. She'd brought a bottle of homemade sloe gin as a gift for them. Made by herself from the sloe berries she'd picked in early November, after the first frosts, from the hedgerows in the nearby lanes. There was a particularly good patch she'd noted on her summer walks, and had revisited at just the right time.

'Hello. Happy Christmas, petal!' The door swung wide, to

reveal Andreas sporting a slightly crumpled red-paper party hat, no doubt from a Christmas cracker.

'Merry Christmas, gorgeous.' Dan appeared alongside. 'Entrée, entrée, come on in from the cold.'

They shared hugs and kisses, then she followed them up to their flat. Shirley, wearing a holly-patterned green festive neckerchief, greeted her on the landing area, with the waggiest of tails and a woof.

'She's been spoilt today,' said Andreas.

'Isn't she always?' Dan added, with a knowing yet tolerant smile. 'Had her very own portion of turkey dinner, with gravy and stuffing,' he explained.

'Loved it. I'm surprised she's moved from her place on the sofa. You're honoured. She's been snoozing soundly since she finished that off.'

'Actually, I think that was you, Andreas.' Dan chuckled. 'You've been snoring for the past twenty minutes.'

'Surely not!' He looked affronted.

Dan quirked an eyebrow, knowing better. 'It was the doorbell that woke you up.'

'Oh, well, that's all part of the tradition. Eat far too much and then sleep it off, with the telly on as background.'

'Absolutely,' Cath agreed with a grin.

'Anyway, let me fetch you a festive tipple,' offered Dan. 'Champagne?'

'That'd be wonderful, thank you.' She began unwrapping herself from her thick coat and scarf.

Andreas took her things to hang on the coat rail, then ushered her into the sitting room, whilst Dan whizzed off to the kitchen.

'How are you, my lovely? And how's today been for you?' Andreas asked kindly.

'I'm doing okay, thanks.' Cath made light of it. There was no need to dwell on the tricky parts … or Will's message, which had made her stomach swirl like a washing machine. How did he manage to take her right back to her teenage angst? 'And in the end, I didn't spend this morning on my own, after all,' and Cath began to describe Adam's surprise visit.

'Oh, how lovely,' exclaimed Andreas on hearing the tale, and about Adam's new job. 'He's such a nice lad, and I'm delighted for him and you.'

'Thank you. It was so wonderful that he turned up to be together for Christmas morning. We've never yet had a year apart … Oh, sorry, Andreas. I'm being insensitive. Of course, Maria …' And their thoughts all turned to Andreas's marvellous mama.

'Oh, don't be worried, petal. It's lovely to think and talk about her. I remember Christmases back in London when I was a child,' Andreas began to reminisce. 'Mama there, such big family celebrations … Enough food to feed the whole street. Christmas Eve, it was carolling around the neighbours, dinging my little triangle as my sister shook her tambourine. By the end of it, we had pockets crammed with *kourabiedes* and *melomakarona* – the most delicious biscuits.'

'Oh yes, were they the ones you made for the Greek-style supper night?'

'They were indeed. The little icing-sugar dusted ones, and the cookies with cinnamon, orange, honey and nuts.'

'They were delicious.'

'Yeah, the *melomakarona* are my favourites. I should have made some more for Christmas time, come to think of it. But the time's just run away with us. What with the shop, and the lunch event, we've been so busy.'

'I know,' Cath agreed. 'And the big Christmas lunch took some and organising, didn't it?'

'Yes, well worth it, though,' added Dan, as he came in with a tray of three filled champagne flutes. 'I loved seeing everyone's faces. It was so joyful somehow. And the dancing … Reggie doing the hand-jive … it was just fabulous.'

'Yeah, it was a fantastic day, even if my feet throbbed by the end of it,' Cath admitted.

'Oh, and I hope you don't mind me asking, but I couldn't help but notice that things seemed rather awkward between you and Will that day. Is everything all right there?' Andreas observed.

'Not really, no.' She might as well be honest about it. 'We're not together anymore. Well, I'm not sure we were ever together, but we're not even trying now. We'd only just got started.' She gave a sigh. 'It's been really difficult, especially with his family. I think they are all very much struggling to come to terms with Jane's death.' She didn't think it fair on Will to go into any more detail.

'Oh, that's such a shame. And I'm sorry. That must be so tough on you, too,' Dan said empathetically, as Andreas reached over to rub her shoulder.

'Thank you. And yes, it's been tricky ...' She underplayed it. 'The whole situation really.'

'We thought you made such a good pair,' Dan added. 'And we so wanted you both to find happiness again.'

'Hey, all that matchmaking for nothing,' Cath quipped, trying to keep her tone light, and not reveal her minced-up heart. Darn it, she hadn't escaped from thinking about Will by coming over here, either.

'Are you really okay, petal?' Andreas asked.

His caring words suddenly got her feeling all choked up. 'Ahm, I'll be all right. Worse things have happened in my roller-coaster life, of late.' She tried to brush it off before she got teary-eyed. Losing a marriage after thirty-two years had been so hard, but this situation with Will had really got to her. Maybe it was because she'd got her hopes up, all over again, and had recklessly opened her heart. It was a bruising she hadn't needed at a time when she was still trying to heal.

'We're always here, you know. Anytime ...' Dan started.

'If you want to chat, or gorge yourself on baklava, or drink strong coffee …' Andreas continued, with a gentle smile on his lips. 'And hey, we know Will cares for you – that much is plain to see.'

'Thank you, lads, I really do appreciate that.' And their warm friendship bolstered her. She felt thankful for that, at least.

'I could box his ears, the silly man.' Andreas was shaking his head. 'However sad the situation is.'

'Maybe it's just too soon.' Cath found herself sticking up for Will. 'It's not an easy situation with his girls just now. I think he's trying to protect them.' She held back from sharing the details of the Christmas tree evening with them. It seemed far too private.

'Well, some other hunk will be sure to pick you up in the new year, if Will doesn't watch out.'

Cath had to laugh at that. It was the last thing she'd consider … someone else, someone new on the scene. No, she'd had it with romance. No more hurt, no more being let down. She'd look forward to a very quiet new year, learning to love this new life on her own, enjoying her cottage, and anticipating the spring breaking though, with its bulbs and birdsong.

'Now then, with all that doom and gloom, we've forgotten to have our Christmas toast.' Dan passed the glasses of bubbly out. 'Cheers, Cath. Happy Christmas, lovely.' Dan raised his flute.

'Cheers, petal.'

'Cheers. Merry Christmas to you both. And thank you for all your kind support since I've moved in.'

'You're most welcome, lovely lady,' said Dan.

'Oh, I'd almost forgotten, I have a little gift for you.' With that, Andreas nipped out of the room, coming back with two sheets of A4 card with printed twirls of festive holly to each corner, each with a beautifully handwritten recipe on. 'A couple of my favourite Northumbrian-Greek-Cypriot recipes, for you.'

'Oh, wow. This is so thoughtful and lovely, Andreas. Thank

you.' She read aloud, 'Lamb Kleftiko and Melomakarona cookies. I'll have to give these a go.'

'In fact, I've made two cards for every member of the supper group. You've all got something different. I hope you enjoy testing them out.'

'It's a ploy, you know, to get you all cooking, and invite us around again next year.' Dan's eyes crinkled with mirth.

'Hah, I like your style. And I'm certain our supper club will still be going strong next year.' She couldn't imagine being without this fabulous friendship group.

Shirley was nestled beside her on the sofa, resting her head on Cath's thigh. Cath stroked her soft white fur. It felt reassuring. The log fire was burning in the hearth. Andreas topped up her glass, as Dan went to make a Zaza cocktail for them all.

He was soon back in and passing out pretty glass goblets filled with the dusky-red delight. 'Well then, let's settle ourselves down. It's almost time for the king's speech.'

'Perfect.'

She felt bolstered by their care, their kindness. She was okay, Cath told herself. She'd manage. Last Christmas was a tough one, and she'd made it through that. Though her heart was aching once more, the disappointment that she and Will weren't meant to be was bound to fade in time. It had to. She had lots to be thankful for, and she needed to keep positive.

But why, when she was back in her own cottage bedroom, late that evening, was it all still tugging at her heartstrings? Will was still there in her mind. Memories of young Matty and her, in their youth. Then the Trevor years. All that wasted time. And now just recently, Will's kiss … his arms tenderly wrapped around her in this very bed. It really had felt like they had a future. Even her body seemed to be missing him, dammit. Why couldn't she just think of these past few weeks with Will as a 'good time', a notch on her bedpost? And let it go?

284

But she'd never really let it go … let *him* go, not even after the first time.

Some people held a special place in your heart, your soul.

And there were some people you were never meant to forget.

Chapter 35

Miss you too xx

That was the message Cath woke to on Boxing Day.

It was from Will. She held her phone in the palm of her hand, not quite sure what to think as she propped herself up in her bed. It sure did melt her heart though.

What was she to make of that? Was there more to this, to *them*, yet? Or was it more an acknowledgement that yes, though this was hard for them both, and perhaps they did miss each other, they were doing the right thing being apart.

She rested her head on the soft downy pillow, feeling the prickle of confused tears. She fumbled for a tissue on her bedside table. You couldn't tell anyone how to grieve. Or how to be in the aftermath of such devastation within a family. But God, she so wanted to turn up at his house and give him a huge bloody hug – and possibly a bit more. She just didn't think it would go down at all well with Sophie or Maddie.

Time for coffee and a shower, get herself dressed, and see what she felt like doing.

Boxing Day lay ahead. Hours of it. There were no online

maths sessions today, no one to cook for, other than herself. She didn't even have many ingredients in; it had hardly seemed worth stocking up for one. A walk, yes – she'd get out and get some fresh air in the frosty fields. And her sister had given her a new book for Christmas too, the latest Maggie O'Farrell … she could get stuck into that later.

At least she'd been brave enough to make this move to her Northumberland village, she reminded herself, on her way down the stairs. To buy her dream cottage and make a new life for herself. She managed to brighten herself up. There was enough doom and gloom in the world, without her adding to it.

The first coffee of the day was good, rich and strong with hot frothy milk. Sat in her kitchen, the sun coming out, casting golden rays over her crisp-with-frost back garden, turning the ice on the grass and bare shrub branches to a million melting mini-globes. Nature was pretty damned cool. She loved the changing seasons, the contrasts of the ice-blue winter chill to the warm heady breezes of summer. Everything was waiting, the bulbs underground, on hold for now, but primed for that rise in temperature. Soon enough the first snowdrops would come. Green shoots and the prettiest, delicate white flowers. She hadn't had a January here in the cottage as yet, but she'd bet that Reggie had some of those green harbingers of hope planted in his borders.

It was then that her phone rang.

It was Will.

'Hi,' he started cautiously.

'Hello … ah, Merry Christmas,' Cath responded, feeling the strings of her heart pulled tightly like a violin.

'Ah, we've been talking, the girls and I … Last night, we had a real heart-to-heart,' Will started, diving right in.

It was so lovely to hear his voice down the line, that he was reaching out to her, even if it was only to offload a bit. Their friendship had obviously survived, and that meant so much to her.

'Ah, well, that's good. I'm glad you've been able to talk. It helps when times are tough.'

'I didn't want to do anything to upset them; it's been hard enough for us all. But, well, they can see how miserable I've been lately. And that maybe having a new focus ... getting to know you ... how that had been good for me.'

There was a pause, Cath nodded, then realised he couldn't see her so added an 'oh', wondering where this might be going.

'And Cath, it's not just them ... I *was* starting to feel more myself. Meeting you, I felt that perhaps I'd been given the chance to be happy again, in a whole new way.'

'Oh ...' she repeated, but she daren't let herself get any hopes up.

'The thing is, the girls are still here. Sophie feels awful about how she reacted with you that day. And well, do you fancy coming to the beach for a walk with us this afternoon? Perhaps we can all have a coffee or something afterwards. Nothing too intense, just a stroll and the chance to chat. What do you think?' He sounded nervous.

She thought it was incredibly brave of him to be asking. And if his girls were holding out an olive branch, however nerve-racking it might be to meet them in the circumstances, she needed to take that branch and make sure it became something positive. Small, careful steps, but they might just be the start of a wonderful new journey.

'Yes, I'd really like to meet your girls properly, Will. That sounds great.'

'We were thinking of Low Newton. Around one-thirty, while there's still plenty of daylight? Shall we pick you up or meet you there?'

It was a beach Cath knew well. In fact, the beach where they'd had their bacon sandwich brunch and that gorgeous walk together, not so long ago. 'I can meet you there.'

It felt rather like a step too far for a first meeting, all four of them up close and personal in the confined space of his car. And having her own vehicle meant she could hopefully time her exit without any awkward moments. This was a delicate situation that might need a little careful handling.

'Sure?'

'It's fine. I'll drive over and see you there at the car park. The one on the brow of the hill above the beach, at one-thirty then?'

'Great.'

'And Will … thank you.'

'Hey, I should be thanking you, for being so patient. For understanding.'

'One-thirty, then. Great. Bye.' *Wow*.

'Bye. See you later, Cath.' She could hear the smile in his voice. She closed the call.

This was a big step forward. Whoop! Okay, so she wasn't going to let herself get too hopeful, of course. But bloody whoop!!

Cath was the first to arrive. She found herself drumming on the steering wheel as she waited anxiously. Each car turning in to the car park sent her pulse rate shooting up. Until, yes, there was Will's blue hatchback, and two women were in there with him.

She waited until they had got out of his car, before stepping out of her Mini. Sophie's glance was a little cool, but she remained polite as Cath approached. Will introduced them all calmly, as if this was the first time they'd met.

Maddie was tall and slim, dressed casually in black jeans and a sporty-style puffer. Her wavy hair, dark like her dad's, was peeking out from below her green woolly hat.

'Maddie, Sophie, this is Cath.'

'Hi.' Did she shake hands at this point? But that seemed rather too formal. 'Nice to meet you,' she added. Then thought to say, 'Thank you for this.' It must have been difficult for them, after all.

The girls nodded. As Maddie said, 'Nice to meet you, too. Dad's been telling us about your supper club evenings. That sounds so nice.' She gave a friendly smile.

And that broke the ice, as Cath could then talk about her love of cooking, and mentioned the lads from the village stores, whom Maddie and Sophie naturally knew. Even teasing that Will was the weak link on the cooking front, which the girls smilingly agreed with.

'Yeah, we wondered how he'd ever got asked into a cooking group.' Maddie gave a grin.

It took the pressure off Will and Cath, and the conversation rolled on from there.

They began to stroll down to the beach, passing the old Coastguard's lookout and the rows of white cottages, which harboured The Ship Inn at one corner. Their leaky port in the storm that day. Leaving the village behind, they made their way down to the golden sands of the bay.

Once they were farther along the beach, and at a point where Will was chatting with Maddie, Sophie caught up with Cath. 'Umm, I think I owe you an apology ...' Her pretty grey-green eyes looked sad, and oh so awkward as she spoke. 'For how I was that day. I don't know ...' The young woman gave a heavy sigh. 'The Christmas tree ... and finding you there in our house. I kind of flipped, I suppose.'

'Hey, it was understandable, Sophie. I'm sure it was a bit of a shock, someone different being there in your home ...' Cath's tone was soft, forgiving.

'Yeah, but I was rude ... and I'm sorry.' Sophie pulled a shame-filled grimace, followed by a hopeful smile.

'Well then, apology accepted. And thank you. Let's put that behind us and move on, shall we? And,' Cath ventured, 'just for the record, I want you and Maddie to know that I do think an awful lot of your dad. We're only just getting to know each other, of course, but I really don't want to see him or either of you hurt.' Cath gave a hopeful smile, feeling that was enough said relationship-wise. But she hoped those words might help put them forward as a team. After all the heartbreak they'd endured, they had to be.

Sophie's smile softened, and that was lovely to see. 'Thanks, that's good to know. Umm, it's made me think. The other night … Dad's been miserable for long enough. No one can ever replace Mum – we all know that – but maybe it's time he did try and find a bit of happiness.'

Cath felt like she'd been handed a huge olive branch. She nodded. 'I think so.'

There were a few seconds where each stayed with their own thoughts, then Cath asked, 'So, how's uni been going? Are you enjoying your course?' Moving the conversation on. 'It's law you're studying, isn't it?'

'Yeah, it's getting a bit more intense this year. We deffo have to knuckle down more. There are exams coming up next term. Then we have to narrow down our modules again for next year, and think about possible placements.'

'It sounds a lot to keep up with. And do you like it?'

'Yeah, especially all the family law stuff. It's cool. Ahm, and you were a teacher, Dad said,' Sophie added, as they strolled around the headland of the bay. The stunning view across the pewter-grey sea to the ruins of Dunstanburgh before them.

'Yeah, maths.'

'Ah, that must have been a nightmare. Maths is always a tough subject. Can't imagine having a whole classroom of kids to try and keep focused.'

'Hah, yeah, it had its challenges …' Cath agreed, glad the conversation was flowing naturally between them, 'but you know what, I really liked it. Finding ways to keep the class engaged, helping all those kids who wanted to learn … and those who didn't. Maths is key to so many courses and job requirements these days. I still do maths coaching now … online tuition.'

'Ah, that's cool. I suppose you can do that from home, in the village?'

'Yep, as long as the internet is working.'

'So, how are you finding good old Tilldale?'

'I really like it there. It's feeling very much like home,' Cath answered, honestly.

Maddie and Will caught up with them, then. As though they'd given them a little time together on purpose.

'Hey, are you getting the third degree from my youngest?' Will asked, with a smile on his face.

'Nope, we're just having a nice chat,' Cath replied. 'We were just talking about Tilldale.'

'Oh, that hive of activity,' Maddie countered, the irony clear in her tone.

'Well, I'm sure it must seem quiet compared to the city. It's Newcastle you're based in, Maddie, isn't it?' Cath asked.

'Yeah, it's such a cool place. So buzzy and friendly. I love it. Loads of great bars and restaurants there, too.'

'You're certainly spoilt for choice,' agreed Will.

'Yeah well, it's The Star or … *oh*, perhaps The Star in good old Tilldale.' Sophie giggled.

'It does have its charm. The village and the pub,' countered Will. And by the look in his eyes at that moment, perhaps he meant some of its inhabitants too, Cath hoped.

'I was in Leeds before,' explained Cath, 'and after years of city life, I have to say it's nice to be able to chill a bit.'

The four of them strolled the beach, chatting away. And Cath was so grateful that after the first few minutes, it hadn't seemed awkward. She was super-careful not to appear lovey-dovey with Will, however, merely catching each other's gaze now and again. They had plenty of time. They needed to tread sensitively with this, after all.

Four sets of footprints were set beside each other in the sand, and for Cath a 'seaside' bucketful of hope. Anyone looking on might have thought they were a family.

Before they left the beach, Maddie and Sophie had paired up ahead of them and were deep in conversation. Will seemed to be hanging back.

'I've told them to go ahead and start getting a round in at The Ship,' he explained.

'Sounds good.'

He stopped, turning to face her. His toffee-hazel eyes set gently upon hers. No one else was on this part of the beach. 'Is it too late to say I'm sorry, Cath?'

'Oh, Will, you've said sorry a thousand times. It's not sorry I need from you …' Cath had to be honest here. She couldn't bear to open up, just to get hurt and be turned away again.

He took a breath, his brow creased with confusion. 'What is it, then? That you need from me?'

Cath gave a gentle sigh, giving herself time to find the right words. 'I need you to give yourself permission to love again. To be able to be loved.'

'Oh.' He looked out to sea for a few thoughtful moments. Then, no doubt feeling nervous, the pressure of the moment hitting him, he quirked an eyebrow cheekily, lightening the mood as he said, 'We could always have a sneaky kiss in the dunes?'

She couldn't help but smile before answering, 'Nope, that's a step too far for day one. The girls have made a big concession, suggesting you bring me along today. Let's not put things back by affronting them. Anyhow, you know where that led last time, back when we were young.'

'I do, indeed.' Will's eyebrow arched.

'Behave,' she scolded, giving him a playful punch on the arm.

They stood side by side for a few more moments, looking out across the bay.

Will took a slow breath. 'Cath, these past few months, meeting you, I have come to realise something … That you can truly love two people. And importantly, that one love doesn't diminish the other.' He turned to her, his tone so damn earnest, his dark eyes again holding hers. 'Cath, I've always loved you. From meeting you way back when you were just sixteen … to finding you again. This is our time now. I feel it in my bones.'

'I feel it too, Will. And thank you …'

'For what?' He looked confused.

'For taking that risk, for letting love in. That's so hard to do when you've been hurt.'

'So, let's take that risk together.'

He glanced up, checking his girls had turned the corner, taking them past the first row of cottages, out of sight. Will took both her hands in his. He couldn't hold back any longer. Their kiss was brief yet beautiful – she felt it in her fingers and her toes and a whole lot more – and it was filled with the promise of a thousand tomorrows.

Epilogue

'Cheers, everyone! Merry Twixmas!' Will was holding his glass aloft. The fizz was flowing, and they'd just finished voting on the Turkey Leftovers Supper Club Challenge.

Cath scanned the room – which was in fact Will's living room – whilst the folded paper-napkin votes were counted. Lily was there along with Nikki, Kev and the three boys – who were sat together on the sofa, Dan and Andreas were stood deep in conversation, and Will was here standing beside her. Wonderfully, Sophie had stayed on for a few days after Christmas to spend some time with her dad, and Maddie had arrived back, just an hour ago, after a nursing night shift and a few hours' sleep.

There had been lemony Greek turkey pilaf rice from the lads, Nikki had made a fabulous turkey curry – finally confessing the sauce was from a jar, but hey, there was no judgement here. Lily was on filo pastry tarts with a creamy turkey, thyme and mushroom filling, and Sophie and Maddie had whizzed up some delightful pan-fried turkey quesadillas stuffed with chopped turkey, grated cheese, green chillis, and spring onion, served with crème fraiche and guacamole. Cath, who didn't actually have any turkey leftovers, had cooked a Bailey's cheesecake for pudding, and Will, who had put out crisps and nibbles, kept everybody's glasses topped up and had very much enjoyed testing all the tasty dishes. Cath warned him that he needed to up his game, and get cooking himself for next time.

He gave her a quick, joyful peck on the cheek.

And she felt confident there would be a next time, and many, many more.

Cath then spotted the photo of Jane on the wall, watching over them, and made a silent promise from deep in her heart to do her very best to look after her family.

'And the winner is ...' Will performed a drum roll on the coffee table '... Sophie and Maddie. The turkey quesadillas were the favourite by far.' You could tell he was having a proud dad moment.

And Cath knew that even though they hadn't entered the competition, it was she and Will who were the true winners, having found each other again.

The Recipes

Supper Club 1: Cath's Cosy Beef and Northumbrian Ale Casserole

Supper Club 2: Nibbles and Natter – Nikki's Sticky Honey-Mustard Sausages

Supper Club 3: In the Greek Midwinter – Lamb Kleftiko and Melomakarona (Christmas Honey Biscuits)

Supper Club 4: Carols at the Care Home – Lily's Mince Pies

Supper Club 5: Lily's Savoury Crostini and Cheeseboard Wreath

Supper Club 6: The Village Christmas Lunch – Dan's Special Stuffing Balls

Supper Club 7: Twixmas Get-Together – Sophie and Maddie's Turkey Quesadillas

Cath's Cosy Beef and Northumbrian Ale Casserole

1 large onion, or 2 small, chopped
2 tbsp sunflower or olive oil
2 carrots, peeled and roughly chopped
1 large parsnip, peeled and chunkily chopped
750g stewing steak, cubed
2 tbsp plain flour
Salt and pepper
450ml brown ale (Alnwick Brown Ale or Newcastle Brown
    work well)
450ml beef stock
1 tsp sugar
1 tsp English mustard
1 tsp horseradish sauce
Preheat oven to 180°C/160°C fan.

In a large pan (or oven-proof casserole suitable for hob too) fry onion in 1 tbsp oil on a medium heat for 5–8 mins until golden brown. Add the carrot and parsnip for a few more mins and then tip everything into a casserole pot.

Toss the meat cubes in seasoned flour. Add a further tbsp oil to same pan, and turn up the heat. Fry the meat cubes until browned, then slowly add the ale and stock, stir in the sugar, mustard and horseradish. Once smooth and starting to bubble, pour over the onion and carrot mix. Stir through, cover with lid, and cook in oven for two hours. Give it all another stir-through and put back in oven for a further hour, until the meat is meltingly tender.

Gorgeous served with buttery mashed potato and greens, or alternatively in a bowl with a hunk of crusty bread. Proper autumnal comfort food.

Nibbles and Natter – Nikki's Sticky Honey-Mustard Sausages

500g of chipolata or cocktail sausages
2 tbsp runny honey
1 tbsp wholegrain mustard

Heat oven to 200°C/180°C fan. Place sausages in a baking tray, ideally non-stick. Mix together the honey and mustard, and then drizzle over the sausages. Toss to coat.

Bake for 20 minutes. Ideal as a canapé or with a buffet. Serve with drinks and friends.

In the Greek Midwinter – Lamb Kleftiko

1 leg or shoulder of lamb, bone in, cut into 4 – ask your
   butcher (or 4 shanks)
Olive oil
Salt and pepper
½ tbsp dried oregano
3 bay leaves
6 garlic cloves
1kg Maris Piper or waxy potatoes, peeled and chopped into
   large chunks
2 onions, cut in thin wedges
1 red pepper, deseeded and chopped into chunks
250ml white wine
1 stick cinnamon
A few sprigs of fresh oregano (optional)
2 lemons, juiced

Put the lamb into a large bowl or dish and drizzle over some olive
oil. Season generously, and sprinkle over the dried oregano and
crushed bay leaves. Take 2 garlic cloves and cut into 4 pieces,
make two small slashes in each chunk of meat and poke in the
garlic. Rub in all the flavours, cover and refrigerate.

*If you have time, marinate the lamb overnight in a fridge,
otherwise for at least 3 hours.

Heat oven to 190°C/170°C fan. Take lamb out of fridge. Tip the
potatoes, onions, pepper and remaining garlic, roughly chopped,
into a large roasting tin, then pour over the wine. Remove lamb
from marinade, briefly set aside, and pour leftover marinade
over the veg. Toss to combine, then poke in your cinnamon
stick and oregano sprigs, if using. Arrange lamb on top of veg,
and squeeze over the lemon juice. Cover tightly with foil (you

would traditionally wrap in baking parchment like a parcel, but this method is slightly easier) and bake for 3 hours. Remove foil, toss everything and spoon over the juices, drizzle over a little more oil if the tin seems dry, leave uncovered and bake for a further 20–30 mins until the lamb is falling off the bone, and the potatoes are golden at the edges.

In the Greek Midwinter – Melomakarona (Christmas Honey Biscuits) (makes around 36)

Syrup
200ml water
200g caster sugar
150ml runny honey
1 orange, cut in half
1 cinnamon stick
2 cloves, whole
60g butter, softened
175ml olive oil
100g caster sugar
100ml orange juice
Grated zest of 2 oranges
2 tbsp brandy
2 heaped tsp ground cinnamon
Large pinch of nutmeg
500g plain flour
150g fine semolina
1 tsp baking powder
1 tsp bicarbonate of soda

Garnish
100g finely chopped walnuts

Firstly, bring the syrup ingredients to the boil, skimming off any foam. Boil for 2–3 mins. Leave aside to cool.

Heat oven to 190°C/170°C fan. In a large bowl, mix the softened butter, oil, sugar, orange juice, orange zest, brandy, cinnamon and nutmeg, and beat well. Mix the sifted flour, semolina, baking powder and bicarbonate of soda, then add gradually to the liquid mixture, stirring initially, then forming into a light dough. Shape into small egg-sized ovals, flatten slightly with a fork and put onto two lined baking trays. Bake for 22–25 mins until lightly browned and cooked through.

As soon as the biscuits come out of the oven, strain the syrup, and then pour half of the cooled syrup over the biscuits with a spoon and sprinkle with the chopped walnuts. Reserve the remaining syrup to drizzle over just before you eat them. Delish!

Carols at the Care Home – Lily's Mince Pies

225g butter, diced (keep cold)
350g plain flour
100g golden caster sugar
Pinch of salt
280g good quality mincemeat
Splash of sherry (optional)
1 small egg
Icing sugar to dust
Preheat the oven to 200°C/180°C fan.

To make the pastry, rub the cold, diced butter into the plain flour, then mix in the golden caster sugar and a pinch of salt. Combine the pastry into a ball – don't add any liquid – and knead it briefly. The dough will be fairly firm, like shortbread dough.

Using a 16-hole tartlet tin, press small walnut-sized balls of pastry into each hole.

Spoon the mincemeat, mixed with a splash of sherry if using, into the pies.

Take slightly smaller balls of pastry than before and pat them out between your hands to make round lids, big enough to cover the pies. Top the pies with their lids, pressing the edges gently together to seal.

Beat 1 small egg and brush over the tops of the pies.

Bake for 20 mins until golden. Leave to cool in the tin for 5 mins, then remove to a wire rack.

Dust with icing sugar before serving.

These will keep for 3 to 4 days in an airtight container.
* Festive alternatives!

Star topped: Make and fill your bases, then roll out the remaining pastry. Make star shapes with a small cutter, and pop one on the top of each pie, pressing lightly down.

Marzipan flavoured: Grate some chilled marzipan over the top of these star shapes, before baking.

Lily's Savoury Crostini and Cheeseboard Wreath (makes around 24 crostini)

2 ready-to-bake baguettes
2 tbsp olive oil

Topping suggestions: Stilton and walnut, roast beef and horse-radish cream (half horseradish to half crème fraiche), brie and olive/grape or cranberry sauce, smoked salmon and cream cheese with a sprig of dill.

Heat oven at 170°C/160° fan. Slice the baguettes into even discs around ½ cm thick. Place on a baking tray, brush lightly with oil on each side, and then bake for around 5 mins. Take out and turn over, then cook for another 5 mins until lightly golden. Remove from oven, set aside and allow to cool.

Create toppings as above, or make up your own combinations. They are so versatile.

Cheeseboard Wreath
Use a large chopping board or tray, and cover in silver foil.

Place some rocket (and fresh basil leaves, optional) in a circle shape, and use your crostini, cheese selection, grapes and fresh cherry tomatoes to make a colourful festive foodie wreath. Drizzle with a little balsamic glaze if you like it.

You can then place your savoury biscuit selection in the middle!

The Village Christmas Lunch – Dan's Special Stuffing Balls (makes 12 balls)

1 onion, chopped
Knob of butter
450g pork sausage meat
120g fresh breadcrumbs
1 tbsp fresh sage, chopped (or 1 tsp dried sage)
8 dried apricots, chopped
50g flaked almonds, roughly chopped (optional)
1 egg, beaten (use around ½ of this to bind)
Salt and freshly ground pepper

Fry the onion in the butter on a medium heat for 5–10 mins until golden and softened. Set aside to cool.

Put sausage meat, breadcrumbs, sage, apricots and almonds – if using – and the cooled onion into a bowl. Season and mix everything together with a little of the egg until combined.

Shape into golf-ball-sized balls, and place on a baking tray. They can refrigerate for up to 24 hours, or make ahead and freeze on the tray, then transfer them to a freezer bag for storage up to 3 months.

To cook, preheat oven to 200°C/180°C fan. Bake for 20–25 mins until cooked through.

Christmas dinner scrumptiousness!

Twixmas Get-Together – Sophie and Maddie's Turkey Quesadillas

1 tbsp vegetable oil
6 large tortilla wraps
200g grated Cheddar cheese
300g leftover cooked turkey meat, chopped
4–5 spring onions, chopped
2 fresh green chillis
Salt and black pepper
Ready-made salsa, crème fraiche and guacamole to serve

Heat a large frying pan with a little vegetable oil. Lay one wrap down and top evenly with cheese, turkey meat, a sprinkling of spring onion and chilli. Season with salt and black pepper. Top with another wrap.

Allow to cook on medium-high for around five minutes until the base is getting golden and slightly crispy. Carefully slide a fish slice under the wrap – this is the tricky bit! – whilst holding the top and filling together, and quickly turn and place back down in your pan for a further five minutes.

Slide out onto a board, and chop into wedges rather like a pizza, and serve accompanied with your salsa, crème fraiche and guacamole. Ideal for a Twixmas lunch!

A Letter from Caroline Roberts

Thank you so much for choosing to read *Christmas at the Second Chance Supper Club*. I hope you enjoyed it! If you did and would like to be the first to know about my new releases, please follow me on Instagram @CarolineRobertsAuthor and on Facebook/CarolineRobertsAuthor, and sign up for my newsletter at https://carolinerobertsauthor.substack.com.

Christmas at the Second Chance Supper Club is inspired by my beautiful Northumberland village, my love of food and the way it brings people together, and also by the twists and emotional turns that life can take us through. I think we all deserve a second chance and some good friends to buoy us up when times are tough.

I hope you loved this novel, and if you did, I would be so grateful if you would leave a review. I always love to hear what readers thought, and it helps new readers discover my books too.

Thanks,
Caroline

The Second Chance Supper Club

Could a new start heal her appetite for life?

When Cath moves to a rural Northumberland village to escape her husband's betrayal and a life that no longer feels her own, she's determined to embrace a fresh start. But the quiet charm of her new surroundings seems only to magnify the loneliness of being on her own for the first time.

On a whim, Cath suggests starting a supper club, transforming her garden shed into a cosy, twinkling haven where neighbours can gather. What begins as an effort to ease her solitude becomes something far greater – a circle of friends, each bringing their own stories, struggles, and laughter.

As bonds deepen over shared meals and mishaps, Cath discovers the healing power of community and dares to believe in love and joy again.

Acknowledgements

Huge thanks to Mum and Dad, whom I've dedicated this book to. Much of Reggie's forces background is my dad's real story. Whilst he was away, my dad also wrote to my mum every day. And as this book is about to be published, they are about to celebrate a remarkable sixty-nine years of marriage. A true love story. Congratulations to you both, and thanks for everything.

A book is nothing without a reader, so heartfelt thanks to all my readers and the book blogging community for your wonderful support over the years. I do love hearing from you on my Facebook and Instagram, so please continue to keep in touch.

The Second Chance Supper Club is very much inspired by Northumberland village life and my local community, who welcomed me into their fold over twenty years ago. Once again, I have to thank Chatton Village Stores for their support, and especially Pat and Sarah, who let me interview and observe them as they served, chatted and baked.

Thank you to Yianna and her Greek-Cypriot dad for their help with Andreas's family's phrases and the gorgeous Greek-inspired recipe ideas.

Thanks to Maths teacher Rebecca Moss for her helpful insights into Cath's profession, whose dreams of becoming a teacher came at the same point as I was trying hard to get my books published – we both very much achieved our goals.

Any mistakes you may find are wholly my own. I endeavour to try my best but sometimes a typo or a piece of information slips the net! Writers are only human, too.

My writing community friends are so appreciated. Thanks to my Romantic Novelists' Association comrades for their support, kindness and inspiration over afternoon teas, kitchen parties, conferences, and pooled lunches! Thanks also to the hard-working librarians, especially Michelle Watson here in Northumberland, and the bookshop staff and owners (thank you, Helen Stanton from Forum Books) for promoting our books, supporting so many writers on the way.

My publishing director and editor, Georgina Green, and editor Priyal Agrawal, plus the editing, marketing, sales and creative teams at HQ, thank you so much for giving me an exciting new chapter with your publishing house. The cover design is beautiful and captures the spirit of the book so well, all credit to Anna Sikorska. It's been wonderful working with you all.

Big thanks to my agent Hannah Ferguson for believing in and guiding me with this new Supper Club series, and the team at Hardman & Swainson.

Last but never least, my family, and our friends, for their patience and support. I spend many, many hours on a laptop upstairs in the spare room in a world of my own with make-believe people. Thanks for giving me the time and space to create these characters and stories.

All best wishes,
Caroline

Dear Reader,

We hope you enjoyed reading this book. If you did, we'd be so appreciative if you left a review. It really helps us and the author to bring more books like this to you.

Here at HQ Digital we are dedicated to publishing fiction that will keep you turning the pages into the early hours. Don't want to miss a thing? To find out more about our books, promotions, discover exclusive content and enter competitions you can keep in touch in the following ways:

JOIN OUR COMMUNITY:

Sign up to our new email newsletter: http://smarturl.it/SignUpHQ

Read our new blog www.hqstories.co.uk

X: https://twitter.com/HQStories

f: www.facebook.com/HQStories

BUDDING WRITER?

We're also looking for authors to join the HQ Digital family! Find out more here:

https://www.hqstories.co.uk/want-to-write-for-us/

Thanks for reading, from the HQ Digital team